Praise for
New York Times bestselling author
Kasey Michaels

"Kasey Michaels aims for the heart and never misses."
—*New York Times* bestselling author Nora Roberts

"Michaels holds the reader in her clutches and doesn't let go."
—*RT Book Reviews* on *What a Gentleman Desires*,
4½ stars, Top Pick

"Michaels…outdoes herself… For lighthearted fun, you can't do better than this."
—*RT Book Reviews* on *An Improper Arrangement*

"This mistress of the genre is on the peak of her career."
—*RT Book Reviews* on *A Scandalous Proposal*,
4½ stars, Top Pick

"A poignant and highly satisfying read…filled with simmering sensuality, subtle touches of repartee, a hero out for revenge and a heroine ripe for adventure. You'll enjoy the ride."
—*RT Book Reviews* on *How to Tame a Lady*

"Michaels' new Regency miniseries is a joy…. You will laugh and even shed a tear over this touching romance."
—*RT Book Reviews* on *How to Tempt a Duke*

"Michaels has done it again…. Witty dialogue peppers a plot full of delectable details exposing the foibles and follies of the age."
—*Publishers Weekly*, starred review, on *The Butler Did It*

KASEY MICHAELS

A Reckless Promise

HQN™

ISBN-13: 978-0-373-77972-7

A Reckless Promise

Recycling programs
for this product may
not exist in your area.

CONTENTS

A RECKLESS PROMISE   9
Kasey Michaels

WINTER'S CAMP   301
Jodi Thomas

Dear Reader,

A promise is a promise is a promise.

Darn.

Darby Travers, Viscount Nailbourne, may have used stronger language to express his reaction to discovering that a promise made has become a promise he must keep.

Not that he considers reneging, not even for a moment, for he is an honorable if suddenly suspicious gentleman.

Darby is also a sigh-worthy hero: witty, urbane, sophisticated, rakishly handsome, apparently carefree. But scratch the surface and find the man beneath: the steel, the loyalty…and the carefully guarded heart.

Now imagine this man saddled with a female ward…because of a promise.

Grab a box of chocolates, curl up on something comfy and come along as seven-year-old terror Marley Hamilton turns the viscount's life upside down, while her unimpressionable and secretive aunt, Sadie Grace Boxer, confounds his head and heart at every turn.

Is *A Reckless Promise* the next great American novel? Nah. Sometimes a girl just wants to have fun!

Happy reading!

Kasey Michaels

A RECKLESS PROMISE

Kasey Michaels

To Jennifer Stevenson
Great writer, fantastic friend

PROLOGUE

March, 1814
Somewhere near Montmort-Lucy, France

RUMOR HAD IT in the camp that their guards were nervous. That Bonaparte's victory over the Allies at Champaubert had only served as a temporary delay in toppling the French emperor from his throne.

Indeed, Jeremiah Rigby had returned from his morning constitutional around the perimeter of the prisoner-of-war camp to report that he'd counted ten less guards than had been at their posts the previous day.

And eight more bodies. The wounded were succumbing with disturbing frequency over a month into their captivity, thanks to the lack of food, clean water and medicine.

"The time couldn't be better for a moonlight flit," Gabriel Sinclair said as he and Rigby joined Cooper Townsend and Darby Travers inside the sagging lean-to they'd constructed to help shield them from a fading winter and early spring rains.

Surgeon John Hamilton didn't look up from his work, inspecting the healing wound sustained when Cooper had taken a ball in his side at Champaubert and they'd been captured along with over a thousand others. "There'll be a nasty scar, sir, but it's all healing nicely now that we're rid of that infection. You're next, my lord."

Darby Travers, Viscount Nailbourne, pushed himself up on his elbows as the surgeon approached, duckwalking across the damp ground, bent nearly in half thanks to the low roof and his tall frame. "No need, John. No angels visited overnight, no miracle was delivered by dimpled cherubs and even the devil hasn't bothered to tempt me. The eye is all but finished, and that's that. I'm already fashioning fetching eye patches in my idle moments."

That was Darby. He would make a joke out of most anything. Not even his closest friends were privileged to know if he was truly as reconciled to his injury as he seemed. Being his closest friends, they didn't ask, but only followed his lead.

The surgeon, however, ignored the levity and began unwrapping the fraying linen bandage that held a clean square of the same material against the viscount's left eye. "It's early days yet, my lord, and the swelling was profound. I can only hope I didn't do more damage by removing the ball, hoping to relieve the pressure."

Darby spoke quietly, so that the others couldn't hear. "I don't remember any of it, thank God, once I'd supposedly told Rigby I needed to sit down moments before I fell down. I was all but a dead man until you showed up with your scalpel and box of leeches. I have my life thanks to you, and my gratitude is without bounds. Now, I know you overheard the captain. We four go tonight. You'll come with us."

Hamilton shook his head as he began rewrapping the bandage. "I can't leave my patients, my lord."

"Those who can manage have been sneaking off

every night for the last week. The guards may not have noticed yet, but soon our thinning ranks will become obvious. At least a few of us will reach our lines, and a rescue will be mounted. But we all know it could come too late. Our skittish captors might dispatch the wounded before they either run off home or go to join Bonaparte. As it is, they're damn near starving us to death."

"My lord, your duty is to return to our ranks in any way you can, as is the duty of every soldier. Mine is to remain with the wounded." Hamilton looked behind him, where the others were deep in conversation, and leaned in closer. "You say you don't remember anything, my lord, and I agree that can be a blessing. But you did speak while you were lost in delirium. Only I heard."

"Well, goodness me, John, you put me to the blush. Was what I said all that terrible?"

"You spoke of your childhood, my lord. A particular time in your childhood. I...I only wanted to say that what happened was not your fault. Children often assume guilt that does not belong to them. You're a good man—you are all extraordinarily good men."

"Thank you, John," Darby said. "I'm sorry you had to hear my ramblings. Truly, I'm long past those years. I can't imagine why I spoke of them all this time later. I would much rather have regaled you with stories of my adventures with the ladies."

The physician smiled. "You were not without amusing anecdotes, my lord."

"Well, thank heaven for that. John, if you can't reconsider and come with us, I want you to know that I'm aware of all I owe you, not the least of which is my fairly worthless, ramshackle life. If there is ever anything I can do for you in return, no matter how inadequate that thing might be, you must not hesitate to ask, because it is yours, on my word as a gentleman."

"You have more goodness in you than I believe you realize, my lord." The physician hesitated, looking out into the camp that was deteriorating daily. "I have every hope of returning home, sir, but if I don't..."

Darby pushed himself to a sitting position and held out his right hand. "Yes? Name it, John, and it's yours."

CHAPTER ONE

London, the Little Season, 1815

"WHAT DO YOU think of Spain, Norton? I've heard intriguing things about the Alhambra, once termed a pleasure palace. But no, you have no interest in pleasure, do you?"

"I take vast pleasure in my duties, my lord," the valet supplied in his usual monotone. "Even more so when His Lordship refrains from speaking whilst I am shaving him."

Darby Travers, Viscount Nailbourne, longed to inquire as to whether his man's words could be construed as a threat, but quickly discarded the notion. Until the straight edge moved from his neck, he prudently refused to so much as swallow.

"And we're done, my lord," Norton said in some satisfaction, stepping back even as he handed his employer a warm, moist towel. "Until this evening, that is. I would ask you to consider again the advantages of a well-trimmed beard."

Darby wiped at his face, then tossed the towel in Norton's direction as he got to his feet and walked over to the high dresser topped with an oval mirror. "Not if you'd continue to force your barbering skills on me, no. It wounds me to say this, Norton, but your mustache appears chewed on, and I'm convinced you employ that wirelike appendage on your chin to brush dried mud from my riding boots. The fact that both are shoe-black dark and your hair red as a flame makes me wonder what you do to amuse yourself when I leave you alone."

Norton, a man of at least forty summers, smoothed a hand over his hair, parted neatly in the middle and tied back into a tail at least six inches in length, and then tugged at his goatee. "Red facial hair is unattractive, my lord."

Darby would have asked his new valet why he didn't expand his use of the dye pot to include the hair on his head, but then the man might tell him. Norton was his third valet in as many months, and the only one who didn't perpetually suppress a flinch when he saw his employer without his eye patch. For that small mercy alone, the viscount didn't really care if Norton sought his jollies by wearing his pantaloons on his head.

He picked up his brushes and ran them through his own coal-dark hair. "I believe I'll refrain from comment on that, Norton. But back to Spain. I'm devastated to inform you that we can't go, much as I'd like to escape my fate. For one, I'm promised to a birthday celebration at the end of the month. Either that or a funeral. Nobody's quite certain yet. My jacket, if you please."

"Yes, my lord. Will we be returning to London today?"

"Don't care for my cottage, Norton?" he asked, shrugging into his handsomely cut tan hacking jacket, for he was anticipating a ride yet this morning. "I know it's quaint, but I believe it provides most of the necessities of life."

Nailbourne Farm, or the "cottage," as Darby termed it, was a large estate just outside Wimbledon, and only an hour's drive from London. Along with an extensive breeding stable and three hundred acres of Capability Brown's better efforts at landscaping, the estate boasted a unique, sprawling stone-and-timber mansion. There were sixteen bedchambers, a dining hall that comfortably sat fifty and a dozen other rooms, all beneath a whimsical thatched roof that kept four thatchers gainfully employed year-round. It even boasted a royal bedchamber, which had actually been slept in by no less than two English monarchs.

It was the smallest of the half dozen Nailbourne holdings.

"Well, Norton? Do you agree?"

"It's…serviceable, my lord."

"How greatly you relieve my mind. I wouldn't want to have to order it torn down and rebuilt to your specifications."

Sarcasm was totally lost on Norton, Darby knew, winging over his head like a bird in flight, but at least the viscount was amusing himself. He was in some need of a smile at the moment.

"Your pardon, sir, but I feel I must remind you that I accepted this temporary position on the understanding that we would be in London for the Little Season."

Darby made one last small adjustment to the black eye patch he'd tied to his head, and turned to give a slight bow to his valet. "And alas, I've failed you. I'm so ashamed, and must hasten to make amends. Since I'll be traveling to London this evening for an engagement, you have my permission to ride along with me. I'll have you dropped at your favorite tavern, as I'm certain you have one, and come back to take you up before I return here, to the wilds. I most sincerely hope that meets with your approval?"

"Yes, my lord!" Norton exclaimed, bowing deeply at the waist, perhaps the first display of emotion the man had allowed in his master's presence. "The Crown and Cock, my lord, just off Piccadilly. And may I say, my lord, you look exceptionally fine today. You flatter that new jacket all hollow."

"Oh, shut up," Darby said amicably as he brushed past the valet on his way to the stairs, only smiling once he was out of sight. "For a moment there, I thought he'd ask to kiss my ring," he mumbled to himself.

His mood may have been temporarily lifted, but the knowledge that Norton was right served to bring it crashing back down once more. He'd been at the cottage for nearly a week, cooling his heels as he awaited the arrival of the consequences of his forgotten promise to John Hamilton. Granted, he'd escaped to London, twice, for evening parties, but the days here were nearly interminable when he wished only to be with his friends before everyone adjourned to their country estates until the spring Season.

Darby supposed he should have put a qualifier or two into his promise to the good doctor before agreeing to take guardianship of the man's daughter should anything fatal befall the man. He'd thought that meant if John had perished at the camp before it could be liberated. He hadn't counted on any responsibility outliving the promise by more than eighteen months, which was when the good doctor had cocked up his toes.

Yet here he was, about to become guardian to his very own ward. His *female* ward. If there could be any one person less suited for the position, Darby believed a person would have to search far and wide to find him. His friends had all laughingly agreed, and looked forward with some glee to watching him deal with this unexpected complication to his smooth-running life.

Marley Hamilton. Age unknown. Would he be able to send her off to some young ladies' academy and forget about her for at least a few years, or would he be laying down the blunt for a Season for the girl? Was she dewy and young, or already past her last prayers?

John had been a country doctor. Of good family, one could only hope, but would his daughter be up to snuff for a Season, or would she come to the cottage still with hay in her hair and mud on her half boots, and speak in some broad country accent?

Would he be forced to rebuild her, as it were, from the ground up, in order to be rid of her?

Would she feel it necessary to address him as Uncle Nailbourne?

Egads.

"Coop's right," he told himself as he reached the bottom of the stairs. "I do get myself into the damnedest situations. If only John's solicitor would arrive, and get the waiting over with before I drive myself mad."

"Milord?" the footman asked, holding forth his employer's hat, gloves and small riding crop. "You be talkin' ta yerself again, the way you said you wuz yesterday?"

"Exactly, Tompkins," he responded, accepting the articles. "And as was the case yesterday, and probably will be for some time yet, you may feel free to ignore me."

"Yes, milord. Mr. Rivers brought the new stallion 'round. He's a big 'un, milord. You do mind ta be careful."

"Since it would upset you, I'll do my best not to break my neck," Darby promised the young lad, and then stopped in the action of pulling on his gloves when there were three loud raps on the door knocker.

His entire body instantly went on alert.

"Ah, perhaps the time has come. Strange we didn't hear a coach pulling up. Attend to that, Tompkins, if you please."

The boy, freckle-faced and towheaded, and more accustomed to his usual chores in the kitchens, looked at his master in some distress. "But, milord, Mr. Camford says he's ta greet all His Lordship's guests to be sure where ta put 'em, and yer'r ta be summoned ta the drawin' room only after he—"

"Tompkins, I can't be certain of this, of course, but last I looked, I do believe I still outrank my butler. Open. The. Door."

Tompkins blushed to the roots of his hair. "Straightaway, milord."

"Clearly I have to develop more of a commanding air with the staff," Darby told himself, replacing hat, gloves and riding crop on the large round table and stepping back two paces, ready to surprise his guest with his unexpected presence. Or perhaps he'd be mistaken for Camford, come to vet the uninvited guest so he'd know where "ta put 'em."

A mental picture of the portly butler dressed in riding clothes brought a small smile to Darby's lips as Tompkins opened the door and then stood directly in front of the opening, blocking any view of the visitor. Apparently Camford hadn't had time to complete the lad's lessons in footmanship.

"Let whoever it is pass, please," he told the boy, unnecessarily it would seem, as Tompkins was rather handily pushed out of the way as a tall, heavily cloaked and hooded figure breached the human barrier and stepped through the portal, dripping water onto the tile floor.

When had it begun to rain? Did Norton so sincerely loathe the country that he didn't even peek out the window to be certain his employer would be correctly dressed? Darby waved a figurative goodbye to any notion of working the new stallion.

He took a closer look at the figure. The words *drowned rat* scuttled into his brain.

"If you hadn't yet noticed, young man, the doorway lacks a portico. How long do you usually have His Lordship's guests stand unprotected in a deluge?"

A woman? It was definitely a woman's voice. Tall, for a woman, able to wear a man's cloak and not have it be six sizes too large. Only four, he estimated, taking in the many-caped cloak once again. Bossy, for a woman, especially one who had arrived uninvited, unaccompanied and apparently on foot.

"Tompkins, offer to take the lady's cloak before she drowns in it, both literally and figuratively."

"Yes, Tompkins, do that. And when it's dry, consider burning it. I feel as if it could stand on its own after five days of travel on the public coach. And then please inform His Lordship that his ward has arrived."

"Oh, bollocks," Darby muttered under his breath, feeling the worst of his many suppositions had just sloshed through the doorway. Past her last prayers, unmannered, tall as a stick and clearly— "Well, hello."

The woman had finally thrown back her dripping, drooping hood to reveal a head of more than merely damp blond hair, eyes that could be any color from blue to green to even gray, probably depending on her mood.

At the moment, as she looked directly at him, they were definitely leaning toward a stormy gray.

Her nose was straight, her lips full—with an intriguing pout to the upper one—her skin pale and flawless, a slight dimple in her chin. Her slim neck could only be judged as regal.

Furthermore, she was tall enough to tower over young Tompkins, and was only a few inches shy of being able to look Darby straight in his eyes, which would make her very nearly six feet tall.

Amazing. One can only wonder how much of her is legs.

"And you are…?" she asked him, definitely imperiously, and with no hint of a country accent. In fact, her English was probably more precise than his own, as he had a tendency to drawl when amused, and he was often amused. He'd best pull out his most precise accent.

He also probably should stop grinning.

"Astounded," Darby said, bowing. "Perplexed. Nonplussed. Oh, and dry. And you?"

"You're Viscount Nailbourne," she countered as Tompkins finally realized he should close the door. "John told me about the eye. You received my letter? I sent one to every address John had provided. You weren't at the first one and I was forced to continue my search."

Typical female. Somehow everything apparently has become my fault.

"Clearly a lapse on my part. A thousand apologies," he said, bowing yet again. "Would you care to continue this conversation upstairs, or are you more comfortable in foyers? I'm amendable either way, and I'm certain

Tompkins here wouldn't mind watching this small farce unfold."

"I'm more comfortable *dry*. Our trunk momentarily lies abandoned just inside your gates. I would appreciate having it fetched and taken to whatever quarters you might assign. Once I have your ward settled, *I* would be more than amenable to continuing our conversation."

"You're...you're not my ward?"

Then who in bloody hell are you?

She looked at him as if he had just popped out a second head. "Certainly not. I'm above the age of requiring a keeper. Marley? You can come out now, please, and allow me to introduce you to your new guardian."

The young woman pulled back one side of the oversize cloak to reveal a female child of no more than six or seven. The child was clinging to her apparent protector with both arms, her face buried against the damp muslin skirts.

Yes, the legs were that long...

"Marley," the woman urged, "if you're quite done with your impersonation of a barnacle, make your curtsy to His Lordship, as I've taught you to do."

"Will not." The words were rather muffled, but clearly understood.

I don't blame you, Darby thought.

"She's prodigiously fatigued, poor poppet," the woman said through only slightly gritted teeth she still couldn't manage to keep from chattering with cold. "Unless I gave him a copper, the coach driver wouldn't bring us any farther. We were forced to walk from the gate. And then it began to rain."

And there is that glare again. Apparently the rain is also my fault.

Considering that the gate and house were separated by nearly a mile of gravel drive, Darby mustered some sympathy for the child. "I understand. And she's probably a bit shy, aren't you, Marley? Tompkins, fetch Mrs. Camford at once, and have her attend to our guests. But first—you still have the advantage of me, ma'am, in more than one way. If I might have your name?"

"Forgive me, my lord. I am Mrs. Boxer. Mrs. Sadie Grace Boxer, sister to the late John Hamilton, and Marley's paternal aunt."

More and more curious…but it might help explain her unusual height. John, he remembered, had been quite the beanpole himself. They also seemed to share their blond hair.

"Boxer? S. G. Boxer? *You* wrote the letter I received last week? I was under the impression that I had been contacted by John's solicitor."

"Then you were laboring under a mistaken impression. I never claimed any such thing."

"No? Well, you certainly implied it, madam. Did you pen the note with Mr. Johnson's lexicon at your elbow?"

"Are you now implying that perhaps Marley and I aren't who I presented us to be? Are you questioning that Marley is indeed John's child, and now your ward?"

Sadie Grace Boxer had stepped forward a pace, her dimpled chin raised. When she spoke, there had been the hint of a drawl in her voice, as if she was pouring cream over steel. Odd, that they both should have the same failing, but for different reasons. Or perhaps she was secretly amused? No, that wasn't it. What he saw in those eyes was a mix of confusion and…could that be fear? Had his intended joke struck a nerve?

Darby tipped his head slightly. "I wasn't, no, not completely. But now that you mention it, have you any proof that you and the child are who you say you are?"

Speaking of rats, did he sound like one searching for any way off a sinking ship? Yes, he probably did. But the woman was not what he was expecting, and until he figured out why that bothered him, he wouldn't be too hard on himself for his suddenly suspicious nature.

Mrs. Camford had just bustled into the foyer, followed by two housemaids, and was already *tsk-tsking* and issuing orders about clean linens and tubs to be drawn and fires to be laid in both one of the bedchambers and the nursery.

"Can this wait, my lord, as I tend to this small darling?" the housekeeper interrupted, having known Darby since he was in short coats and apparently already half in love with the now visibly shivering blonde poppet with the huge green eyes sparkling with heart-melting tears. "Oh, just look at the little darling. Come to Camy, sweetheart. Camy will make it all better."

Darby raised a hand to his forehead, rubbing at the headache he could feel advancing on him. "Scolding me, Mrs. Camford? And with good reason. I can't imagine what I was thinking. Take them off, with my compliments. I'll be in my study if anyone needs me."

"Yes, m'lord, you do that. You're clearly of no use here."

At last, Mrs. Boxer smiled. Of course she would. No woman could resist a little crowing when a man has been put solidly in his place.

"I'll take myself off, then, Camy, before I'm sent to bed without my porridge."

Sadie Grace Boxer turned toward the stairs, following

the housekeeper. "How gracious, my lord. Come along, Marley," she called over her shoulder.

Instead, Marley walked straight up to Darby, stopping just in front of him. "You're mean," she announced. "I don't like you, and I hope you die."

"What a charming infant you are," he said, and inclined his head to her.

The charming infant kicked him straight in the shin with all her might.

"Tired *and* hungry," Mrs. Boxer said, perhaps in apology—and perhaps not—hurriedly coming back to take Marley by the shoulders and steer her toward the staircase.

Tompkins quickly suppressed a giggle, and even Mrs. Camford smiled as she brushed past the guests, to lead them upstairs.

"She's just a child, my lord," Mr. Camford said from behind him. "Mrs. Camford will soon take her in hand. Didn't take any sass from our four boys, nor from you, either, begging your pardon. I couldn't help but see you rubbing at your head. Shall I bring you some laudanum, sir?"

"No, thank you, that won't be necessary. I'll leave you and your good wife to sort things out, if I may, and retreat to my study to lick my wounds. Please have Mrs. Boxer brought to me when it suits her."

Mrs. Boxer. If she looked that good wet, cold and bedraggled, how would she appear in velvet and diamonds? *Mrs.* What in bloody hell was he to do with a *Mrs.*?

And why had her demeanor gone from aggravated (truly, aggravated) to apprehensive when he had asked her for proof of her claim? Both the legitimate and the imposter would have come fully armed with documentation. So why had that one question upset her?

It wasn't as if he had demanded said proof or else order Tompkins to toss both her and the child back out into the rain. You didn't just toss innocent children around from pillar to post all willy-nilly, as if they didn't have feelings.

The headache was closing in on him now, and thinking hurt, so he'd stop doing it.

CHAPTER TWO

"I ALREADY TOLD YOU I was sorry. Three whole times," Marley whined, her bottom lip stuck forward in a defensive pout. "But he was mean to us. I could tell, because you were using that voice you use when you're ready to go *pop*. That's what Papa used to say. You get all sweet as treacle, Papa told me, and then you go *pop*."

"I wasn't ready to pop," Sadie told her niece as the two sat on the hearth rug in front of the nursery fire, finally dry and warm once more, Sadie still brushing her niece's thick blond hair.

"Yes, you were. *Pop!*"

"All right, perhaps I was. But His Lordship has to be the most insufferable—no. I didn't say that. He's your guardian now, Marley. That means you will be polite, well-behaved, obedient when he speaks to you and that you never again kick him in the shin. What would your papa have said if he'd seen such naughty behavior?"

"Papa's dead," Marley answered flatly, hugging the rag doll that was the most beloved of her possessions.

Yes, John was dead. A truth not easily forgotten. Her brother was dead and Marley's world had been turned upside down in an instant.

"I know, sweetheart," she said, gathering the child close. "We've spoken about this many times. He had never been well since he returned from the war, had he? Now he's with the angels, and we're thankful he's at peace, reunited with your mama. Isn't that right?"

Marley turned those huge green eyes on her aunt. "You're not sick, are you, Sadie? You aren't going to go see Papa and Mama?"

And there it was again, the fear Marley carried with her, the one Sadie couldn't seem to make go away.

"No, I'm not about to do that. I promised, remember? Why, I'm going to stay so close to you that one day you'll be forced to lock your door to keep me out."

Death was a tricky subject all by itself, but explaining the finality of it to a child could break a person's heart.

And now, apparently, Marley had a new worry.

"That's what you say. He can't send you away, can he?"

"That's His Lordship to you, young lady, not *he*." Sadie tapped her niece's pert little nose. "That being said, no, *he* won't do that. Only an unfeeling brute would separate you from your very last blood relative, and your papa said the viscount is a good and honorable man."

Had she sounded convincing? Marley gave her a quick squeeze and got to her feet, looking much relieved. If her papa had said it, then it must be true.

If only I could feel equally certain, Sadie told herself. *Because here we are, nearly out of funds and completely devoid of options*.

"Ah, and here comes Peggy with your milk and cakes, just as promised. You tuck into that while I go see His Lordship and thank him for his fine welcome. Peggy?"

"I'll watch her, missus," the young maid said, bobbing a curtsy. "I got two bitty sisters of my own. Mayhap we'll sing songs, won't we, young miss?"

"I suppose so," Marley answered, seating herself at

the child-size table in the center of the room, and her rag doll in the adjoining chair. If nothing else, the child had taken to the luxury of her new surroundings without a blink. "I know lots of songs. Lots and lots."

"But *not* the one you overheard one of the outside passengers singing yesterday," Sadie warned as she stood in front of a small mirror and inspected her appearance. Her hair looked presentable enough, brushed back severely and twisted into a figure-eight knot at her nape. The knot itself was damp, but if she'd waited until her hair was completely dry it would be nearly time for the first dinner gong.

She had never heard a dinner gong, but she'd read about them, and fine houses such as this one. What a lovely place for Marley to grow up, surrounded by such beauty and ease. Marley was young, and already adapting to her new surroundings, seeing the housekeeper and Peggy as new friends.

While Sadie felt out of place, an interloper. A fraud.

It was best to get over potentially treacherous ground as quickly and painlessly as possible, and that meant she could not allow His Lordship any more time to think up objections or inconvenient questions, or more time for her to doubt her ability to answer those questions in a convincing manner.

Her niece needed her; it was as simple as that. As complicated as that. She could not fail.

"But it was so silly," Marley complained around a large bite of cake. "'It's of a pretty shepherdess, kept sheep all on the plain,'" she sang in a high, childish voice. An innocent voice. "'Who should ride by but Knight William, and he was drunk with wine.'"

"Marley Katherine—stifle yourself."

"'Line, twine, the willow and the dee.' That's all I remember before you clapped your hands over my ears."

"And thank the good Lord for that," Peggy said, breaking off a piece of cake with her fingers and all but shoving it into her new charge's mouth.

"I'm so sorry, Peggy. She...she picks up very quickly on anything she hears. And has no problem repeating each word, verbatim. You are to consider yourself warned, I suppose," Sadie said, taking one last moment to smooth down her plain, pale blue gown before heading for the stairs.

"Mrs. Camford said to tell you she'll be waiting on you in the entrance hall, to escort you to His Lordship's study, and act as chaperone," Peggy called after her.

"Oh, wonderful. So very kind of her," Sadie said, and thanked the maid.

And then muttered to herself for the first two flights of her descent from the attic nursery to the entrance hall. Was the viscount in the habit of physically pouncing on his female guests...or did he worry that his unwelcome guest might become so overwhelmed by his masculine attraction that she'd assault *him*?

She wished she didn't feel she was on such shaky ground. Until a few short hours ago it had never occurred to her that she might not be believed. Everyone knew her; everyone knew she was honest and truthful. What a shame that *everyone* remained in the village.

"Mrs. Boxer," the housekeeper said when the last flight of stairs ended at the tile floor of the entrance hall.

"Mrs. Camford," Sadie returned, along with a matching nod of her head. Only a fool wouldn't believe they were sizing each other up, deciding on how to go on. "Thank you again for your kind and generous welcome.

I promise you that Miss Marley is usually much better behaved. She's frightened, you understand, having so recently lost both her papa and her home."

"And you, Mrs. Boxer, if I might ask?" the house-keeper said as she motioned for Sadie to follow her to the rear of the house. "Have you also lost your home?"

Lost my home? Yes, let's go with that, since apparently it's easy to believe, women being so inherently fragile and in need of protection that nobody would ever suppose they could get by on their own.

So recently reminded by Marley of her betraying tendency, Sadie attempted to tamp down the sweet drawl as she bristled at the woman's curiosity, as it wouldn't do to go *pop*. Still, she would stick to the truth, or as near to it as possible.

"As I resided with my brother in lodgings provided by his patients, yes, that accommodation was no longer open to either Miss Marley or myself. But that's not why I'm here. I'm here to deliver my brother's daughter to the man who promised to care for her in the event of my brother's death. If asked to leave, I will do so, the moment I feel my niece is in good hands."

She couldn't keep the smile and drawl at bay as she ended, "I do most sincerely hope that aids in your information, Mrs. Camford, but if there's anything else you feel the need to know, please don't hesitate to ask."

The woman's blush told Sadie that she'd made her point—that she knew she was being questioned, measured, perhaps even judged. The staff was very protective of the viscount apparently. Odd, because he certainly didn't seem in need of protection.

"That was rude of me, and uncalled for. Forgive me, Mrs. Camford. I'm horribly nervous about meeting with

His Lordship. I know what an imposition this is for him. Not many gentlemen would be willing to take on a young female ward."

"He'll manage just fine, missus. It's *you* he wasn't expecting, or so I say. And here we are," Mrs. Camford said, putting her hand to the handle of a dark oaken door. "I will see if His Lordship is agreeable to seeing you."

Sadie nodded, realizing they'd passed by several rooms she normally would have loved to see, totally oblivious to her surroundings. "I suppose I was a bit of a surprise."

"More like a shock, missus, to tell the truth, and so I told Mr. Camford." The housekeeper quickly rapped on the door and then stepped inside, holding it nearly closed behind her as she said, "My lord, Mrs. Boxer is without."

"Without what, Camy? Nothing vital missing, I hope." Sadie heard the man question, humor in his voice. "And since when have we become so formal here at the cottage? I have enough of that everywhere else. Let her in, and then close the door behind you. Please."

Sadie did her best to school her features into some semblance of calm as she stepped into the room…only then realizing she might just be voluntarily entering a lion's den.

The door closed behind her even as the viscount pushed himself up from the black leather couch he'd been sitting on. Lying on, she mentally corrected, noticing the sleep marks on his cheek, put there by a quilted satin pillow. Apparently he'd been relaxed enough to nap as he waited for her. How lovely for him.

"With you on the other side of it, Camy, please. I doubt she bites."

Sadie turned to see the housekeeper directly behind

her, and gave her a sympathetic look and shrug of her shoulders.

The door opened and closed again, and Sadie was alone with Darby Travers, the man who held Marley's fate in his hands, even if he'd yet to know that, and wouldn't, not until she was assured the man wasn't planning to wriggle out of his new responsibility.

She decided to prove her relationship to John before the man could repeat his earlier suspicions, spoken of so jokingly at their first, unfortunate meeting.

"John told me much about you, my lord, and those days in that horrible camp. You, and your friends, and so many more fine English soldiers, all the victims of the consequences of inferior leadership. How are the others, if I might inquire? Captains Sinclair, Rigby and Cooper Townsend, the latter injured in the same battle as Your Lordship. John said you four were close as inkle weavers and always ripe for adventure. He seemed to swell with pride at having known you. May I be seated?"

There. Now she could only hope that mentioning the names of his friends carried any weight for him in proving she was who she said she was. Or had she been too obvious?

She sat down before he could answer, moving the quilted pillow out of the way. The satin was still warm to the touch, and smelled faintly of the same shaving soap her brother had favored. She resisted an urge to clasp it close to her chest, as a sort of protection.

She'd already noticed that the man really didn't look well, certainly not displaying the same vibrant presence he'd projected earlier. His complexion was rather pale now beneath a healthy tan, his hair a bit ruffled, as if he'd been running his fingers through it, or perhaps massaging his head.

He had the headache, perhaps? A lingering reminder of his wound? She felt some pity for him, but wasn't so silly that she didn't see the advantage could temporarily reside in her corner during what would probably turn out to be a sparring match between them. With luck, whatever ailed him would put him off his game, as John had told her the viscount was wickedly intelligent, witty and didn't suffer fools gladly. Her brother had admired the man, his courage and even self-deprecating humor in the face of his terrible injury.

"They're all in good health, thank you for asking. We were all quite fond of John, and saddened to hear of his death." Lord Nailbourne didn't retake his seat, choosing instead to lean against the front of an ancient carved desk some feet distant from the couch.

What was the protocol in duels? Ten paces, then stop, turn and fire? Sadie could feel the tension in the room, and wondered if it was all coming from her, as the dratted man still seemed very much at his ease.

Well or in pain, he was a handsome man, possibly made even more so by the eye patch, and his height would have been intimidating to most. Sadie gave a quick thank-you to her parents, who had combined to make her the empowering height she was. If she'd been a petite thing, she might feel completely overwhelmed and overmatched by the man. In truth, she still would have felt more than slightly intimidated, save for the quilt marks on his right cheek, which made him seem more human. Rather like a young boy, playing dress-up.

She wasn't sure now what she'd been expecting, as John had never mentioned the viscount's age, but it was clear he still lacked a few years before he was on the shady side of thirty. So young, and yet one of the wealthiest men in England, with all the benefits and burdens that sort of thing entailed.

And now she'd added to his responsibilities.

"My lord," she began, searching for the correct words to show she knew of the imposition John had placed on him, but he stopped her simply by raising his hand.

"Forgive me for doubting your identity earlier."

That sounded rather like a demand, but she was too relieved to challenge him.

"I looked at the letter again, and clearly nowhere did you suggest that you were a solicitor acting on John's behalf. In fact, you didn't identify yourself at all."

That was definitely an accusation. Even if he'd cut off her apology, clearly he wasn't going to take all blame onto his shoulders.

"No, I suppose I didn't," she said. It had taken her some time and several attempts before she'd been satisfied with the letter. She certainly could not have given him the one John had written. Yes, John. A safer subject than the letter, no question. "I imagine you'll want to know more about my brother."

"I say again, a good man."

"Yes, but you're wondering why he would ask me to hold you to a promise you made him so long ago. That's understandable. John was injured in the camp, shortly before the Russians found it and freed their men and the British who were there. What you might know as being *belly shot*. He—" Sadie hesitated, as the wound to her heart was still raw "—never fully recovered, and this past summer—the heat, you understand—was a torture to him. We both knew it was only a matter of time. His passing was a blessing in many ways."

"You're saying he as good as died in that camp. Again, I'm sincerely sorry, Mrs. Boxer. I tried to convince him to leave with us, but he wouldn't desert his patients. Your brother died a hero, and I can do no less than stand by my promise to him."

Sadie's shoulders finally relaxed. One hurdle passed over safely. Marley would have a home.

"He said you were an honorable man, that you all were brave and honorable gentlemen. Thank you. I know Marley will be safe with you."

The viscount pushed himself away from the desk. "Safe, Mrs. Boxer? That seems an odd choice of word."

Wickedly intelligent. I shouldn't forget that, must never fully relax my guard.

"John left little money, and owned no property. Everything he had came courtesy of our village, and hopefully there will be a new physician installed within a few months. It was only because I could manage the surgery on his behalf while he was away, and yes, after he returned, that we weren't put out on the street months ago."

"Really? It would appear you are a woman of hidden talents. How fortunate for the villagers."

Was he mocking her? Applauding her? Doubting her? His tone, his smile, could be interpreted many ways.

"One does what one must, especially with so many doctors and surgeons gone to war, but I am no physician. Once John truly was gone, a more suitable replacement was in order. Marley is homeless, near-penniless and alone save for me. In today's world, would you call that safe, my lord?"

There, that should satisfy him!

He rubbed at his forehead. "I seem to go from bad to worse with you, Mrs. Boxer, so I might as well push on. Where is your husband? May I assume he also is deceased?"

Or did he run, screaming, into the night, to be shed of you? He didn't say that, but Sadie was fairly certain he was thinking it.

But she'd prepared herself for this question. "You're correct to believe I am without a husband, my lord. Maxwell has been gone for more than two years now."

So much truth, taken separately. It was only when the two were put together that her words could be seen as a whopping great lie.

The viscount appeared to consider those words for long moments, as if repeating them in his mind. He then walked around the desk, to stand, his back turned to her, before the impressive expanse of windows that looked out over the rear of the estate.

"My condolences on your loss. But back to my new ward. I was raised here at the cottage after my parents died," he said quietly, so that Sadie sat forward on the couch in order to hear him. "She and I have something in common, as I imagine I was about her same age at the time. Eventually I went off to school, spending all my holidays here with the Camfords until I reached my majority. Your niece will be in good hands with them, unless you believe I turned out badly."

There. It was settled, and out of his own mouth. But could she relax now? She doubted it, for she was still in the room, and what on earth had he planned for her? Truly, he couldn't have planned for her at all, could he? The inconvenient aunt.

"Thank you. I am sure I'm not prepared to make any

conclusions on such short acquaintance, my lord, and have placed my full reliance on John's opinion."

He turned away from the window. "A careful answer, Mrs. Boxer. Shall we return to you? Do you plan to remain here with your niece?"

And here it was, with her knowing she was still totally unprepared for the question.

"Have I been invited?"

"No, I don't believe you have. You do realize you've put me in an awkward situation. You're obviously too old to become my ward, yet you're too young and, yes, too attractive to remain here as my guest without tongues wagging all over Mayfair. Not that I've ever been opposed to that, but there is your reputation to be considered. Therefore, if you're agreeable, I believe I shall have to employ you in some fashion. Which do you prefer? Governess? Companion? Tutor?"

He was going to let her stay with Marley. Not that he had much choice, so she couldn't consider his offer a win on her side of the invisible tote board that had apparently been set up somewhere in the room.

She straightened her posture to the point that her spine protested. "Companion, I would think, seeing that I am her aunt. The position includes a wage, I presume?"

His smile took her quite by surprise, and seemed to serve to remove the tension both in his face and in the room itself.

"You move quickly, Mrs. Boxer. Do you have a figure in mind?"

"I wouldn't presume to—"

"Of course you wouldn't."

Now he was definitely being condescending. He had a burr under his saddle, most definitely, but Sadie still wasn't certain what it was. It almost seemed as if her very existence bothered him.

"I have to rethink this business of companion. Not quite right, I believe, or believable, for that matter. Never mind, I'll think of something."

"I'll await that decision, then, my lord, grateful that you'll allow me to remain with my niece."

"So happy to ease your mind, Mrs. Boxer. And now, unless you have more to share with me, beyond my painfully acquired knowledge that my ward has a predilection for violence, I believe you may retire for the nonce. If my ward has been suitably instructed in her table manners, you and she can begin taking meals in the small dining room. I can remember refusing to be constrained to the nursery for my meals by the time I was her age. However, alas, I am committed elsewhere this evening, and will be departing for London within the hour, to return tomorrow. Or perhaps next week."

Sadie leaped to her feet, speaking before she could think better of it. "You won't be here? Oh, no, that won't do, my lord. Marley is your ward. She remains with you. I must insist."

Could she have been more clumsy?

The viscount, his hands behind his back, walked up to her, stopping much too close to her, and looked into her eyes. "You must insist? And why is that, Mrs. Boxer?"

Sadie scrambled for an explanation that would seem reasonable. "She, um, Marley has just lost her father. She…she needs to know someone still cares about her."

"Other than yourself?"

"Yes! Yes, that's it. A…a *male* presence."

"A male presence," he repeated, and the words sounded no more convincing when he said them. "I see.

And a male presence would make her feel—what was the word? Oh, yes—*safe*. Mrs. Boxer, forgive me, but a thought occurs. Could you have perhaps kidnapped your niece?"

That question came close enough to the target to be uncomfortable.

"Of course not! Why would I do any such thing?"

"Oh, I don't know. Perhaps to find yourself a deeper gravy boat than the one you might be offered—if any— by John's other relatives?"

"I thought I'd told you. I am Marley's only living relative."

"And that would be her only living relative on John's side. Is the child as unfortunately lacking in family on her late mother's side?" He leaned in even closer. "Mrs. Boxer? Cat caught your tongue?"

Everything now rested on her answer. Marley's future, and her own. And the lies were piling up.

"My sister-in-law had no family of her own, as they'd perished in a fire while she was away at school. There is no one else, my lord."

"Poor imp, her entire life has been one long litany of tragedy and loss. Save for her dearest aunt, that is."

Would he just stop smiling and shut up!

"But she is not without hope. You promised John. John is dead. As her aunt, I have decided where her best future lies, and that is with you. Please don't force me to rethink my decision."

He stepped back a few paces, and Sadie realized her hands were shaking.

"I would never do that. At least not until I understand what the devil is going on here. Are you going to tell me the truth?"

It wasn't easy, but she kept her gaze locked with his. "I've told you the truth."

"Very smoothly, yes. Very nearly as if you'd rehearsed every word, save for a few unsettling stumbles. Perhaps a few tears might have made it all more convincing."

Tears? She was more than ready to box his ears. How dare he be so clever.

"I have no time for such miss-ish indulgences, my lord. I have a responsibility."

"As do I. Yes, Mrs. Boxer, you've driven your point home. Make yourselves comfortable in my absence. And then we'll have us another small, hopefully more enlightening conversation." The viscount strolled to the closed door and opened it with a flourish, inviting her to leave.

If she were Marley, she would have kicked him in the shin. But she wasn't, and since their newly acquired safe haven hung in the balance, she would do her best to behave.

"I can't help but wonder. Did you kill him?" His Lordship asked as she walked by, her chin once again held high.

Sadie stumbled, nearly fell, so that he grabbed her elbow to steady her. She felt light-headed, her knees nearly turned to water, her vision blurry, and for a moment she thought she either might vomit on His Lordship's shoe-tops or faint at his feet.

"Steady on, Mrs. Boxer."

She had no choice but to pretend to have not understood the question.

"Forgive me, I stubbed my toe on the carpet. Did you mean my husband, my lord? I suppose you would think his death a happy release, married to me. How very droll of you."

"No, Mrs. Boxer. I was referring to my friend John. You've been a puzzle to me since you first stormed into this house. It would seem your lot in life has improved immeasurably thanks to your brother's demise, no longer forced to care for him as he continued to linger on after his wound. I hadn't considered your husband. Should I? No, don't answer, not on either head. I'm certain I'll find out soon enough, as I do so love a puzzle. In the meantime, I have no fears for my ward. After all, she's your golden goose, isn't she? In any case, I've now changed my mind about keeping her here. Be ready, both you and my charge, to leave for London in two hours."

"Her name is Marley, my lord. I suggest you become familiar with it. And I will add that you're extremely insulting. Everything is just as I told you."

"So you say, and I've carefully noted your vehemence as you denied my purely idle question without really answering it. That said, I'm equally as certain you won't mind if I satisfy my curiosity by doing a bit of investigating on my own. I feel I owe that to John."

"No, I most certainly don't mind. And then, sir, you can apologize." With that her only parting shot, she curtsied rather rudely and turned for the door.

"We shall see, won't we, Mrs. Boxer? Remember, two hours, no more."

Sadie was halfway to the nursery before she calmed herself enough to realize that one of the things he'd do would be to search out any information he could about one Maxwell Boxer.

And good luck to you with that, Lord Nosypants!

CHAPTER THREE

IT HAD BEEN a decidedly odd journey to London, with Darby leading the way in his curricle, followed by his traveling coach containing Mrs. Boxer, his new ward and—Good God, how had he forgotten?—Norton, dressed in his best clothes and visibly eager to visit with his chums at the Crown and Cock.

He would have enjoyed being privileged to overhear any conversation transpiring within the coach during the hour-long drive.

It certainly had been interesting when Mrs. Boxer and his ward—Marley, he really should think of her by name—had stepped out of the house to see Norton holding open the door to the coach and the latter had immediately inquired as to the valet's odd hair coloring.

"Sadie, why is that man's hair red if his beard is black? Remember when we found that baby woodpecker that had fallen out of a tree and the top of his head looked as if he was wearing a red cap, but the rest of him was black and white, and you said that was because he was a baby woodpecker and—"

"Marley, shhh."

"But his hair is red and his beard is black."

"I heard you the first time. 'Shhh' means to stop talking. And I would imagine it's because he prefers it that way."

"You mean he did it on purpose? Like the vicar's wife when she painted her hair orange, and wouldn't take off her bonnet for six whole months? Why would he do that?"

"I'm certain that's no business of ours, just as I told you it was no concern of yours just before you asked Mrs. Thompson that same question before vespers."

"But he looks silly. Shouldn't we tell him?"

"I believe you already have. Lower your voice."

"I think I like the red better than the black."

"An opinion you will keep to yourself."

"I don't understand why people can't ask questions. If someone doesn't want questions, someone shouldn't paint his hair. That's what I think. Sadie, what do you think?"

"I wouldn't dare tell you," Mrs. Boxer had said, taking her niece's hand as they made their way down the marble steps to the drive, and the waiting Norton.

Who had smiled quite genuinely at Marley and tipped his hat before offering to lift her up and into the coach, already having launched into an explanation about his black mustache and beard.

Mrs. Boxer had turned her head to encounter Darby standing there, still doing his utmost not to laugh, and she'd shot him a smile clearly meant to imply that children were such a treat, weren't they?

At that moment he had very nearly changed his mind about choosing his curricle over his coach. But he had too much to think about as they made their way to Mayfair, and clearly Mrs. Boxer would prove a distraction.

And now they were here, having dropped Norton at the Crown and Cock as promised, probably not more than three hours after his hastily scribbled appeal to the Duchess of Cranbrook had arrived in Grosvenor Square.

Vivien, darling lady, my ward has arrived at last, and trouble travels with her in the form of her aunt, who appears too nervous by half and, I believe, is not being entirely truthful with me for reasons I've yet to discern. In any event, they cannot stay with me in my bachelor residence, nor can I leave them at the cottage since I refuse to remain there while everyone else is kicking up their heels in Mayfair. In my desperation, I am bringing them to you yet today, falling on your mercy and that of my friends.

To compensate for any inconvenience, I feel certain you'll all find much to amuse you in my dilemma, one most probably made more pronounced by the fact that the aunt is also quite beautiful, something I'm doing my utmost to disregard, at least for now.

As he tossed the reins to one of the duke's grooms and hopped down to the flagway, he pretended not to notice the draperies twitching in three of the long windows facing the street. He could count on Gabe's duchess aunt to be peeking from behind one of them, Rigby's Clarice from the second, and could only hope Coop's mother didn't make up the remainder of the trio. But since he couldn't think of a worse combination—as far as his sanity was concerned—he made a silent wager with himself that he was correct.

He waved a footman away and opened the door of

the coach himself, smiling into the interior to ask if the ladies had enjoyed their coach ride.

His answer came from Marley, who launched herself at him, so that he was forced to catch hold of her or else she'd fall to the flagway. "Here now, is that any way for a lady to exit a coach?"

"I suppose there are others," the child answered matter-of-factly, her arms wrapped around his neck, definitely putting paid to his carefully tied neck cloth, her legs scissored around his waist. Oddly, rather than being annoyed, he somewhat enjoyed her enthusiasm. "Thank you, thank you, thank you, Uncle Nailbourne. That was quite the most pleasant coach ride I have ever had. Norton pointed out all the sights, and even promised to take me to the park to see the swans. I never saw a swan, did you? Their necks are exceedingly *long*, Norton says, and then he explained about his hair. Would you like to know *why* he paints his beard black?"

Darby was still attempting to regain his breath— apparently a slight but well-aimed child had the power to partially knock the wind out of him. And she'd actually addressed him as Uncle Nailbourne. Oh, wouldn't his friends delight in how far, and how quickly, the mighty had fallen. "Well, I suppose I—"

"Think carefully before you answer, my lord," Sadie Grace Boxer warned as she made shooing motions with her hands so that he would move away from the coach and the footman could put down the steps for her. "How badly do you want to know about your valet's personal grooming choices?"

He looked at the aunt, who was now standing beside him, and then to his new ward, who now had her cheek pressed against his shoulder as she blinked up at him, and came to a decision.

"Another time perhaps, poppet. We'll go inside now."

"A prudent answer," Mrs. Boxer whispered as she preceded him up the marble steps and into the foyer of the mansion, just as if she entered mansions every day of her life. "What a lovely residence you have, my lord," she remarked as she turned in a full circle, admiring her surroundings.

"I do, yes," he said, finally able to detach Marley from his person. She immediately began hopping—jumping from one large black tile square to the next, careful not to land on any of the white tiles. "This, however, is not it. Make her stop, if you please."

"The ladies await in the main drawing room, my lord," the Cranbrook butler said, eyeing Marley as if she might have been a puppy who'd tracked in mud from the streets and now expected a reward.

Mrs. Boxer snapped her fingers twice and, unbelievably, Marley came to her at once, slipping her hand into her aunt's. From the faintly surprised look on that aunt's face, she had been as astonished by her niece's quick obedience nearly as much as had Darby.

"She's been cooped up in too many coaches for too many days, my lord. Your ward is only showing a healthy, youthful exuberance. Were you never a child? And what do you mean, to say this isn't your residence? Where have you brought us?"

"I'd say a den of iniquity, were it not very nearly true. I'll explain once we're upstairs." He snapped his fingers twice as he headed for the wide staircase, sadly without the same obedient result, as Marley ignored him to goggle up at the huge chandelier that hung in the foyer.

The butler was already halfway up the stairs, on his way to announce the visitors. "If you and Marley will follow me, please."

"Marley, follow your uncle Nailbourne."

Once had been enough, and at least the child only repeated what she was told. But the aunt, as well? *Go to Uncle Nailbourne. Curtsy to Uncle Nailbourne. Slow down, darling, so poor Uncle Nailbourne can catch up.* No, he wouldn't allow it. He stopped on the second step and turned back. "Darby. She is to address me as Darby."

"That's quite impossible, my lord, and definitely not acceptable. She is a child, and you are her guardian."

"Darby," he repeated. "She calls you Sadie, and she can bloody—very well call me Darby. Is that clear?"

Sadie shrugged. "You're in charge, I suppose."

"There is no *suppose* about it, Mrs. Boxer."

He wasn't made for this. He wasn't prepared for it, had no idea what to do with a child or the child's aunt. Neither fit into his life, his idea of what his life was about...and as soon as he figured out exactly *what* his life was about, he'd be a happy man. He'd been a boy, and then a soldier, and since he'd returned from the war he'd been pretty much nothing but a man happy to move with the tide of events as they occurred. Not quite a grand example for a man now in charge of a young female ward.

To be fair, he had been giving at least a cursory thought to setting up his nursery, as titled gentlemen were expected to do, as Gabe and Rigby and even Coop were in the process of doing—all but tumbling over one another to do, as a matter of fact. It did seem the next logical step.

But if he was going to one day be *Uncle Nailbourne*, it

would be to his friends' children, and if he were to take a wife, it certainly wouldn't be— Lord, he needed a drink.

"Darby, there you are, you scamp. What a deliciously confusing message you sent me. We're all agog to learn more."

"Aunt Vivien," he said as the petite woman and her usual filmy draperies and ruffles exited the drawing room, to meet him in the large first-floor foyer. He quickly motioned for Sadie and Marley to sit themselves down on a nearby ornate bench—hopefully out of ear-shot of whispers—while he dealt with Her Grace.

Within a moment he was engulfed in butter-yellow silk and tulle, kissing the top of the woman's bouncy silver curls and inhaling her powdery scent. "You've saved my life."

"I have? Well, isn't that clever of me. How have I done that?"

"By inviting my ward and her aunt to reside with you until I can bloody well figure out what to do with both of them," he whispered into her ear. "You know they can't stay with me."

She whispered right back at him: "They could, if you were in mind of creating a scandal, but I suppose you aren't. Is that them, plopped down way over there on that uncomfortable bench the fourth duke dragged home from Lord only knows where, saying the elephant feet were all the *mode*? Pretty, the pair of them, definitely not the bench, which is horrid. Country mice, though, definitely not up to snuff for the Season. May I have the dressing of them, as well?"

"You, Aunt Vivien?" he asked, once again finding himself having to disengage from a clinging female. The woman, dear lady that she was, dressed like a confection suited to be displayed in a bakery shop window. "Only you?"

The duchess gave his chest a playful slap. "No, silly, *all of us*. Well, except for Coop's mother. Minerva has the oddest taste. Perhaps we'll allow her to choose gloves. Not a whacking great lot of damage one can do with gloves, isn't that right? Now bring them inside. Have you no manners?"

"So you'll do it? You'll take them off my—that is, you'll ask them to join you here until the end of the Season? I know I'm asking a lot, especially with the duke's birthday fast approaching, but—"

"Must I cross my heart and swear, you scamp? It's going to be the greatest fun, and give Basil something else to think about beyond discovering himself to be either horizontal or vertical come his birthday morn. Although what you'll do with them afterward is a subject for delicious conjecture. We've already discussed it among us, you know. Clarice says—"

"Another time, Aunt Vivien," Darby interrupted, well able to image what Rigby's beloved said. He'd already been put to the blush, as it were, enough for one day, and he still had to face the rest of the ladies.

"Come say hello to your aunt Vivien, my dears," the duchess trilled, and he watched as Marley leaped to her feet and ran straight up to the duchess, dropping a curtsy that nearly ended with her stepping on the duchess's full skirts. Mrs. Boxer approached more cautiously, eyeing Darby, clearly in hope of some explanation for a very curious five minutes.

"Your Grace, may I present to you Mrs. Sadie Grace Boxer and my ward, Miss Marley Hamilton. Mrs. Boxer, Her Grace, Vivien Sinclair, Duchess of Cranbrook."

Sadie's mouth fell open—to her credit, only slightly, and she quickly recovered. "Your Grace," she said, dropping into a perfectly respectable curtsy. "It is indeed an honor."

"Yes, I suppose so. Everyone seems to say that, although I'm no different than I was before all this curtsying and bowing business became a part of our lives. Please, call me Aunt Vivien. Everyone does. And I shall call you Sadie and Marley. I had a cousin Sadie, years ago, but I've lost track of her since she ran off with her husband's man of business. And far from penniless, as they took all of poor Robert's funds with them."

Darby cleared his throat. "We're still standing here, Aunt Vivien. Perhaps we should introduce the ladies to the rest of the company?"

"Oh, fiddle, of course." The duchess turned to reenter the drawing room, having taken Marley's hand in her own, but Sadie stood her ground, refusing to budge when Darby offered her his arm.

"The duchess is your aunt?"

"A courtesy title only. My friend Gabe is the duke's nephew and heir. She and the duke feel much more comfortable with informality. I'll explain later."

"Yes, you will. My imagination was running wild. For a moment I thought you'd brought us to a well-to-do brothel, and the duchess was the madam, or procuress, or whatever such people are called."

Darby's bark of laughter caused her to flinch slightly.

"It's her gown," she went on quickly. "I've never quite seen so many ruffles."

"She wants the dressing of you," Darby said, offering her his arm once more. "Apparently she and the other ladies have decided you and Marley are to move about in Society while you're here."

"You aren't going to allow that, are you?"

He was actually becoming used to the idea, odd as that seemed to him. The sight of Sadie Grace Boxer in fine silk and pearls might prove interesting. In fact, the more he thought about how displeased that same Sadie Grace appeared to be, the more he approved the ladies' plans.

"The dressing of you, no. I'm afraid the ladies are quite set on the rest of it. You could have remained at the cottage, not that I'd be so crass as to point that out to you."

"No, you'd never be that, would you? And where will you be, my lord, once you've successfully dumped your responsibility in that sweet old lady's lap?" she asked, taking his arm and forcing a smile to her face as they at last entered the enormous drawing room.

He had one thing to say for the woman. She could hold her own in a give-and-take of words. Of course, he wasn't sure that could be listed as a compliment, not when she was also so clearly concealing something from him.

"Hiding in a cupboard under the stairs most quickly springs to mind, Mrs. Boxer, but I do believe that won't be allowed. Shall we be on with it? I'll introduce you to the ladies and be off about my business for a few days, giving you and my ward time to...settle in. You'll be *safe* here. In every way."

"Her name is Marley, and we're both in mourning. It would be highly improper for us, me most especially, to go into Society."

"I'm convinced John would understand, under the

circumstances. Well, Mrs. Boxer? I don't hear any argument coming from your direction, which is refreshing."

"That's only because you're correct. John specifically asked that Marley not be subjected to a year of mourning."

"And?"

"And I agreed," she muttered before Clarice Goodfellow, never one to wait patiently for anything, came at them, all but cooing in pleasure over the smiling Marley she carried along with her, the child's legs wrapped around her hip.

Darby quickly counted noses. Besides the duchess and Clarice, Minerva Townsend was present, along with Gabe's Thea and Coop's Dany. More than needed for a witches' coven.

Five against one. Seven, if he counted Sadie and Marley.

Darby introduced, bowed, kissed hands and excused himself within five minutes, lamenting that he could no longer keep his cattle standing.

Marley, he was certain, was the only one who didn't know he was lying through his teeth.

CHAPTER FOUR

WHAT A DIFFERENCE a few days can make. From sorrowful country mouse, to panicked hare on the run, to pampered pet curled up snug as a bug in a rug in the middle of fashionable Mayfair, Sadie's entire life had seen change after rapid change.

Could she relax now? It seemed so, at least for the moment. Except, of course, for the fact that Marley's curious guardian had been noticeably absent for five entire days, but would be calling on Sadie in a few minutes, supposedly to take her for a stroll in the square.

What pleasant surroundings for what was sure to be an inquisition, at least thankfully without the thumbscrews or rack.

Five days. More than enough time for him to have stuck his nose where she wished it would never go. Time to think up a dozen questions she'd have to answer without hesitation, without fear. Without telling him the whole truth.

"Did you kill him?"

Yes, her days with the ladies had been chaotic, bordering on delightful, but her nights had been filled with those four carelessly drawled words and the memories they evoked.

The viscount had this *way* about him, Sadie had decided. Even in such short acquaintance, she had recognized his intelligence, for one, and his curiosity, for another. He had a rather *silken* way about him, saying things that seemed innocuous and even slightly silly on the surface, but with an intensity of purpose behind every carefully careless thing he said. He didn't goad her, as he'd done at the cottage, because he was a mean man, but because she hadn't had sufficient time to produce a more convincing story, and he had seen straight through her.

Not to the lies themselves, thank goodness, but to the fact she was telling them.

She'd actually believed herself to be on relatively solid ground until he'd asked her why he should believe her as to Marley's identity, her own identity. He'd certainly had every right to ask the question, but she hadn't been prepared to have her word doubted. She had proof, certainly she did, but to show it to him would open the door to everything else.

"There you are, Sadie. He's downstairs. Don't forget your new cloak and bonnet. And just you wait until you see what he's brought with him!"

Sadie snapped out of her uncomfortable reverie, surreptitiously wiped at her damp cheeks and unfolded herself from the window seat overlooking the mews. Smoothing down the same light blue morning gown she'd worn the first time she'd met the viscount, she looked at Clarice, who was all but hopping from one foot to the other, apparently in some anticipation.

What a lovable creature she was, and lovely into the bargain, from her blond curls to her saucer-size blue eyes, to her...interestingly curved figure. But it was her open and carefree nature that made Sadie feel so comfortable around her, and she knew she had found a friend.

Clarice Goodfellow viewed most everything to be either delicious or wonderfully exciting and worthy of exclamations—be it the materials the ladies had picked for Sadie's and Marley's new wardrobes or the fact that the Cranbrook chef had prepared sugared berries for dessert.

"My goodness, Clarice, did the man bring a pony with him, or perhaps a monkey on a chain?"

Her new friend looked crestfallen for a moment. "No, neither of those." Just as quickly, she brightened once more. "But very nearly as wonderful."

Sadie patted at her hair as she did a quick inventory of her appearance in the mirror—she must have looked into the mirror more often since arriving at the cottage than she had done in her entire life—picked up her borrowed cloak and bonnet and followed Clarice out into the hallway. "Then we must settle for very nearly as wonderful. I will do my utmost to hide my disappointment."

"Oh, he didn't bring anything for *you*, silly. He brought it for Marley."

Sadie found herself tipping her head slightly and smiling. The viscount had brought a gift—a very nearly as wonderful as a pony or a monkey gift—for his new ward? Wasn't that sweet. And thoughtful. Perhaps she'd been judging him too harshly, and he was more delighted to have a ward thrust upon him than he was interested in asking questions.

No, she doubted that. He had probably brought the gift just so that she would relax, feel in charity with him, and then he'd start in on the questions once more.

Oh, he was a tricky sort. And not above using Marley to get to her, soothe her into lowering her guard, even liking him. She'd thought he'd assign the ladies the mission of asking penetrating questions, assuming she would tell women things she would not tell him. They'd gathered around like mother hens over Marley, and taken Sadie into their circle without a blink. She had never much cared for the company of women, truth be told, but these ladies were so open, so sincere and definitely unique that Sadie probably would have confided in them if they'd asked.

Yet none of them had, not in five whole days.

"You've been lulled into feeling comfortable, Sadie Grace. This unexpected gift to Marley is probably the man's coup de grâce, and he'll expect you to spout the truth now like a garden fountain."

"You said something, Sadie?" Clarice asked from behind her.

"Just cudgeling my brain as to what this gift could be," she answered, realizing she still had her hand on the newel post, and had not begun a descent to the lower floor.

"There's only one way to find out, you know, and dragging your feet like some silly looby isn't one of them. Come on now, it doesn't bite. Well, at least it hasn't yet. Follow me."

Clarice brushed past her, leaving Sadie to follow. But slowly. She was girding her loins, or stiffening her upper lip, or whatever anyone could hope to do when faced with a worthy adversary.

But she possessed her own measure of intelligence. She had long ago cultivated a rather admirable backbone. She had to remember that; she was not without defenses of her own. The viscount was no match for her, not when she didn't allow herself to be distracted by anything. Not by this so-called gift. Not by the generous inclusion offered by the ladies. Not by the soft bed, nor the more than ample meals. Not the new gowns she and Marley would soon have hanging in their wardrobes.

And most certainly not the smiling, one-eyed viscount who was much too attractive for her to think about him the way she had been these last days, just as if she'd never before encountered anyone quite like him.

Even if she hadn't.

Sadie approached the drawing room slowly, listening to the voices coming from the interior, and paused in the doorway to see the duchess, Clarice and Mrs. Townsend all leaning forward in their seats, looking at something on the floor.

Some*one* on the floor.

The viscount, clad in his impeccable London finery, was actually sitting cross-legged on the carpet, watching as Marley sat there, as well, attempting to hold on to a squiggly tan puppy with long drooping ears and a tongue currently employed in placing slobbering kisses all over her niece's face.

"Oh, stop, puppy, stop!" Marley exclaimed, still holding on tightly. "That tickles!"

"Perhaps if you let him go he'd stop," the viscount suggested, his smile easy and relaxed.

He looks younger again, the way he did with the pillow marks on his cheek. And he genuinely seems to be enjoying himself.

Marley tightened her grip on the puppy, and Sadie quickly recognized a now-familiar panic rising in the child. She would have gone to her, but wanted to see how His Lordship reacted to this new problem. Besides, the shin-kicking episode was still fresh in her mind.

With her aunt by her side, Marley might just feel protected enough to say or do something that would ruin the lovely scene.

"Go on, sweetheart," Clarice soothed as she settled into a chair. "He really seems to want to roam now."

"You won't take him away, will you? He gets to stay with me forever and ever, doesn't he? Auntie Vivien," she implored, looking to the duchess, "he's my puppy now, isn't he? He won't go away?"

Even as the duchess and the other women all spoke at once, fervently agreeing the puppy would stay (Clarice adding, "Even if he pids on the carpets"), the viscount inched closer to Marley, patting the dog's golden head.

"Marley, look at me, please," he said quietly.

The child sniffled, but then did as she was told.

Sadie held her breath.

"I told you the puppy is yours, didn't I? I wouldn't lie to you, on my word as a gentleman. I realize you don't know me well, but I trust the good ladies here will vouch for me."

As one, the ladies "vouched."

"Thank you, ladies. Do you believe me now?"

Marley bit her bottom lip, but then nodded. "I suppose so, Darby."

Dear Lord, he had the child calling him Darby? Against her wishes to the contrary? First the puppy, and now the unseemly informality. What next from this unpredictable man? Would he bounce her niece on his knee while reciting nursery rhymes?

The viscount held out his arms and the child released her death grip so that he could deposit the fuzzy and undoubtedly relieved little thing on the carpet, where, as if fulfilling a prophecy, he immediately sniffed the carpet and then piddled.

He was a small puppy, so it was a small piddle, and nobody commented.

"Good. And now that that's settled, perhaps you'd feel even better if you gave this scamp here a name. We can't keep calling him 'puppy,' now can we? Do you have a name in mind? Reginald, perhaps?"

Once again the ladies spoke in near-unison:

"George, after our beloved king."

"Bouncer. See how he bounces when he walks?"

"Major. Look at those paws. He may be small now, but he'll grow. He needs a name worthy of the man— that is, the *dog* he will become."

"I shall name him Max," Marley announced above the friendly argument.

There was an immediate chorus of agreement. Sadie imagined the ladies would have lauded the choice if her niece had chosen to name the thing Doorstop.

But did she have to pick *Max*?

"Max," the viscount repeated, looking to Sadie, proving he'd known she'd been standing some distance away all along.

Did she look like someone whose stomach had just hit the floor?

"His name is Max," Marley said again, rather forcefully this time. "Max is a very good name for a dog. Papa named his dog Max, so this one will be Max, as well. Only I won't let this Max escape his leash and get run down by a cart, or leave me the way Papa did. Mama died, too, but I don't remember her. You promised, Darby."

The ladies variously sighed, or dabbed at their eyes

or, in the case of Minerva Townsend, loudly blew into a handkerchief.

"Then it's agreed," the viscount said, again looking toward Sadie.

Had he noticed that she'd backed up two paces since he'd last glanced her way?

The duchess, carefully keeping her skirts out of reach of the dog, asked Marley if this Max looked like the last Max. "I know your uncle Basil gave the same name to two of our birds, but that was only because we had so many that he forgot we already had a Punjab. Extremely common name, Punjab. Well, at least in some areas. I believe we were in—but that doesn't matter at the moment, does it, Minerva, so you can stop worrying that I'm about to launch into a story not fit for young ears."

"I know I'll hear it later," the lady grumbled, and sat back on her chair, clearly finished with the subject. "Just don't linger on the birds and leave out the good parts."

Marley, seemingly oblivious to everything save the duchess's first question, shook her head, her newly trimmed blond curls swinging about her cheeks. "Max was so big I could ride on him. Papa said he looked like a horse, so that was all right, at least until I grew."

Sadie backed up another step, turned her head to judge how far she was from the hallway, the stairs.

The dratted man couldn't have brought her a kitten, could he? Or even a monkey.

The viscount scooped up the puppy and returned it to Marley's arms. "I've recently purchased a very handsome black horse. Was he perhaps black, this *horse* of yours?"

Marley began petting the puppy. "No, Max was brown, but much browner than this. And he had little ears that stood up, and white feet like the grocer's wagon horse, and some white on his face even though a lot of it was black. Papa called him *sleek*. He was so handsome."

"Brown—clearly dark brown," Clarice said, apparently enjoying a puzzle. "White feet, black muzzle—oh, and small ears. Do you know what I think? I think Marley means the dog was a boxer. My cousin Lester had a pair of them for hunting. Handsome things, when they weren't slobbering all over my shoes."

Sadie had resumed covertly backing up when the viscount asked the color of the dog.

She'd turned toward the foyer at the words *even though a lot of it was black*.

And she had tossed both cloak and bonnet in the general direction of one of the duke's footmen before she'd hitched up her skirts and was already halfway up the stairs as Clarice had clapped her hands and asked, "Do you know what I think?"

By the time she reached the landing she could hear the viscount's Hessians on the marble stairs, and increased her pace, praying there was a key on her side of the bedchamber door.

Skirts still above her ankles, she ran down the hallway, sliding around a corner thanks to a small rug on the floor that apparently wanted to travel along with her.

"Whoa there, Sadie. In a rush, are you?"

She skidded to a halt. "Your Grace," she gasped, dropping into a curtsy as she came face-to-face with the Duke of Cranbrook. "I'm so sorry. I forgot something in my room. Please excuse me."

"Yes, yes, run along. I'm only sorry to have impeded your progress."

"Oh, no, Your Grace, you haven't—" The footsteps were getting closer. "Yes, thank you."

As she picked up her pace she could hear the viscount's voice, but not his words. His tone was light, even friendly. He was probably attempting to talk his way around the duke, which certainly wouldn't happen. She stopped, leaning her back against the wall, her chest heaving after her effort, sure the duke would turn the man around and send him about his business, for he certainly had no *business* in this private area of the mansion.

"Sadie? Why, yes, son, she just blew past me as if shot out of a cannon, matter of fact. You two up to some mischief? A little hide-then-seek, eh? I remember those days with my Viv like it was yesterday. Come to think of it, it was last week, when Clarice and her Rigby were out for a drive. Don't worry, son, I'll keep mum. Us men have to stick together, don't we? Just go to the end of the hall and turn to your right—mind the carpet, it slips— and then the third door down."

Shock that the duke would aid and abet, as it were, seemed to have stuck Sadie's shoes to the floor. Admittedly, she wasn't as shocked as she would have been five days ago, since the duke and duchess were quite *open* with their affection ("randy as a pair of old goats," Clarice had called them, winking).

Then she was off again, realizing for the first time how long the hallway was and how defenseless she seemed to be. She hadn't heard any of the ladies following, calling after the viscount, and now the duke had as well as given the dratted man carte blanche.

Her original plan of hiding behind the locked door of her bedchamber seemed ridiculous now, if the viscount had dared come this far. He'd probably just bellow through the door and everyone would know what she had done.

So thinking, she left the door open behind her and hastily flung herself into a pink-and-white flowered slipper chair, folding her hands in front of her as she attempted to catch her breath.

She heard his footsteps, the hunter carefully approaching his prey.

He did in fact stop just in front of the opening, very nearly posing there, drat him, and then so unnecessarily *knocked* on the wooden door before stepping inside and closing the thing behind him.

Now she knew how the mouse felt when the cat had it cornered.

"With your kind permission, Mrs. Boxer," he drawled before dragging the desk chair into the center of the large room and sitting down, his long legs crossed at the ankle, his arms folded against his chest.

"Let me think for a moment. You are without a husband. And, in almost the very next breath, you told me Maxwell died two years ago," he said.

He had a memory as good as Marley's, drat him!

"Both truthful statements, yes. Um, taken separately, that is."

"So you didn't lie to me. Precisely."

"No, I did not. Not precisely." Her heart was pounding half out of her chest. If the man became any more *relaxed* he might slide right out of the chair!

"Pardon me if I don't figuratively shower you in rose petals in reward for your selective honesty."

He had every right to be angry. Incensed. And yet he seemed somehow pleased. What was wrong with the man?

"I had a reason."

"Oh, I'm certain you did, and a prodigiously good one at that. Please share it with me. I'm all agog to know."

"Not if you continue to be so facetious. And…and smug. I would have told you. Eventually. Someday. If left with no other—and now you're grinning. How dare you!"

"I dare, madam, because you're not married, have never been married and are definitely not a widow. You certainly aren't a Boxer. So what do I call you now?"

"I don't believe we have a choice, unless you want to tell those kind ladies downstairs that they've been lied to, which I sincerely do not wish to do. Especially after the duchess and Clarice, believing me widowed, insisted on sharing some rather, um, *pointed* jokes about the joys of…"

He was sitting forward now. "Yes? The joys of what, Sadie? I've settled on informality, you'll notice."

"They considered me equally…experienced. And I won't say any more than that because it would only make you happy. I just thank heaven I spent enough time in my brother's surgery to understand what they were referring to much of the time."

"Pertaining to the male anatomy, I'll assume. When you dig a hole, Sadie Grace Whomever, you dig it deep, don't you? I suppose we should both thank your lucky stars that Maxwell wasn't a Pomeranian."

Sadie's mouth twitched upward at the corners, but only for a second. There was much more to come, and she knew it. He was being entirely too congenial for a man who'd been tricked into thinking of her as Mrs. Boxer, addressing her as Mrs. Boxer in conversation, introducing her to his friends as Mrs. Boxer. In fact, he should be hopping mad!

So why wasn't he?

"I shouldn't mention this, as it reveals my sad lack of trust in you, but I wasted a good part of the last four evenings pestering friends and acquaintances, hoping one of them would remember a Maxwell Boxer, perhaps from the war. Oddly enough, none did."

"You can't blame me for your suspicious nature, my lord," Sadie pointed out, because she could take his *facetious* and raise him two trumps, blast him!

"I suppose you have me there." He put his thumb to his cheek and stretched out his fingers to begin massaging his forehead above his left eye. His lips thinned noticeably and his complexion had gone rather pale.

For all his outward composure, clearly inside he was struggling to control his temper. She'd given him the headache, and felt instantly ashamed.

She rushed to explain.

"Marley is John's daughter—I didn't lie about that. She's here because John instructed me to bring her to you. And I'm John's sister, just as I said I am. Sadie Grace Hamilton. I simply felt it safer to travel the public coach as a soldier's widow than as who I am, that's all."

He looked at her with his one eye. That single piercing blue eye. What was he waiting for now?

"Now you want to know why I simply didn't identify myself in my letter. I…I felt I had a good reason for that. It seemed sensible to have my letter to you carry more weight than one penned by a grieving sister."

He was still staring.

She squirmed in her seat. What else did he want her to say?

And why couldn't she simply *shut up*?

"And yes, I will say it did occur to me the precariousness of my position. I was bringing my niece to what I believed, rightly, to be a male household. Alone as I was, with only a child with me, I did not want to be perceived as…as fair game."

At last, a reaction.

He allowed his hand to drop into his lap. "By *me*? Good God, woman, what in bloody hell did John tell you about me?"

"Lovely things, all of them," she hastened to assure him. "But that doesn't mean I wasn't, am not, an unmarried woman straight from the country, with limited resources of my own, without the slightest protection and determined to do anything I could to assure my niece's well-being."

"And safety. Let's not forget her safety, as that's what piqued my curiosity in the first place. Are we finished now? Is there anything else I should know?"

Sadie thought for a moment. Was there anything else she should tell him? Probably. Anything else she *wanted* to tell him? No, definitely not.

"Yes, there is. I want you to know that I have agonized over what I've done and am heartily sorry. My plan was hastily formed and badly flawed. And…despicable."

"Surely not despicable. Unfortunate perhaps. Poorly conceived. Misleading at the least, and maddening at the most. You've caused me several uncomfortable hours, Sadie Grace, for reasons I will not discuss. Yet at the same time, you've eased my mind considerably. You are who you say you are. Marley is whom you say she is. I suppose I'd rather your misguided lies than know I've foisted a pair of imposters upon my friends."

"How you comfort me."

"I won't even point out that your last remark could be

construed as facetious. I'm a gentleman that way. Now we will put all of this behind us. She likes the dog, you know," he said. "The stable bitch whelped over a month ago, and suddenly it struck me that Marley might feel *safer* with a companion. I think I did well."

"You could have brought her a kitten. A female kitten," Sadie pointed out, getting to her feet, so that he did also. "It would have made everything so much easier."

"Don't look a gift puppy in the mouth. You've saved yourself a rather intense grilling, Sadie, and should be thankful Marley and the ladies were present when the magic penny finally was dropped into my suspicious brain."

Was that it? Was he done? She'd like to believe so.

"I suppose I did, yes. I knew you didn't believe me. I'm…I'm not at all used to not being taken at my word. It came as a terrible shock, especially when I realized you had to either take my word on faith or toss us both back into the streets. I began to regret my lie in earnest then."

"I wouldn't relax just yet. I'm fairly certain those ladies downstairs have been busy putting two and two together and coming up with a solid four. In other words, no, you can't continue as Mrs. Boxer. You have considerable explaining to do, I'm afraid, but I know they'll keep your secret."

"I'd much rather hide in shame up here for eternity than disappoint them, but if I must, I must. I imagine they're appalled to know I haven't been totally honest with them."

Now Darby actually laughed out loud. "On the contrary. Knowing the ladies, I imagine they'll be too busy complimenting you before pointing out ways you could have done it better. But we can discuss this in greater depth once we're out of this room and safely public in the square. For now, let's go see how Marley and Max are rubbing along."

She was more than happy to leave the subject of her lies behind them, and latched on to the subject of the puppies. "You said a litter, didn't you? What are you doing with the rest of them?"

"Naturally, needing only the one, I had the rest drowned in a bucket. Is that what you want to hear?"

Since her relief wasn't exactly total, she could forgive him for his lingering anger.

"I'm not that eager to make you into a monster, my lord. I only hope they find good homes if you can't keep them in the stables."

"There were only four. Arrangements were made. Come along, we were going for a stroll, remember?"

Sadie looked at the closed door in horror as another thought struck her with the force of a slap to the face. "You followed me upstairs. They all saw you. The duke saw you. We've been gone for a long time. What are they thinking? Oh, Lord, Clarice will giggle, and the duchess will probably ask me outrageous questions. Or worse, *wink* at me."

"I applaud you on your belated ability to see too late what you should have realized sooner. But I'm afraid it's worse than that. It was one thing for me to have a private talk with the widow Boxer, my ward's aunt. Not precisely proper, considering this is your bedchamber, but rules are meant to be bent. Some of them, but not all."

Sadie felt a figurative pit opening beneath her feet.

"But that's ridiculous. You can't possibly mean—"

"No, actually, I don't. Knowing these particular ladies as I do, I imagine they'd all think it simply deliciously naughty. Lord knows the duchess doesn't care a snap for convention. Coop's mother believes conventions were invented by men simply to annoy women, and Clarice, bless her, has no real idea as to what they are."

Sadie sagged back into the chair. "Thank God. For a moment I thought—"

"You thought I'd say convention dictates that we marry. Yes, I know. However, the idea has merit. Speaking practically."

Sadie believed her eyes just might pop out of her head.

"I beg your—*what?*" To look any more smug he'd have to push out his chest like a pouter pigeon, drat him.

"Speaking practically," he repeated, retaking his own seat. "Marley is now mine. You? You're rather just *floating* about, aren't you? Neither here nor there, neither fish nor fowl, as it were. The aunt. The spinster aunt, well past her first blush of youth."

"I beg your pardon!"

"You cut your wisdoms years ago, Sadie Grace, even if you are not yet at your last prayers. I can't hire you as governess and pretend you are no more than a paid employee, not when you're the aunt. I can't allow you to wander about my household in the aforementioned neither fish nor fowl category until Marley is grown and gone—or until you molt. If I were to marry, how on earth would I explain you to my bride? Oh, and one thing more—I'll be damned if I'll give you a Season. So what does that leave us, Sadie Grace, hmm?"

"You can't mean this."

"I can't do myriad things. I can't fly. I can't swim across an ocean. I can't pat my head and rub my stomach at one and the same time—but you might want to apply to Rigby on that one, as he believes the feat extraordinary when he does it. I *can*, however, see the merit in a marriage of convenience between us. Purely a business arrangement. And think how pleased Marley will be, to know for certain that you're not going to leave her. Consider the child, Sadie Grace."

"I can't believe this is happening."

"Oh, come now, am I that terrible? I'm fairly attractive, even with the patch. My teeth are good, I bathe on a regular basis and am complimented on my abilities on the dance floor. Oh, yes, I'm also so very wealthy I could grow old just counting my money. In short, I'm quite the coup."

"And so modest with it all, although I suppose I do appreciate the bathe regularly part of your self-serving description. You did, however, neglect to mention that you can be exceedingly annoying, entirely too enthralled by your own wit, not to exclude the fact that you don't really *do* anything, do you, my lord?"

"Do anything? I'm a viscount. That's what I do."

Why couldn't she stop talking? Was she trying to get herself booted out the door?

"That was an accident of birth. But what have you done that you can point to and say, 'I did this thing. I made this difference'?"

He pushed at his left temple. "Are we having our first fight, Sadie Grace?"

"Do you feel useful, my lord?"

"At the moment? No. Shall we make it a part of our *business arrangement* that you save me from my feckless ways and point my toes in the direction of good works?"

"There could be worse fates," Sadie said, suddenly feeling more in control of her own future, which she hadn't done for a long, long time. "I do not wish for Marley to grow up believing she is nothing more than a fashionable ornament."

"So you're accepting my proposal?"

She looked at him curiously. Why so suddenly formal? "I thought I had no real choice."

"There are always choices, Sadie Grace. I need to hear you tell me that we will marry."

"Perhaps you'd like me to write it down?" she asked, yes, facetiously.

"I've already seen one example of your letter-writing skills. A simple *yes* will do."

"Very well, then," she said, getting to her feet once more. "Yes. Yes, my lord, I agree to our arrangement."

"Not my lord, but Darby," he said as he rose, as well. "And I like to think of our marriage more as a bargain, with benefits on both sides."

"That only seems fair. A bargain, with benefits on both sides, I imagine, although I'm not quite certain what you believe to be your benefits. But we really must rejoin the ladies now."

He followed behind her, down the hallway, down the stairs, and only said as they stepped into the drawing room: "About my benefits, Sadie Grace. Did I perhaps fail to mention that I'll want an heir?"

CHAPTER FIVE

THE AIR WAS COOL, the breeze brisk, but most of Grosvenor Square was still washed in sunshine, making a stroll reasonably pleasant. Save for a few nannies and their charges, the area was also conveniently devoid of possible interruptions. Residents of the square who did leave their homes headed directly into carriages, and visitors to the square did much the same in reverse.

Society was social only when it wanted to be, and when it had specific destinations in mind it might as well be wearing blinders.

Darby had counted on that when he'd first suggested the stroll. Propriety ensured, the chance of interruption slight, *Mrs. Boxer* feeling assured she was within easy reach of the duke's mansion, the safety of her new friends.

Now he could kiss Miss Sadie Grace Hamilton senseless smack in the middle of the square and, save for a few raised eyebrows and giggles from the nursemaids, nobody would so much as give a damn.

And the stroll no longer a reason for an inquisition meant to pry her secrets out of her. What a lucky turn of events bringing the puppy to Marley had been, but then Darby knew himself to be a lucky man.

A lucky, apparently useless grasshopper of a man in Sadie's eyes.

"You have the headache again," Sadie said, the first

words she'd spoken since they'd escaped the mansion ten minutes earlier. "And again, it's my fault."

Darby realized he was rubbing at his forehead beneath his curly crowned beaver and quickly dropped his arm to his side. Yes, he had the headache. The familiar vise had gripped his head while they were still in her bedchamber, and he doubted it would let go anytime soon.

"I believe there's enough blame to go around."

"You're correct. There is. You certainly didn't have to take my hand and drag me into the drawing room to announce that we had realized our *attraction* and were now betrothed. You made it sound as if we had been upstairs all that time because we were being…being…"

"Indiscreet. Try that one. Anyone who can't think beyond Maxwell Boxer probably needs all the assistance she can get."

"You can stop chewing at that bone now, my lord, if you'll pardon the canine reference. I know what I did, and it wasn't my most shining hour. However, *indiscreet* only serves to pretty up what they all must have been thinking."

"You'll have to admit it certainly eased us through your small deception without much trouble, as the ladies were so delighted to hear our other news. Apparently you've found new friends there."

"*Your* friends were no help when they arrived with their ladies. Patting you on the back and congratulating you. I would think gentlemen would stand together."

"You mistake them. They did stand together, believing they know what's best for me, most especially since their ladies, as you refer to Thea and Dany, clearly approved. If each of them weren't so obviously in love I'd think they were of the belief that misery enjoys company."

"Or perhaps it was revenge for the puppies."

Darby smiled. Gabe, Coop and Rigby had all arrived during the time he and Sadie had been absent. With them, they'd brought their *gifts* from him, the remaining spaniels in the litter, just so recently delivered to each of their domiciles with the viscount's compliments.

The ladies were delighted. Marley was nearly over the moon when all the puppies were put on the carpet and they immediately began crawling over her, licking her, reducing her to helpless giggles.

It had felt so strangely wonderful to hear Marley's giggles. That was what childhood should be. A time of giggles and puppies. And innocence. Or so he would like to believe.

"Shameless toadeater," Gabe had said to him jokingly as the four men stood together, away from the fray, "making certain all the ladies love you. Now explain yourself. How the devil did you go from reluctant guardian to engaged man in five short days?"

Later, he'd promised them, over drinks at their club, and before Sadie was happily attacked by the ladies, much like Marley had been by the puppies, he managed to extricate her and, well, here they were.

He'd left Sadie to contemplate her future, their future, as they circled the square, but now it was time to move on to the next step. She hadn't responded to his whispered announcement to her that he expected an heir from their bargain, but he was in no rush to push her on the subject. After all, he did know how to *nudge*…

"I gave the ladies only vague instructions. How many gowns did you order?"

"*I* have not ordered any gowns. *I* never asked for any gowns. Or the shoes, or the gloves or the bonnets or the scarves or the cloaks or reticules. *I* did not agree to having my hair trimmed, nor my fingernails buffed. *I* neither need nor want anything."

"All right," he said, trying not to smile. "Let me rephrase that. How many gowns—and the rest of it—have the ladies ordered for you?"

Sadie sighed. "Too many, too much. And for Marley, as well, but I saw the point in that, as she is growing very quickly right now and complained that her half boots have begun to pinch. The duchess assured me every piece was necessary, or else I would be an embarrassment to you, as your ward's aunt. All the bills for the small army of tradespeople who have been tracking in and out of the mansion these past days will be sent to your direction. I should thank you, I know, and I do, but please understand I only agreed because of Marley."

"Yes, Marley appears to be at the center of everything you and I have done these past days. So young and defenseless, and so clearly troubled. John's death affected her greatly, didn't it? I would imagine it would, at her age."

I know it would, at her age. But I won't think about that. I never think about that.

He guided Sadie to one of the benches situated along the square and invited her to sit down, then spread his coattails and sat beside her.

"She's afraid. You've noticed that, as well. Susan, Marley's mother, passed away when Marley was only just three, and she barely remembers her, which is sad in itself. I did my best to step in for her, coming to live with them, helping in John's surgery, taking it over for the time he was away and…and until he died."

She seemed open to telling him things now, so he decided to see just how much information might be forthcoming. "You never mentioned where John and Marley lived. Where he had his surgery."

She looked up at him curiously, and he noticed that her eyes were shining with unshed tears. It hadn't been the best of days for her, not for a many number of weeks and months, and he felt his heart soften toward her. She was quietly brave, and he admired her for that, as well. He could even forgive her lies—her one lie, for that's all it had been, really. She had done what she had thought best under the circumstances. As had he, come to think of the thing.

Careful, Darby, you're in danger of turning into a softhearted ninny. What would your friends have to say if they suspected any such nonsense? Well, that's simple enough. They'd think you'd once again fallen into a mud puddle only to come up smelling like the first roses of spring, that's what they'd think, because Sadie Grace is an exceedingly beautiful woman, apparently both inside and out.

"I didn't? I certainly wasn't hiding that information. We resided in Dibden, in Hampshire. I doubt you've heard of it."

Darby shook his head slightly, for he'd gotten lost in his own thoughts and for a moment didn't have the faintest idea what Sadie was saying. "Oh, Dibden. No, I can't say that I've heard of the place. Not quite the thriving metropolis, I'll assume. But you didn't always live there?"

"No. I remained in our parents' cottage in Huyton, not

much distance from Liverpool, after they'd passed, happy with a small allowance. Papa had been a tutor and Mama a fine seamstress, and they left me as well-provided-for as they could. But that was only until Susan died. I'm a country mouse, and content. I've really never been anywhere, and yet now here I am in London, and soon to be a viscountess. I still can't quite imagine it. You're marrying quite beneath you, my lord Nailbourne, but with your friends' support, I believe there's still time for you to come to your senses. Ah, and here they come now, marching to your defense, I should hope."

Darby looked across the square to see Gabe and Coop approaching, Rigby and his Clarice bringing up the rear. He suppressed a smile at the sight of Rigby's betrothed, who apparently had discovered a love for furs, as the ermine muff she carried rivaled the size of a bandbox. She certainly had adapted well to her new station in life.

"Miss Hamilton," Gabriel Sinclair intoned, bowing in her direction, as did the others, while Clarice shooed Darby from his seat and quickly occupied it, giving a surprised Sadie a quick hug that left her to surreptitiously pick a few bits of ermine fluff from her tongue.

"Excuse us, Sadie," Darby said as he joined his friends a safe distance away from Clarice's happy chatter. "Gentlemen? You've come to thank me for the puppies?"

"What?" the red-haired Rigby said, momentarily confused. "Oh, yes, yes, indeed, the puppy. Quite the surprise, that. Not so much as Gabe's birds, but Clarice is happy enough. Can't walk a parrot in the park, you know, although Lord knows we did the next best thing. Clary's already named him Goodfellow. Er, yes, thank you very much."

That was the beauty of Jeremy Rigby; he was easily distracted.

Gabe and Coop, however, were not.

"You want to tell us what the devil's going on?" Gabe asked.

"Why, Gabe, gentlemen, whatever would make you think something is *going on*? I will admit I have only a faint hope that the ladies swallowed that farradiddle about Sadie and I discovering a mutual affection, but they won't question it. In truth, Miss Hamilton made a foolish mistake, I committed a worse faux pas, thus compounding the error, and now we are constrained to marry. It happens every day. Or at least it seems to. As I recall, Gabe, it nearly happened to you. Oh, wait a moment, it did. To both of you, to one degree or another. I suppose I'm simply following in your footsteps, taking my hints from watching you."

"Thea was deliberately putting herself in danger. I had no choice."

"There are always choices, Gabe. And you, Coop, you and Dany were on your way to the altar within four and twenty hours of your first meeting, which I was so fortunate to witness."

"There were unusual circumstances, and you know it, and the engagement was meant only as a ploy, a temporary solution."

"I was rather in on *that*, as well, wasn't I? Perhaps the fates are having their fun with me now, as a sort of punishment. Do you think we'll tumble into love when we least expect it, Sadie and I, as you fellows did? I doubt it, but at least my ward won't have to worry about losing her aunt."

"Yes, at the bottom of it, it's the child, isn't it," Coop remarked, not as a question, but as a statement he felt certain was correct. He always had been the most level-headed of their group. "This all has something to do with John's orphaned daughter."

"It may also have something to do with the obvious beauty of that young lady over there."

"I admit to an attraction, Gabe, yes," Darby said, laughing. "In fact, marriage to Sadie has seemed the only logical solution since we first met, if she's to become a part of my household, and clearly Marley loves her. The events of this morning only gave me an opportunity to avail myself of that solution. There. Are you all happier now? I'm not exactly throwing myself away strictly for the child, or on impulse. I may have only the one eye, but it sees quite well."

"But marriage, Darby?" Gabe shook his head. "Out of your own mouth, you didn't even know her true name an hour ago, if she really is John's sister. We'd hate to see you hoodwinked."

Darby raised a finger to wipe at a nonexistent tear. "Ah, my friends, how you warm my heart with your concern."

"We could also be worrying about that young lady over there. If you're convinced she is who she now says she is, someone should warn her that you're not the first man any of us would choose to easily take on the role of spouse."

"Then perhaps, Gabe, you ought to toddle on over there and tell her. 'Beware, beware, Miss Hamilton, you are sticking your head into a lion's mouth.'"

"Oh, shut up," Coop muttered, stepping forward. "Look, Darby—we're here, just as you've always been for us. But damn it all, what are you doing?"

The top of his head was very nearly ready to explode.

"I made a promise to John, and I'm a man of my word. I'm protecting the child."

"From what?"

Darby pushed his fingers against his forehead, vainly attempting to shove away the headache. "I agree, there is that, isn't there? Sadie hasn't told me yet, but there's something."

"Oh," Rigby said, smiling. "There you go, gentlemen, he does have a good reason. Wait, no, he doesn't, not if he doesn't know what Miss Hamilton knows and hasn't told him."

"You're all forgetting Marley," Darby reminded them, knowing they wouldn't let him alone until they'd dragged everything he knew out of him. "She, unlike her aunt, is happy to talk about most anything, according to my housekeeper at the cottage. It would seem that poor John was barely in the ground before Sadie came to her niece in the middle of the night, rousing her, dressing her and leading her off into the dark, dragging their only piece of luggage with them a good distance from the village, to a posting inn."

"Escaping John's creditors?"

"No, Rigby," Gabe pointed out. "Female relatives aren't tossed into the Fleet for a male's debts."

Darby chanced a quick look to the ladies, who were still deep in conversation, although he doubted Sadie was getting a word in sideways.

"According to Sadie, John's surgery, complete with living quarters, is owned by the village, and she and Marley had to leave in order for the council or whomever to install another doctor. That explains why she brought the child to me, but nothing explains a moonlight flit."

"Did you ask?"

"No, Coop, I haven't as yet had the opportunity. My well-meaning friends keep interrupting me whenever I think I have a moment to broach the subject."

"Sorry," Rigby mumbled. "Do you think she took the silver with her? Being penniless and all. She was penniless, wasn't she? I would think so."

"I doubt John owned much silver or anything else of value. What I believe, gentlemen, is that Sadie wasn't so much running to me as she was running *from* someone else. With Marley somehow smack in the middle of it. I feel certain every step Sadie has taken revolves around my new ward."

"The child's gotten to you, hasn't she?" Gabe patted Darby on the shoulder. "You've never really spoken about it, but we all know you were orphaned while still quite young."

After which I was also whisked from the only home I'd known and plunked down among strangers, if that is also something to consider...

"Sadie said something the day we first met, something I don't think she wanted to say. She wants Marley to be *safe*. When I pressed her, she gave a reasonable answer, but I didn't believe her then and I don't believe her now."

"Safe? He's right, nobody could be safer than to be under our friend's protection," Rigby declared. "Look at him. There are times even I wonder at how dangerous he could be. Probably the eye patch, don't you think?"

"Thank you, Rigby—I think. So, at the end of the day, and to hopefully put an end to this discussion, what I *believe* is that a marriage between us would be a comfort to Marley, who clearly is terrified that more people will leave her, and protection for both of them, whatever that may entail. In other words, my friends, I am being noble. Except, of course, for the part where I admitted to the fact that Sadie is definitely a beautiful, even desirable woman. I don't have the makings of a martyr."

"Since you didn't ask for our advice before you embarked on this course, I suppose we would only be wasting our breath now."

"Bless your practical mind, Coop. I can always count on you to think with a clear head."

"But not me?" Gabe asked, grinning. "What have I ever done that would make you doubt my sensibilities, if not my intelligence?"

Darby believed his friends, although clearly not happy, had satisfied most of their curiosity. "Do we really have to discuss the birds again?"

"No, I suppose not. Rigby, are you insulted?"

Their friend shook his head. "Since the only opinions I have lately all come to me via my sweet Clary, I don't think so. Carry on, Darby, since you will, anyway. Just don't let on that this betrothal of yours is devoid of affection, or Clary will drive us all into Bedlam attempting to change your mind."

"I'll second that," Gabe said, "tossing in my aunt, as well. Coop?"

"Dany and Minerva, putting their heads together with the others? Wasn't it bad enough while I was dealing with those damn chapbooks? Rigby's right, Darby. Warn your Sadie. For all our sakes, yours and hers included, don't let any of them get even so much as a whiff of any idea that yours isn't a love match."

CHAPTER SIX

THE FIRST OF Sadie's new gowns had arrived just in time for her initial public appearance with her betrothed. Her soon-to-be husband. Under the law, her lord and master. The love of her life and the father of her future children, or so her new friends had been led to believe.

Darby had explained that it was important that their friends felt confident the betrothal had been the culmination of a whirlwind courtship, and she'd seen the sense in that. Vivien and Clarice, in particular, were such happy romantics, and wanted everyone to be in love. If they thought for one moment that the marriage would be purely a business arrangement, they'd do their best to *fix it*.

So Darby kissed her hand and then held it a little too long when he visited. He brought gifts of flowers and bits of jewelry for her. He always sat beside her on the couches, his arm draped over the back, inches from her shoulders. He whispered sweet nothings in her ear and called her *my dear* or *my darling*.

He called for Marley to be summoned so that he could bounce her on his knee and escorted the pair of them for drives, going so far as to arrange for Norton to meet them there, to take the child for a walk while Darby and Sadie took a more private turn around the park. He always had a twist of licorice in his pocket after learning the treat was Marley's favorite. And his laugh was genuine when Marley chattered at him like a magpie about the adventures of her days.

The ladies were delighted.

Sadie had at first wanted to box his ears, but the attention was flattering, he was witty and fun and she knew her defenses were weakening.

She also felt certain he was patiently waiting for her to tell him something, something she knew and he didn't. He gave no hints to that effect, so perhaps it was her own guilt that made her think this way. She only knew that, without her secrets haunting her, eating at her, she would have tumbled deeply into love with the dratted man by now.

The duchess had chosen carefully from the invitations on the mantel, and Sadie's entrance into Little Season Society would be that evening, at a small party hosted by one of the duchess's friends.

She didn't know which made her more nervous—the party itself, or being introduced to the curious as the affianced bride of the handsome, wealthy, clearly above her touch viscount.

Yes, back to thoughts about Darby. Her thoughts always seemed to circle back to him.

Her new friends had told her how thrilled they were by the match. Just like something out of a fairy tale, Clarice had cooed, clasping her hands to her generous bosom.

Darby Travers was a fine and loyal friend, Clarice had added, and not one to judge what other people did. Ridiculously popular with the ladies, but didn't rakes make the best husbands (that from Minerva)?

He was always the gentleman, the duchess trilled, even when she wasn't always the lady.

He saw the humor in most everything, Thea had added, telling her more about "the birds" and how they had all worked together to cheer the duke, who was certain he was dying, but now was nearly as certain he wasn't.

Sadie knew she would like to hear more about that, and the duke's upcoming sixtieth birthday, but Dany was already chiming in about Darby's clever mind that saw something neither she nor her Coop had seen, and then made certain he helped them see it.

There simply was nothing *bad* about Darby. She wished he could be more serious, yes, but he had been raised to be who he was, to step into his father's shoes, and she could understand that, as well. He was very good at being a viscount, she supposed. Everyone else seemed to think so.

Marley was his staunchest champion, having been wooed and won by his gift of Max the not-a-boxer. And she was full of questions. Where would they live? Would he do more than come to visit and then go away again, as he did now? Would he help her with her sums, the way Papa used to do? They'd gotten to five times six before Papa died. Why did Papa die? What was he doing, now that they'd left him behind in Dibden with Mama?

Poor Marley. She was such a mix of emotions, and too young to understand if she should be happy with her new life, or sad about the one she'd so recently lost. Sadie felt much the same.

Dany and Coop and the purple-turbaned Minerva had set off that morning for a week in the country with Dany's parents, whom Coop had yet to meet. Thea and

Gabe both resided in the mansion, but had also departed London, so that Gabe could oversee some sort of alterations to the great hall at Cranbrook Manor. Something having to do with those birds again, although Sadie chose not to inquire too deeply about that.

That left Clarice, who certainly couldn't reside with Rigby in his bachelor lodgings, along with Marley and herself. Clarice and Marley had struck up quite the friendship. Even now, with Max and Goodfellow in tow on their new leashes, they were enjoying themselves in the square, with Clarice demonstrating how to properly roll a hoop.

The mansion was quiet, unaccustomedly so, now that the duke and duchess had made some sort of garbled excuse directly after luncheon and taken themselves upstairs, giggling and holding hands like children.

It was, Sadie realized, the first time she'd been left to her own devices since stepping into the mansion nearly two weeks ago. It was rather nice, this quiet, although she hoped her thoughts would leave her alone, as some of them tended to be unsettling. Could she really bury the past along with her brother, and continue to live with her secrets? It certainly would be simpler. But then there was Marley... Darby had to know about Marley, sooner rather than later.

"Oh, John, why did you do it?" she whispered as she continued to busy herself putting fine stitches into repairing a seam Marley had managed to tear open on one of her night rails.

"Talking to yourself, Sadie Grace? Have you other bad habits I should know about?"

The needle jabbed into the soft flesh of her fingertip and she quickly raised it to her lips to suck at the resulting blood before it could stain the night rail. "Don't *do* that," she said, looking at Darby as he made himself at home on the facing sofa. Apparently he didn't feel the need to play the doting fiancé when they were alone.

"Arrive unannounced? I run tame in this household now, hadn't you noticed? I'm no longer announced, I simply appear. Rather like with the snap of my fingers."

"I'd never done that before, you know. Snap my fingers at Marley as if she was a pet being called to heel. I don't know why I did it then."

"Perhaps you were nervous. What with being brought to a house of ill repute and all."

She shut her eyes on that particular memory. "You're like Marley, and forget nothing. Or refrain from repeating it. Did you see her out in the square with Clarice?"

"I did. Rigby is with them now, and a sorrier sight with a hoop has yet to be discovered, especially with Goodfellow and Max winding their leashes about his ankles. Of the three, I believe my ward is the most adult. We were on our way to one of our clubs, but apparently Rigby can't abide not seeing his beloved at least twice a day."

Sadie smiled at that. "I like all your friends, but I will admit to a special affection for Clarice. She's so simple and open, isn't she?"

"She is that, yes. Has she told you much about herself?"

"If you mean do I know she came here from America as Thea's childhood friend and personal maid, yes, she has. Rigby took one look at her, and she at him, and figurative clouds parted and a dazzling sun appeared, so now she has joined Society as Clarice Goodfellow of the Fairfax County Virginia Goodfellows, and isn't love wonderful—I'm all but quoting her, you understand. I think it's sweet."

"Clarice's background is also a secret. She did tell you that?"

"No." *Also?* Sadie put aside her mending, certain her hands would tremble if she tried to take another stitch. "I suppose most everyone has a secret or two, don't you?"

He crossed one leg over the other, apparently settling in for a visit. "Don't I think so, or don't I harbor secrets?"

"Either one, I suppose. What brings you here today? Are we supposed to go for a drive in the park, and I've forgotten?"

"I don't think so, no. Perhaps we've both forgotten. I was merely making idle conversation."

She didn't know Darby well, but she was certain of one thing at least—he did not make idle conversation. She was, as Clarice had said so wonderfully, as nervous as a long-tailed cat in a room filled with rocking chairs.

And he knew it.

She retrieved the night rail and hunted for the needle, which she'd carelessly left dangling, something her mother had taught her never to do. *Never leave a threaded needle dangling, dear, or else you'll find yourself stuck.* Words to live by, Sadie supposed, although she hadn't realized their full significance at the time. She'd been too busy weeping as her mother extracted a partially buried needle from her rump.

She spoke only to fill the silence he clearly had no intention of breaking.

"My mother taught me to sew," Sadie said as she located the needle and wove it halfway into the material before folding the night rail and putting it down beside her once more. "It hadn't occurred to me that one day my skills would be needed to sew up people who came to John's infirmary. In fact, John believed I was better at stitching than he, but he was only being kind. I'd be interested in seeing how he did sewing you up, as working around the eyes and skull must be approached with some delicacy. May I see?"

"Another time perhaps," Darby drawled, touching his fingers to his patch as if assuring himself it hadn't slipped.

"Forgive me. I shouldn't have asked anything so personal."

"You're forgiven, and if I barked, I hope you'll forgive me. It's not lovely, if that's your question, for all John's hard work. He'd harbored hopes for a full return of my sight in time, but thus far that hasn't happened, so I doubt it will. I wear the patch as to not terrify small children—or valets—but mostly because the vision I do have remaining in that eye is doubled and therefore most annoying. But that isn't what you want to know, is it?"

"I did, but I suppose I really want to know how you feel about…about the injury."

"Damned mad," he answered with a smile that belied his serious tone. "Wouldn't you be? Our so-called commander had let his guard down, and we could have suffered a massacre that day. Excuse me for a moment."

She watched as he walked over to the drinks table and poured himself a glass of wine before he returned to sit down across from her again.

"For a time," he said quietly, "for many months in fact, and sometimes even now, I will be struck by a sudden, sick terror that something will happen to my good eye, leaving me blind and in the dark. Never to see the sun again, the faces of my friends. The scars are one thing, but…but that *fear* is what I resent most of all. There, have I answered your question?"

"I'm sorry, Darby. I'm so sorry."

"Don't apologize. If you'd simply been curious I wouldn't have answered you. I was lucky to get off so easily, but the patch is a constant reminder of the thousands who weren't so fortunate. Including your brother."

"You look at the patch and are reminded of those men. I understand. In some way, looking at you will always remind me of John. He was a very good man."

"We'll agree on that. But now I'd hope you'll satisfy my self-admitted curiosity about you. What else did you do for him, besides caring for Marley and stitching up the villagers? Did you cook his meals, tidy his house, wash his socks?"

"We couldn't afford a maid of all work, if that's what you mean. I also kept his books. Why? Would that disqualify me from being wife to a viscount, or should we just add my domestic skills to an already long list of reasons?"

"On the contrary, I believe your experiences will stand you in good stead when overseeing a staff, although I would advise against making any suggestions to Mrs. Camford. I'm fairly certain she considers the cottage hers, and I'm only allowed to visit on sufferance."

Sadie smiled. "I believe Mrs. Camford and I understand each other."

"I wouldn't relax my guard until and unless she invites you to call her Camy."

Since they were having a real conversation today, perhaps their first real conversation, she dared to probe further. "That first day, you said you were raised at the cottage, after the deaths of your parents. I suppose the

Camfords feel proprietary toward you in many ways, even now that you're the viscount."

"I became the viscount at the tender age of seven, Sadie. But no, that didn't save me from a good spanking when I deserved it. They'd raised four sons before I came along, and I soon learned my limits."

"So that you could exceed them, I'm sure. I'd like to reiterate about Marley's behavior that first day if I might. She was tired and hungry, and upset. She's always a well-behaved child. She'll give the Camfords no problems."

"She kicked me in the shin because I managed to make *you* angry," Darby told her. "She's as protective of you as you are of her. I was in the wrong."

"Thank you. Um…" She cast her gaze around the room, hoping to give her mind time to latch on to another subject while silently praying the others would join them and Clarice could fill the empty air with her usual happy chatter before she was tempted to share more with him. "The, um, the duke and duchess are here, but they…they retired upstairs just before you arrived."

"Chasing each other, or simply cooing and cuddling as they went?"

Sadie felt her cheeks grow hot. "They're very happy people."

Darby threw back his head and laughed out loud. "Yes, they are. Often bordering on delirious." He looked at her curiously. "Has anyone told you about Basil and his sixtieth birthday?"

"Oh, yes. I know there is to be a small family party that day, followed by a ball that same night. At the very end of the month." Then she frowned. "Unless there isn't. I would have asked about that, but everyone else simply nodded as if they understood, and I didn't want to pry."

Darby leaned forward, his hands on his knees. "We'll still be in town, so you probably should know. Basil was never meant to be the duke. In point of fact, Basil never aspired to the dukedom. As the fourth—or was that fifth?—son in line, he wasn't raised to be the duke, and was allowed to marry whomever he wished, whomever he wished being the totally unsuitable candidate for duchess, our own Vivien. They were handed a generous allowance and told to please go off and amuse themselves, which they did, for many years. They traveled far and wide, collecting exotic birds on all their travels—but that story will keep for another time—and very definitely *enjoyed* each other, if you take my meaning."

"I think I do," Sadie said, the blush still burning her cheeks.

"Yes, well, frivolity of any sort came to a screeching halt when Basil realized that his brothers were turning up their toes just as they approached their sixtieth birthdays. One was sad. Two was coincidence. Three? Again, I'm not sure—there may have been a fourth. Suddenly, in his fifty-eighth year, word of the most recent death reached him and he found himself the duke. Oh, and clearly destined for a similar fate."

"What a terrible thing to contemplate. He really believes that?"

"Alas, yes, he did. He retired to Cranbrook Manor, locked himself in his chambers, shutting Vivien out for the most part, and prepared to meet his Maker. Which, according to Vivien, turned him into the dullest, most depressing man in nature, and when all else failed she ordered Gabe to do something about it. My friend tried his best, but I believe it was Thea who finally convinced Basil that, if he was going to die, which she doubted, he might as well *live* in the interim. Basil has been, shall I say, making up for lost time these past weeks, as you may have noticed. Personally, I believe if he does end up cocking up his toes, it won't be because of some Cranbrook curse, but more because he's been cocking up something else with a bit too much enthusiasm. As the sister of a doctor, I do hope you take my meaning, and my apologies for my clearly inappropriate joke."

Sadie lowered her head, doing her best not to smile. It was senseless to pretend she didn't understand what he'd meant. "But they are sweet, aren't they?"

"Cute as a pair of rabbits in the spring," Darby said, leaning back once more. "Now, as we may have exhausted most subjects, unless you've a mind to talk about our unseasonably mild weather, I have a question for you."

She slowly raised her head, tipping it slightly to one side as she looked at him. "I knew you were being too nice. You wanted me relaxed before you pounced. Very well, what do you want to know?"

He smoothed down his sleeves and got to his feet. "Nothing too terrible. I'd like to know why you felt it necessary to drag my ward from her warm bed in the middle of the night and march her to a posting inn."

Sadie's insides turned to jelly and she drew in a quick, painful breath. "How…? *Marley.*"

"She told Camy, that first day."

Sadie's mind was whirling. That first day. He'd known since the beginning. She and Marley hadn't been separated that day, except for the time she was in her own borrowed bedchamber, submerged in lovely, warm water for at least an hour. Was an hour long enough for Marley to chatter to the housekeeper, or Peggy? Of course it was. Marley always told the truth and, worse, never hesitated to tell it.

"Cat got your tongue, Sadie? Or are you doing as the ladies did the other day with your name, putting two and two together? In this case, Marley's retelling of her last night in Dibden, and your blurted insistence that the child be kept *safe*. Yes, there are reasons for everything I do, Sadie Grace. Other than the sad diversion, time spent searching for the nonexistent Maxwell Boxer, I have thought of little else."

"And your answer to it all was to marry me? Even if you had not discovered my fib, and come chasing up the stairs after me?"

"I did not chase. I walked, slowly and deliberately. There will be no more moonlight flits, and there will be answers. The answers can wait—I'm a patient man. But it was necessary to ease the child's fears, which marriage—and a puppy—have seemed to do."

"You could have stopped at the puppy," Sadie grumbled halfheartedly, knowing she'd no one but herself to blame for finding herself about to be bracketed to a man who would not stop until he had every last truth from her—and probably have her tumbling into love with him along the way. "As for the rest of it, if we hadn't started out before dawn, we would not have arrived at the posting inn in time for the public coach. All you had to do was ask me."

"Yes, and there was no one in the village who would have agreed to drive the late doctor's poor sister and orphaned daughter to the posting inn."

He had her there. "I...I didn't want to bother anyone."

He dropped to his haunches in front of her, his face close to hers.

"You're a terrible liar, Sadie Grace, most especially when you've had no time to prepare. You didn't want anyone to be able to say they knew the direction you were about to travel. Now hear this. I've asked you for the truth for the last time, and you've lied to me for the last time. When you're ready, I'll listen, but in the meantime, no more lies. I will protect you both from whatever or whomever it is that sent you running into the night, but sooner or later you'll have to trust me. Do we understand each other?"

Sadie bit her bottom lip, and nodded. There was no sense in pretending he was mistaken. "John… No, I can't do it, it's too soon. First I must come to grips with it all, as you say you have with your injury. Except for those… moments. But I will thank you for what you're doing for Marley. And for me. I had no expectations beyond acting as companion to her until I could be assured she no longer needed me."

"You'd have given up any chance of a life of your own for her. I admire that, Sadie Grace. But that's not what John asked you to do, is it? You were to bring her to me. What did he suppose was to happen to you after she was delivered into my custody?"

His words hurt. She'd asked that same question of her dead brother at night, when she couldn't sleep. *How could you leave me this way?*

She blinked at the tears stinging at her eyes. "I don't know. He… He was very sick. All he could think about was Marley, what would happen to her after he died. I can understand that. I've tried so hard to understand…"

She felt Darby's fingers beneath her chin as he gently raised her head so that they were eye-to-eye.

"Don't cry, Sadie Grace," he said quietly. "We were off to a rocky start, you'll agree, but we're working this out, aren't we, step by cautious step? We're doing it together, no matter our initial reasons. For John. For Marley. And for you. You have my word."

She could barely breathe. He was so entirely sincere.

"Your brother saved my life, even when I'd have rathered he not bother. Whatever he may have done since then is nothing compared to that, except for the fact that he's made you cry, and kept you frightened for some reason you'll tell me when you're ready. I hope that's soon, because a new world is opening for you, Sadie, and I want you to enjoy it. Now, do you feel better?"

She nodded, unable to speak. He was so close, and somehow she wanted him closer. She wanted to bury her head against his broad shoulder and weep like a baby, tell him everything, cling to him, as somehow he had become her one safe haven in the storm that had raged inside her since waking that terrible morning and finding the letter John had slid beneath her door.

"Good, then that's settled." He tilted his head slightly, saying, "Do you know, Sadie Grace? No matter what, I believe I've gotten the better side of our agreement. The chance to give little Marley a happy, secure childhood, something that matters to me more than I would have suspected…and marriage to her beautiful aunt."

"I'm not…"

"Ah-ah, we agreed, no more lies."

He was going to kiss her now. She may never have been kissed in her three and twenty years, but she knew she was going to be kissed now. Perhaps to truly seal their bargain. Perhaps so that he could prove himself to be her lord and master. Perhaps—and wouldn't that be lovely—he actually *wanted* to kiss her.

Sadie looked down at his mouth, and saw no smile there. She looked into his eye, that beautiful eye, and saw no wry humor in its depths.

There was only an intentness she could feel all the way through her as he held her chin steady and came closer, even closer…

"Well, that turned out to be a fine mess," Clarice announced from the hallway. "Just as he finally had the hoop going, poor Rigby got tripped up in Goody's leash and went sprawling onto the cobbles, putting paid to his pantaloons and scraping his knees and hands like some little boy who—oh! Good Lord, Rigby, it seems we've interrupted something. See, I told you if we left them alone they'd be just fine. Better than fine, I'd say."

Darby and Sadie had moved apart hurriedly, with Darby just getting to his feet as Clarice fully entered the drawing room.

He looked down at Sadie with a smile and a what-can-you-do shrug of his shoulders. "That will teach us to leave the children unattended. Sounds as if your skills might be needed, Sadie Grace."

"What?" Sadie blinked, attempting to regain her focus, as she'd been about to have her first kiss, and she felt rather bereft to have missed it frankly. "Oh! Oh, yes, I should think so." She took Darby's offered hand and stood up just as Rigby came limping into the drawing room, Marley holding tight to his arm and looking very nearly frantic.

"Sadie, Sadie! Uncle Rigby fell down and broke his crown. You must save him!"

"Not my crown, sweetheart," Rigby corrected, grinning sheepishly. "I've told her I'm fine, save for a few scrapes. Darby, you'll never guess who saw me take my tumble. Lady Appleton. It will be all over Mayfair by suppertime, how that bird-witted Jeremy Rigby made a proper cake of himself in Grosvenor Square. My knees are beginning to sting. I think I might want to sit down."

"I know this seems unfeeling of me," Darby said, helping his friend to a chair, "but where are the dogs?"

"One of the footmen took them to the kitchens for something to eat. They're very sorry, really they are, and have promised not to do it again," Marley said as she sat at Rigby's knee and looked up at him. "Does it hurt very badly, Uncle Rigby?"

"Yes, Uncle Rigby," Darby said, shaking his head at the sight of the ripped and bloody pantaloons. "Tell us where it hurts, other than your pride."

"Oh, stop," Clarice scolded, taking Rigby's hand in hers. "You're just out of sorts because we walked in on the two of you. They were *kissing*, Jerry," she told her betrothed. "I told you it all would work out. You owe me a new bonnet."

Sadie shot a quick look toward Marley, but the child was fully occupied in stroking Rigby's arm and telling him Sadie would fix everything.

"Where are you going?" Darby asked her, following as she turned for the doorway and the stairs.

"It's you who pointed out my skills are needed. I brought John's medical bag with me, the one thing of his I kept. Please have Rigby moved to the kitchens, as I'll need water to clean his wounds of any dirt or small stones. He won't like that, I'm afraid. Oh, and ask the housekeeper for some bandages. I don't know what to say about the pantaloons other than that they need to be gone by the time I join you there."

"The general, barking out orders. I was only teasing. You're not actually going to—no, never mind, I can see you are. But truly, one of the servants can take charge, especially if treatment necessitates the removal of Rigby's pantaloons."

"Darby," she said, attacked by a sudden need to be truthful about something. "I've been sitting about ever since you brought me to London, useless as a wart on the end of the king's nose. I'm not accustomed to that, and I really don't much like it frankly. At least, for the moment, I can be of actual use to somebody."

"Yes, of course. Many others, whole multitudes in fact, would be delighted to become ladies of leisure, but not you. I apologize for not realizing that. Do what makes you happy, Sadie Grace, with my blessings. As long as I'm in the room while you're mucking about with Rigby's dimpled knees."

She looked at him in some surprise, but then smiled. "For a moment, I thought you were being serious."

"For a moment, I believe I was." He leaned in and planted a quick kiss on her cheek. "Go along now. I'll meet you in the kitchens."

CHAPTER SEVEN

"Is THE CANE really necessary?" Darby asked as he and Rigby went off to find tame liquid refreshment for the ladies during a blessed intermission between Lady Clathan's daughter Emily's singing and daughter Amelia's promised proficiency with the harp. "It's your knees, not your ankles."

"You only say that because your knees aren't stiff as two boards and wrapped in miles of bandages. I think Clary might have overdone the bandages. But the gloves are a nice touch, don't you think? I thought I'd faint dead away while Sadie was digging for that last stone in my palm."

"A faint would have been a blessed relief from the moaning and whimpering when you saw her coming at you with that wire brush, to scrub away the bits of gravel. Since she refused to leave your side, I was forced to cover Marley's ears. She was amazing, wasn't she?"

"Marley? Yes, I suppose so. You would have heard a lot more than a few moans if she hadn't been there to act as my supporting prop."

"My ward was quite the little soldier, yes, but I meant Sadie. It was rather like watching a field surgeon at work."

Rigby grinned at him. "And don't you sound the proud fiancé. Not that anyone can know, as I've explained to Clary. The Viscount Nailbourne's betrothed, mucking about with a gentleman's bare knees, and with said gentleman's pantaloons butchered above the knee so that his entire lower legs were exposed. Save for my hose, that is, and she tugged those down over my protests, to make sure I wasn't scraped anywhere else. Quite put me to the blush, the entire episode."

Darby plucked two glasses of lemonade from the tray of a passing servant. "She's bored, you know. Apparently being fitted for gowns and such, and having tea with the ladies, is not enough to keep Sadie from feeling she's wasting her days. Marley has her nurse, the duchess's staff tends to her every need, and she's nothing to do. I caught her out earlier, mending what appeared to be one of Marley's night rails. A servant's job. Ladies knit, or embroider. They don't *mend*."

"And you're angry about that?"

"No, Rigby, I'm not. I'm angry with myself for not realizing she might feel useless, as she's certainly hinted as much. Useless as a wart on the tip of our good king's nose, in fact."

"Here now, you can't blame yourself." Rigby leaned in close, to whisper his next words. "Clary went from lady's maid to swimming in Society overnight, remember? Doesn't bother her any to spend her days shopping and gossiping and whatever else ladies do. Took to it all like a duck to water. It's true. One of her favorite things is sitting in a bath she neither carried the water up two flights for nor would have to scrub afterward. I can't say as I blame her."

Darby searched his brain for a response, but couldn't find one. He certainly wasn't going to tell him Sadie had apparently decided wealthy, titled men were, as a species, lazy layabouts with nothing more to do with their lives than enjoy them. "You and Clarice are a match fashioned by the heavens, my friend."

They went off to rejoin the ladies, who apparently had deserted their chairs. "Could be hiding out on the balcony," Rigby suggested. "I know that's where I'd like to be. Vivien didn't mention that this was to be a musical evening. I loathe musical evenings, and so do my ears. Oh, wait, here comes Sadie, heading straight for us. But where's my Clary?"

"Quickly—do I curtsy?" she asked in a whisper as she stopped in front of them.

Darby gave a slight shake of his head as he handed her one of the glasses. "Nor do I bow over your hand, since we've been sitting together on those chairs over there for the past excruciating hour."

"Still, I believe I'll need lessons. Clarice tried to help, as we were making our way to one of the withdrawing rooms, but she admitted to not being certain, usually relying on the duchess or Thea or Dany."

"None of whom, now that I consider the thing, are overly conversant on all the nods and curtsies and such," Darby said, smiling. "We should perhaps hold group lessons."

"Where's Clary?" Rigby asked. "This lemonade is growing warm. Is she with the duchess?"

Sadie looked at Darby, and gifted him with a quick, grimacing smile. "Yes, Rigby, about Clarice..."

"What? She's ill? She's been cornered by Lord Haslitt again? Damned old lech keeps trying to look down her gowns, every time we see him. Where is she? I'll put that man to the right-about this time, and I don't care if he is older than dirt and Clary says he probably can't even remember why he's looking."

Ah, the joys of being in Rigby's company. They never ended.

"Clarice is on her way back to Grosvenor Square, Rigby," Sadie explained. "She…she has the headache, and the duchess was about to leave, anyway, since the duke said he'd rather *erp*—whatever that means—before he'd stay here and listen to Althea's offspring murder a perfectly fine harp. I'm sorry, but that's what he said. They took Clarice up with them, and I was commissioned to tell you she is horribly sorry, but she is definitely sick as a toad that swallowed a mouse whole, and she didn't want to chance casting up her accounts in Darby's town coach. The duke didn't seem to care either way about his coach—he just wanted to leave."

Again she looked to Darby, who was doing his best not to laugh.

"I'll go to her immediately."

"Oh, no, don't do that. She specifically asked me to tell you not to come. She doesn't suffer often from the headache, but told me she can be sick for a day, even days, and she will send you a note when it's safe to visit. I'm sorry, Rigby. But she'll be fine, I'm sure of it."

Poor Sadie Grace. She really needed to learn how to lie if she planned to remain in Society for long.

"I don't care," he exclaimed, waving his cane in the air as if prepared to strike down anyone who would stop him from going to his beloved's side. "I'm going to see her, if I have to beat down the door." He bowed quickly to Sadie before striding toward the hallway, completely forgetting to lean on his cane.

"He's upset, poor fellow, but I promised Clarice. I was

quoting, you understand, both Clarice and the duke," she said. "I wanted to get it all right. What's an *erp*?"

"Supposedly, it's what each of the duke's brothers uttered just before planting themselves facedown on the floor."

"But that's terrible!"

"On the contrary. Gabe will be delighted to hear that his uncle is now able to joke about his fears. She's really ill? You convinced Rigby, which is no great feat where Clarice is concerned, but I'm sensing there's something deeper going on here."

Sadie shook her head. "There is. But not here. Is there somewhere we can be more private?"

Darby gave in at last to a grin as he offered her his arm. "Off the top of my head, hundreds. Sadly, propriety greatly limits that number. You have your shawl with you. We could step out onto the balcony for a few minutes, as long as we return in time for the remainder of the recital. If we run off, as well, we may instigate a stampede for the door, and poor Lady Clathan will go into a sad decline."

They passed through the small crowd without much notice, as the other guests apparently already had their fill of attempting to guess whom the viscount had on his arm this evening. After all, no female stayed on that arm for long, and the Little Season was awash in hopeful country misses who would most probably end up bracketed to a local landowner before the spring Season, which none of their families could afford. Besides, Darby knew—as he knew Society nearly too well— Sadie was no dewy infant of no more than seventeen or eighteen, but clearly had kissed her debutante status farewell several years ago. Sadie might be beautiful, but if she hoped for a marriage, Society certainly wouldn't think she'd find one with Darby Travers. She'd best decide to settle for a middle-aged widower in need of a mother for his children.

Announcing their betrothal the day of the duke's birthday celebration should put the capper on what would afterward always have been the highlight of the Little Season. Unless, of course, Basil *erped* into his birthday toast; then Darby and Sadie's news would fade into oblivion.

"You're feeling comfortable here?" he asked her as they stepped out onto the balcony.

"I suppose I am. Thankfully, nobody is paying me much attention, and a few seem to deliberately pretend neither the duchess nor Clarice exist. No one has given them the cut direct, I believe it's called, but they're politely distant. Although the gentlemen can't seem to keep their eyes from straying to Clarice's bosom."

"Partially explaining why the ladies don't seek her acquaintance, as making comparisons are one of the many failings of most men."

"But not you? And how can we be having this conversation?"

"We're having this conversation because, once you've seen Rigby's dimpled knees, and whatever you saw in John's infirmary, I no longer see any reason either of us should feel the need to dance around most subjects. Especially since you've admitted you watched the gentlemen…watching."

"They're rather difficult to ignore, especially the one with the quizzing glass. But you're right. No wonder the wives aren't eager to be in Clarice's company. The… comparisons."

"There's also the fact that our beloved Vivien is a fairly loose screw, bless her, and being cornered by her when she's of a mind to tell one of her stories could have a marble statue reaching for the hartshorn and burnt feathers. Now, tamping down my curiosity, I want to apologize for not realizing sooner that turning you overnight into a lady of leisure might bore you senseless."

It was dark on the balcony, with only a few flambeaux burning in the gardens below them, but Darby could see the embarrassment on Sadie's face. "Oh, no, it's I who should apologize. How could anyone be so crass as to complain at having been dropped into what is certainly one of the deepest gravy boats in all of England? I'm delighted for Marley, and couldn't have hoped for a better situation for her, not in my wildest dreams."

"We're not talking about Marley."

She lowered her head. "No. No, we're not. And I know she'll…gravitate back to me once we're returned to the cottage, or wherever we'll be, no longer surrounded by so many who are bound and determined to make her feel loved, and wanted."

"It's just that you're now left to twiddle your thumbs, with nothing to do," Darby pressed. "So I want you to think about what you would like to do, as I'm afraid that, as part of our *business agreement*, you'd be expected to do more of that same *nothing*. At least by your standards. There will be the estate residences to oversee—I've a few—and parties to hostess, parties to attend. Oh, dear, and gowns to buy, such as this lovely creation you're wearing tonight, in case I forgot to compliment you."

"Thank you, yes, you continue to play your role nicely. You remarked on how well the color brings out the green in my eyes, and I appreciate that, truly I do. I doubt there is a woman alive who doesn't wish to be thought of as…as attractive."

"You're much more than attractive, Sadie Grace. I'm well aware I've gotten the better half of our bargain."

"You can't mean your eye," she said, her shyness gone, replaced by a touch of anger. "I won't say the patch doesn't make you appear dashing and even slightly dangerous, which it does. It's the reason behind your sacrifice that fills me with pride. Besides, and I don't mean I take your injury lightly, I've seen much worse in John's infirmary. Those who came back missing legs, arms, even their wits. Victory has its costs, and often those who helped attain that victory are left forgotten, barely able to fend for themselves. Soldiers, those brave men, should never be left to beg passersby for coppers, or sleep in the streets. John and I had many conversations about that, and he remained as frustrated as did I."

There was such conviction in Sadie's voice, in the earnest expression on her face. She hadn't been to war, but she'd seen its consequences, and not only in the way John was affected by it. "I can only agree with you, and have been thinking about just that since we spoke this afternoon," he said, taking her arm once more and heading to the end of the balcony as other couples began returning inside, all of them looking as jolly as those condemned to the hangman. "I promise you we'll discuss this again. Sadly, I'm afraid we'll have to return our attention to Clarice's sudden indisposition that has so greatly upset her devoted Jerry. What happened while you ladies were in the retiring room?"

"How did you know it happened there? Oh, never mind, where else could it have happened? There was a woman there as we walked in, the only other occupant of the room, thankfully. She was leaning close to a mirror and rubbing rouge into her cheeks, although she already looked very much like an apple, which is probably why I noticed her. But then Clarice noticed her, as well, and I don't think an entire pot of rouge could have raised apples in her cheeks at that point. She rather swayed where she stood, so that I felt it necessary to support her. She whispered that we had to leave, but before we could the woman must have caught out our reflections in the mirror and called out Clarice's name. Actually, she called her *Goodfellow*, and then ordered her to hop to it and fetch a damp cloth, so that she could wipe the rouge from her fingers. Just *ordered* her, as if she were a servant."

"She was a servant, remember? How did Clarice respond?" This wasn't good, this wasn't good at all.

"She didn't. Well, that's not true. She grabbed my hand and pulled me out of the room, warning that she could be sick at any moment, which she thankfully was not, and the rest you know."

"We all knew this could happen at some point, but Rigby was adamant. The problem, you understand, is that for weeks we've been parading Clarice around Mayfair as a member of the supposedly prestigious Virginia Goodfellows, and if the ton were to discover her true background now, I doubt she or Rigby would ever be forgiven. People have been bowing and curtsying to her, for Lord's sake. No, this isn't good. Deception rarely leads to a happy ending."

Sadie lowered her head. Once again, he was coming close to whatever it was she continued to hide from him. But now was not the time for profound statements, was it? Their friends clearly needed help.

He went back on point, the dilemma at hand.

"The question is, however, since the deed is done, what the devil do we do about it?"

"Hope the woman decides she didn't see what she actually saw? I think that's what Clarice is counting on, although not enough to remain here. That's why she ran away, and why she's already planning to retire from Society until the woman takes herself home. Oh, I forgot that part, didn't I? Clarice told me the woman is from Fairfax County, Virginia, just as you probably already guessed. Her arrival in London is woefully inconvenient, but I suppose we can't keep Americans at home, can we, even for Clarice's sake. How are you going to tell Rigby?"

"It's not how, Sadie Grace, it's *what* will I tell Rigby. At the moment, that's not much. And here I had hoped for a romantic interlude with my betrothed sometime this evening—the current secrecy of said betrothal only adding to my anticipation."

"You don't mean that."

"Ah, but you can't be sure, can you? Perhaps I do mean it, Sadie Grace. I adore your name, you know, that much is true. Sadie Grace. I may even write a poem about it. 'Sadie Grace, so fair of face…'"

"Please be serious."

"Ah, Sadie Grace, but I am being serious, deadly serious. We've yet to share a betrothal kiss, and once we leave here, I doubt there will be time for much more than thinking about our distressed lovebirds." He took her hands in his and leaned in. This time not Clarice or a bleeding Rigby or anyone else was going to interrupt him.

Kissing an untutored mouth had never been so sweet. He was careful not to startle her, keeping his grip on her hands in order not to pull her into his arms. The kiss, he admitted to himself, was purely experimental, a sort of test to see if his recent thoughts about the subject, or marriage in general, and a marriage to Sadie in particular, had only come to him because his friends were all rushing to the altar.

After all, there were certainly other ways to protect Marley, if she really did need protection.

He did not expect his reaction to be more than mild amusement at best, or feeling no reaction at all.

He couldn't have been more wrong.

"Well," he said, drawing away slightly. "That was interesting."

He watched as she drew in her lips, moistening them with her tongue. "We should go back inside."

"Or down those stairs over there, and deeper into the gardens." He let go of her hands and touched a fingertip to her nose.

"You don't have to do this, you know. The kiss, the betrothal, any of it. Nobody knows. There has been no announcement. There's still time to make good your escape. I won't mind."

"God, woman, was the kiss that terrible? I can do better, you know."

"Actually, I don't know what it was, but you've probably realized that. You're an extremely maddening man, my lord, which you also most probably know. I wouldn't be surprised if you believed it one of your charms."

"It's not?"

"I won't answer that, as you'd probably counter with something else equally maddening. You must terrify the debutantes."

"But not you."

"No, I don't believe so. I am, however, still attempting to understand why you've gone so far in your guardianship of Marley as to propose marriage to her aged aunt."

"Yes, there is that. How long in the tooth are you, Sadie Grace?"

"You'll notice that I refuse to be insulted. I'll be four and twenty next June. Decrepit by Society's standards, I believe."

"Egads, on your way to being twenty-four, with me merely two years from thirty. Whatever will the ton have to say to that? Oh, wait. I don't care. Do you care, Sadie Grace?"

Her smile was genuine—he'd teased her into saying what was on her mind. "I don't believe so, if you're content with an aged spinster, and at least I won't be doomed to an eternity spent leading apes in hell."

"Yes, there is that," he agreed. "And the caps. We can't forget the caps. I supposed they're meant to warn the men away, an outward sign that the female wearing said cap is beyond her last prayers and consigned firmly to the shelf. We are a brutal bunch, aren't we? I'd never thought of that before. And what a miserable waste of fine women, I'm sure. You are a fine woman, Sadie Grace—I decided that days ago, even before I knew how aged you are—and I truly believe we're on our way to becoming true friends."

"Yes, I suppose we are. At least I don't actively dislike you anymore."

"Now who isn't being serious?"

"I have no idea," she said, and he suddenly longed to kiss her again.

"Minx. We'll take this up again at another time. For now, let's step inside and you can point out our Mrs. Apple-cheeks. I need a name to go with the face if I'm to help Rigby."

"If *we're* to help Rigby and Clarice. Don't think to exclude me."

They hadn't taken five steps into the music room before he caught sight of the woman; Sadie had described her rather well. "All right, I've got her in my sights. You return to your seat—why in God's name Vivien chose the first row will always be a question—and I'll seek her out."

"Seek her out? You mean engage her in conversation? But what will you say?"

"It appears she has a daughter in tow. I imagine my title alone will make it unnecessary for me to say anything else for at least five minutes."

"You're rather full of yourself, aren't you?"

"To the brim, my friend. Another of my charms you may one day come to admire. Don't forget to secure a seat for me. I shouldn't wish to miss a moment of the harp recital."

"Only if you promise not to make faces, as Rigby did throughout that other poor child's attempt at opera."

"May I feign falling asleep?"

She laughed aloud. "And you're certain you're not younger than I, perhaps by several years? As for my answer, only if you don't snore. Now go."

He watched after her as she made her way through the other guests, idiots all, who didn't marvel at the way the chandelier set sparks in her blond hair, or how she moved, those long legs not only putting her above many of the other ladies but even some of the gentlemen—a goddess, somehow rendered invisible, passing unnoticed among the mere mortals. Did none of them see what he saw? He might have only one good eye, but they obviously were blind.

His *friend*? Had he actually said that? Yes, he had, and he'd meant it. He wasn't accustomed to having females for friends, as equal partners in any conversation beyond the complexity of whether or not it was coming on to rain. In his experience, women were for other uses. He'd been attracted to Sadie purely by her physical appearance, which made him guilty to the crime of being insufferably shallow. He still admired her beauty, but more and more he found himself attracted to her mind. This fact amazed him, and he spared a moment to wonder if the same had been the case for Gabe and Coop. Rigby's reasons for pursuing Clarice had been simpler to understand. He'd been attracted to her face and body, and then fallen in love with her simple but pure heart.

My, but wasn't he growing philosophical, if that meant having deep conversations with himself at the oddest of times.

He watched as Sadie reached the front row of chairs and settled herself, placing her reticule on the empty seat beside her before he headed straight for the garish twin beacons of his target's cheeks. He probably could have located the woman in the dark.

He relieved a servant of two glasses of lemonade, having decided to use them as part of his entrée to the ladies' company.

The pair stood rather on their own island, ignored by the others in the room, their unfashionable gowns clearly not the work of any competent London modiste, their hair in braids wrapped around their heads like mousy brown crowns, their fairly frantic looks about the music room betraying their mutual discomfort. The younger one held a folded fan, and was tapping it against her thigh as if it was a riding crop. The elder was plucking at the tips of her gloves, as if repeatedly counting her fingers, just to make sure all ten were still there.

Engaging them in conversation could almost be considered a kindness.

"Pardon me, madam, miss, but did you see two ladies standing here a few minutes ago? They sent me off for refreshments, but now I can't seem to locate them. Ah, well, perhaps you and your daughter would care for some lemonade, as it's dashed warm in here, don't you think?"

"I… We…" The lady seemed lost for words, probably because a strange man had dared to approach them without a proper introduction. Then again, perhaps it was the patch, or perhaps it was protocol be damned and she wasn't about to shoo away what could be an eligible gentleman come to flirt with her darling daughter. In any case, either thirst or common sense ruled in the end, and she held out her hand for the glass, urging her daughter to do likewise.

He treated them to one of his most elegant bows. "You are saviors, dear ladies, else I might have been forced to drink them both. I abhor lemonade. I'm Nailbourne, by the way. Viscount, for my sins. Here, here, careful with that curtsy, miss, your glass is in danger of tipping." He quickly reached out to steady her hand, at which point the hopeful debutante fell into giggles.

Really, sometimes it was all just too easy.

"Good evening, my lord," the mother said, her curtsy only slightly less painful to watch as her daughter's. "I am Mrs. Henderson, widow of the late Henry Henderson of Fairfax County, Virginia, and this is our daughter, Belinda. We've traveled here to London for the Little Season, on invitation of my husband's cousin, Jackson Henderson. You perhaps know him?"

Darby feigned cudgeling his brain, already knowing he'd never heard of Jackson Henderson. "A hint, Mrs. Henderson, if you could? I'm afraid I can't place him."

"Jackson resides in Exeter, my lord, but we've taken up lodgings in Half Moon Street for…for the nonce. He kindly offered to bring my Belinda into Society, for which I'm most grateful. Our invitation to this lovely soiree came courtesy of Lord Clathan, a long-time patron…er, that is, friend of Jackson's from Exeter."

"Ah, a splendid and most proper connection, Mrs. Henderson. I'm convinced your daughter's appearance here this evening will lead to many more invitations of this sort."

When desperate hostesses would reach out to any reasonably presentable hopefuls needed to fill otherwise empty chairs.

"Will you and your daughter remain in London for the spring Season, Mrs. Henderson? Company is always thinner now, and such a charming young lady as Miss Henderson would do well with a wider exposure."

There had to be someone desperate enough to take on the child, whose unfortunate doughy resemblance to her mother might be overlooked if the dowry was sufficient.

"We were hoping she'd…that is, we haven't quite decided if we should stay on until the spring."

"But, Mama, you promised we would be back in Virginia before Christmastime."

Interesting. And much better than Clarice having the headache until Mrs. Henderson snags a suitable candidate for her little darling.

"Is Christmas a special time for you in Virginia, Miss Henderson?"

"No. I just don't like it here. I miss my horses and

need to be there when the foals come in the spring. My lord." She curtsied again.

Her horses. He'd guessed well about the fan as riding crop.

"Belinda, finish your lemonade, dear," Mrs. Henderson said quickly. "My lord, perhaps you could assist me in something odd that occurred earlier. Do you see that rather tall blonde woman sitting in the front row?"

Darby didn't have to look, but he did, anyway. "Why, yes, I see her. That's Miss Hamilton. Do you know her?" He had nearly added "my companion for the evening," but stopped himself in time or else the woman would probably ask to be introduced.

"No, my lord, but it was the oddest thing. She entered the withdrawing room with her maid, and I was certain I recognized her."

"Miss Hamilton?"

"No, my lord. The maid. I was astonished to see her. I even called out her name, but she rudely ignored me and all but ran from the room. Clarice. I remembered then that she'd traveled to England in service to Miss Dorothea Neville. I was hoping she could give me Miss Neville's direction. It would be so pleasant to see someone else from Virginia, but apparently Clary has left her employ. Sacked, I would imagine, and for good reason, I'm certain. In return for transport home, I thought she might consider serving as our maid. Wretched girl, but I recall she was quite accomplished with hair. Ah, well, I'm sure I'll see her again."

"I wish you luck with that, of course, and I'm sorry that I couldn't be of more assistance. Will you ladies please excuse me now? It would appear our harpist is about to begin, and for the sake of my ears, I needs must effect my escape."

He bowed to both Hendersons and made his way back to the balcony, as it was now impossible to take up his seat beside Sadie. He walked the length of the balcony until he came to a set of French doors leading to what appeared to be His Lordship's private study, and stepped inside.

Thus did he learn that Lord Clathan and one of the housemaids had found a way to pass the time without having to listen to his daughter murder a harp.

"Nailbourne!"

"Clathan," Darby responded affably with a tip of an imaginary hat as the maid simultaneously leaped off His Lordship's lap and pulled up the bodice of her uniform. "Don't mind me, I'm merely passing through on my way somewhere else. You're free to continue as you were, although I would advise locking the door. Oh, and this one, as well, once I'm gone."

"Damn you for a one-eyed—"

Darby chuckled as he closed the door behind him, neatly pocketing the key he'd slipped from the keyhole, rendering the door impossible to lock.

Who knew a musical evening could be so enjoyable?

He headed down the hallway, depositing the key in a potted palm as he passed, unerringly led to the music room by the sound of what might have been a clutch of hens laying square eggs.

He stood just to the side of the doorway and waited for Sadie to notice him, which she did in short order, bless her. He put a finger to his lips, and then tipped his head in the direction of the hallway before disappearing.

She was a bright girl, and would soon follow.

CHAPTER EIGHT

"NOT ONLY DID our Mrs. Henderson recognize Clarice. She wants to hire her away from you."

"From *me*? Whatever would make her think Clarice is my—oh, yes, of course. What else would she think? Do you know how annoying it is for women to have to move about in packs, it would seem, or have a maid in attendance? What would a maid do if the lady was attacked on the way to a withdrawing room, pull a hidden saber from some unknown pocket and slay him dead?"

"I'd rather like to see that. However, right now, were she privileged to see us, I'd imagine Mrs. Henderson would be thinking how strange that the so-handsome and kind viscount is currently occupied in a dark coach with the unknown-to-him blonde woman from the front row, with not a maid or chaperone in sight."

Sadie nodded. She'd thought of that, belatedly, as she'd watched the duchess and Clarice following the duke out of the music room. They had dispensed with the idea of bringing along one of the maids, allowing the duke to act as chaperone, for both Darby and Rigby had arrived separately.

"Yes, if the withdrawing room is bad, I suppose being alone with you in a coach could be likened to an unforgivable sin. But, to be sensible about the thing, it's not as if we're heading into the wilds. We're only a few blocks from Grosvenor Square."

"True, leaving us without sufficient time to formulate any sort of plan to deal with our Mrs. Applecheeks, which is why I've instructed my coachman to drive around the perimeter of the park before returning to the square. You did say you wish to be involved."

"I did, yes. I do. Clarice is always so bright and sunny, and has been endlessly kind to Marley. Seeing her so suddenly terrified was heartbreaking. I've already thought about sending Thea a message, asking her to return."

"I don't think that's wise. Thea's reappearance would only cause the woman to approach her, asking about Clarice. Lies lead to more lies, and eventually we'd trip over at least one of them, especially if the woman's daughter doesn't take before the Season ends—which I seriously doubt—and they decide to stay for the spring Season."

Sadie tapped her foot as she considered his words, studiously ignoring his reference to lies leading to more lies, and then agreed. "Still, we can't ask Thea to hide along with Clarice, can we?"

"Gabe might cut up stiff at that idea simply on general principles. Besides, there's this business of the ball to celebrate the duke's birthday, remember? Everyone who is anyone will be there, to either help Basil celebrate or to be able to say they were present when he *erped*. We must all be there that night, to lend him support."

"The duke isn't going to *erp*, er, die. There's no such thing as the Cranbrook curse. After all, who would have cursed them?"

"Sadie Grace, I never thought of that. None of us has. Indeed, who would have put such a curse on the family?"

"A wicked witch? *Fie on you, you damned Sinclairs. I curse you all, seed, breed and generation. No male shall reach his sixtieth birthday, this I decree by all the devils in hell and Beelzebub himself.* Nonsense!"

Darby applauded softly, but only briefly. "Nonsense or not, please don't reprise that fairly impressive performance anywhere near Basil, or all Gabe's hard work convincing him there is no curse will have gone for nothing. Shall we get back to Clarice?"

"Yes, certainly. But first I'll say that I'm impressed by your loyalty to your friends. John had told me you were all very close, but I see it goes beyond that. How fortunate you are, all of you are, to have such a strong bond."

Darby put his fingers under her chin. "You're a part of us now, Sadie Grace, remember that. Thea, Dany, Clarice and now you. We're all here for you."

She closed her eyes for a moment. "For when I finally tell you this truth you keep talking about. Yes, I know. I can't do that, not tell all of them. It's painful enough to know that someday I need to tell you. No one else can ever know, please. Not that part."

"There's more than one part?"

"Please. Not now."

"You're right. I did promise not to press you. Forgive me."

Oh, how she wanted to tell him, tell him all of it. Every moment she was with him she trusted him more, liked him more. Admired him more. They had become, as he'd said, friends. The longer she waited, the more difficult it would be to confess the truth. But the pain was still too raw for her to relive it again this soon. Her mistakes, her haunting feeling of guilt.

Still with his fingers beneath her chin, he leaned in

and kissed her. Like the first, it was maddeningly gentle and wretchedly brief, before he leaned back against the squabs once more, the coach traveling on through the dark.

He was no fool, Darby Travers. He was wearing her down by inches, tiptoeing rather than crashing into her life, seemingly content to proceed slowly, and with caution, until she felt an actual need to tell him everything she'd hidden inside her since John's death. Would telling him lift at least a part of the guilt that weighed so heavily on her?

She'd even had time to wonder if he'd understand, and felt she had reason to hope he wouldn't judge her. Or was that wishful thinking on her part?

Whoever and whatever the viscount was on the outside, he was an entirely other person on the inside…the part of him he probably shared only with his friends. If she had secrets, she had already decided that he harbored a few of his own, as there had been both sadness and anger in his voice the day he told her about his childhood at the cottage.

She sensed rather than saw him raise his hand to his forehead, a sure sign that the headache he suffered from had made its presence known.

"Turn your back to me," she told him, already stripping off her evening gloves.

"I beg your pardon?" he returned with a smile. "Are you about to do something I would be shocked to see? Adjust a garter perhaps? We're engaged, Sadie Grace, and I'd like to consider observing such a delightful exercise a privilege of our approaching union."

"You really can be impossible, you know. You have the headache again, which may account for some of it, but I believe you actually enjoy being outrageous. Now turn your back, slip off the patch and let me see if I can ease the pain."

"I don't think so, no." His voice was clipped now.

"Don't be so prickly. I won't look, if that's your concern. John suffered from the headache when he returned from the war, and I massaged his head many times. He taught me how, after learning from one of the Spanish doctors he met. Not to be immodest, but he told me I have magic in my fingers. Please, you've done so much for us. Let me do something for you in return."

He looked at her for some moments, and then shifted on the squabs, turning his back to her as he reached up to untie the ribbons of the eye patch. "You can be much like a dog gnawing away on a bone. I can't believe I'm doing this."

Sadie was suddenly nervous. What if it didn't work? What if she touched her fingers to his bare neck and head, and swooned away like some silly child? That certainly had never happened before, but massaging her brother and massaging the viscount were as unlike as chalk and cheese.

The space inside the coach was so intimate, the darkness melting away inhibitions she might not be able to overcome in the daylight. She would do what she had to do, what her fingers had itched to do each time she sensed he was in pain.

She ordered herself to be calm, be sensible, and put her hands on his strong, broad shoulders. A thrill went through her, all the way to her toes. How absurd. He was wearing his evening jacket; it wasn't as if she was touching his bare skin, even if she could feel his muscles through the fine material. His tense, tight muscles.

"Relax, for goodness' sake. I'm not going to hurt you," she said as she began to push her thumbs against either side of his spine, slowly working her way up his back until she could feel those muscles relax beneath her touch.

With her hands bent inward toward her palms, she continued her ministrations, with thumbs and her flattened knuckles never leaving his body, moving in a hopefully soothing rhythm as she inched slowly upward, applying pressure directly against either side of his neck.

Darby bent his head slightly forward, most definitely relaxing. "Delightful. Are you certain it was a Spanish *doctor* who introduced John to this sort of thing?"

"What do you mean by—oh. I didn't press him, no. For the sake of my blushes, we'll make no assumptions."

"You won't, no. All I can say is good on John. *Ahh*, yes, that feels oddly wonderful."

She had slid her spread fingers up and into Darby's thick dark hair and was pressing the balls of her thumbs just behind the base of her ears. Holding the position, the pressure, and then sliding her thumbs upward. She repeated the action until she could feel Darby's head drop even lower, a sure sign that he no longer had any thoughts in his head beyond the rhythmic ministrations of her fingers.

Only then did she dare slowly adjust her approach, until her thumb pads rested on his temples, lightly dragging her fingertips from the center of his forehead to his temples, her strokes light, even, measured. A gentle stretching meant to relax him, ease the tension and pain.

He didn't resist, not even when her fingertips encountered the rough scarring along his left brow, the small puckers of skin that had been roughly drawn together to close a wound. She could tell that half his eyebrow was gone, replaced by scars, even though John had already told her that he'd regretted the necessity, but it was the only way to get to the ball that had lodged in the bony protection around the eye, a heartbeat above instant death. The scar, John had believed, was a small price to pay. Darby raised his head, probably not even realizing what he was doing, and she gently pulled him back against her breasts, so that it was easier to reach him.

Her touch became lighter as she stroked his forehead and into his hairline. Only with great effort on her part did she control her breathing as the weight of his head had served to bring a not unpleasant pressure as well as an awareness of Darby as a male, and not a brother or any patient. There was this feeling of closeness, oneness, here in the darkened coach, a stirring of emotion she had never felt before, an unspoken rapport between the two of them, a strange, silent communion that both pleased and worried her.

Was she about to become a victim of hopeful wishes she'd not acknowledged from the moment of their first meeting in his study and she'd felt so drawn to him—him and the silly sleep marks on his cheek? Had her lonely spinster heart begun to melt as she watched him sit on the floor, being the man, not the viscount, playing with Marley and the puppy? Was it his easy affection for the outrageous duke and duchess, his teasing nature with Rigby, his acceptance of Clarice and the flash of real anger she'd seen in his eye when he realized the maid-turned-lady was in danger of being exposed?

He *cared*. He pretended he didn't, laughing and joking about most anything, including his own wound, but she didn't doubt he would lay down his own life for any of his tight-knit circle of friends.

And now he'd included her in that circle. She and Marley both.

Sadie knew her heart was involved now, an emotion totally separate from her gratefulness toward him because he'd taken Marley as his ward. He'd protect her now as he did his friends, with all of him, heart and soul and body.

She could only pray it didn't come to that.

Darby's slow, even breathing told her he had fallen asleep against her, hopefully to wake sans the headache. For a moment she was tempted to move her hands down onto his shoulders, leaning over him as she stroked his chest, dropped a kiss on the top of his head while he wasn't awake to make a joke of her actions. Or question them.

The side door of the coach opened, and the steps folded down as the groom unnecessarily announced that they'd arrived in Grosvenor Square.

Sadie had been so caught up in her thoughts that she hadn't even noticed the slowing of the coach.

"Darby," she whispered gently. Then, "Darby! We're back at the duke's mansion."

He roused then, rather all at once. "Love a duck," he said, sitting up, his features now partially illuminated thanks to the light thrown by the twin flambeaux burning on either side of the mansion's grand entrance.

Sadie watched as the groom, seeing his employer without his eye patch, swiftly put a hand to his mouth, his eyes all but popping from his head as he backed away from the coach.

"Bloody hell," Darby said as he searched the squabs for his patch and quickly positioned it over his eye, fumbling with the ribbons. "He'll probably have night-mares."

"He's probably merely shocked to have opened the door to see his employer intimately lolling against a lady's bosom, soundly asleep," Sadie improvised quickly.

He turned to look at her, his hair smoothed, the familiar patch covering the scar and accentuating the perfect handsomeness of the rest of his face. "I was lolling? And I don't remember it? Shame on me."

"Indeed. How is your headache?"

He raised a hand to his forehead. "Gone." He smiled in her direction. "It's totally gone. John was correct— you apparently have magic in these fingers." He raised both her hands and, over her protest, kissed her fingertips. "You should hang out your shingle, Dr. Hamilton. Thank you."

"You're welcome," she said quietly, embarrassed and rather thrilled at the same time.

He helped her down to the cobblestones and escorted her to the door.

"I have to go inside now, don't I? Do you suppose Rigby is there?"

"If he is, have one of the footmen come inform me and I'll drag him away by his coattails, promising all four of us will put our heads together tomorrow morning. The last thing any of us needs is a strategy session that includes helpful suggestions from either Vivien or Basil."

Sadie nodded her head. "They're both very fond of Clarice."

"They also both have strangely inventive minds. I can hear Basil now, contemplating a possible assassination. He's already come to her defense, you know, much to

Gabe's astonishment, but that's a story for another time. Besides, I think we may want to further explore your remarks concerning who might have put a curse on the Sinclair men. I'll have a coach sent 'round for you both at eleven."

Sadie was confused. "All right, I suppose. But I was only being silly."

"Sometimes, my dear Sadie Grace, being silly is actually achieved by highlighting possibilities other, more sober brains may have overlooked."

"Do you really think—"

"'There are more things in heaven and earth, Horatio, than are dreamt of in your philosophy'? Yes, I do."

"Shakespeare. Hamlet, to be exact. Quoting the bard doesn't make the idea any less absurd, you know. Look," she said as the door opened, "here comes Rigby now. Oh, dear, he doesn't look happy, does he?"

"Rigby?" Darby inquired as their friend brushed past them and down the steps.

"I'm going home with you," the ejected swain called back to them. "She tossed me out on my ear, and I'm told Sadie knows why. If she knows, you know. Hurry up, I want a drink."

"Several drinks would be my guess," Darby said, smiling at Sadie. "We'd better make that noon." He bowed over her hand, turning it at the last moment to press a shiver-inducing kiss against her palm, and then he was gone.

Sadie squared her shoulders and entered the mansion, wondering if the duchess might allow her a few sips of her favored gin. She could pour it into a teacup, and nobody would know...

CHAPTER NINE

CLARICE ARRIVED HEAVILY VEILED, and quickly raced ahead of Sadie and their maid-cum-chaperone to enter Darby's Park Lane townhome, even while he stood at the window, watching as Sadie stopped to admire the facade that boasted a first-floor balcony facing Hyde Park. He'd spent many a pleasant hour on that balcony, smoking cheroots with his friends, or just idly watching Society go by inside the park…many of them making cakes of themselves as they did so.

Poodle Byng, the Green Man, wet-behind-the-ears young dandies perched precariously in their yellow-wheeled curricles while being dragged along by their showy yet fairly useless cattle. And not to forget the ladies, each attempting to outdo the other as they feigned ennui with the whole process even as they prayed to be noticed.

Sadie would enjoy sitting out here with him, half-hidden behind the greenery from a few strategically placed pots. He was as interested in hearing her comments as he was eager to compare them to his own thoughts. One thing about Sadie Grace Hamilton… the lady did not suffer fools gladly. She hadn't had the time, had she? But now, even as her world changed around her, he had the distinct feeling that she would never change to suit it.

He remained amazed that he'd allowed himself to be

talked into removing his patch, even more taken aback to have fallen asleep under her ministrations. When was the last time he had been that close to a woman's bosom without taking full advantage of that happy happenstance?

That, he knew, was a rhetorical question.

He moved away from the window as he heard Willie Camford beg the ladies to please follow him upstairs to the drawing room "where His Lordship awaits."

Sounds as if I'm here in my lair, prepared to pounce.

Strange how he suddenly found himself looking at his world through the eyes of a person who had never had the time, and probably the use, for half of the nonsense Society used to measure the acceptability of others. If he'd had his own way, he would have met Sadie at the door; indeed, probably helped her down from the coach and escorted her inside so that he could see and hear, firsthand, her reaction to his townhome. Instead, Society dictated that he *await* her in his lair.

"Your Lordship," Willie announced with all the formality his father had impressed on him and his brothers, Lawrence, Thomas and Quentin, all raised to be butlers, all now in charge of Nailbourne holdings. "Misses Hamilton and Goodfellow are here to see you."

Since Clarice had already bounded into the room, the ridiculously long veil still hiding her features as she proclaimed, "He knows who we are, you silly man," and Sadie stood in full sight just behind the butler, the announcement was half formality, half comedy.

"Thank you, Camford," Darby said. "You may retire. Please have refreshments sent here for the ladies."

"As you wish, my lord." Willie bowed himself out of the drawing room, just as if he and "my lord" hadn't spent an hour or more last night, their jackets gone, their shirtsleeves rolled up, playing two-handed whist and reminiscing over shared days at the cottage in their younger years after they'd finally managed to get a by turns sorrowful and belligerent, definitely drunken Rigby upstairs to one of the guest chambers.

"Are you just going to pose on the threshold, Sadie Grace, not that you don't make a pretty sight?" Darby asked as he crossed the room to greet her.

She lifted her hand, more to wave off his words than anything else, but he managed to secure it, bow over it and place a kiss on her gloved fingers. He leaned in close to say quietly, "You and the memory of these magic hands served to keep me awake most of the night. Pleasantly, I might add."

She ignored his smile, and his intimate tone. "Clarice and her tears kept me from my bed well past three. Where's Rigby?"

Clearly the interlude in the coach was not to be discussed. Just as clearly, he was to adjust his behavior accordingly. His circumspect lady of the day...but perhaps not so much the lady in the dark? An intriguing prospect.

"Banished to his own lodgings until he can make himself presentable. I expect his return at any moment."

"We had to almost physically boost Clarice from her tub. The duchess feared she would try to drown herself, but Clarice swore she thinks better in the tub."

"And does she?" Darby asked as he escorted Sadie to one of the couches.

"Not noticeably, no. She did end up looking rather prune-y, but no brainstorms rained down upon her head." Sadie looked up at him, a frown furrowing her smooth brow. "She's here to offer Rigby his freedom."

"She's what? She couldn't blast our Romeo from her side with a cannonball. Strange. I hadn't thought of Clarice as a martyr. In fact, I initially worried she might only be taking advantage of Rigby for his title and deep pockets, but that thought soon faded. They're ridiculously, almost embarrassingly in love."

"Yes, and only a woman in love would consider such a sacrifice. My heart is breaking for her, and the duchess retired to her rooms in tears, to demand the duke *do something.* From the little you said last night, that alone should be enough to give us all pause."

"Most definitely, and I speak from Gabe's experience. We have to come up with something, and do it quickly. Ah, here comes our worse-for-drink friend."

Rigby burst into the room, nearly knocking down Camford, who had returned carrying a tray of refreshments. The butler hastily deposited it on the table in front of Sadie and was gone as quickly as he'd arrived, probably to stand in the hallway and laugh himself crooked, Darby decided, since *he* didn't have to deal with any of it. Sometimes it was wonderful, having Camy's sons established as butlers at his various estates, and sometimes he believed he was still a youngster, and prone to be laughed at by much older cousins.

Darby reluctantly turned his attention to the reunited couple.

Clarice got to her feet, fighting free of her veil. "Oh, Jerry, my heart, my soul!"

"Oh, Clary, my life, my love!" Rigby sent his curly brimmed beaver flying, nearly scattering a collection of jade pieces displayed on a nearby table.

"Oh, bollocks," Darby muttered as the two lovebirds

came together in the middle of the room, nearly taking each other to the floor with the force of their collision.

"Don't be so cynical. They're happy to see each other."

"Happy, Sadie Grace, doesn't begin to describe it," Darby said as the dramatic reunion appeared likely to escalate into passionate lovemaking. "I should have Camford send up a few buckets of cold water. Either that, or you should close your eyes."

"Nonsense. They'll stop soon enough, when Clarice tells him her plan."

"In other words, when they finally feel the need to take a breath. You're right to keep your eyes open, as this should be interesting. It's probably too late to call Camford back to watch with us. There aren't many who can say they've witnessed a man's head spin about in a full circle while still attached to his shoulders."

Sadie looked up at him. "I know, Darby. You're as worried about them as I am."

"Did I say I was—oh, all right. Yes, I'm worried. Rigby is by nature a gentle creature, which is another way of saying nobody wants to see him when he's finally provoked into anger. We were out on a stroll in a small Spanish town we'd captured when he ran off down an alleyway, having spied out soldiers from another regiment assaulting one of the village females. Two of them, and neither small men. By the time the rest of us arrived on the scene, one man was howling with a broken arm, and the other was dazedly looking about on the cobbles to locate several of his teeth."

"That's very interesting, even edifying, but he can't mill down Mrs. Henderson to keep her from speaking. Oh, look, they're talking now. At least Clarice is."

Darby directed his attention to the pair, now sitting

close together on a settee beneath one of the windows, their hands tightly intertwined as they half-faced each other. *Lovers in a Window.* A pretty picture, save for the fact that Rigby, who hadn't looked all that splendid when he'd stumbled out the viscount's door this morning, looked five times worse now.

"He's not taking this well," Darby said as he sat down beside Sadie.

Sadie watched along with him. "No, but since Clarice is being strong, he rather has to be, doesn't he? It's what I told her I'd hoped. She did have that small lapse when she first saw him, but I believe she's doing much better now."

"Pardon me? Are you saying you and Clarice — most apparently, you—came in here with a plan to keep Rigby from making a scene? Save for that small lapse, of course."

"Yes. Nothing is ever solved by ranting and raving, now, is it? Why should any of us have to deal with Rigby crashing about, spouting invectives, gnashing his teeth and so forth, all to no avail, as histrionics seldom are? Once I pointed out that she'd be helping Rigby, Clarice was in complete agreement."

Darby looked at her, saw the quick twitch of her lips as she hid a smile. "Whoever said women are devious creatures didn't know the half of it. Are we always managed so easily?"

"I don't know. I was only using the strategy I employ with Marley. It's awkward to know yourself hysterical when those around you maintain their calm. The hysterical one either storms out, which does no one any good but at least clears the room, or that person calms down, as well. It's really a simple remedy. But it's the only plan we had, and it goes only this far. Now it is up to you and I to present both of them with an alternative that doesn't rip them apart forevermore in order to save Rigby's reputation—I'm quoting Clarice now. So, what are we going to do? And hurry, because I think I see Clarice's chin wobbling."

"All right," Darby said, "let's run down our options."

"We have options? Why didn't you say that earlier? I'd be grateful to hear a single idea that has some hope attached to it."

"Oh, that's unfortunate. I'm merely guessing, you understand, but I suppose that means you don't want to consider kidnapping the two ladies, stuffing them into sacks and tossing them onto a ship bound for the port of Virginia. A pity, because I believe that was my best idea."

"You're impossible."

Darby kissed her on the cheek before she could protest, or perhaps she didn't notice. She was clearly concentrating all her efforts on the problem at hand.

He took a moment to reflect on this new level of association with his betrothed. *Friendship.* The word had never entered his head when the subject was females. She'd even accepted his kiss the way a friend or even sister or cousin might do. Did he have no romantic effect on her at all? How lowering.

There was still no real noise coming from the devastated lovebirds other than the occasional heartfelt sigh, so Darby pressed on.

"I suppose we could pay her to forget she saw Clarice."

Sadie shook her head. "Considered and discarded, as soon as the duke offered his own purse. Clarice told us the Hendersons already are swimming in lard, or some such thing."

Darby laughed. "My dear naive Miss Hamilton. *Nobody* ever has enough money. That's a universal rule of the wealthy, especially the odiously wealthy. Money itself, or something they want that is owned by someone else, and therefore unattainable."

"I don't understand that, but I suppose you'd know better than I on the subject, having already admitted to being one of the odiously wealthy. I also wondered if perhaps we could offer Mrs. Henderson our assistance in finding a husband for her daughter in exchange for her silence. She doesn't seem to be doing very well on her own, does she?"

"Thought of it," Darby said. "Not enough time. It would take more than a fortnight to bring anyone up to snuff, I'm afraid. There is her dowry, which by Clarice's description of the Henderson wealth is probably considerable, but do we really want to stoop so low as to bracket the poor girl with a fortune hunter? Sadie? You're hesitating."

She sighed. "I know. Just for a moment I—we have no more ideas, do we? What is the daughter like, by the way? Just so I can feel more guilty for having entertained the notion, if only for that one moment."

"Miss Belinda Henderson? Horse mad, I'd say, like many English girls, as well. She was employing her fan as a riding crop—a most betraying habit—and insists she be back in Virginia for the foaling season. Frankly, other than to be momentarily titillated by my title, I doubt she could have cared a fig that she'd been introduced to my most impressive self."

"How that must have stung," Sadie responded, her expression marvelously bland.

But Darby was deep in thought and didn't react.

"Darby? I didn't mean to insult you."

"That's all right, you're forgiven." *What the devil had she said?* "It's just that I may have had another idea. Oh, and by the way, you're brilliant. I never would have thought of this if you hadn't asked me about the girl."

So saying, he cupped his hands on her cheeks and caught her mouth with his own. This time a longer kiss, a lingering kiss that could lead to so much else.

But not now, even if the lovebirds across the room wouldn't have noticed.

Besides, Sadie hadn't exactly objected. She also hadn't wound her arms around him and called him her darling, but she hadn't slapped his face. He'd take that as a victory over mere friendship, and perhaps later think more about what he'd done, and how ridiculously pleased he was with himself for having done it, how natural his reaction had been. Feel happiness, kiss Sadie Grace. A lovely combination.

He stood up, suddenly anxious to be on their way to doing something, which was not as wonderful as sitting here with Sadie, but at the moment was a very close second place finisher. "Rigby? Pull yourself together, my friend. I think I've solved our problem."

Clarice all but flew across the room to fling herself into his arms. "Darby! Oh, sweet, wonderful Darby! I *told* Rigby you'd think of something because Sadie swore you're brilliant."

"You swore that?" he asked Sadie, who rolled her eyes rather comically as he attempted to disengage the clinging Clarice and steer her back into Rigby's arms.

"I had to do something to stop her tears. You...you were handy."

"Really? My name popped straight into your mind... combined with the word *brilliant*. Didn't I just say the same about you?"

Sadie plucked at the folds of her gown. "It's a common enough description. I was desperate. Are you desperate, as well, or do you really have an idea, a plan?"

"An idea, Sadie Grace. It takes a bit longer to formulate a plan. Now come along, ladies, let's find your maid, escort you to the duke's coach and get you on your way to Grosvenor Square. Rigby and I have some things to do, but I promise to send 'round a note this evening, to apprise you of our progress."

"Since Clarice refuses to attend any parties this evening, that seems reasonable enough. The duke has promised me a chess lesson, and I am more than satisfied with that."

"But—but, oh, Rigby, will you be safe?"

"Safe as houses, as it's said, Clarice," Darby assured her, silencing Rigby's quick question as to what was happening with a shake of his head, as his idea was still too new and fragile to share just yet, in case a certain long-legged someone said something else *brilliant* and shot it down.

"You're feeling rather full of yourself, my lord," Sadie commented as he escorted her down the steps to the duke's town coach.

"You're displeased?"

"Actually, I rather like you this way. I've held the reins for a very long time in one way or another, and I look forward to riding in comfort from time to time while someone else manages the horses."

"But only from time to time?" he asked as he bowed over her hand before assisting her up the step and into the coach.

"Indeed. And by the way, your establishment is most impressive, most especially that balcony above us. I look forward to one day sitting there to watch the world wander by."

Darby laughed and closed the coach door behind her, stepping back to stand with Rigby as the coachman drove off. How had she known he'd wanted to hear her opinion of his residence? How did she know anything about him, because it seemed she knew more than he believed he'd shared? But she'd let him handle the reins, would she? Was it a far step from that to entrusting him with her secrets? With more than her secrets?

"You know something, Rigby?" he said, putting his arm around his friend's shoulders and turning him back toward the door. "If it weren't for your dilemma, I can't remember the last time I've enjoyed myself quite so much."

CHAPTER TEN

"I SAW HIM kiss you, you know," Clarice said as she sat cross-legged on Sadie's bed, and then reached for another lemon square.

They both had pretended to turn in for the night, but once they were snug in night rails and dressing gowns, Clarice had tiptoed down the hallway, to meet in Sadie's chamber without any fear of being interrupted. There had been enough of that from Vivien and Coop's mother, Minerva, all evening long, especially after Darby's note had arrived with the evening tea tray.

"It wasn't really a kiss, Clarice, not in the way you think. He was excited about his idea. Feeling exuberant, as it were."

Clarice snorted. "You really are a looby, aren't you, for how smart you are?"

Sadie squirmed a bit on the soft mattress, folding her long legs beside her, and began absently running a hand up and down her calf. "Don't see things that aren't there, Clarice, please."

"Yes, yes, I saw straight through that nonsense about the two of you suddenly tripping over some mutual affection you'd managed to discover in two very brief meetings. Darby only said that to mollify Vivien and the others. The marriage is for the sake of sweet Marley, who will now feel safe and loved and unafraid of the future, knowing her guardian and her aunt will be walking hand in hand with her through the sweet meadows of her life."

Sadie felt a blush stealing into her cheeks. "That was embarrassing enough when Vivien said it. You don't have to repeat it word for word."

"I do if I want to see you hide your eyes from me and pretend you see marriage to Darby as a sacrifice you're both making for Marley. Every time you say it, you sound less sure, do you know that? Besides, I think he likes you."

Sadie's head snapped up. "Why? What do you know? Did Rigby tell you something? Has Darby said anything? What did he say?"

"Aha, you fell straight into my trap," Clarice said, pointing a finger at her. "I knew it. You do care, don't you? That's another bonnet my Jerry owes me. I'll soon have more than I'd need if I had a dozen heads. I think I'll start in on reticules next."

"You're much too clever for me, you know," Sadie said, sliding off the bed and heading for the desk holding the note from Darby. Her betrothed, but far from her beloved. Why did everyone in love want everyone else to share their same condition? Didn't most couples marry for much more pragmatic reasons? Wouldn't she be smart to remember that?

Still, she'd never really had a friend back in the village, neither male nor female. She'd had acquaintances, yes, good people all, but she'd never felt the least desire to confide in any of them, share secrets, giggle in corners, exchange knowing looks that communicated without words. To do so now, even with Clarice, seemed foreign to her, and vaguely uncomfortable.

She'd had her parents, but that was long ago, and her father had believed in strict discipline, her mother in teaching her daughter how to sew a fine seam and keep an orderly house. Sadie's education, although much more extensive than that of most young girls, hadn't extended to anything either of her parents thought objectionable for young ladies.

Which was why the day Sadie had discovered one of John's anatomy books had come as such a revelation to her. Working with him in his infirmary had taken care of most everything else, for good or ill. But she'd never seen her parents share a kiss, never heard either utter an endearment, never been the object of a warm hug or a declaration of love.

John had been no different, and had chosen a bride cut from his same straightforward, no-nonsense cloth.

Sadie knew that was why, from the moment she'd entered Marley's young life, she'd made certain that things would be different for her niece. Marley didn't steal a glance up from her lessons to watch from the window as the village children played on the green; she joined them in their games. She was allowed to sit on a bench in the blacksmith's shop to watch the smithy at work, say "thank you very much" and accept a treat from the town baker, hold hands with the shoemaker's apprentice as he taught her how to skate on the ice-covered pond.

And that was never going to change! Not because of any promise to John, but because of one she'd made to herself. She'd had some worries the first few days, but when Darby had arrived with the puppy, she had finally mentally unpacked, believing she could do no better for her niece.

All the rest of it? Well, that was just Clarice's wishful thinking.

Wasn't it?

"Sadie? Yoohoo, Sadie—have you frozen in place? Did I upset you? I'm so sorry. I suppose I simply want everyone to be happy." Clarice paused a moment, then added, "And I like being right. That's wicked, isn't it?"

"No," Sadie said kindly, climbing back onto the bed, this time with Darby's note in hand. "I want everyone to be happy, as well. For the moment, that means you and Rigby most especially. Shall we read this again?"

Clarice shrugged. "I don't see why. Darby will come for you in his curricle tomorrow at eleven, so dress warmly, while Martha and Belinda Henderson will be driven in his coach, with you all meeting at the cottage for luncheon. He doesn't mention then tapping the ladies over the head with a shovel and burying them in the gardens, but clearly he has something planned. I'd come along, to act as chaperone, except that I'm not a maid anymore. Sometimes that's a shame, because people speak in front of maids just as if we haven't got ears under our caps. The things I heard about people that way when I'd accompany Thea's mother to engagements would shock you to your toes."

Sadie didn't believe she was interested in gossip, especially about people she didn't know, but if it would turn Clarice's attention away from her romantic imaginations about Darby, she'd ask for details her new friend clearly wanted to share.

How nice it was to have a friend, to be a friend.

Clarice scooted backward to reseat herself propped against the pillows. "Now, let me think. All right. There was the time Winnie Fowler had me help boost her out the window at a party, off for some slap and tickle with her lover. I didn't think that was very nice to do to her husband, so I decided not to wait around to help her climb back in, even though she'd given me a copper when she told me to stay right here by the window, Clary Goodfellow, or you'll be sorry. I wasn't sorry, especially when it started to rain."

"Clarice, you're incorrigible."

The girl had slipped into a pleasant drawl, probably the same one she was working so hard to conquer, but Sadie thought it charming.

"I know. I also know that Jacob Smith pawned his gold watch and some of his wife's jewelry to pay a gambling debt, then had his manservant locked up for stealing when everything was found under the poor fellow's mattress. Fakes by then, glass for real stones, of course, save for the watch, because he must have found it too dear to copy, and with his wife never the wiser. Struts about with all that glass hanging around her neck, still thinking they're diamonds."

"I feel sorry for the manservant."

"Don't waste a moment worrying about Skippy Baxter. He'd been stealing Jacob Smith blind for years. He pretty much had to, seeing as how he had one wife in the village and another in some holler over in the next county."

Sadie sighed. "I've missed so much of life, not being privy to gossip. Please, is there more?"

"You're like the duchess. She loves my stories. Here's another one. I know that Daisy Fisher did the beast with two backs with her sister Sally's betrothed, except he didn't know it because Daisy and Sally are twins and look as alike as two peas in a pod. Oh, and I can tell you that nose-in-the-air Elizabeth Rumple stuffs her bodices with lambswool wadding, and won't her husband be surprised on their wedding night!"

"Clarice, stop," Sadie said, laughing, but then an idea struck her. "Do you know anything about the Hendersons? I mean, other than that they're quite wealthy and own a horse farm?"

"Oh, everybody knows about them, no secrets there," Clarice said with a dismissive wave of her hand. "The Hendersons were nothing but dirt farmers up until Sissy Henderson, not a day past sixteen, waved her bottom at that old fool Silas Winkle, telling him the bun in her belly was his—and him, eighty if he was a day, believing her."

"They married, I imagine. I take it Silas Winkle was a wealthy man?"

"More money than God, that's what they said. And deader than dead not a year later in a tumble down the stairs. Before the cat could lick its ear Sissy was bracketed to her second cousin Fred, and all the Hendersons were deep in clover."

Sadie shivered. "Murdered?"

It was Clarice's turn to laugh. "Not exactly. The way I heard it, the old bugger was chasing Sissy down the stairs with his breeches at his knees, her in her petticoats, giggling and daring him to catch her. But I only heard that because nobody notices the maid, who saw it all. Everyone said he'd simply lost his balance and fell. It was Fred's sister-in-law Martha—*our* Martha—who swore she saw it all, and sure enough, next thing anyone knew, Martha's Henry was the proud owner of a horse farm, and Martha's been strutting around like the cock of the walk ever since."

"Some would call it murder. Clearly Sissy lured him to the stairs, and his death."

"How do you figure that?"

Because I've seen eighty-year-old men stripped down to the buff in John's infirmary, that's why. Seduction wasn't the game Sissy had been playing!

"I don't know for certain, silly. I was only guessing. Is there anything else you know about the Hendersons?"

Clarice thought for a moment, popped the rest of the lemon square into her mouth and closed her eyes in bliss at the taste. "Nothing nobody else knows…or guesses at, the way you just did. Sissy and Fred sure did spread Silas's money around to all the Hendersons, and there's a passel of them. Now there's Judge Henderson and Pastor Henderson and Banker Henderson and Livery Stable Henderson. One of them—Jackson, I think it is—took himself off to England with his share, and now he sends rugs over to his kin all the time. No more dirt floors for the almighty Hendersons! The rest they sell in Henderson's Emporium and Fine Imported Carpets, la-di-da. And it all started with Sissy's wagging tail. You ought to see it now, Sadie, broader than a barn door."

Sadie ignored that last statement, preferring to return to the subject of Jackson Henderson. "Darby told me that Martha told him—oh, now I sound like a gossip! Clarice, I think you're telling me that Mrs. Henderson's cousin Jackson is in *trade*."

Clarice shrugged. "You're smiling. Is that good?"

"Not if said cousin is sponsoring Belinda, hoping to snag her a title, I'm sure. I may not know very much about Society, but there's something about any *lingering smell of the shop* that apparently is considered even worse than murder—when thinking about English his-

tory and all the murders that have been winked at over
the centuries. I have to tell Darby. This might be useful information for him. Clarice? Did I say something
wrong?"

Her friend shook her head and sniffed, a pair of enormous tears beginning their journey down those wonderfully rounded cheeks. "I miss them so much."

"The Hendersons? No, of course not." Sadie pushed
herself back against a mound of pillows and slid her
arm around Clarice's shoulders. "You mean your family, don't you?"

Clarice nodded, pulling a handkerchief from her
dressing gown pocket and noisily blowing her nose.
"Cousin June should have birthed her baby by now, and
Mama isn't getting any younger. And I wanted to tell
Uncle Soggy that he's a privy councilor, because he'd
be so proud he'd pop his buttons."

"Ah, Clarice. You can do all of that."

"No, I can't. I...I used to think, oh, what fun, showing
up one fine day on my Jerry's arm, the Lady Rigby, and
now you all curtsy to me, you who used to look down
your noses at all us Goodfellows. But someone will just
tell Jerry everything, like I just told you about the Hendersons and all, and he'll never forgive me."

"For goodness' sake, Clarice, what did you do? Nothing can be that bad."

"That's because it wasn't. Not for Clary Goodfellow. It
was all in fun, and what else was there to do in Fairfax—
that's how I saw the thing. And I never took any money, I
swear it. Not even from Georgie Henderson."

"Who?"

"Belinda's b-brother. Sadie, don't you see? Him and
a lot more."

"How…how many more? Wait, don't answer that. I shouldn't have asked."

"Too many more, that's how many. Jerry knows something, but he doesn't ask, and won't let me tell him. I don't have to, do I? Everyone else will tell him. There goes Clary Goodfellow, always *good* for a tumble. Oh, God! Thea said it would be all right, and she and Gabe would be with us when we visit, and I'd be all dressed in fine clothes and keeping my chin high and everyone would be wanting to talk to me and say they know me. But it won't be all right, it will never be all right. Not if Martha Henderson tells everyone here about me, and not if Jerry and I go to Virginia and everyone tells him. I can't be anywhere—not with Jerry, not if he isn't to be fighting duels or coming to hate me for who I was. Oh, Sadie…"

Clarice cried for a long time, Sadie holding her close until she gently disengaged herself and called for a tub to be brought to Clarice's chamber. It had already gone past midnight and she apologized profusely to the maids and footmen who dragged out the tub and filled it nearly to the brim with kitchen-fire heated water, and then perched on the edge of a chair while Clarice soaked… just to be certain the girl didn't decide sinking beneath the surface was the only real answer left to her.

She woke several hours later at a slight sound, as she'd never really allowed herself to go into a deep sleep, still propped in the same chair, her neck protesting when she attempted to lift her head from her shoulder, and then panicked as she didn't see Clarice's head and shoulders above the water.

"Clarice!" she called out, turning in a circle in an attempt to locate her. There was the dressing gown and night rail, where they'd been put, and the turned-down bed was empty. "Please don't tell me she's run off to protect her Jerry. And where would she go?"

Sadie raced down the hallway to her own chamber, not bothering to rouse her maid as she'd dressed herself for many years and certainly could manage the exercise one more time. She did stop to slap cold water left in the basin from the previous night against her cheeks, and clean her teeth because a person did have to maintain some standards, even in an emergency, twisted her hair into a figure-eight bun that in truth ended looking more like a figure-six, grabbed her new cherry-red cloak, slipped her bare feet into half boots and headed for the stairs.

A liveried footman snored on a bench in the grand entrance of the mansion, but somehow managed to jump to attention at the sound of her footsteps on the stairs.

"Did you see Miss Goodfellow pass by here?" she asked the boy, who shook his head even as he yawned widely, showing his molars to the world. "Are you quite certain?"

"No, miss," he confessed, rubbing at the back of his neck as he got to his feet and bowed. Sadie understood; sleeping while sitting up wasn't comfortable. "I think I might hadda nodded off there for a space. Don't tell Mr. Hobson."

"I won't. I need you to open this door."

"I can't do that, miss. Only Mr. Hobson has the key, and he locks us all up nice and tight every night."

"But—but that's ridiculous. What if there was a fire? How would anyone get out?" And why was her practical brain thinking so practically now, when she should concentrate all of it on Clarice and her whereabouts?

The footman puzzled on this for a moment, and then brightened. "Oh, *that* key. I have the fire key right here in my pocket. But I can't use it or Mr. Hobson will have my ears. No, miss, not lessin' there's a fire."

"I'll light a fire right under you, young man," Sadie threatened. "Open the door. I need to see into the square."

"You could just peek out one of the windows, you know. What a fuss. I could hear you before I could see you."

"Clarice!"

The girl was walking toward her, dressed in her cloak and a silly straw bonnet, a half-eaten chicken leg in her hand. Belatedly, Sadie noticed a large round bandbox sitting on the floor behind her, beside the staircase.

"I'm sorry, Sadie. I was hoping I could sneak back upstairs before you noticed I was gone."

"Well, young lady, I did notice, and you're not gone. Where on earth did you think you were going to go? No, don't answer me, not yet. Get yourself back up those stairs right this minute."

Honestly, it was like dealing with Marley. When the child had been three.

Clarice dropped a rather cheeky curtsy, not helped by the chicken leg she flourished rather like a wand. "If you could bring the bandbox, Sadie?"

Relief had made Sadie's knees go positively weak. "First I have to promise myself I won't beat you around the head and shoulders with it. Do you know how frightened I was when I woke to find you gone?"

"I'm sorry. Does it matter that I was desperate?"

"Only a little, and definitely not yet," Sadie told her, shooing her on ahead of her on the stairs.

"Well, I was. First I thought I could talk the coachman into driving me to Thea so I could hide there, but he wouldn't. And I shouldn't bother her, anyway, since she and Gabe are finishing up with the grand entrance hall and all. I hope they keep the fountain. And the banana trees."

"Clarice!"

"I'm sorry. Then I thought I could go throw myself on Martha Henderson's tender mercies, but I don't know where she is and I don't think Hendersons have any tender mercies. So, Clarice, I thought, Clarice, it's about time you stopped thinking, because you're going dotty with fear and you really aren't all that good at it right now, and trust someone else to do it for you. That," she said as they reached the second landing, "was when I realized that I didn't really eat my dinner, so I went to the kitchens and—"

"—and forgot that there are people who care about you," Sadie ended as they walked down the hallway toward Clarice's chamber. "My heart is still beating half out of my chest, if you must know."

Clarice turned to her, tears in her eyes. "Oh, Sadie, I'm so, *so* sorry."

"I know. It's all right, Clarice. I…I know what it's like to feel desperate."

Honestly, if it weren't for the bonnet covering them, it was entirely possible Clarice's ears might have begun wagging. "You do? Oh, you poor thing. Do you want to tell me about it? When you felt desperate, I mean."

"Clarice, go to bed. Please. And take this with you—good Lord, it's moving."

"Of course it is. You didn't think I'd leave without Goody, did you?"

Sadie opened the lid to have the tongue-lolling spaniel stick his head up out of the box. He put his front paws on her chest and licked at her face before leaping to the floor.

"Here, Goody-Goody," Clarice called softly, waving the chicken leg. "Let's not bother your auntie Sadie any more tonight."

Sadie summoned a weak smile before heading off to her own bedchamber. She had a lot to think about, didn't she? What it was like to be desperate. The unthought-out things people tended to do when they were desperate.

The way secrets had a nasty way of poking up their heads just when you began to relax, lower your guard and even began to daydream about happy endings.

"Please, God, I'm not dotty, but I've been a fool. There's no more thinking about running from what you've done, Sadie Grace," she told herself as she stripped off her clothes and pulled the night rail over her head. "You won't take Marley away from Darby's protection and her new life. You've always told yourself you could still leave, releasing him from his practical and outrageous proposal. But you forgot something... Marley isn't the only person in your life, not anymore. You can't upset her or any of these good people who accepted you without a blink, who care for you, who'd worry about you...and most probably follow after you, anyway, run you to ground and demand to know what sort of idiot you were to have run off in the first place."

She crawled into bed and looked up at the canopy above her. "It's just as Clarice said. The time has come to trust someone else to know what's best..."

CHAPTER ELEVEN

DARBY HAD TO silently applaud Sadie. She'd waited until he'd handed her up onto the seat of the curricle and walked around to take up the reins from his tiger before turning on him, most probably to demand he finally share his idea with her.

So he spoke first. "You look tired, Sadie Grace. Beautiful as always, but tired. Has Clarice proved the same handful to you as her beloved has to me?"

"I didn't sleep well, no."

"That was succinct. Well, at least we can relax now. They're both safely tucked up with Vivien and Minerva for the afternoon."

Sadie looked at him for a long moment. "Do you listen to what you say when you speak?"

Darby threw back his head and laughed. "You're right, what was I thinking? With both Thea and Dany gone, you must feel as if you're the only adult in residence. My plan had better work, hadn't it?"

Sadie pulled her cloak more firmly around her. "*Your* plan. And that's another thing, my-lord-knows-everything. I may be tired, and I'm painfully aware I'm being cranky, but I still have no idea what this grand plan of yours entails. What is my part? Why am I here?"

Poor sweetheart. Clearly she didn't like being kept in the dark, as it were. A woman with secrets who didn't like secrets. Did she realize how contradictory that was? "It isn't enough that I desired your company?"

"No. That is… Thank you. But no. You're either obtuse, my lord Nailbourne, or consider yourself clever. I'm not pleased with either, by the way." She shook her head. "I'm sorry."

Again, he laughed. "No, you're not, and I'm surprised you haven't yet to attempt to choke everything out of me. Very well. You're here, Sadie Grace, because a luncheon with just the ladies Henderson could be considered too intimate, and may even serve to make said ladies nervous. As my hostess, you can be sweet and pleasant and natter on about nothing with the ladies, putting them at their ease."

"That would be reasonable, if I were Clarice or the duchess. If you've yet to notice, I don't know how to natter about nothing. Besides, the first thing they'll ask me will be the whereabouts of my *maid*."

"No, they won't. That's why we're arriving separately, so that I've time to tell you what I've done. That, and the fact that I didn't want to spend any more time with Martha and Belinda than I already have. The matter of Clarice is already settled, if Belinda is satisfied with my offer. In fact, most everything is settled. You really must learn to trust me, Sadie Grace."

"Yes… I know. I've waited too long as it is."

It was his turn to look at her for some moments. "Does that mean…?"

"It does, and you'd please me by not looking quite so smug as to have long ago realized that I haven't been… haven't been totally honest with you. I decided last night—early this morning actually—that today is the day I give you the answers you seem to believe you need."

He could hear a slight tremor in her voice. What had brought her to this decision? His charm? No, he doubted that. Somehow, some way, Clarice and Rigby, their situation, had turned the trick in his favor. That thought made what he was soon to do even sweeter.

"I'm honored, Sadie," he said sincerely. "Thank you."

"I wouldn't thank me yet, were I you. But first we— you—settle this mess for poor Clarice before she feels the need to make some grand confession to Rigby concerning her past. She told me he knows…some of it, but that the whole of it would send him turning from her in disgust."

"I believe he knows more than he lets on, and he doesn't care. He loves the Clarice who walked into his life. To him, nothing else matters. As it should be for those in love, don't you agree?"

"It would be comforting to think so, but that can't always be true. We are, after all, human, and we might say what we truly believe at the time and with the best of intentions, only to, upon reflection, find we were incorrect."

They were no longer speaking about Clarice and Rigby, even as they both pretended they were.

"I see you've been giving this subject quite a deal of thought."

She sighed. "Perhaps too much thought. My affection for Clarice hasn't changed, even after the confidences she shared with me last night, because it's not what she's done that matters, is it? It's Clarice herself, and her good heart."

This was neither the time nor place for such a heavy discussion, but Darby knew her statement couldn't go unanswered. "You also have a good heart, Sadie Grace.

No one and nothing could convince me otherwise, not even you. Does that help?"

She turned her head away from him, the brim of her bonnet obscuring her features. "Yes. Yes, it does. Can we speak of something else now?"

"That something else being my plan, my all but accomplished plan. Yes, let's do that, and before you can point out any flaws let me say that Rigby already knows what I'm about, and will doubtless tell Clarice and the others. Once this day is over, we need not ever speak of any of this again. To which I'll add—thank God, for we've more pressing matters to discuss now, don't we?"

She laid a hand on his forearm. "There are still flaws? But you said everything was all but settled."

"The first is that you'll attempt to talk me out of it, which would only waste time, because everything *is* all but settled. Just let me say I'm proceeding with an open heart and no regrets. Rigby's my friend, and would do as much for me. I'd tell you about the time he saved my life during the war at great risk to his own, but since that didn't happen, I won't. It only matters that I know he would have had the necessity arisen."

"Now you're being flippant, even as I know you mean every word you're saying. But before you begin, I just remembered that I wanted to tell you that Jackson Henderson is in trade. He manufactures rugs. Carpets. I don't know if that helps, or if it might change your plans, but Clarice told me."

"I already called on Lord Clathan yesterday afternoon. My understanding is he and his wife received two lovely new patterned carpets for their country estate in exchange for agreeing to invite the Hendersons to a few tame events, and ask friends to do so, as well.

He did whisper to me that Belinda's dowry is immense, in case I'd be interested."

"Oh, my goodness. And what did you say?"

"I thanked him, of course. I suppose next we'll be hearing I've lost half my fortune in the Exchange. You have to marry me now, Sadie Grace, if only to save me from the gossips."

"Because I'm penniless, which would prove you're not? But I thought you said the wealthy are never wealthy enough. Miss Henderson might be a better match."

He smiled at her, enjoying their banter, which seemed to have lifted her spirits out of the doldrums. "You'll not cry off that easily, as we both know our marriage to be best for Marley."

Sadie looked off into the distance, as if her mind had traveled miles away. "Yes. Best for Marley. Everyone agrees. Absolutely."

He didn't like the way that sounded…or perhaps he liked it more than he should. Because Sadie had sounded almost disappointed.

Yes, he preferred the latter, and would consider her reaction progress.

"Besides, with any luck, and I'm most usually lucky, the ladies Henderson will be on the first ship bound for Virginia, eager to tell everyone how delighted they were to meet the future Lady Rigby, who is a dear and treasured friend of all Hendersons."

He had her attention again. "You know about *all* the Hendersons?"

"Sissy Winkle and her talented derriere? Yes, I've heard the entire story, as told to Rigby at some point. The parson, the judge, the banker, on and on. I doubt many dare cross the Hendersons, don't you? If they accept Clarice with open arms, and I'm certain Thea's family will do the same, I see no reason for Clarice to believe she can't visit her family without Rigby being subjected to a barrage of sordid winks and whispers. In fact, Martha is honored beyond measure to hostess a welcome ball for Sir Jeremiah and Lady Rigby."

"They'd do that?" Sadie said, and he could hear the disbelief in her voice. "Good God, Darby, what are you offering them? The cottage?"

"Not quite that much, no, but the offer is considerable. You won't try to talk me out of it?"

"No. I promise. But I need to know."

For Darby, it had been one of the more difficult decisions of his life, yet the one he'd made most quickly.

"You've already reminded me that I said the wealthy never think they're wealthy enough. Do you remember the rest?"

"Yes, I think so. The frustration, even with all that wealth, in not being able to acquire something someone else has. Darby, what do you have that the Hendersons can never hope to have?"

"You, for one," he teased, and laughed as she rolled her eyes at him. "You're not flattered?"

"Not when you're avoiding answering me, no."

Other than his three closest friends, no one had ever dared to speak to him so candidly, had ever seen him so clearly. Sadie didn't know how to play games, clearly had no time for them, and he wouldn't have her any other way.

"Very well. Have you ever heard of Marengo?"

Her brow furrowed as she thought about his question. "Is it a place?"

"It is, actually, but I'm speaking of a different Marengo,

the name Bonaparte gave to his favorite war horse, a magnificent gray Arabian nearly as well known as Boney himself. Marengo served the emperor from the Battle of Austerlitz to the retreat from Russia, to his final downfall at Waterloo, where it was finally captured and brought to England. He is and was worth five thousand men, to hear Bonaparte, and was used often in gallops of up to eighty miles in distance, a feat the stallion achieved in five hours."

"I really don't know much about horses. Is that impressive?"

"Beyond impressive. Both speed and stamina, a rare combination, and a splendidly beautiful animal into the bargain. Word is, Marengo was wounded eight times while carrying Boney, and never faltered. Heart, Sadie, the stallion has heart. Naturally, his new owner has put him to stud, as any foals would bring him a fortune, although at Marengo's advanced age, I don't see much future in that hope. However, the stallion did manage to woo and win a few mares through the years, and I happen to have come into possession of one of his offspring—I won't bother you with how I managed that, but only that I have. A magnificent black stallion, and he has many years at stud ahead of him."

"I'm sorry, I still don't understand."

He explained. "Miss Belinda Henderson is horse mad. More importantly, her parents own one of the foremost horse farms in Virginia—indeed, perhaps in the entire country. One of Marengo's stallions, put to stud there, is a prize beyond price."

Sadie nodded. "Something even the wealthy cannot buy unless you are willing to sell. You're going to sell her the stallion."

"No, Sadie Grace, in return for the cooperation I've already mentioned, and if Belinda is satisfied with her inspection, I'm going to *give* her the stallion."

He waited for her reaction, which wasn't long in coming.

"That's…that's the most generous gesture I've ever heard. I'm so proud of you, Darby. So very proud."

"And worth everything, to know I'm in your good graces. I suppose I shouldn't ruin the moment by telling you five of my best Arabian mares are already carrying said stallion's foals, who will be romping the meadows here at the cottage in the spring. I'm hoping for at least two grays with a resemblance to Marengo, and with luck, at least two will be stallions I will delight in one day seeing take cups at Royal Ascot, and then being put to stud."

Sadie's bottom lip trembled as she put her fingers to her mouth in an unsuccessful effort to cover a smile that rapidly turned into a grin, which almost immediately accelerated into a full-throated laugh.

He'd never felt so pleased in his life…a realization that made him wonder if he'd ever been really happy until Sadie Grace Hamilton had crashed uninvited into that same outwardly charmed life.

"You never lose, do you?" she asked at last, wiping at tears of mirth that ran down her cheeks even as he reined the curricle to a halt in front of the cottage. "Your wound could have been a disaster, but you jokingly make that patch a part of your not inconsiderable charms. You took on the promise to John, and instead of seeing a burden, you've embraced the role of guardian and are clearly enjoying your new responsibility. You unselfishly give away a prime stallion to help your friends, but will have dozens to take its place. No, you never lose. You simply find other ways to win."

Darby had fairly well stopped listening after she'd said "your not inconsiderable charms," content to merely sit beside her, look into her beautiful eyes and hope he could count himself a winner just one more time.

Not because I want to win...but because it suddenly occurs to me that I've at last found what I didn't know I've been searching for my entire life...

CHAPTER TWELVE

THERE HAD BEEN the day Roscoe Thatcher had come strolling into John's infirmary with a shoeing nail stuck smack in the middle of his forehead. He'd walked out thirty minutes later, the nail extracted, and gone back to the blacksmith shop to finish shoeing the horse, apparently not realizing that, by rights, he should have been dead.

That had been a strange day.

But nothing had been as strange as watching Belinda Henderson inspect the black stallion.

After a luncheon passed comfortably enough thanks to Darby's polite inquiries about the Henderson Horse Farms, which had elicited lengthy and effusive descriptions of the land, the weather, the stables and the quality of the horseflesh from Miss Henderson, they'd adjourned to the stables for the all-important inspection.

Sadie no longer had any qualms over what was about to occur, if she'd harbored any in the first place, as Clarice's well-being had always been foremost in her mind.

There could be nothing more apparent than Miss Henderson's love of her home, and her horses. Whatever had Mrs. Henderson been thinking, to bring the girl to England, to marry her off to some impoverished peer, just so that she could boast of another Henderson accomplishment, adding a title in the family? Belinda would have wilted under the English sky, under the strictures of English Society, and would probably never be accepted, not when her entire conversation was horses, and more horses.

The stallion, already saddled, had been brought out even as Belinda had bounced on her toes, her eagerness apparent. She'd even clapped her gloved hands together when the black appeared, and no wonder. The stallion was beautiful. Sadie knew she'd never seen the like— that sleek body, the rather dish-shaped face, an air of delicacy belied by the smooth ripple of the muscles beneath the jet-black coat as a groom walked the horse in a full circle in front of its audience.

There was a look of intelligence in its soulful eyes, and Sadie told herself she wouldn't have been surprised if it took a bow, acknowledging its admirers.

"He's magnificent," she'd said to Darby, who was watching, looking rather proud himself.

"Looks aren't everything, Sadie Grace. Now we get down to business. Watch."

She'd done as he'd said, and that's when this strange day had proceeded to beat Roscoe and his shoeing nail all hollow.

Miss Belinda Henderson had stripped off her cloak, exchanged her white kid gloves with a pair of strange black leather gloves with the fingers incongruously cut off. She approached the stallion, walked completely around it, twice, and then began barking orders to the groom.

Walk him in a straight line. Now in a larger circle. All right, let's see what he can do.

The groom looked to Darby, who only nodded. The groom walked the stallion to a mounting post and hopped on its back. Everyone adjourned to the fence to watch as Darby unlatched the gate and stallion and rider entered the grassy meadow. Belinda shouted orders: "Walk him...trot...canter— spring him!"

"What's his name?" Sadie had asked, her heart pounding at the speed and grace suddenly on display.

"I doubt you mean the groom. Marrakesh."

Sadie had heard the pride in Darby's voice, along with a whisper of wistfulness. She'd slipped her hand into his and squeezed his fingers. "Maybe she won't like him."

"She'd be a fool not to. He's putting on quite the show for her, but the inspection is far from over."

Never had there been such an understatement.

Once back in the stable yard, and without a comment as to the stallion's performance, Belinda ordered the groom to hold its head and asked for a second groom to stand at its flank as she moved in for what would be a much closer inspection.

Her hands-on hooves-to-tail examination was both extensive and, at times, rather *personal*. Sadie felt herself becoming impatient, both with the examination and Belinda's *ummp*s and *hmm*s, sounds impossible to interpret. Even Darby had begun to look worried.

"She gives nothing away, does she?" she asked Darby.

"She doesn't even remember we're here," he told her in a whisper. "I know Marrakesh is sound. I'm only hoping she knows what she's seeing. Good God, she isn't going to—stand back, Sadie."

Sadie turned to see what had alarmed Darby, just in time to watch as Miss Belinda Henderson of the Fairfax County Virginia Hendersons slid one of her oddly gloved hands along the underside of Marrakesh's belly before disappearing between the stallion's hind legs.

"Ezekiel 23:20, Mama. He'll do," Belinda said from the ground, where she had landed ignominiously on her rump when Marrakesh had reared in protest before slipping its lead and escaping to the meadow.

"She's quoting the Old Testament?" Sadie asked, shocked.

Darby shook his head, laughing. "Indeed. Crudely translated, my dear sister of a physician, Miss Henderson has just informed her mother that Marrakesh is indeed hung like a stallion."

"You, boy, bring me a stick," Belinda was saying then. "I want to poke about in this manure to be sure there are no worms. Can't be too careful."

That's when Sadie had turned on her heels and stomped all the way back to the house, entering through the kitchens and immediately requesting hot water and soap so she could wash her hands, as if she had been a part of the *inspection*.

Mrs. Camford had found her there and invited her into the small private housekeeper's parlor, calling for tea and cakes. "You'll want to hide out here until they're gone," she'd said with a wink. "I was watching from the upstairs window, even if I couldn't see much. Pitiful, that's what I say. Tell me everything, dear."

"They've taken themselves off, Mrs. Camford," a kitchen maid said an hour later, poking her head into the room, and Sadie had said, "Thank you, Camy," and allowed herself to be escorted to the main drawing room, where she now sat, awaiting Darby. She hoped he wouldn't expect an apology for having deserted him, because one would not be forthcoming.

Yes, a strange day, a very strange day, and oddly, another friend made in the housekeeper. She'd also learned that His Lordship favored roasted potatoes above turnips with his joint of beef, was indifferent in preference when it came to other vegetables, but actively abhorred beets, as he never seemed to be able to eat them without ending the meal with small red stains dotting his neck cloth.

With the thought of the so-perfect viscount being outdone by a mere beet still in her mind, it was easy to smile as Darby entered the drawing room.

"Camford told me I'd find you here. I made your apologies to the ladies, who hadn't really cared either way, and they're gone. Marrakesh will be sent to the docks tomorrow, ready for his trip to Virginia, as I'd already made arrangements for passage there before gathering you up this morning. Clarice is safe, as I'd also prepared a bill of sale that reads more like a contract, with the caveat that the Hendersons owe me return of Marrakesh and all foals he may have sired, plus twenty thousand pounds sterling, if the terms are not met."

"And Mrs. Henderson signed this document?"

"Dearest Belinda would have held a pistol to her head, I believe, if she'd dared to object to any of the terms. At any rate, when she does return to Virginia, Clarice will be greeted as no less than visiting royalty, or I don't know my Hendersons. And before you doubt me, you may not have seen them, but my man of business and a London solicitor witnessed the signatures. Lastly, and at the moment most importantly, if you'll excuse me for a moment, I bloody well need a drink," he ended, walking over to a nearby table holding various crystal decanters and pouring himself a glass of wine.

He downed the contents in a few gulps before turning to smile at her, rakishly handsome in his breeze-tousled hair and dangerous eye patch. "What, no applause?"

"Only a question, I'm afraid. However did you accomplish so much in the space of not quite four and twenty hours?"

"Remarkable, aren't I? In truth, there are few problems a title and enough coins passed into the correct hands can't solve."

She hoped he was right. She prayed he was right. John had depended on just that, as well.

Hearing footsteps in the hallway outside the drawing room, and remembering what she'd recently learned about servants and ears, Sadie got to her feet, her cloak in her hand, ready to slip it over her shoulders. "Could we possibly take a walk?"

Darby hastened to help her with her cloak. "I'd be honored to show you the grounds, and will promise our stroll will bypass the stables."

"It's not that I don't like horses, you know. I've never ridden one, but I think they're beautiful. I just don't think I could come face-to-face with Marrakesh at the moment. He must be so embarrassed."

Darby laughed. "I'm sure he appreciates your discretion."

They passed through the entrance hall where they'd had their first, rather awkward encounter, and out onto the gravel drive.

"I should order the construction of a portico, correct?" he asked as they turned to their left and crossed onto a neatly bricked path.

"I was being rude."

"You were being *wet*," he corrected. "In fact, I've already consulted a London architect, and will soon have his drawn plans for a covering that will be compatible with the rest of the cottage. That's important, you know, or you will, once you see the hodgepodge of additions my forebears inflicted on Nailbourne Manor. In truth, I haven't visited there in years, but tradition demands we be married there, in the family chapel. It has gargoyles. The chapel, that is."

"It sounds…lovely."

"The exact opposite of lovely, and something else to speak with the architect about at some point, I suppose. Until now I haven't really thought about effecting any sort of remedy, preferring to simply ignore the ugliness, but Marley need not be subjected to gargoyles, and so much more. I don't believe you need worry about being without anything to fill your days, Sadie. Perhaps we should consider writing up a list?"

"Beginning with the gargoyles? I wouldn't wish to be part of dismantling anything important, but I believe the gargoyles can be excluded from any inventory of important, um, decorations."

"And not just the gargoyles. There are a few dragons and imps with outrageously bulging eyes in the mix, as well, all eminently dispensable. In any event, I named them, the gargoyles, that is, which gave me something to do rather than just sit there on Sundays, rubbing at my cold bare knees for hours while the vicar droned on and on about sin and hellfire and my father nodded in fervent agreement. On second thought, perhaps we'll break with tradition, and marry here at the cottage."

"Whatever you decide," Sadie said nervously. Was he only making idle chatter so that she'd relax, or was he showing part of himself to her, to encourage a like exchange of confidences? She believed it was the latter, for this wasn't the first time, consciously or merely by his tone, that he'd hinted his had been far from a bucolic childhood.

There definitely were things no amount of money and prestige could buy.

They'd reached the gardens off to the side of the immense building and she spied out a sun-dappled stream and a pretty white, curtained gazebo near its banks.

"Our destination, I'll assume?"

"As good as any other, wouldn't you agree? Lovely surroundings, none but the birds to hear us or see us. Or have you changed your mind, and would rather continue our stroll? The gardens aren't at their best this late in the year, but we may find a few hardy roses for the plucking."

"No, I've put this off too long as it is, and a promise is a promise. If Clarice's dilemma taught me nothing else, I've realized that delaying the inevitable, pretending nothing bad will ever happen, is a sure path to disaster."

He held her hand as she raised her skirts and climbed the steps to the gazebo, immediately seeing not only a large, comfortable-looking chaise, but also a low table loaded with a silver tea set, cups and a tray of small cakes.

"You're not precisely lacking in confidence, are you, my lord Nailbourne," she said, careful to take up her seat on one of the built-in, padded benches that lined the octagonal perimeter.

"Guilty as charged. Tea?"

"Thank you, no. Where should I begin?"

He sat down on the edge of the chaise, his elbows on his knees. "It's not my story to tell, Sadie Grace. Begin where you feel comfortable beginning."

She smiled weakly. "Then I wouldn't begin at all, would I?"

"You've never been comfortable? In your entire life?"

She clamped her lips together and thought about his question for a few moments. Of course she'd been comfortable, happy, at some point in her life. Several points in her life. Hadn't she? If so, why did she suddenly realize she could count those individual moments on her fingers, not in years?

"A girl child is born to duty and obedience, Darby, at least a daughter born into the Hamilton family. Levity? Informality? No, neither John nor I were encouraged to cultivate either. There had to be something that kept us above our neighbors, even if our father's attempts to find teaching positions more suited to his opinion of his talents never came to fruition. We had standards to uphold, you understand. We were encouraged not to even speak with anyone above a nod in passing, for fear we'd corrupt our diction."

"You had no friends? I'm sorry, I keep interrupting."

"That's all right. No, we had no friends. Not outside of the house, or inside it, for that matter. Our mother never referred to our father other than as Mr. Hamilton, and neither did we. To be fair, we never lacked for anything, and our parents were only doing what they thought best for us."

"In other words, your childhood was a bloody bore."

She smiled. "That would sum it up nicely, yes, along with constantly fighting the impulse to break at least one rule, one time. To my everlasting shame, I never did."

Darby chuckled softly. "I'm sorry. I'm just imagining your thoughts when first presented with Vivien and the others. You must have thought them all mad, at the least, and me into the bargain."

"Oh, no," she corrected quickly. "I may have been shocked when you first introduced them to me, yes. But Marley and I had also stepped into a fairyland. I don't believe I've ever been so happy, or even imagined such exotic creatures existed, and I love them all so much. You may think what matters is the mansion, the clothing, simply being in London. But it's not—it's them, how they've taken us to their hearts. I...I keep waiting for that happy bubble to burst."

She hadn't meant to be quite that honest. She had so, so much to lose, not the least of which was this maddening man who sat smiling at her as if she'd just said the most wonderful things.

But then he sobered, and she knew the time had come.

"I know where to begin. I'll begin the day John arrived home from the war. He'd been in hospital in Calais for months, until he was deemed recovered sufficiently to survive the Channel crossing, so that it was late October of last year when we finally saw him."

She closed her eyes, and an image of her brother, reduced to a bent old man too weak to walk without his cane, made her wince. "I thought my nursing would help him, that months of good food would serve to make him stronger, but he never gained much ground, no matter what I did. Although his mind remained clear, I had to continue managing the infirmary, so that we could remain in the cottage, so that he could sit in his office in his bath chair and give me orders on how to attend to everyone's needs, outwardly in charge once more."

Darby came to sit beside her, take her hands in his. "I'm certain you did the best you could."

"I wanted to take us back north to Huyton, to the cottage my parents left to us. But not only had I leased it to the church when Marley's mother, Susan, died and John summoned me to Dibden, but the journey might have proved too much for him. No, that's not the whole truth. He wouldn't have allowed me to take him there in any rate, which you'll soon understand."

"In your own good time, Sadie Grace. I'm not going anywhere. Nothing will change that."

We are, after all, human, and we might say what we truly believe at the time and with the best of intentions, only to, upon reflection, find we were incorrect.

She smiled wanly. "You feel sympathy for me now, but that's because you've yet to hear the rest." She tugged her hands free and got to her feet, asking him to please remain seated. She couldn't look at him as she told her story, nor could she sit still.

"With this past summer's heat, John grew weaker. He said nothing, never letting me see how he suffered, but I knew. He barely ate, and he looked nearly skeletal. That tall, strong man. He took to prayer." She sighed at the memory. "So much prayer. Sermons. Readings from the Bible. There were nights I prayed he'd die, just to be freed of his quiet misery. And then...and then he was gone."

"You didn't *pray* him dead, Sadie. He was slowly dying from the moment he was shot in that camp. You can't feel guilty about that."

She turned to look at him. "I know that, but thank you. That last month I actually believed he'd begun to rally. Not recovering, for that was always impossible, but he had gained some weight. I could see the difference in his face. He'd begun to avoid the bath chair, which he'd always hated. He even took Marley for short walks. I thought, perhaps all those prayers were working."

"Yes, and your good food and even better care."

This was hard. This was so hard…even more difficult than she'd imagined.

"No matter the reason, I…I had hope again. But then suddenly, he took to his bed, telling me the pain was unbearable. It was I who brought him his laudanum, for the pain. He couldn't get to it, you understand, was too weak to leave the bed on his own. He'd beg me for more laudanum, and more often. Day and night, he demanded I obey him. I believed his pain made him…unpleasant. He'd never before spoken to me that way, had never raised his voice around Marley or anyone, not ever. He was a good, kind man, Darby, you know that. But he kept telling me that he had to die, that he had to die *now*. I feared for him, for Marley, for my own sanity, because I couldn't help him anymore, nothing helped him anymore but the laudanum. Watching him suffer like that, turning away from him when he called me stupid and swore I didn't love him or else I'd do what he asked. Three days and nights, without sleep, losing hope…"

"Sadie, that's enough. I understand."

"No, I have to say it. That last night, I gave him what he wanted. I poured the laudanum straight into the glass, not diluting it in water, as he'd taught me to do. I lifted his head and held the glass to his lips as he drank. Me, I did that! I felt as if I was someone else, watching a person in a dream. I kissed his forehead—something I'd never done, we'd never done—and sat in the dark in my small bedroom, in the blessed silence that had been absent those other days and nights. I sat there until dawn before I went to check on him."

She wiped at her eyes and turned to face Darby. "Your friend, my brother, Marley's father. I knew what would happen, and I did it, anyway. I killed him."

"No, damn it, you didn't. You were very brave. You granted his last wish, took away his pain, gave him peace," he said, gathering her close.

She remained stiff in his arms.

She wanted to stop now, cling to his sweet sympathy, keep his memories of John pure, not tell him the rest, even as she knew that wasn't possible.

He had to know the rest. She'd confessed her secret, but now it was time to tell him John's secret.

She pushed away from him, to gain the strength to finish. "I've told you only what I *thought* had happened. I didn't know. I didn't realize... I should...I should have sensed something. He was growing stronger. How had that suddenly changed? Why, after fighting for so long, was he suddenly so desperate to die? What hadn't I seen?"

"Ah," Darby said, and his soft tone had turned harder. "So now you're God, Sadie Grace? He who sees all, knows all? Humans make mistakes, but helping John gain peace wasn't a mistake."

Suddenly Sadie was filled with the rage she'd felt after John died, and the same wild anger and hurt that he hadn't asked for her help, hadn't confided in her, had turned himself into a martyr and her into a murderer.

"You don't understand. He *lied* to me! He made *me* do what he couldn't do himself, and left me alone to deal with everything. I'll never forgive him for that, for not trusting me to help him, for not allowing me to help find some way other than the one he chose."

"Sweet Jesus, Sadie, what are you saying?"

She'd held her jumbled emotions inside ever since

that fateful night. Comforting Marley, struggling with her own grief…trying to separate her anger toward John from the love she felt for him.

She wiped at her tears with hands that trembled, and then reached into the pocket of her cloak to hand him the letter. "When dawn came and the room lightened, I saw this had been slipped under my door. Delivered to me by the man who couldn't walk, the man too weak to so much as lift a spoon to his mouth. I found him slumped in his bath chair, probably because the drug had over-taken him sooner than he'd supposed and he couldn't make it back to his bed. Here. Read it."

Darby took the folded page from her as she avoided his gaze. "Are you certain?"

Sadie nodded. "Only because you have to know. For Marley."

She folded her arms tightly against herself and turned her back.

"So I am dead. Finally I have convinced you to do what I could not do for myself, or else never be reunited with Susan in heaven. Her parents have somehow found us. I could not run, and Marley must be made safe. You cannot help her and would be foolish to try. Deliver the child into Lord Nail-bourne's keeping. He will stay true to his prom-ise. Even the Dobsons haven't the power to defeat him. Bury me beside Susan and leave this place. Tell no one you're going, or where."

"A list of your residences was with the letter." She turned back to Darby, needing to see the expression on his face. It wasn't a kind expression, not by a long chalk.

But where was he aiming his anger? "He'd long ago told me about your promise to him."

"You think he tricked you into dosing him with the laudanum. Taking to his bed those last days—also part of some insane plan?"

"You read his letter. I also found a letter from a solicitor in the drawer of his night table, demanding the return of Marley to Sam Dobson, her grandfather. It had arrived a week earlier, and put the last pieces together for me."

"Yet there still are a few things missing, aren't there. Not a word of thanks to you, and without asking your forgiveness in the way he tricked you. He doesn't even seem concerned about what would happen to you once you *delivered* Marley into my hands."

Sadie felt now as she'd done when she'd read the letter. *Used and discarded...and yet guilty.* "I know. I've had a lot of time to think about that."

"Damn it, Sadie Grace, look at me." Darby waved the paper in the air. "This is not the John I knew, nor the John you knew. Everything he did, everything he wrote and didn't write, means nothing. Do you understand, Sadie? Less than nothing."

He crushed the paper into a ball and flung it out onto the grass. "And now it's gone. It's the past, one we can't change, but we can begin to understand for what it was. It's not you who needs forgiveness, but John, and only you can forgive him. That will take time, I know, but one day you'll be able to remember him as the man he once was, and not for that damned letter."

"Will I? At the moment, that doesn't seem possible."

"I know," he said, and something in his tone told her he did know. But how?

Sadie looked at him, at the concern and kindness in

his face, and felt the heavy weight of her own guilt that she'd carried since John's death slip from her shoulders. She should have told him sooner, on that first day, except that she'd bungled everything, hadn't she? Mrs. Boxer indeed. He'd questioned her identity, and Marley's, as well, as rightly he should have done, and thoughts of anything else had disappeared from her head in her sudden panic.

Lies, hidden truths. Betrayed by her own brother, she had lost the ability to trust in anyone, and by doing so had made a bad situation worse.

But still she had been welcomed. Marley had seamlessly slipped into the affections of everyone, and Darby had proved, again and again, that he was a good man, worthy of her trust.

"I swear to you, Darby, I've learned my lesson. I will never lie again." She attempted a smile. "Except, perhaps, if the duchess asks my opinion on one of her new gowns."

"Good girl. There are always exceptions to any rule." He held out his arms to her. "Nothing that's happened has been your fault. If I know nothing else, I know that you need to hear that, believe that. Everything else will sort itself out, I promise, and Marley is safe. Now come here."

She wasn't about to protest, say he needn't worry about her. That she didn't crave the healing comfort of his strength. Because that would be the worst sort of lie.

She walked into Darby's arms, and finally allowed herself to mourn.

CHAPTER THIRTEEN

THEY SAT SIDE by side on the padded chaise, both lost in their own thoughts as Sadie composed herself once more. He'd never before held a weeping woman, whispered inane words of comfort, felt the shudder of her shoulders as she gave in completely to grief he could understand, even as he fought anger at what she had been forced to suffer alone.

As he had suffered alone, surrounded by the best of intentions, but too young to sort out the feelings inside his head, the conclusions that seemed so reasonable to that young mind. And too frightened to share those conclusions, for fear he could lose so much more than he'd already lost.

She would never be in that position again, not as long as he drew breath.

Darby longed to put his arm around her waist, tell her just that, draw her even closer, but he knew it was time to move on, for there were still questions that needed answers.

He'd begin slowly, and then follow her lead.

"It's grown cold, hasn't it?"

Darby watched as Sadie took a second sip of tea he'd poured from the pot. "It's fine as it is."

"Liar," he said jokingly as she put down the cup. "I

believe we've already established that you're not exactly proficient at that. For most, it's an acquired skill."

She smiled at him, her eyes only slightly reddened from her tears. She still seemed fragile to him, even as he was amazed by her strength and courage. "I've decided there's a difference between lying and being polite. Just now, I was being polite."

"You'll improve the more you're in Society. But first you need to be educated on the different sorts of lies most employed in that society, and how they are intended."

"I don't think my recent vow of truthfulness is quite up to such intricacies. How many sorts are there?"

"There are two, I believe, although there are many levels of lies within both categories. The polite lie, as we'll now call it, is the first. *Vivien, don't you look all the crack in that most delicious gown. Lord Havistock, what a coup to have purchased that magnificent animal for a mere two thousand pounds. Nonsense, Miss Melbourne, that wasn't my foot. You're as light as the proverbial feather on the dance floor.*"

Sadie smiled as she balled up the handkerchief he'd given her and slipped it into the pocket of her cloak. "I feel better now, thank you. There's no sense in telling the truth when it serves no good purpose and that truth can only bring unhappiness with it. Yes, that's what I meant. Please, tell me about the second type of lie."

He had to admit to himself that he, too, was feeling much better than he had only minutes ago. How could he not be cheered by that brave, beautiful smile?

"You'll realize I'm betraying myself, telling you this. But very well. The second type of lie used in Society is meant to teach a lesson to the overly confident braggart, such as—*You've so impressed me with your self-confessed mastery at cards that I believe I've lost count of trumps.* Most, however, are meant to depress pretensions—*My dear man, I'm convinced you're delighted to see me, but I'm mortified to inform you that I've quite forgotten your name.*"

"I'd sink into the floor if anyone said that to me. You've done that sort of thing?"

"Both accomplished with great flair and accompanied by a touch of panache, yes. I'm an evil man, Sadie Grace. Shame on me. Although I'll admit I mourn the loss of my quizzing glass, used for effect in such situations, I believe the patch is nearly as impressive."

"You're an impossible man, do you know that?" Sadie said, picking up the cup and sipping from it again before making a face and replacing it on the tray. "That really is horrid. Can we spill the pot onto the ground so that Camy believes we drank it?"

"Camy, is it? And how did you manage that?"

Sadie busied herself folding one of the linen serviettes. "I didn't *manage* anything. The pot boy came into the sitting room with a large splinter in his palm, poor thing. I removed it. And I may have sung to him as I worked, and then kissed his palm to assure him he was all better now, as I do with Marley when she suffers a scrape."

"You should have thought of that with Rigby—the singing, that is. He enjoys a good tune, although I would have balked at you kissing his knees."

"I enjoy feeling useful, and said as much to Camy, and suddenly I became Miss Sadie and Mrs. Camford is now Camy. I hope it doesn't disturb you that I told her about assisting John, and acting as his housekeeper."

"On the contrary, I've probably just grown in stature in Camy's eyes, having had the genius not to bring home a brainless debutante who'd insist on a French cook and drive the staff batty with demands, all while emptying my pockets on gowns and jewels."

"I wouldn't know what to do with a French cook, and it's already clear to me that Camy and her husband have everything here well in hand. I wouldn't change a thing."

"Which makes you, to Camy, a treasure beyond price, especially since you bring Marley with you."

"Yes, Marley. I suppose we've avoided that subject long enough, haven't we?"

Darby took her hand and held it between his. "I was content to wait until you were ready."

"I know. As you may have already guessed, Susan's parents did not approve of the marriage. Sam Dobson is quite wealthy, up to his hips in coal mines, and with that money Mrs. Dobson planned to marry Susan well, holding out for a minor peer, much in the same way Mrs. Henderson planned for her Belinda, which is the only reason I have any sympathy for her after what she did to poor Marrakesh. In any event, a country doctor was a totally unacceptable match for her only daughter."

"It's a common failing among mothers. What did John do? Take his Susan and run off to Scotland, to marry over the anvil?"

"How did you guess? I believe that was the only rule John ever broke in his lifetime, but he and Susan were wildly in love. We didn't realize what had happened until Sam Dobson arrived at our door demanding my father produce Susan at once or he'd have John run down and personally take a whip to him."

"Lovely man. And your father?"

"There was nothing for him to say, since John hadn't confided in us. Mr. Dobson offered money, quite a generous amount of it, if we told him John's whereabouts. I believe my father would have taken it without a blink and moved us to Cambridge, where he'd once studied. I was not allowed to say John's name again after that."

"John never contacted you?"

Sadie shook her head. "Not for years. And a good thing that he didn't, because Mrs. Dobson never ceased to come knocking on our door with her threats and demands. My parents died within months of each other during a particularly nasty winter, so that when a letter to me arrived the following spring, I actually saw it, rather than have one of them intercept it, which would have been terrible."

"And what did John have to say in that letter?"

"Only that Susan had died, and that he had already agreed to join the king's army as a surgeon. They had a daughter, Marley, who had just reached her third birthday, and I needed to tell no one, but hasten myself to Dibden to care for her in his absence. I left immediately, and spent three months working beside John before he was called to his new duties, learning all he could teach me so that we could remain in the infirmary during his absence. It…it has been a whirlwind in the four years since then, I'll admit to that, but we managed. Frankly, I never gave a thought to the Dobsons."

"But Mrs. Dobson never gave up, did she?"

"John never believed she would. The solicitor's letter, the one he hid from me, contained the information that Mr. Samuel Dobson knew of the death of his daughter and demanded the return of his granddaughter, with the promise that she would be given every advantage she deserved, along with a loving home."

"Marley, but not John."

"But not John, no, although he would have been *compensated*," Sadie agreed. "The solicitor believed John would see the advantage of not having to concern himself with Marley's future, not in his current sad state of health. But if he did not agree, other action would be taken, proving John was not capable of remaining Marley's guardian, of giving her the life she, as granddaughter to the great Sam Dobson, deserved. It was all rather threatening, but wrapped up to sound as if they'd be rendering John a great favor by assuring him Marley would have a good home after he was gone. John would never have the strength, or the money, to fight him, of course. I…I copied that high-nosed tone when I composed my letter to you."

"Ha! I knew I was right. Clever girl. John believed he had two choices, as we've already established that he didn't believe you capable of caring for Marley on your own, fighting the Dobsons on your own. I agree with him on that, by the way. People with money tend to run over those without it, and you're a female into the bargain. John was left with either the grandparents he apparently despised, or the promise I made. In the end, he chose me. All he had to do was to die. Damn it, he should have come to me. He had to know I would have helped him."

"As you've made me understand, he wasn't the John I knew anymore, the John either of us knew. He chose you because you have a title and probably much more money and power than even one of the wealthiest mine owners in all of Lancashire. For myself, I had no idea if you'd even remember the promise, let alone honor it, or if Marley would be in good hands. You could have been married, with a wife who didn't approve and children of your own. Or you could have been a terrible rake. I'm sorry, Darby, but I had to consider all these things before giving Marley over to you. I only knew the Dobsons shouldn't have her. Not after the way they attempted to use Susan for Mrs. Dobson's ambitions."

"And so here we are."

"Yes, here we are," Sadie said, getting to her feet. She picked up the teapot and held it over the railing, allowing the cold tea to pour onto the ground. "Once I'd assured myself that Marley would be safe with you, I would have gone, you know. The solicitor's letter was accompanied by four five-pound notes, to pay passage for Marley. Sam Dobson was very sure of himself, wasn't he? I could have used that money until I could find a place of employment as a seamstress, or perhaps as a governess. Now, because of my lies and your insistence on being a gentleman, everything's…complicated. This betrothal? I know you've given me what you believe are valid reasons, but…"

"We're going to be married. You haven't taken me in total disgust, or you wouldn't allow Marley to stay with me. You wouldn't be here with me now." He took the teapot from her and placed it back on the table. "You're not going anywhere, Sadie Grace. We've already established that."

"I know you've said that, keep saying that. But with Marley safe and clearly happy, we've yet to really establish *why*, other than the fact that Clarice and the duchess seem to think it's a whacking great idea."

She didn't know. Admittedly, how could she, as he'd

engaged in all that nonsense about business arrangements and convenience. She enjoyed their friendship,
yes, but marriage? That remained a far stretch for her,
didn't it?

Unless she knew he wanted more from her than
friendship. Unless she wanted more than friendship from
him. He wouldn't ask for declarations of undying love,
not from either of them. But they were adults, there was
something between them that had been growing every
day, with every touch, damn it, and it was time they addressed that subject.

Darby walked closer to Sadie, and took both her
hands in his, just in case she felt the need to back away
from him. "Lovely ladies, both of them, but I'd volun-
teer to be chained to a wall in Bedlam if I ever thought
to take advice from either of them."

Sadie smiled weakly. "That's not kind."

"Ah, but true. I make my own decisions, Sadie Grace,
and while we're on the subject of truth, I decided I
wanted you from the first moment I saw you dripping
all over my foyer, Marley clinging to your knees. I don't
know why, since I'm being so self-damningly honest, but
when I thought you were Mrs. Boxer, a married woman,
I was immediately plunged into despair."

"Is…is that a polite lie, or the sort where I should be
looking for hidden meanings?"

"I'm not hiding from you. I don't think I've ever been
so candid in my life. Seeing you wet and angry, seeing
you glide across a room in fancy dress, oblivious to
your own unique beauty. Watching you tend to Rigby's
scraped knees, knowing how much you enjoy and care
for my friends. Listening to you lamenting your idle
state, making me see how much there is to be done in

this world while I fritter away my life looking for something I only now know I need. You have to marry me, Sadie Grace. I've still so much to learn, and I want to see it all through your eyes. Those wonderful, honest, beautiful eyes. I want to see the expression in them as you look up at me from my pillow. There, have I embarrassed you?"

"Yes, actually, quite a bit. But I will admit that I've been drawn to you from the beginning," she told him quietly. "When I didn't want to box your ears. I don't really understand it, this feeling I experience when you're near. It…you…you're nothing I've experienced before. I…I don't know what to call it."

"Desire, Sadie Grace. It's desire. May I dare to hope it's mutual? I've already said it, but I'll say it again. I want you. I want all of you. I lie awake nights, wanting you. That makes me a bad man, but we've already established that. You're a grown woman, so I don't expect you to not understand what I'm saying. I can only hope you want me in return—everything else be damned— and I dare now to believe you do."

"I didn't know, didn't realize you could ever… Are you certain? Even after everything I've told you? I…I don't know what to say to any of that."

Darby's hopes soared. "You could say yes."

"You're right. I could do that. Yes, I'm doing that. I'm saying, yes, I do want you…in that way. I do. Wait— where are we going?"

He'd led her down the steps of the gazebo and onto the grass, still holding her hand, pausing only to bend down and scoop up John's letter and shove it in his pocket. "We'll burn this, together."

"Wait. We should take the tea tray back to the kitchens so no one has to come fetch it."

He leaned in to kiss her, but only briefly, because his plans included much more than a kiss: she'd just agreed to much more than a kiss, and tea trays be damned. "Sadie Grace, you're a wonder in so many ways. But if you want Camy and the servants solidly in your corner, you won't usurp their duties."

"Oh. You're right, of course. I have so much to learn, don't I?"

"Don't worry about that as I am more than delighted to play tutor in all things. I know just where we should begin, and it's definitely not in thinking of everyone else's needs before your own."

"Darby!"

He grinned at her, not Society's impressive and powerful Viscount Nailbourne, but merely a marvelously carefree man who was about to be even happier.

Shame on me.

"Darby, where are you taking me?" she asked him, lengthening her stride to nearly match his own.

Ah, an added benefit of those long legs I can't wait to see.

"There's a side door that leads to a rarely used flight of stairs. But we must be quiet."

"I'm beginning to think…"

"No, don't think, Sadie Grace. We're all done thinking for today."

"Perhaps you are, but what on earth will everyone else think?"

"I don't care. I'm the master of this house and you are soon to be its mistress."

"Did you have to say *mistress*?"

He squeezed her hand as they finally left the grass
and moved along the brick walkway leading to the small,
deeply shaded door he'd used in his childhood when he'd
wanted to avoid Camy and the servants.

"Stand here," he told her. "I'll just be a moment. Now,
where the devil did I hide that key?"

"Pardon me? When did you hide this key?"

Darby was already lifting bricks one after the other,
while attempting to jog his memory. "I don't know. I
couldn't have been more than fifteen. Ah, here it is."
He held it up for her inspection. "I've wondered since
if they knew, and only allowed me to think I was brilliant in finding a way to be out and about on my own."

"And what did you do, out and about on your own?"
she asked as he cleaned off some clinging mud and slid
the key into the lock.

"Probably broke every rule you wanted to break when
you were that age. Now we must be quiet."

"I feel silly."

"Good. So do I. We all deserve to feel silly from time
to time." He took her hand and led her inside, then motioned for her to precede him up the narrow wooden
staircase, and then passed ahead of her once they reached
the landing.

Her hand was cold in his as they sneaked along the
carpeted hallway and slipped into his chambers.

"Oh, my," she said as he locked the door behind him,
and then locked the door to his dressing room even
though Norton was happily ensconced in London. "This
is quite huge, isn't it?"

She was probably commenting on the size of the
chamber, which was considerable, or else the size of

the Tudor-style four-poster canopy bed, which could also be very likely.

"Here, let me take your cloak."

Sadie was still looking around the room, and rather absently untied the cloak and handed it to him before walking to her left and the large sitting area he hadn't planned on as her destination. Perhaps the warmth of the fire had lured her, or the fact that the couches were quite distant from the bed.

As if he'd be so overt.

"*Paradise Lost*?" she questioned, picking up a large leather-bound tome he'd been reading while waiting for the arrival of his ward. "Our father read this to John and me, night after night, verse by verse. I believe I may have been six. I can't tell you how badly I wanted to throw it in the fire." She put down the book and wiped her hands together, as if wanting to remove even the feel of it from her memory.

Darby joined her as she sat down on one of the couches. "Do you want to do that now?"

"No. I imagine it would be less frightening if I were to read it now. But I won't. I much prefer the works of Miss Jane Austen the duchess loaned to me."

Darby slipped his arm over the back of the couch, resting his hand on her shoulder. "'One half of the world cannot understand the pleasures of the other.'"

Sadie looked at him curiously. "You've read *Emma*?"

"My dear, everyone reads the works of Miss Austen, whether they admit to it or not. To be honest, I had only been reading Milton in order to put myself to sleep."

"That's certainly not the effect it has on a six-year-old. But you could burn John's note. I think I'm ready for that."

"Done," he said, taking the note from his pocket and

unerringly launching it into the burning fire. "See? It even wanted to go there. Now we look to the future."

She rubbed her hands up and down her thighs. "Yes. The future. There's still much to discuss."

He lightly placed his knuckle beneath her chin and turned her toward him. "I was referring to the very near future."

Her hands stilled in her lap. She looked into his face, her gaze unflinching. "I know. Are you going to kiss me now? Because I really do think it's time, don't you?"

He moved closer. "Before you change your mind, Sadie Grace?"

She was watching his mouth now, her eyelids lowered slightly. He could feel the tension growing between them. "No. I won't do that. I'm not a child, but not yet a woman. If anyone is going to change that I…I want it to be you."

Darby Travers, you remain the luckiest man in the world…

"I'd be honored," and then he captured her mouth in their first real kiss. A kiss that was more than a tease, or even a small experiment on his part A kiss that claimed, that promised. A kiss she returned with maidenly fervor as he slipped his arms beneath her and lifted her high into his arms and carried her over to the bed, before setting her down on her feet.

He broke the kiss then, but only for a moment, sliding his arms around her small waist, running his hands up and down her long back, along the enticing dip at her waist, the magnificent curves of her buttocks, amazed at her sleek perfection.

In another lifetime, she could have been the purest of Arabians. Wonderfully constructed, beautiful to look at, deceptively strong. Built not merely to be admired, but with hidden strength and a great heart ready to go the distance, whatever distance was required.

He allowed his hands to travel upward again, gently searching for and finding the pins holding her long blond hair and releasing them, sliding his fingers into her soft curls as they fell nearly to the middle of her back.

She sighed into his mouth as he lifted her arms from his shoulders.

"I'm not going anywhere, Sadie Grace," he promised, smiling into her eyes. "But there are practical matters that must be addressed."

She lowered her forehead onto his chest. "I...I'd wondered about that."

He chuckled softly. "My ever-practical Sadie." He swept her long hair over her right shoulder and drew her close, his normally confident fingers fumbling slightly as he released the row of buttons on her gown. "Clearly a garment not constructed with seduction in mind," he joked as he was finally able to ease the gown from her shoulders, to fall in a puddle of sunflower silk at her feet.

He leaned in to kiss the side of her neck, silently marveling at how well-matched they were, her height bringing their bodies together in all the most interesting places. He felt her hands against him as she undid the laces of her final concealing garment, wordlessly telling him she was ready for whatever was to come next.

"A moment, Sadie Grace," he said, leaving her only long enough to rather ruthlessly pull down the heavy covers on the bed, exposing the soft cotton sheets he'd favored since childhood.

When he looked back, it was to see her toeing off her kid slippers, so that now she was clad only in white silk hose that enhanced the perfection of her long legs, and the chemise she held tight against her waist, her freed hair tumbling over her breasts as a sort of living curtain of modesty.

"I still feel rather silly," she said as he simply stood there, unable to do more than look. "Too tall by half and, unlike Clarice, sadly lacking in…attributes. I hope you're not disappointed."

"I believe I'll manage. Now turn your back, if you please, for I'm about to rid myself of my own outward trappings."

Her cheeks colored most adorably. "I've seen men's bodies before, in the infirmary, as well as cared for my brother."

"Not the body of a man who clearly isn't at all disappointed, Sadie Grace. Please, turn your back."

She looked at him for a moment in question, and then her eyes widened. "Oh. Um…*oh*."

Darby's laugh sent her scurrying onto the bed and beneath the covers, but not before he caught a quick glance at her firm bottom as the chemise slipped from her hand.

Had there ever been a seduction quite like this? He doubted that highly. What a shame for the rest of the world.

Darby made short work out of employing the bootjack to remove his Hessians—Norton would probably never forgive him—and then stripped off his neck cloth, tossing it to the floor. Shrugging out of his well-tailored jacket was nearly as difficult as removing his boots, but he easily picked up the pace as first one, then the other white silk stocking was pushed out from beneath the covers and onto the floor.

Next time, we'll leave her stockings in place, he

thought as he removed his own and slid into bed beside Sadie.

"Hello again," he said as she lay near the middle of the wide bed, having scooted across the mattress in order to give him room.

So thoughtful. Clearly she could keep her head during most any circumstance.

"I feel so—"

"Silly. Yes, I know. I'm here to remedy that. Although I do warn you that if you were to laugh at any time during the coming procedure, I would probably be immediately crushed."

She put a hand to her mouth, obviously to stifle a giggle, and he knew the worst was over. She was ready for whatever would come next, or at least believed she was, probably thanks to John's anatomy books.

But now, to my delight, and with only a whisper of trepidation, I am about to prove her wrong.

He'd begin where they'd left off, with kisses meant to both relax and inflame. At least that's how their first kisses had affected him. Turning onto his side, he braced his palm against the mattress beside her and smiled down into her eyes.

They had somehow gone deliciously blue. He liked that.

"You have the most intriguing mouth, Sadie Grace. Plump, and curved, and eminently tempting. Let me teach you how to use it."

She parted those lips slightly, perhaps to contradict him, but he didn't give her the chance. Mouths were meant to mesh, to engage, to serve as the initial portal to that most deepest intimacy. Tongues were meant to taste, to tease, to mimic that same intimacy, flood the body with sensations that, once aroused, could not be denied.

As she began to move beneath him, he knew that, even if her mind did not yet fully understand, the most sensitive parts of her had taken the message to heart.

As had his. Darby knew he had to ignore the messages his own body was sending, at least for a while, but that would be one of the most difficult things he'd ever do, especially when he began exploring her body, first with his hands, and then with his mouth playing accompaniment to the music singing inside them both, growing to a crescendo.

If she had first been shy, unsure, even embarrassed, the Sadie coming alive in his arms was none of those. She matched him kiss for kiss, caress for caress, her touch even becoming slightly frantic as she wrapped her arms around him, drew him to her, up and over her.

Another intimate kiss, her lips drawing together around his tongue, sucking him in, a slight shifting in their bodies, and the deed was done. The last barrier gone, he was inside her, trying to calm himself, allow her to become accustomed to this new fullness, to even say no, although it was eons too late for no.

He would take even this slowly. For her, most definitely not for himself. His movements were slow, allowing her pleasure to build, struggling to control his breathing even as he knew, for all his experience, that he had never experienced this depth of feeling and wanted to explore it more himself.

But when her grip on his shoulders tightened, her fingertips pressing into his flesh, and he felt those long legs that had previously only done so in his dreams wrap high around him, Darby most willingly lost the battle.

CHAPTER FOURTEEN

"CLARICE, YOU HAVE to stop laughing, or else you'll wake the entire household. And *that* was a snort. I'm certain ladies don't snort."

Sadie and her friend were sitting cross-legged, facing each other on Sadie's bed, which had become their nightly ritual, it seemed, discussing the events of the day and at times nattering about nothing, really, which was also fine with both of them.

Tonight had been no different, even if Sadie's world had changed irrevocably that day. She wanted to tell Clarice about it all, and would. Once she'd finished telling her about Belinda Henderson's inspection of Marrakesh... and once Clarice stopped laughing.

"Truly, Clarice, it wasn't all that amusing. Marrakesh was clearly mortified."

Clarice wiped at her eyes. "I'm sorry. But remember, I know Belinda. I'd wager my last two new bonnets that that's as close as she'll ever come to any sort of male naughty places. And wouldn't she be disappointed if she did."

"Clarice, stop, please," Sadie said, laughing in spite of her best intentions.

"And another thing. I don't see anyone ever wanting to hoist up her tail to take a peek at her underpinning, neither."

Sadie allowed her upper body to fall forward, burying her face as she dissolved into giggles.

"See?" Clarice said rather triumphantly once they'd both recovered their composure. "You were being all serious about everything—oh, the poor, poor horsey—and there is nothing that is all serious, Sadie. That stallion will live higher on the hog than half of the people in Fairfax County, and have all the humping and bumping he wants. Belinda is going back to where she wants to be, to do whatever it is that makes her happy, and her mama sent around a note earlier reminding me to be sure to pen *her* a letter once His Lordship decides when we're to visit Virginia, as she wants to give a ball in my honor. In *my* honor, Sadie. Yesterday, that woman wouldn't have thrown me more than the empty shell after she'd chomped on her morning egg. Really, I'm going to give Darby the biggest kiss when I see him, because he's a true wonder, isn't he? Don't you think he's a true wonder?"

Sadie could feel hot color rising in her cheeks, and turned to look across the chamber at nothing in particular, showing great interest in that nothing. "Yes, that's just the word I would have chosen. A wonder."

"My Jerry said he refused to be thanked, because friends *do* for friends, which is just the— Sadie? Is something wrong? All of a sudden you look all—wait a moment. I know that look. That's the same look Thea gave me, or tried not to give me, after she and Gabe— *Sadie!*" Clarice pushed herself to her knees and began bouncing on the bed. "Tell me. Tell me *everything*."

"There's nothing to say, is there, as you've clearly guessed. However did you do that?"

Clarice gave a dismissive wave of her hand. "It's a

talent, I'll admit. I've precious few of them, but I've certainly got a nose for sniffing out April and May. Was it today? After he shooed off the Hendersons? Yes, it had to have been today, or I would have noticed yesterday, wouldn't I? So-o-o...you stayed at the cottage, and I'll wager he *introduced* you to the gazebo. That's where Dany and Coop first...and then it was where he—well, never mind about that. I must have Jerry ask Darby if we can drive out there one day. You know, before it gets too cold." She tapped her hands against her cheeks. "Oh, shut up, Clary, and let the girl *talk*!"

"Why, when you were doing so well on your own?" Sadie said, realizing that she had a true friend, and true friends can say most anything to each other. It was remarkably freeing, really, after a lifetime spent keeping her thoughts to herself, depending only on herself. "And it wasn't the gazebo, although it may have begun there. We...we sneaked up to his bedchamber. He had a key buried under the bricks, you understand, so that's how we— I can't believe I'm telling you this!"

Clarice shrugged. "Who would you tell, if you didn't tell me? Vivien? Believe me, her questions would probably even put me to the blush. And a woman has to tell *someone* or else burst. Are you all right? Was it wonderful? Please say it was wonderful."

"I'm fine, more than fine. And it was wonderful. Silly, then wonderful—and I'll say no more on that because you're much too eager to listen—and then silly again. At least Darby found it all amusing."

"Why? What was so amusing?"

"I said Darby found it amusing. I...I was concerned about...other things."

Clarice leaned forward. "What other things?"

"The sheets, Clarice," Sadie whispered, again feeling heat rising in her cheeks. "Darby wasn't in the least concerned, but he wouldn't, would he. He didn't care what anyone might think, would know what had happened, but *I* wasn't about to go crowing it from the rooftops."

"I still don't understand what you're—oh, *that*. Sorry, that was a long time ago for me, and I didn't have to worry about what might have been left behind on a haystack, now did I? Sadie, you're much too worried about what other people might think. I know that sounds ridiculous, coming from me, after Mrs. Henderson and all, but it's true. There are times we must do what makes us happy, and be damned to everyone else."

"Yes, that's what Darby said, and I certainly can see his point, and yours, as well. But as I told him, I believe I'll have to slowly *ease* my way into thinking differently than I have for all of my life."

"That's because you're not selfish, Sadie. Everyone needs to be at least a little bit selfish, or else the world will trample right over you. You also have to sometimes step back and let others *do* for you. Just follow my lead. I've taken to letting others do for me quite handily, Jerry says, but that's because I knew my place when it was my place, and I know what those who are in my place expect of me now that I'm in a different place. I may still be learning exactly what those in my new place *do*, but I certainly know what I should no longer be doing, because I'm not in that place anymore. Do you understand that?"

Sadie nodded. "Unbelievably, yes, I do. I shouldn't save someone else steps by carrying a tea tray back to the kitchens. That is what you mean, isn't it?"

Clarice pointed a finger at her. "In a nut's shell. And

not because you're lazy, or tipping up your nose at everyone like you're *so good*, but because it makes people nervous, thinking mayhap they aren't doing their job the way they should and could be out on the streets without a reference. You're in Society now, not mucking about in your brother's infirmary or under your parents' roof. For the love of ducks, Sadie, you're about to become Lady Nailbourne. You ring for tea and then serve it. You don't go lugging the tray from the kitchens. You leave your shoes right where you are when you take them off, and don't brush them clean yourself and carry them back to the wardrobe, leaving nothing for your maid to do but suck her thumb. You don't climb out of bed and lickety-split turn back to pull up the covers and—oh, Lord. Oh, sweet Lord, tell me it isn't true. You insisted on making up the bed afterward, didn't you?"

"You needn't sound as if the world is ending, Clarice. Besides, the bed couldn't be simply straightened after—should I tell you how he kissed me? Because I'm beginning to think I'd be less embarrassed to do that."

"No, no. I know about kissing, and the rest of it, and my imagination can do the rest. I want to hear about this bed."

"Darby says he'll remind me of it annually for the remainder of our lives," Sadie said quietly. But then, slowly, she smiled.

First had come the small argument about the whole thing, with Darby pointing out once more that she really needed to stop worrying so much. But she'd won that particular argument, explaining that she simply couldn't *do* that to Camy or any maid who would immediately come tell her what she'd seen.

She just couldn't, that was all, and she didn't care

what lordships and ladies did because Sadie Grace Hamilton had her limits.

Besides, once he'd agreed with her, he'd pointed out that a good half of the large bed had remained pristine, without so much as a wrinkle, and that seemed a cruel waste of fresh linen.

Sadie didn't tell Clarice that part, but concentrated instead on how she'd had to instruct Darby on how to remove and fold up sheets…once he'd freed her after having playfully rolled her up in one of them, not giving her a chance to first hop down from the bed.

Really, there was a lot of the naughty boy in Darby Travers, for all his sophistication.

Then again, apparently there was a good amount of naughty in her, even if she'd only discovered that fact this afternoon. How lovely it was to finally be a woman.

"Sadie? You can stop smiling at any time, and tell me the rest," Clarice prodded.

"Oh, I'm sorry. The sheets. At any rate, only once the bed was stripped did I realize that we now had to go sneaking about the hallways to find the linen cupboards. Thankfully, Darby remembered he had hidden in one of them as a boy, to eat a peach tart he'd nipped from the kitchens. Then it was explaining to him just *how* to replace the sheets and smooth them just so—and to that I'll only say it is a wonder how men rule the world when they seem to have six thumbs when it comes to something so ridiculously simple. At one point, as we fussed with the heavy coverlet, he said a word I didn't think gentlemen said, but then decided the entire household staff deserved a raise in wages."

"I believe I adore your Darby." Clarice had been munching on a seed cake while Sadie told her story, but now asked, "So where are the betraying sheets now? Surely you didn't pack them up and bring them back here."

"I confess I hadn't thought of what we'd do with them, not until we'd done it," Sadie said as she slid off the bed. She picked up the gown she'd worn that day, currently hung over the back of a slipper chair, as she'd dismissed her maid and Clarice had helped her with the buttons, and headed for the large cupboard.

"Put that back down," her friend ordered. "What did you do with the sheets?"

"We didn't stuff them up the chimney, if that's what you're asking." Sadie rolled her eyes, but obeyed the order, being careful to place the gown so that it wouldn't become too wrinkled. "And I just want you to know what we did wasn't my idea. Darby rolled open the window and tossed them to the ground. Once he determined it was safe for us to leave his chambers again, we retrieved them and took them to the washhouse, and used one of the paddles to submerge them in a large washtub already filled with water. No one will know how they got there, he said, and someone would simply wash them and put them back in the linen cupboard."

"And you think this Camy person doesn't count the linens every week and won't be any the wiser?"

Sadie returned to the bed. She was accustomed to having only one sheet for every bed, and those sheets were washed and replaced in the same day. "Why would she count the sheets?"

"Because that's what housekeepers do, you ninny. They're forever counting things. Linens, silver, china. They also have eyes in the backs of their heads, at least the good ones do. You did all of that for nothing, Sadie.

Camy will know. She won't say a word, but she'll know. Just as I'd wager she knew about the key, and even the peach tart."

For a moment, Sadie was mortified. But then she remembered how Darby had looked exasperated yet boyishly flummoxed as he wrestled with the bedclothes—with the heavy satin spread clearly winning—and she broke into a grin. "I can't wait to tell him."

Clarice began bouncing on her knees again. "No. No, no, no, Sadie. You never tell him. Because he knows. He knew all along, yet did what you wanted, anyway, and made a rare cake of His Lordship's self as he did it, to hear you tell it."

Sadie didn't understand. "But...but why would he do that?"

"There's nothing else for it, you silly. The man is dotty for you." She reached for the now totally flummoxed Sadie and gave her a tight hug. "Now, good night. I'm certain you have much to dream about."

Sadie didn't sleep much for the entire night after that impossible revelation, and was up and dressed and fed and was now sitting by herself in the drawing room, although she still felt far from awake or even able to form proper sentences.

The man is dotty for you.

No, he wasn't. He was dotty for *parts* of her. He'd made that clear enough, and since she felt rather the same about him (embarrassing to admit, even to herself), she'd had little difficulty believing him.

But *dotty* was clearly Clarice's definition of love, or something very close to love, and that was ludicrous.

Their marriage was to be one of convenience, granted one now apparently including rather more convenience than simply to give Marley a feeling of home and security, but convenience nonetheless.

The mantel clock counted out the hour of eleven, and she realized Darby wasn't being his usual prompt self. Had his night been as disturbed as hers had been, or was he perhaps reluctant to see her again after what had transpired between them?

No. Not Darby. He'd either behave as if nothing untoward had occurred, or he'd bounce into the room his jolly, witty, well-dressed self, and make her blush by saying things that might sound perfectly reasonable to others, but not to her.

There was a noise just outside in the hallway, and Sadie tensed, turning to see if there would be a bounce in Darby's step, except that it was Marley who came skipping into the room, followed by the duke himself.

"Look at me, Sadie!" the child exclaimed. "Escaped from the nursery and Miss Potterdam's lessons in globes." She pushed down her chin, doubling it, and proclaimed in a deep voice, *"I don't care a goat's bladder what you say, missy, if I want the child with me, the child is with me! I'm the duke, blast it all, and that has to be good for something!"* She turned to beam up at His Grace. "Isn't that right, Uncle Basil?"

"Regular little parrot, ain't she?" the duke said as Sadie quickly got to her feet and dropped into a deep curtsy. "Never saw the point of keeping the kiddies all locked up, fed pasty porridge and put to bed before sundown. Don't you agree, heh-heh?"

"Why, yes, Your Grace, I most certainly do," Sadie said, since there was undoubtedly nothing to be gained by disagreeing. "And may I say, Your Grace, that is a lovely parrot."

The duke turned his head to look at the large white bird perched on his shoulder, almost as if he'd forgotten it was there. "Not a parrot, Sadie girl, not in the truest sense, I could say. Cockatoo straight from Siam, this gal is. Bought her from a nabob, as I recall, or did I trade him my watch for her? No matter. Name of Putri, which means princess."

"So we call her Princess," Marley interjected—thankfully, or else the duke was bound to go on for hours on his own. "And she's going to be mine someday years from now, unless Uncle Basil dies next week, but he's not going to die, Sadie, is he?"

Oh, dear. And here everyone thought the duke had cast aside his worries, and was even looking forward to his birthday and the ball to be held in his honor. Vivien would be crushed to hear he still harbored worries of some sort of Cranbrook curse. We really need to do something about this.

"No, sweetheart, he's not," she said, giving as close to the evil eye to His Grace as she could muster.

"No, no, o' course I'm not," the duke blustered, puffing out his cheeks even as the cockatoo's magnificent white crest popped up as if it was on a string. "Can't say what I was thinking, to even hint at such a thing. Come along, pet. We'll take Princess here to the solarium, just as I promised, and let her hop about in the greenery, hunting up beetles. Ah, Darby, my son, how are you today?"

Sadie relaxed. He looked perfectly normal. She could only hope she looked the same. But then, what had she been expecting?

"Basil," Darby said, bowing, and Sadie quickly composed herself as she watched Marley run into his extended arms for a hug. "Well, look at you, poppet, sprung from your jail. And where is Max?"

"He barks like a berserk banshee when Princess is about," Marley told him seriously, "so he's banished to the kitchens for the nonce, happy enough with a marrow bone."

"Berserk banshee, is it? For the nonce?" Darby looked at Sadie. "And what, pray tell, is a banshee, Marley? For that matter, what is a nonce?"

The girl grimaced. "You always know, don't you? How do you always know?"

"When you're being a parrot, you mean?" he countered, winking at Sadie.

"This one's a cockatoo," the duke corrected, looking abashed. "Come along, Marley, before we're both banished to the nursery."

They watched as Marley slipped her hand into the duke's and the pair went happily off to the solarium.

"She gets the cockatoo if the duke dies next week," Sadie said as Darby joined her on the couch, lifting her hand to plant a kiss on her palm. "When do Thea and Gabe return to the city?"

"Not until next week, I'm afraid. I had a note from Gabe yesterday, informing me that Thea slipped on a banana, took a tumble and sprained her ankle. And before you say another word, that can be easily explained, as they've been supervising the dismantling and reconstruction of the great hall at Cranbrook. We're not to let Vivien know about Thea, and then I somehow forgot. I had other things on my mind yesterday."

"I *knew* you'd say something!" Sadie pressed a hand to her mouth. "Oh, I'm sorry. You didn't really say anything, did you?"

Darby smiled. "According to many, I rarely do. Perhaps if I were to kiss you, it would help settle your nerves. You appear poised to leap from this couch if I so much as sneeze."

"I do not!" Her shoulders slumped. "Yes, I do. I spent half the night wondering how I'd feel seeing you this morning, if you would even come here at all."

"I never had any intention of not coming to you this morning, but I will say I, too, was awake most of the night. I woke only a little past nine after falling asleep in my study, and then I had to eat, bathe and, most naturally, change my linen."

"*There!* See? Now you said it. You had to say something, didn't you? Are you done now, because we have other things to—oh. You were awake most of the night, and fell asleep in your study?" She put a hand to his forehead. "Was it the headache again? Is it gone now?"

He took hold of her hand and kissed it. "Yes, it's gone, but I admit to nearly ordering my carriage and coming here, begging for your magical ministrations. Norton tried, but even with my instructions, I'm afraid he failed miserably. That crushed him, as the man appears to have his pride, but although he was to be but a temporary valet while I'm here in London, he's informed me that, as long as Miss Marley is to become a part of my household, he will consider the possibility of making his position permanent. My opinion on that was not consulted."

Sadie shook her head. "What a strange man. But they did seem to strike up a friendship in the short time they were together in the coach on our way here, and in the few times they've seen each other since then. That's probably because she gave her approval on his reason for *painting* his beard black. Are you quite certain you don't want to know why?"

"And risk another headache? Thank you, but no. But now, about that kiss…"

She closed her eyes and met him halfway, welcoming the thrill that ran through her as their mouths engaged. She was better at kissing now, having had several hours of practice, and only sighed in pleasure as he cupped her breast in his hand, lightly stroking her nipple through the soft cotton of her morning gown.

"Oh, dear. I'm so, *so* sorry. I'll leave now. Don't let me interrupt, just carry on as if I wasn't ever here."

Sadie pulled back, touching her neckline to be sure it hadn't slipped dangerously low.

"Vivien, my love," Darby said, getting to his feet to sweep the duchess an elegant bow before escorting her to the facing couch, kissing her hand as she sank into the soft cushions, her tiny feet dangling a good three inches above the carpet. "Even your interruptions are a delight. If you're looking for Basil, he and Marley are entertaining a cockatoo in the solarium. Or perhaps that's the other way 'round."

Vivien gave a wave of her lace-edged handkerchief. "Looking for him? Gad, I'm *escaping* him. We were merely nattering over breakfast when I happened to mention our travels in Italy and that *lovely* terrace overlooking the red roofs of Florence and the night we—well," she ended with another flourish of the handkerchief, "just let me say that Harris, my dresser, didn't seem best pleased to have the dressing of me *twice* this morning."

Darby leaned close beside Sadie's ear. "And you were fretting about the linens. We can only goggle at the thought of what Harris has to say in the servants' hall."

Sadie bit her bottom lip to hold back a smile. Odd, but Vivien's references, however veiled, to her and the duke's dalliances carried much more meaning this morning than they had heretofore done.

And all I can say to that is brava, Your Graces!

"Oh, did I tell you both that Minerva, dearest Minerva, has deserted me to join Dany and Coop, in order to meet Dany's family now that he's prepared them for her? She was invited, you understand, by Dany's sister and her husband, as they were headed there, anyway, to surprise the family with news of the impending birth of the Cockermouth heir. None of them will return until the night of the party for Basil, and although I will miss my friend, I must say, her insistence on purple as the color for all the flowers and bunting was depressingly funereal. Now we'll have pink!"

"Your Grace—"

"No, no, I'm quite settled on the color. And that's Vivien, darling. I shouldn't have to keep reminding you that you're family now. Yes, dear?"

Sadie hesitated. She probably should wait until she could confer with Darby, and with Clarice, as well, but since Gabe was not going to be available and she'd had an idea, and since Marley was now involved, she felt it might be unwise to wait.

"I don't know everything, or even very much at all, about the duke's fear of his coming birthday. But from something he said minutes ago, something Marley said—about a bird, ma'am—I fear His Grace is not entirely confident he'll survive to see it."

Her Grace sighed. "Giving away things again, is he? Two days ago it was the watch fob he purchased in Paris that he pressed on his valet, and yesterday he gave the

cook his best set of suspenders. At least I could understand that, as the cook is nearly as round as he is tall
and anything that might relieve the strain on his trousers should be appreciated."

"Vivien," Darby said soothingly. "Focus, please.
Sadie is telling us that Basil still thinks he might die
before his birthday. Is it possible he'll take to his bed
again, even retreat to the country again?"

"He seems fairly happy with Marley, bless her heart,"
Sadie added. "But that isn't to say he isn't putting on a
brave face for her. I...I've seen people die simply because they're fearful that they're going to, especially in
the elderly."

Oops!

Sadie's eyes widened as the duchess's eyes narrowed.

"Not that the duke is elderly. Goodness, no, Vivien,
that's not at *all* what I meant. Why, he's just—you're *both*
just entering your prime. Aren't they, Darby?"

"'Indeed, the prime of a man's life lies in the ageless-
ness of his mind,'" he responded profoundly.

"Precisely!" Vivien pointed a finger at him before
hopping to her feet and making her way across the room
to the drinks table, clearly aiming for the decanter of gin.

Sadie whispered to Darby. "That really doesn't make
sense. Who wrote that? Surely not Shakespeare."

"Hardly. I just made it up. It seems to have worked to
pull you out of the briars, and I certainly wasn't going
to point out that Basil, although gifting others with his
possessions, appears hardy enough to live the romantic
life until he *erps*."

*If only I wouldn't appear to have gone mad if I were
to dive beneath the couch...*

"You're impossible. And I didn't just make that up—

you've been impossible since the day we first met. Still, thank you."

"You may thank me later. Or do you think I'm devoid of a plan to abscond with you for a few private hours this evening?"

There wasn't much she could say to that without betraying herself. Besides, the duchess and her glass of gin were back.

"All right. Now where were we? Nowhere near *elderly*, I'm sure," she said, taking a sip from her glass.

Sadie rushed into speech. "I just feel, Vivien, that it may be necessary to ease the duke's mind now, rather than risk his trepidation growing with each passing day."

And to ease Marley's mind, poor baby.

"It isn't that I haven't tried to keep him occupied," the duchess said on a sigh before busying herself arranging her skirts into flowing pleats. "Lord knows how I have tried," she repeated, as if talking to herself.

Darby leaned in to whisper in Sadie's ear. "Day in, day out, and very possibly twice on Sundays, goodness, how the poor woman has tried."

"You're im— No, I'm not going to say it."

Sadie stood up and walked around the large low table to sit down beside the duchess.

"Vivien," she said, taking the older woman's hands in hers, "do you think His Grace truly believes there's a curse on the Sinclair men?"

"My dear Sadie, his brothers all—well, as Basil so inelegantly puts it, they did all *erp* on the eves of their sixtieth birthdays. What would you think if you heard the story?"

"Yes, and how did that go again, Vivien, if it isn't

too upsetting for you to tell us? Truly, Sadie, it is rather remarkable."

"No, Darby, it doesn't upset me, except that I sometimes get the names mixed up." Vivien politely tugged her hands free from Sadie's sympathetic grip, and began counting on her fingers. "The first duke stuck his spoon in the wall with the swiftness of a blown-out candle days before a celebratory hunt in his honor upon his sixtieth birthday. That began it all, although no one thought so at the time. After all, he'd been a hard-living rascal, which is the way nice people say hell-raking libertine. Then came the first of his five sons—the first duchess popped out sons on nearly a yearly basis, you understand. The oldest, and now the second duke, Boswell, was leading a sweet young thing onto the dance floor when, as the story has it, he rolled his eyes heavenward, said something akin to a startled *erp*, and the next thing anyone knew, he was facedown on the floor and gone… also mere days away from his sixtieth birthday. He was quickly followed to his heavenly reward by Bennett, Ballard and Bellamy, each succumbing quite suddenly and, yes, also within days of *their* sixtieth birthdays. Basil began to worry with Ballard, but when we got word about Bellamy having *erped*? The man hasn't been the same ever since."

Sadie didn't even attempt to memorize all the B's Vivien had been counting off. "So the curse, if there is one, had to have been directed at the first duke."

"'Fie on you, you damned Sinclairs. I curse you all, seed, breed and generation. No male shall reach his sixtieth birthday, this I decree by all the devils in hell and Beelzebub himself,'" Darby said with an evil smile.

"Marley isn't the only one who can parrot someone else's words."

Sadie glared at him. "We were doing quite nicely without you, my lord, thank you."

"Yes, Darby, stifle yourself," the duchess scolded. "I don't believe in curses, myself, but Basil does, even if he's been bravely pretending he doesn't, and Sadie here seems to have an idea. You do have an idea, don't you, my dear?"

"Yes, my dear," Darby said, leaning forward, his elbows on his knees, clearly feigning intense interest. "We are all ears."

"I suppose I do, although thinking it and actually voicing it out loud are two very different things and, upon reflection, I don't know if it would work, in any case. And for another, where would we find someone to *do* what I thought of doing?"

"Are you perhaps thinking of a séance, Sadie Grace?" She frowned. "I don't know what that is."

"Oh, a *séance.* I know," the duchess said, all but bouncing in her seat. "Basil and I attended a party in Paris, oh, years ago, and the hostess put on a séance as entertainment. We all had to sit around a table, clasping hands, with only a few candles to light the room. There was this veiled woman at the table with us—a Gypsy, I suppose, but perhaps not—and she had us all think about our hostess's departed father, asking him to please speak to us from beyond the grave. Our hostess wished to know where he'd hidden her late mother's jewelry, we'd been told, because she couldn't locate it. Personally, Basil and I thought the old bugger had long ago sold it for gambling debts, but the veiled lady began to rock in her chair and moan most earnestly, and suddenly there was this *voice* coming out of her that wasn't her voice at all, oh, no, and the voice said he'd had them sealed up in the mausoleum with his dear wife."

"Really," Darby said, and Sadie saw he was holding back a smile.

"Yes, really, that's what the voice said. Well, that was the capper to *that* party, let me tell you, and we heard the next day that our hostess—what *was* her name?— had gone off to the country in quite a rush. I've always wondered if she'd found the jewelry tucked up with her *maman*."

"Somehow I sincerely doubt that," Darby told her. "But by then the veiled lady was undoubtedly gone, her purse heavier than when she'd arrived. In any event, that's a séance, Sadie. Is that what you were thinking? To hopefully make contact with the first duke, and ask him who had cursed him?"

Sadie was feeling extremely embarrassed. "No, because I've never heard of a séance, and because what could we possibly do with a name all these years later? We have to remove the curse. I...I was thinking more of a...a *ritual*."

"Oh! You mean where we dress ourselves in paint and feathers and prance around a fire? I watched as Basil did that in a small village on Saint Domingue. Casting out demons, I believe it was. Such fun. Oh, the places we've been, children, and the glorious things we've done, while his brothers were busy being duke and we were left to do as we pleased. Basil never wanted to be duke, you know. And how much we've missed this last year and more thanks to his absurd notion that he's dying. I thought returning to Virginia without him would boost him from his deathbed, but even that didn't help. Thank goodness for Thea, who dared to challenge him into coming with us to Mayfair, although Gabe's silly threat about the birds probably boosted him, as well. Do you know something? We should be in Egypt at the moment, for we still have an entire list Basil drew up when we were first married. He said we would ride camels there, but now..."

Vivien paused to wipe at her eyes and then rather heartily blew her nose.

Sadie returned to sit beside Darby. "Clearly we have to do something. For Their Graces, and for Marley, as well. She's had enough of death, and I don't want her fearful."

"We neither of us do," he said. "We can't wait for Gabe's return. I already have plans for us for later this afternoon, but if the idea you and Vivien have sparked in me seems feasible to you, you and I are going to have a few interesting hours between now and then. Have your maid bring down your cloak, as it's breezy today, and request that she accompany us."

"I don't—"

"No, of course you don't, as the idea is only half-formed in my head at this point. Vivien?" he said, getting to his feet. "Dry those tears, darling lady. This very evening Sadie and I will rid His Grace of all his worries. You only be certain that both Clarice and Rigby are here, and His Grace, as well."

Vivien looked hopeful. "Will there be feathers?"

"Alas, I believe not."

"That's too bad. Although probably safer. Last time, Basil danced too close to the blaze and his feathers caught fire. As there weren't many feathers to begin with, seeing him racing to be rid of them caused quite a stir among the other ladies present. Of course, we were much younger then, and Basil could still strip to effect, if you take my meaning."

Sadie hastened into speech. "What shall I tell Clarice?"

"Nothing," Darby answered. "I'd much rather she reacted as her unique self, and Rigby, as well. Now, if you can peel Marley away from the duke, have her cloak fetched, as well. She's an important part of my idea, a major part, for probably nothing will happen without her help. Run along, Sadie Grace, and find Max while you're at it, while I stay here and convince Vivien to keep mum, as well."

"Run along? You really are im— I'm going! I'm going!"

CHAPTER FIFTEEN

DARBY DID NOT agree that the duke could actually worry himself into dying. He had other reasons for encouraging Sadie in her idea of somehow convincing the man that there was indeed a curse, *and* a way to remove it.

He wanted her mind occupied with something other than any lingering concern that this Sam Dobson person might be able to wrest guardianship of Marley from him.

More importantly, he certainly shared her opinion that Marley had been exposed to enough unhappiness for a child of her tender years. Most especially enough of death and loss.

Yes, he certainly agreed on that.

Lastly, selfishly, he wanted Sadie to see him as the center of her universe, as he considered her to be the very core of his own.

Since that had been a fairly recent and rather shocking conclusion on his part, and he'd managed to make a rare mess of things by taking her to his bed on what could now only be termed false pretenses, he wasn't quite certain how to convince her that he loved her, and that she loved him.

Because any two people could make love to each other, but creating love *with* each other, growing that love beyond the mere physical, was an entirely different thing.

Let's be blunt, Darby, old man, you've allowed your body to rule your head, and now you have to fix that.

He could lay the blame for his prior uncertainty squarely at his own door, and he knew that, as well. His damaged eye wasn't the only thing he hid from the world, from even his closest friends. Even from himself…except when the headache claimed him.

Happy, lucky, carefree Darby, always ripe for adventure, always with a ready quip. That was how he wanted the world to see him. How he wanted to see himself.

He'd done well, at least believed himself to be doing well, but he'd never told anyone what had made him the man they thought they knew.

Sadie had bared her soul, her deepest pain, to him, while he still had his secrets.

That had to change, and it had to change soon, or else he would be risking all he now knew he needed to truly feel whole.

Yes, he had to get the apprehensive duke settled, and then Marley.

"My lord?"

Darby had been sitting on one of the benches in the park, watching as Sadie and Marley and the young maid romped on the grass with an ecstatic Max.

He looked up to see his valet standing there, hat in hand, red hair blazing. "Ah, Norton, then you received my message."

"Yes, my lord, that I did. But truly, sir, there's no need to apologize for the bootjack. I was able to rectify the damage with my special bootblack mixture."

Probably the same mixture he uses on his mustache and beard.

Darby was careful to keep his expression neutral.

"How did you know that's the reason I called you out here?"

Norton looked puzzled. Clearly he was the center of his own universe and, most naturally, saw that universe only from his own perspective.

"But, my lord, what else could it be?"

"What else indeed. Still, truth be told, I do have something else to discuss with you. A boon. A favor. Or, if you're reluctant, an order accompanied by a substantial bribe. I'm open to whatever prompts you to offer your assistance in a matter that involves Miss Marley and her continued happiness."

"Miss Marley, my lord?"

"Miss Marley, Norton. You two seem to have cried friends, and you've asked daily how she's enjoying her stay. You have a fondness for her."

"Yes, my lord. We took to each other right quick, we did, and Mrs. Boxer didn't seem to mind."

"Ah, yes. Mrs. Boxer. Quite the story behind that, Norton. Banish the name from your memory. We call her Miss Hamilton now."

The valet wrinkled up his brow. "I don't understand, my lord."

Darby reached into his pocket for his purse and extracted a five-pound note, handing it to the man. "On the contrary, my good man. You understand quite well."

"Oh, *yes*, my lord," Norton said fervently, bowing three times in quick succession. "Mum's the word on the whole of it. The bootjack, the name. Is there anything else? I can forget most anything you'd like me to forget."

He capped off this bit of jolly man-to-man camaraderic with a wink.

"You misunderstand, Norton. Miss Hamilton and I

are betrothed. You are speaking of the future Viscountess Nailbourne."

The valet began to turn a fairly dangerous shade of puce as he stumbled into speech. "I never meant…oh, no, I couldn't have meant… My…my most heartfelt best wishes to you both, my lord." He reached into his pocket. "You'll be wanting this back, my lord?"

"In point of fact, Norton, it's probably lonely. I'd like it to have company, and quite a bit of company at that. We return now to the boon I would ask of you."

"*Anything*, my lord. You have my word as a gentleman's gentleman."

"Do you see that little girl over there on the grass?"

The valet turned to look. "Miss Marley! Oh, my, sir, how happy she looks. And how pretty, all dressed up in pink and ribbons, just as she should be. And would that—oh, my—would that be Mrs., er, Miss Hamilton with her? Such a miracle for them both, my lord. Miss Hamilton will make you a splendid viscountess."

"Oh, good. I can't tell you how I worried I might not receive your approval."

Once again the valet looked panicked, but Marley had spied him out and came running toward him, joyfully calling out a greeting.

"Uncle Ralphie! It's me. Marley!"

Norton turned to Darby. "May I, sir?"

"Of course…Ralphie."

Ralphie? Egads.

Marley stopped a few feet away from the valet and dropped into a curtsy, which Norton quickly told her was not at all proper, and that he should bow to her, which he then proceeded to do.

"I don't care," Marley said with her usual spirit, and

threw herself into his arms, delivering a kiss to the man's cheek. "Uncle Ralphie! You said you'd shave off that silly thing. Sadie can do it for you. She used to shave my papa when he couldn't do it for himself."

Will the wonders of that woman never cease? Should Norton be trembling in his boots that he's about to lose his position?

Sadie had come within earshot, and quickly told her niece to say good day to Norton and return to Max, who was impatiently waiting with a stick clutched in his jaws, ready for another toss and run. She smiled at Norton, and then shot a quick glance toward Darby, mouthing the single word *no*, before taking Marley's hand and heading back to Max.

Apparently Norton's job was safe.

"I don't know why, Norton, but Miss Marley clearly adores you, a feeling obviously returned. But, sadly, her world is not entirely filled with sunshine, and as her guardian, I cannot allow that unhappiness to persist. She's extremely concerned that another of her new and dear friends—the Duke of Cranbrook, to be exact about the thing—is going to die, quite soon, if the curse he believes will be the death of him isn't lifted."

Norton nodded his understanding. "My aunt Mildred was like that, my lord. Only it weren't no curse coming after her, but my uncle Hiram, who wanted to see her planted in the churchyard. And *he's* the one what thought he was cursed, being bracketed to Aunt Mildred."

"Fascinating as that is, Norton, this is rather a different curse plaguing the duke. Time is of the essence, if Miss Marley is to be relieved of her worry—you do want that, I know—so we do what we do this very evening."

He signaled for Sadie to join them, leaving Marley and the maid to continue their play with Max.

An hour later, the child had become a member of their party, to have her part in the evening explained to her, before Norton was sent off to escort Marley and the maid back to Grosvenor Square.

"He seems actually eager, and chock-full of ideas," Sadie said, watching them go, Marley's hand snugly held in the valet's. "Marley has that effect on people, doesn't she, as if she was born to wrap others around her little finger."

"We'll be beating gentleman callers away from the door with a stick when she makes her come-out," Darby agreed, all but puffing out his chest in doting guardian pride.

Truly, he barely recognized himself these days.

Sadie lowered her chin for a moment. "That's years and years in the future."

"Hadn't thought that far ahead, had you, being stuck with me for all those years?" he teased, putting out his arm, indicating they could now be up and on their way. "Of course, she won't be the only one, not if our children favor you at all."

"You say these things only to see how I'll react, don't you? And I suppose I'm now to say that if the boys resemble you, they'll be handsome devils indeed."

"Handsome devils, is it? I rather like that."

"I know," she said, grinning up at him. "How often might you require flattery, my lord, so I can make a note of it?"

If they'd been anywhere but the park, always full of nosey parkers on the hunt for scandalous dinner conversation, he'd have kissed her. Instead, he merely smiled and brought the subject back to the amazing Uncle Ralphic. "Would you ever have expected that my valet was once part of a touring company of players?"

"Not until he disclosed that information, although I should have guessed. It's your luck again, Darby. The Travers luck. In truth, I stand in awe of it."

The Travers luck. But not always good luck. Just one more look back, and then only forward.

"Are you going to ask where we're headed, Sadie Grace?" he inquired jovially as they cut across the plush lawns to a path leading to a gate on the opposite side of the park.

"No. I'm only assuming you have some good reason for ruining my new kid slippers. You should have told me to change to my half boots before ordering me outside."

"I'll buy you another dozen pair."

"Don't be ridiculous. I have only two feet."

"And lovely feet they are, although totally outdone by the legs attached to them. Ah-ah, before you protest, I am well aware that you have no budget for flattery. In fact, compliments tend to embarrass you. Therefore, I've vowed to say only what's true, which I've just done. You, Sadie Grace, have the most magnificent legs in nature."

"I can only imagine you've had the experience necessary to make that statement."

"Ouch! Time to find another subject, isn't it? We are expected at that narrow house just ahead of us."

"Am I allowed to ask why? Does this have anything to do with the supposed Cranbrook curse? Perhaps you're also thinking of hiring a few jugglers to entertain once Norton completes his hour upon the stage?"

Darby laughed as they left the park behind and crossed the street to the tall, narrow house. "Just follow my lead, Sadie. With luck, you'll need do nothing but sit quietly beside me, marveling at my resourcefulness."

"You can be smug, you know. And that is not a compliment."

"Yes, but I'm quite talented in other areas that seem to please you."

Sadie opened her mouth, probably to say something he'd regret, but a footman responded to the knocker and whatever she was going to say remained unsaid. At least *for the nonce*.

"Viscount Nailbourne and Miss Hamilton to see Mr. Hooper," he said, ushering Sadie inside the minuscule hallway. "We're expected."

"Yes, my lord," the fairly aged footman said, bowing. "Mr. Hooper is waiting just up those stairs."

Darby handed the servant his hat and gloves before helping Sadie with her cloak. "Miss Hamilton's maid is awaiting us in the park," he added as he slipped the man a coin. "We'll find our way, thank you. Miss Hamilton, if you'd care to precede me?"

If he were to count up the *telling* looks she had thrown at him in the past two hours, he'd have to employ both hands. But perhaps she'd forgive him once she realized the identity of Mr. Hooper.

Or perhaps not. He'd have to count on the Travers luck again, wouldn't he?

Darby had always been fascinated by this particular row of houses. The rooms all ran front to back, with only narrow hallways and staircases following one after the other to the very top. Being able to both own a sterling view of Hyde Park and an impressive address apparently had many overlooking the notion that one was residing within a well-furnished, multistoried coffin.

"Your Lordship!" the man who could only be Mr. Jasper Hooper all but bellowed, his right hand extended as he advanced toward them when they reached the landing, since it would be silly in any event for him to pretend he couldn't see them from what had to be the drawing room.

No bowing or ceremony for Mr. Hooper, once a young lad picking up coal that fell from the carts for a halfpenny a week, and risen from breaker boy to a wealthy mine owner by dint of his hard work, according to Basil. He'd made his climb, considered himself any man's equal, and Darby took to him immediately.

"Mr. Hooper," he said, extending his own hand for what was bound to be a bone-crossing squeeze, for the man was as tall as he and twice as broad—a man who had hands the size of shovels that would never be clean no matter how he scrubbed them, and was proud of it. "You received the duke's note. Allow me to please introduce my fiancée, Miss Sadie Hamilton. Miss Hamilton, you see standing before you the king of coal, or so says the duke."

"Oh, none of that. Call me Jas, everyone does, save m' Sally, who doesn't call her da much of anything now that she's a fine lady, just as if I hadn't turned her over m' knee a time or three when she was naught but a snively nosed brat spoiled to the hilt by her mama, rest her soul. Hullo there, miss. Here, come have a seat!"

Sadie looked to Darby, who only nodded. "Thank you, sir," she said, dipping into a rather uncertain curtsy before she aimed herself at a small couch in the small room.

Once she was seated, Darby waited for the mine owner to lower himself into a high-backed leather chair that rather moaned under his weight, and then sat down beside her.

"The duke told me a most fascinating story of his travels in Lancashire, and his meeting with you. How well did he do in the mines? He said he thought he had the makings of a fine collier."

"Is that so? Then we'll let it stand at that, won't we, since he's the duke now, and not just a happy soul out to see the world," Jasper said with a broad wink. "Quite the good sport, though. Said he wanted to try everything before he croaked. Another day in the mines, and he might have seen that hope dashed."

"Fortunately, His Grace and his duchess have survived to seek many adventures over the years."

Jasper nodded. "I know. We exchange letters from time to time, him telling me about his travels. Sent me a bird once, said to try it in the mines to see if it was better than the canaries. Good man, good man. Saw him the other night at some damned musicale. Music? I've heard better tinkling in the privy. Sally made me go, you understand, and he invited me to some celebration he's planning, so that was all right. Hadn't seen him in dogs' years. Got the invitation right there, on the mantelpiece, where Sally said I was to put all my invitations so visitors could see them and gnash their teeth because they didn't have as many. I don't know. I still have only the one, and you're my first visitors. Only here at all to visit my grandkiddies. Sally isn't keen on that, but I figure I bought and paid for 'em, just like I did their papa, so I'll see 'em when I damn well want to, begging your pardon, miss."

"Jas's daughter is Lady Sarah Woodley," Darby told Sadie in explanation.

Sadie smiled. Apparently she was going to keep mum until she figured out just what was going on, although Darby was certain she already had some idea about the reason for this visit.

"Basil's note said you had some questions about a mine owner I might know. Know 'em all, I do. Mine owners, coal merchants. Just toss a name at me—I'm sure to catch it, and toss back the good and the bad about all of 'em."

"Thank you. So that would mean you're familiar with a mine owner named Samuel Dobson?"

"Sam? One of the better ones. Always liked old Dobby. A hard man, but fair. What do you want to know?"

"Anything you might be able to tell us," Darby said, since he wasn't quite sure, and a wise man learned all he could about his enemy.

Jasper leaned back and scratched at his ear. "Let's see. Came up about the way I did, going from nothing to something thanks to hard work. Back then you could do that, but not so much anymore. We'd meet from time to time in Liverpool, just us men, but his Alice took my Bessie in dislike, you could say, when she popped off Sally, and that was that. Nothing worse than a jealous woman, I say. Poor Sam. Don't think his life was ever the same."

Darby felt a slight kick to his ankle. Clearly Sadie had questions. He'd attempt to ask them.

"Mrs. Dobson was unhappy about your daughter's marriage?"

"More like she was unhappy about my Bessie crowing about it all the time, like a rooster at sunrise. But that's women for you. About the same time we got Sally popped off, Sam's daughter run away with some fella, just as her mama was about to buy her a baronet, think it was. More ancient than that Bible guy, Methuselah, but that didn't bother Alice. She was fighting mad, and swore she'd get her Susie home and start over. I believe she went so far as to hire some of those robin redbreasts. You know, Bow Street Runners?"

"But she never found her?"

"No, but not for lack of trying. The way I heard it, Sam blamed Alice for the whole thing, his Susie taking off like that. Cursed himself for not putting his foot down. He soldiered on as it were, for a few years, but then he didn't seem to care anymore about the Dobson mines, and all but turned over the running of them to a nephew."

Jasper sighed. "Just didn't care anymore, what with his only child lost to him. Alice turned in her ticket about two years ago, Lord rest her, I suppose, and Sam took himself off to Bath—no, wait, Brighton. Yes, that's it, Brighton. Where Prinney built that silly palace with the turrets?"

"Minarets," Darby corrected.

"If you say so that's fine with me. I took a look at 'em, figuring once my Bessie was gone I could do a bit of adventuring myself, like Basil did. So that's Brighton? Then it wasn't Bath. Saw Sam there, being dunked in the sea, just as I was doing the same."

He shook his head. "Never got much out of that dunking business, but it was good seeing Sam. He didn't say much, but I thought he was still looking for his Susie, wanting to make amends. I told him he'd best take himself back home and see how his nephew was making a mess of the mines, but he said no, he didn't care a spit and was staying right where he was, and the nephew could damn well have 'em when he was gone. Sad. You had to ask me about one of the sad ones…"

"I'm sorry, Jas," Darby said, his mind racing. "I wonder what would happen if Sam was to find his Susie, now that Alice is gone."

Jasper had pulled a huge white linen handkerchief from his pocket and had just lustily blown his nose. "Fall on her neck and beg her forgiveness? My Sally's happy enough, so that's all right with me, but to have your one child run from you because of how unhappy you made her? That's a weight not easily dropped, son, especially as we have more life behind us than we do ahead of us."

Darby looked at Sadie. "Have you anything to say to Jas, Sadie Grace? It's your decision, and yours only."

She nodded, wiping a tear from her eye.

Sadie Grace Hamilton was a good woman, beautiful inside and out. He knew what she was going to say before she said it.

"Sir? The man Susan eloped with was John Hamilton. My brother."

"What?" Jasper leaned forward. "Now, wait—wait, wait, wait. Hamilton? Yes, that's it. Country doctor, poor as a church mouse. I remember now. Then you know where Sam's Susie is?"

"Unfortunately, sir, Susan and John are both deceased."

Jasper fell back in his chair. "Oh, no. Can't tell Sam that."

"He knows, sir, just as he knows Susan and John have a daughter, my niece, Marley. The viscount is now her guardian and she's here in London. Here secretly."

"That's probably sufficient, Sadie," Darby said quietly.

"I don't think it is. Mr. Hooper—Jas—my brother's

dying wish was to keep Marley safe from the Dobsons. To that end, I followed his wishes to bring her to the viscount rather than obey a letter I received from Mr. Dobson's solicitor in Liverpool, demanding her return there. But you say Mr. Dobson resides in Brighton."

"He does. Saw him only last year. Said he'd never go back up north."

"Yes. Then I have a question for you, sir. A most important question, so I'd like you to consider well before answering it. Does my niece need to remain safe from Sam Dobson?"

Darby also felt certain he knew the answer to that question before the man spoke, knowing he wouldn't like it. Jasper Hooper might be rough about the edges, but he wasn't a stupid man.

"To see his grandbaby, look in her eyes, hear her call him Grandda? That's a sad man, Sam Dobson is. He'd give up his hope of heaven for that, miss, just as I would do for mine. The one you should be worrying your head about is Ellesmere."

And there it was.

"I beg your pardon?"

"Ellesmere, missy. Ellesmere Odling, Sam's nephew. Nasty pieces of work, him and his sister both. Edythe, yes, that's the name. Edythe and Ellesmere. They're the ones who stand to inherit every last groat." Jasper looked to Darby. "You look a bright boy, and this old man here didn't just fall from the sky yesterday, neither. This gel says the letter came from Liverpool, not Brighton. What would you do if you knew what Sam doesn't, and can't find the girl because she's been hidden?"

"I'd kill Sam Dobson before he can hear about his

granddaughter, or see her. That is the answer you're looking for, correct?"

Jasper Cooper slapped his ham-like hands against his knees and got to his feet. "Damned right, you would. Sam and the grandbaby both, had I the chance. Glad to have met you two, but I expect you'll be leaving now. When you find Sam, bring him here to me. He'll like this place the way I do. Nice and snug, like the mines. We probably never should have left 'em."

"Thank you, sir," Sadie said as he escorted them to the stairs. "I look forward to seeing you at the duke's party."

"Ah, the party. Ordered a new waistcoat and all. Basil says I need to meet someone. Do you two know a Minerva Townsend?"

Darby waited until they were back on the flagway and strolling in the direction of Grosvenor Square before giving voice to his mirth. "Jas and Minerva? Should we be warning Coop his mother is about to be courted by the king of coal?"

"That's quite amusing, and I'd probably be in stitches if it weren't for everything else. But first tell me how you knew Basil knew Mr. Hooper."

"I didn't. That is, not Jas precisely, but I did know Basil once took himself down a coal mine, so I put a few questions to him last evening. The rest was the Travers luck, I suppose."

"I think I prefer to call it fate, intervening on Marley's behalf."

"Whatever it was, we can thank Basil for his wanderlust. Did you know he and Vivien once bathed, *starkers*— the word Basil used—in the Blue Grotto on the Isle of Capri, or that he slept in the catacombs beneath Rome one night on a dare? We really need to boost them back onto their trail of adventures. The poor man is beginning to repeat himself."

"And to accomplish this, we've put our faith in Uncle Ralphie and a seven-year-old child?"

Darby smiled down at her. "It was your idea, as I recall."

"I never said it was a *good* idea."

"It's the only idea we have. Now, ask me the question you're burning to ask."

"When do we leave for Brighton?"

"To scoop up Sam Dobson, if he's still aboveground?"

"Do we have another choice? He's Marley's grandfather, Darby. We at least need to speak with him."

"I know, and your heart is already melting for the man you so lately, and wisely as it turns out, attempted to escape. We leave at first light, Sadie Grace. At first light…"

CHAPTER SIXTEEN

SADIE WAS CERTAIN their evening meal had been delicious, and only hoped the cook wasn't insulted that her plates had gone back to the kitchens nearly untouched.

Darby had noticed, of course, and had been sure to keep the conversation swirling around her, a feat easily accomplished just by asking the duke to tell everyone about the time he and the duchess had been very nearly shipwrecked, only to end up stopping at an island that had not been on their route.

As was always the case, His Grace was more than happy to launch into one of his stories.

While the ship was being repaired, he and Vivien had gone touring with one of the local chieftains, and eaten something he was fairly certain was snake cooked over an open fire, and Vivien protested it had been nothing of the kind. The friendly argument of snake versus frog had gone on until Clarice had informed them all that everyone knew you fried up a snake but boiled a frog, and if you were so silly as to toss a frog into a pot of boiling water it would hop right out again, but if you put it in a pot of cold water and then placed it over the fire, the silly things would just sit in there and let themselves be cooked.

Rigby had kissed her hand and said, "That's my Clary. She knows such interesting things."

"There's a lesson to be learned there, however," Darby had said, with Sadie grateful to hear about anything that wasn't a suicidal frog. "If tossed into something—for instance, a war—one does one's best to escape it. But if the supposed *reasons* for going to war are slowly fed to us, building one on the other, we may be just as prone to simply do nothing but sit idle until we're...well, until we're stewed."

"Don't think I'd care much for stewed frog, boy," the duke had said. "Now, prunes? Stewed prunes, they're just fine. In moderation."

Somehow Sadie had managed to survive the remainder of the meal. But once the ladies had retired to the drawing room, leaving the gentlemen to their brandy and cigars, she had excused herself and run up two flights of stairs to the nursery floor, closing the door behind her and pressing her back against it in an attempt to recapture her breath. And perhaps her sanity.

"He's here?"

"He is, Miss Hamilton," the governess said, her tone expressing her displeasure. "I do not approve of playacting, Miss Hamilton, nor of encouraging young minds to explore the fanciful."

"The duchess herself has approved this evening's entertainment, Miss Potterdam. In fact, she's quite looking forward to it."

The governess sniffed. "I'm not surprised. I am the daughter of a vicar who was the son of a vicar. I know the devil's work when I see it, and a most distasteful lack of propriety such as abounds in this strange household. You will have my notice in the morning."

Sadie pulled herself up to her full height. How dare the woman insult her friends!

"Thank you, Miss Potterdam. You've relieved me of the necessity to ask for it. However, if you expect to depart this den of iniquity tomorrow with a letter of reference to be clutched to your sanctimonious bosom, I suggest you hold your opinions similarly tight to yourself. You may leave the room now, as your presence is neither required nor desired."

Well, and wasn't that fun! I think I may have begun to know my new place.

Bridget, the young nursery maid assigned to Marley, made a sort of snorting noise from her spot in a corner of the room, and then quickly went about folding a blanket that had been draped over a chair back.

"Where are they, Bridget?" Sadie asked as the governess lifted two of her chins and scurried off to her quarters in the attic.

"Why, they'd be off in Miss Marley's bedchamber, Miss Sadie, sewing up a sheet I fetched the redhead from the cupboard. Hair as red as a flame, but he says he ain't from the auld sod. Told me to keep Miss Poutypuss clear and stay clear m'self, 'cause him and Miss Marley was practicin'."

Odd. Bridget hadn't mentioned the black beard and mustache. What was the sense of mentioning the hair and not the mustache? Perhaps Marley had convinced him to shave it.

Sadie looked to the closed door. "Very well, then I won't disturb them, either. Stitching up a sheet, did you say?"

"Yes, miss. Ripped it clear in half and then whipped out needle and thread from the bag he carried with him. Said he was about makin' a costume for Miss Marley.

You know what I'm thinkin', miss? I'm thinkin' he's about makin' her into a ghostie. Ain't that a treat?"

Not for the sheet, but I'm done worrying about sheets...

"It should all be jolly fun, yes. You know what to do when they're ready, don't you?"

"Oh, yes, miss. Sneak 'em down the back stairs and point 'em toward the street, so they can bang on the knocker."

"Yes, well…yes, then I suppose we're ready, aren't we?" Sadie asked, casting one last nervous look at the closed door between her and her niece. "I need to return to the drawing room. Thank you, Bridget."

She aimed an "all's ready" nod at Darby, who was standing behind a chair, one hand on its high back, the other holding a glass of wine. Clearly, this was where she was to sit for the…performance.

Although the drawing room was impressively large, the other occupants were all gathered around beneath the large, central chandelier. The duke and duchess holding hands as they sat side by side on one of the couches, Clarice tucked up on the floor beside Rigby, her pink silk skirts arranged around her, her cheek against her beloved's knee.

All that was missing from this scene of domestic bliss was Max, but as the spaniel couldn't be trusted not to immediately run to Marley and give the game away, he'd been locked up in the kitchens, probably enjoying the remainder of Sadie's loin chop.

The subject had changed in Sadie's absence, and they were now discussing the continuingly growing guest list for the upcoming celebration. Lord Alvanley had asked if he might bring along his good friend Beau Brummell, and the duchess had immediately accepted, since the Prince Regent had already declined his invitation via one of his secretaries.

"You sent off an invitation to Prinney, Vivien?" The duke shook his head. "Don't you remember me telling you he has no truck with Whigs since the king went all dotty again and the prince was made regent? I'm a Whig, or so my solicitor tells me I am, and so's Brummell. Not to say calling the prince fat didn't have a hand in their falling-out. So the Beau's coming, is he? We sent him a bird, you know, Gabe did, but he didn't take to it like the others."

"Not everyone wishes to walk about Mayfair with a bird on his shoulder, Basil," Darby said, stepping out from behind the chair. "With word of the man's increasing debts, we should probably be happy he didn't boil it for dinner. Now, I have a surprise for you, Your Grace."

The duke sat forward on the couch and clapped his hands. "A surprise? Oh, good. What is it? I love surprises."

Here we go, Sadie told herself, surreptitiously crossing her fingers in her lap.

"I know," Darby said kindly. "I thought to wait until your birthday celebration, but then I realized my small gift might be lost among so many wishing to honor you, and decided tonight is as good a time as any."

"Yes, yes. Good idea there, Darby. Splendid. What is it? Give it over. Isn't this exciting, Vivien?"

"Yes, my love. Now sit still and let Darby speak."

Sadie jumped in her seat as the sound of the knocker banging with the force of a giant hand, it would seem, reverberated through the drawing room. Had Norton ignored the knocker and taken a hammer to the door?

"Ah, that would be my surprise now. I've already left instructions downstairs that the person is to be escorted directly here."

Everyone turned toward the wide doorway.

The duke's butler marched into the room, shoulders back, his expression blank, to announce the new arrival.

"Your Graces, m'lords, ladies," he said, bowing. "Renowned on three continents, revered by kings and princes, feted from the steppes of Mother Russia to the vineyards of France, blessed with ancient secrets and the power to tell all, heal all, the most magnificent, resplendent, er…"

"Glorious." The prompt had come from the hallway.

The butler shot a dangerous look over his shoulder.

"…*glorious* Madame Royale." The butler rolled his eyes before ending flatly, "And Madame's assistant, Henry."

Madame? Sadie looked to Darby, who only shrugged.

"Oh, my, oh, my, oh, my!" the duke exclaimed, leaping to his feet to applaud as Madame Royale, swathed in what had to be a half dozen layers of skirts and colorful shawls swept into the room.

Oh, my, indeed.

He—she—had rings on her fingers and actual bells on her barefoot toes. Thin, colorful bracelets ran from each wrist to nearly her elbows. A belt made of golden coins hung at her waist and there were enough gold necklaces to completely cover her bare chest…and any chest hair that might be there.

But it was her hair that amazed Sadie. Red as a flame, yes, but released from its queue, to spring into a head completely covered in curls.

Her eyes were framed in blue, her cheeks and lips painted a rosy red.

She moved with grace, extending her hand to the duke, who bowed over it with the sincerity of an acolyte.

Oh, and Henry. *He* was dressed all in white, a gold braided sash about his waist, his head and face covered with a hood that exposed only his eyes. One of those eyes shot Sadie a wink. In his hands, Henry carried a square marble base with a glass ball the size of a melon perched on top of it.

Sadie watched as the duke escorted Madame to a chair, before bowing to her again and returning to his seat beside the duchess.

"The beard and mustache are gone," she whispered to Darby.

"As I've heard it said," he whispered back, "there's always a pony in there somewhere, if you look well enough through the pile of—disregard that, please, I believe I'm awestruck. Oh, and I hadn't thought of it until now, but men often took the part of ladies when performing in plays. I'm only wondering how he was able to find all he's wearing, especially in so short a time. I've often pondered what it could be that the man gets up to when I'm out."

"Yes, yes. But look at Marley. She's nearly ready to burst. And what's Nor—Madame, doing now?"

"Reading Vivien's palm," Darby said, straightening. "I fed Norton a few tidbits about everyone while I was dressing this evening, so this should go reasonably well."

The duchess was seated on a padded stool Rigby had placed in front of Madame, and she was intently watching as the fortune-teller traced the lines on her palm with one be-ringed finger.

A finger with red paint on its long nail.

Sadie silently agreed. Darby really should have a talk with his valet.

"Your Grace, my lovely woman," Madame was saying now in a high-pitched, singsonging voice. "You have led a most wonderful life, with much adventure still before you. I see health, and happiness, and deepest love. And camels."

"Basil! Did you hear that? Camels! That's a sign, isn't it? I'm sure it's a sign!"

"Let me try," Clarice said, raising her hand as if hopeful to be called on. "Let's hear what Madame sees for me."

"Ah," Madame said, holding Clarice's hand in both of hers, leaning close to squint at the lines in her palm. "I see a crossroads. No, a bridge. Yes, a bridge taking you from one life to another. Be not afraid, pretty one, but step boldly forward. You and your love will live to see your children's children look up in your faces."

"Thank you, Madame," Clarice said, her eyes bright with happy tears as she rejoined Rigby.

"I believe you're next, Sadie," Darby prompted evilly.

With him having fed Norton information on what to say?

"I think not, thank you, as I'd rather be surprised. But I do wonder what Madame has to say about you, Your Grace. Aren't we all anxious to hear about His Grace's future?"

"I'm of two minds about that, what with the curse and all. Could be sticky," Rigby whispered to Clarice, but being a man, his whisper carried farther than he'd supposed.

Madame gave a snap of her fingers and Henry took a step forward.

"A table for my ball," Madame commanded. "Quickly."

Rigby scrambled to do as Madame ordered, tossing a pair of porcelain statuettes to Clarice, one after the other and pocketing an oval candy dish, comfits and all, before carrying the denuded table over to plunk it down in front of Madame Royale.

Henry immediately placed the base and crystal ball at its very center.

"The words, Henry," Madame said, her arms outstretched, her eyes already closed.

"To see the future the past must be known," Marley said, her voice lowered, as she had done in imitation of her governess. "To Madame Royale, all mysteries are shown. Come shades of past deeds and tell your tale, so peace might find you and all will be wale."

"Wale? Didn't she mean *well*? Wale doesn't mean anything."

"Shh, Sadie Grace. It rhymes. Norton's a valet, not Will Shakespeare. Look at the duke and the others. They're entranced. Personally, I think he's doing very *wale*."

"You're not amusing." Then she smiled. "All right, I concede, Master Conniver. That was funny."

Sadie decided she'd been plunked down in a happy madhouse, fast becoming one with her fellow inmates… and she couldn't be happier and…and Miss Poutypuss be damned!

Madame Royale dropped her chin to her chest, and then began rolling her head up onto her shoulder, then back, then continuing around to her chest again before repeating the movement, moaning softly. "Yes…yes… I hear you… I understand…"

She shot her arms out so quickly even Sadie was taken aback, watching as Madame's hands unerringly came crashing down on the crystal ball. "Done!"

"Done? What's done?" Basil got to his feet. "What does she mean, *done*?"

"Sit down, dearest. I'm certain she'll tell us."

Madame Royale removed her hands from the crystal ball and Henry bowed before lifting it from the table and carrying it out into the hallway, returning with a small silver box she presented the fortune-teller, who didn't take it, but merely moved her ring-heavy hands over it three times, muttering something under her breath.

"Rather dragging it out, isn't he?" Darby whispered.

Norton opened his eyes, glaring at the apparently offending table until Rigby scrambled to remove it.

"There was a duke called One," Madame intoned heavily, her hands still hovering over the silver box. "He took the land and told the Gypsies they must go, never to return, as they had returned for many years. Greedy man. The Gypsy queen cursed him, vowed that he and all his male seed would die before their sixtieth birthdays, a fishbone magically appearing in their gullets. The curse would remain until the Gypsies were invited to return."

Rigby nodded sagely. "That explains the *erp*."

"I'll never eat fish again," Clarice added sincerely, a hand to her throat.

Darby had been right. Their friends' reactions were so much better than if they'd been let in on the secret. *Perhaps I'll tell Clarice one day. And perhaps I won't…*

"But…but Madame Royale," the duke said nervously.

"What do I do? I don't *know* any Gypsies. Darby? Rigby? Where does one locate Gypsies?"

"Yes, Darby," Sadie all but cooed, blinking up at him, as she hadn't been privy to this information before Norton had been sent off with Marley and the maid. "Pray tell, where, oh, where do we find Gypsies before the duke's sixtieth birthday?"

"Be patient, Sadie Grace. I'm a man blessed with a highly inventive mind," he whispered, at the same time lightly running a finger down the side of her throat… which distracted her from the matter at hand more than she would have previously thought possible.

"Stand before me, Basil Sinclair."

"Me? Yes, yes, here I come," the duke said, scrambling to his feet.

Madame Norton—er, Royale rather—waggled her fingers over the silver box. "Gypsy queen, your voice has been heard. The land is now open for your return. I, the most renowned on three continents, revered by kings and princes, feted from the steppes of Mother Russia to the vineyards of France, blessed with ancient secrets and the power to tell all, heal all, the most magnificent, resplendent, glorious Madame Royale, demand you lift the curse from this good man. *Curse—begone!*"

Henry opened the lid of the silver box, reached inside and tossed a handful of silvery glitter in Basil's direction. Because of her small stature, the glitter landed within the area of His Grace's ample stomach.

But Madame Royale wasn't done, and neither was Henry.

"Begone!"

Another shower of silvery glitter.

And yet a third time: *"Begone!"*

Thwack, one last shower, this one delivered as Henry went up on his tippytoes and the glitter smacked the duke square in the face.

"It is done," Madame said, getting to her feet, lifting one of her many colored shawls and tossing one end over her shoulder. "M'lords, miladies, my work here also is done. Henry!"

The lid of the silver box snapped shut. Henry followed Madame out of the drawing room, but only after turning back to the company and giving them a small wave.

"Oh, good Lord," Sadie said, burying her head in her hands.

CHAPTER SEVENTEEN

EVEN THE BEST-LAID plans of mice and men didn't always work out exactly as planned.

Darby had been surprised by Jasper Hooper's revelations; there was no question about that. He hadn't known exactly what he'd wanted to hear, but to think his ward, his sweet Marley, could be the object of a plot to remove her from any line of inheritance had set off an anger inside him the intensity of which amazed even him.

He'd been to war; he'd seen his share of enemies. But to wish a child dead? No. He needed to find and speak with Sam Dobson before he'd believe that.

Except that he already believed it.

Meeting privately with Sadie last night, however, whisking her away on the pretext of a late party and instead taking her back to Park Lane, had been a casualty of that belief, as her total concentration was now centered on getting to Sam Dobson. A romantic dalliance was the farthest thing from her mind, and he could understand that.

He didn't like it, but he could understand it.

My, what a mature fellow you're turning out to be, Darby Travers...

At least his hastily devised plan to ease Basil's mind had come off *wale*. Basil's many travels, and the sights and rites and such that he'd seen, had sparked the idea in Darby, telling him the duke would be at least open to the notion of a curse and a way to banish it.

The man had been positively giddy, requesting that a willing Clarice scoop up "that glittery magic stuff" from the floor so that he could toss some of it over his head, just to make certain all of him was now "uncursed."

Another result of the evening, for good or ill, had been returning to Park Lane to confront Norton, and ask him a few pertinent questions while the man packed his employer a small traveling bag. He probably should have asked those questions earlier, but he'd been too happy to find an at least marginally proficient and temporary valet for the length of the Little Season.

Norton, it seemed, had more than occasionally dabbled in acting. He was a dedicated *thespian*.

An underappreciated thespian, hence his occasional stints as a valet or gentleman's gentleman. After all, even thespians have stomachs. He met whenever he could with kindred spirits at the Crown and Cock in Piccadilly, all of them "wintering" in London and subsisting as best they could via myriad varied endeavors while awaiting the chance to join with other traveling players and be off on the road again come spring.

Norton had run lickety-split to the Crown and Cock that afternoon, where his friends helped kit him out with the paste jewels and draperies that had changed him into Madame Royale, and even given him hints on how to best play the role.

This had necessitated the shaving of his beard and mustache, a sacrifice he'd made in the name of his art, but he would grow both again.

"One never knows when one might come in handy. Cover the hair, or shave off the beard, and I can play most any role, my lord, from lady of the manor to the Sultan of Persia. Madame Royale cost me the beard, but it was a small price to pay for the opportunity to perform before a duke. I'm the envy of all at the Crown and Cock."

Darby said he was happy for the man, and turned in, knowing he'd had a busy day, with another full day stretching out before him.

Unbelievably, he slept quite well.

He was up and dressed before sunrise, penning a note to his friend Gabe, apprising him of the lifted curse, and another to Coop, only to tease him about the duke's plan to play at matchmaker between Minerva and the king of coal.

That would teach them both to leave him here with only Rigby to assist him in riding herd on the duke and duchess.

By six, his matched chestnuts were standing ready in their traces and his hooded curricle awaited him as he bounded down the steps clad in tan buckskins, a hacking jacket, his many-caped great coat, his curly brimmed beaver and riding gloves, easily catching the reins his yawning tiger tossed him.

He expected Sadie to be waiting for him when he arrived in Grosvenor Square, and he wasn't disappointed. She wore a fashionable woolen cloak, a matching green velvet bonnet and apparently Clarice had loaned her the ermine muff. With the pair of heavy carriage blankets already folded on the seat, wrapped hot bricks to rest her half boots on and the top pulled up on the curricle, she should be tolerably comfortable. Not toasty, but she was made of stern stuff, and speed was of the essence.

The tiger strapped her small portmanteau beside Darby's, and they were off.

As it was, employing the chestnuts for the first twenty miles, and then changing horses at posting inns every ten miles after that, and stopping only for luncheon, it would still be past two before they caught their first sight of Prinney's minarets.

They wouldn't be able to muster anything in the way of speed until they'd reached the outskirts of London, so Darby took this time to ask about Marley.

"Marley? Please, she is now Henry, or so she insisted last night as we attempted, without much success, to stop her from running in circles around the nursery, spouting that same *'Begone!'* nonsense Norton had her parroting in the drawing room. She also tossed *magic* glitter on everything from the rocking horse to poor Bridget, when she didn't move out of the way in time."

Darby laughed. "Have we lost her to the stage, do you think?"

"I sincerely hope not, although she was quite good, wasn't she? I don't think His Grace suspected a thing. When I was at last able to settle Marley and returned to the drawing room, it was to walk in on a lively discussion of the plans for his celebration. He wants pipers now, to precede him into the ballroom, and he and Vivien will be visiting an establishment they referred to as Gunter's today to place orders for all sorts of fanciful confections, as well as ice sculptures of Princess the cockatoo for the supper room. Turbot, you will be unsurprised to learn, has been removed from the menu."

"I would have been disappointed if it hadn't," Darby said as he neatly avoided a wagon holding a large mound of cabbages probably meant for Covent Garden Market. "Once we're free of the city, I plan to spring the horses for a bit, if that's all right with you."

"If we could sprinkle glitter over the horses and they could magically *fly* us to Brighton it would be all right with me," she told him. "In the meantime, I've asked Clarice to be certain she and Rigby both accompany Marley if she is to go outdoors, and then only as far as taking the air in the square, to exercise Max and Goody. I'd like to believe the Odlings have no idea where she is, but they did find us in Dibden, didn't they? They're probably paying their own robin redbreasts to hunt her down again. I really should have told you all of this sooner, but I truly believed she was safe once she was in London with you."

Darby reached over to squeeze her hand. "She's safe, Sadie. And we're about to make her safer, remember? Are you ready? The roadway looks clear enough ahead, and my cattle have had enough of this slow pace."

"I'm ready. Rigby's already told me you're an outstanding whipster, as did you, now that I think of it. Although I suppose anyone would be an improvement over that horrible little man who held the reins on the public coach. One of the outside passengers was actually bumped off at one point and we had to wait while his friend went after him, to dust him off and bring him back. He'd paid, you see, so the coachie had no choice but to stop."

"I promise, if my tiger is bumped off, I will personally go back and get him." He raised his voice and called out jovially, "Robinson? Miss Hamilton is up here fretting, and wishes for you to hang tight to the bar, as I'm about to spring 'em."

"You're impossible."

"Yes, I know. I've actually begun to look on that as an expression of endearment. 'Come kiss me, you impossible man.'"

Sadie rolled her eyes, and then grabbed for the strap as he flicked the reins and the chestnuts sprang forward.

Darby was pleased with their progress, and when they stopped for a second change of horses and some luncheon, was even able to tell his tiger to fold back the hood, as the sun was pleasantly warm.

It was quick work arranging a retiring room for Sadie and a private dining room, and he was sipping from a glass of moderately tolerable wine when she was ushered into the room, her nose delightfully shiny thanks to a recent encounter with soap and water, and her gown had been freshly brushed free of road dust.

"Don't you look fine, wife," he said, getting to his feet and walking around the table to kiss her hand.

"Don't you *wife* me," she whispered to him as the innkeeper himself carried in their luncheon platters and set them on the table before bowing himself out again. "When the housemaid sent to assist me addressed me as *my lady*, I had to look about to see if someone else had come into the room. Was that really necessary? You could have warned me."

"I know," he said, pulling back a chair, inviting her to sit down. "I suppose I didn't have to do it, but I do have my reputation to maintain."

"*Your* reputation? It was my reputation you were— oh, all right." She reached for a dangerous-looking knife and attacked the crusty loaf with it. "I concede the point. I have no maid with me, to satisfy the proprieties. But pray tell, my lord, where *do* you put a chaperone when riding through the countryside in a curricle? Do you strap her to the back of the equipage with the luggage?"

"Exactly. Like a stag brought down during a hunt." He watched, amused, as Sadie next set her sights on the ham. "Did the ham do something to annoy you, Sadie Grace?" he then asked, quickly securing a slice with his fork and tossing it onto his plate.

She looked at what she'd been doing, and all but slammed down the cutlery.

The expression on her beautiful face did not bode well for him, perhaps for any man.

"I have been carving ham for all of my life. I've done everything but butcher the pig and render the fat. But I suppose now the slicing of the ham is to be left to you? The way everything seems to be left to you? I'm not silly enough to lie and tell you I want to go back to the life I have so lately escaped, but nor do I appreciate being seen as someone suddenly rendered incapable of crossing the street on her own. A maid for this, a chaperone for that. I'm not even allowed to put up my own shoes in the cupboard!"

"Your shoes? So this has to do with more than I initially thought. You've got an entire budget of woes to expound on, don't you?"

"I suppose I do, and if that seems ungrateful I'm certain it is, but I have to say it. I'm a grown woman, Darby. I have a mind, and yet I often feel a spectator of my own life these past days. Everything's happening so quickly."

"There is that, yes. Things. Happening quickly."

Lord, she was gorgeous when she was angry...and he should be drawn and quartered for thinking such a thing.

"I'm not finished. I'll admit I rather enjoyed being in charge while John was off at war, and it wasn't easy for me to step back when he returned, pretend I had no real mind of my own. And then there you were—there was everyone, and all of them feeling in charge of me, of Marley. All with the best of intentions, and I thank them for it, truly I do."

"They all adore you both."

"As we adore them. But *you*? When it comes to managing my life for me, you, my lord, carry off the prize. 'We're going to London, Sadie. Here is where you will live, Sadie. This is what you will wear, Sadie. Oh, look, Sadie, I've brought my ward a puppy, without so much as asking if puppies might make her sneeze. We will be married, Sadie. Just follow my lead, Sadie. Come lie with me, Sadie.'"

She stopped then, rather abruptly, as if realizing what she'd just said.

Darby got to his feet and moved around the table, to go down on one knee beside her chair. "You're right, and I'm sorry. If I could go back and begin again, I'd do things differently, I swear."

She kept her chin high, facing forward. "How?"

She had him there. He really couldn't change much leading up to the proposal. And to tell her that he was sorry that he'd taken her to his bed? He'd made his mistakes, yes, but he wasn't a total idiot!

"I don't know. I suppose I should have conferred with you more, asked your opinion."

Now she looked at him. "You *suppose*?"

He held up his hands as if to be prepared to defend himself. "I *know* I should have asked your opinion. I should have told you where I was taking you before we set foot in Grosvenor Square instead of springing Vivien and the others on you. Although I doubt you would have believed a word I said about them. I should have conferred with you before landing a puppy in your lap when you were more used to making decisions that affect Marley. I should have prepared you better before announcing our betrothal to everyone. It is my fault entirely that I didn't share Jasper Hooper's name with you before taking you to his residence."

"And…?"

She wasn't about to let go, was she?

"And I should have taken my time courting you, advancing by inches rather than giant steps. But I'm not going to apologize for that, Sadie Grace. It may have been wrong, but it was also very, very right, which you'd admit yourself if I hadn't given you time to have second thoughts last night. That is what's happened, isn't it? Sadie?"

She reached for the small butter pot and began buttering the slice of bread on her plate.

"Sadie, this is a stone floor, and it's not only uncomfortable on my knee, but cold into the bargain. Are you going to answer me?"

"I think I forgive you," she said, ripping the slice in half, and then licking a dab of butter from her fingertip.

"Are you certain?" He was doing his best not to smile.

"Probably. As long as you promise to consult with me before doing anything else that affects either Marley or myself. That way, the next time a maid at a country inn addresses me as *my lady*, I won't turn to her with an expression akin to that of a stunned ox, and ask *who*?"

Darby got to his feet, pretending he'd completed the feat only by dint of much effort, and bent down to kiss the top of her head before returning to his chair. "Do I have your kind permission to refer to you as my lady wife once we reach Brighton and secure lodgings for the night in one of the new hotels?"

"Must you?"

"If it will make you feel more comfortable when I ask that our baggage be carried upstairs to a suite for the two of us, yes. Or would you rather I sneaked down the hallway after midnight, to scratch at your door, begging entrance?"

"There is a third option," Sadie said, stabbing at a slice of ham. "You could ask one of the staff if you might borrow a book of sermons to help lull you to sleep."

He could hear the teasing in her voice.

"And here I thought we were getting along so swimmingly."

"Yes, I imagine you did. Poor Lord Nailbourne."

"Sadie Grace, I was down on my knee when I said I was sorry. Doesn't that count for anything?"

"There was that, wasn't there. Very well, I'll think about it, and give you my answer when we arrive in Brighton. Goodness, isn't this ham delicious? I didn't realize the drive would give me such an appetite. Really, try the ham."

"Might as well," Darby said, lifting a bite to his mouth. "It's either that or step out behind the inn and fall on my sword."

Sadie giggled.

She'd had her say, and now she felt in control of herself again, and his equal. Strangely, he didn't mind that at all. He might even glory in the notion.

"I have to ask you," he said as they continued their meal. "That day in the coach, driving in from the cottage. What did Norton tell Marley about the reason behind the red hair and painted mustache and beard? Last night he informed me that he is a true traveling thespian—his words, not mine—and that he employs both in his various roles. But if you knew he was a traveling player, you never told me."

"I never told you that because he never said anything of the kind until he mentioned it yesterday in the park.

He regaled Marley with a rather long, convoluted tale about his travels through the wilds of India with a maharaja, and their strange encounter with a redheaded snake that—"

Darby held up his fork, motioning for her to stop. "I withdraw the question. Moreover, I regret the question."

"Don't worry that Marley believed him. She just thinks he's wonderfully silly."

"That wouldn't quite be my description. But since we're *discussing* things now, my soon-to-be wife, what do you say to the notion that, come the spring, we provide Norton and his thespian compatriots with a fully equipped traveling wagon and send them out into the countryside to edify the masses?"

"Why, I believe I'd say *huzzah* to that, my soon-to-be husband. I also would not be opposed to having him visit Marley when he is able, if you're of the same mind."

"Agreed. That was simple enough. I believe I can become used to this new, shared responsibility. Now, as to our accommodations tonight in Brighton?"

"Ah, you see, my lord, not every decision can be shared, and I do believe this one is mine, although I will say I'm feeling…much in charity with you at the moment. More ham?"

The remainder of the journey to Brighton was spent *mutually* planning what they'd do once they'd located Sam Dobson, and it was only when Darby entered the lobby of the hotel he'd chosen after giving instructions to his tiger about the stabling of the horses that he was greeted by a bowing servant who said, "Lady Nailbourne awaits you in your suite, my lord. If you'll step this way…"

Step? Darby was hard-pressed not to *skip*!

CHAPTER EIGHTEEN

SADIE STOOD AT the windows overlooking the street, and the sight of the Prince Regent's Pavilion.

She'd expected more, or perhaps less.

"Fancy meeting you here, Miss Hamilton," Darby drawled from behind her.

She'd heard him enter the large drawing room, but she'd decided that he would come to her, and not the other way around. She'd already come more than halfway, hadn't she?

And why was she keeping score? For two people who had so recently been…intimate, there remained a noticeable *divide* between them. It seemed so strange, to be so near, physically and even as declared friends, and yet still so far apart.

She could verbally spar with him, laugh with him, even confide in him, but she still couldn't be completely at ease with him. There were times she had to search for topics in order to avoid what might be an awkward silence, at least on her part. There were times she didn't know if he was serious or joking. She was comfortable with him on many levels, yes, but she wasn't comfortable being with him. She couldn't just be, not when she still had to concentrate on *being*.

She couldn't explain what she felt, not even to herself. Something remained between them, something she couldn't sense or touch. It was *there*, and it shouldn't be. An invisible barrier that needed to come down. And since she'd told him her innermost secrets, perhaps the barrier was on his side. Nobody was as happy as Darby appeared to be, so satisfied with life and his place in it. She knew there was more to him, but even when she thought he was serious, he somehow managed to turn that moment into a joke of sorts, often directed at himself. Was that who he was, or was he still keeping a part of himself from her, perhaps from everyone, even his closest friends?

Or could she simply be a silly female looking for a declaration of love? Would those three words bridge the invisible gap, take down that last wall? It seemed ludicrous. After all, they were only words. Deeds had to count for something.

So now, once again, she searched for something to say. Prinney's palace seemed a safe enough topic.

"I didn't realize the palace wasn't a fully accomplished fact. I thought His Royal Highness has been visiting Brighton for many years."

He joined her at the window.

"He has, which is why we're standing in this grand new hotel, and why you'll see several new buildings as we head to Sam Dobson's place of residence. Society goes where Prinney goes. He began with a small cottage, but then realized it didn't suit his idea of a royal residence. He's been adding to it ever since, both in land and additions, hence the scaffolding and swarms of busy ants crawling all over the structure. But some of it is complete. What do you think of the dome? Sixty feet high if it's a foot, and miraculously standing without incident, which many vowed it would not thanks to the glass roof."

"I think it's amazingly delicate for all its size, nearly fairylike. So that's where His Royal Highness resides now when he's here?"

Darby laughed. "No, Sadie, that large dome rises above the royal stables. His horses are housed there, at a cost to the crown of more than fifty thousand pounds. God only knows what the rest will look like, or cost, before he's done. You can already see the minarets that are completed, with many more of different heights and shapes still in progress."

She turned to him in disgust, her earlier thoughts flown to the winds. "Fifty thousand pounds? Many of our soldiers are barely existing, consigned to the streets, and his horses live in *that*? Fifty thousand pounds?"

"What would you do with fifty thousand pounds, Sadie Grace? Granted, that's a lot of money, but certainly not enough to fix a broken world."

"No, it wouldn't." Sadie gave the question serious thought, because his had been a serious question, and then sighed. "It's not quite so easy, is it?"

"Definitely beyond the power of sprinkled magic glitter and a few *begone*s, yes. I could give away my entire fortune, and the gesture would barely make a splash in the ocean of wrongs plaguing society."

"You're right, of course," Sadie said, pulling the drapes shut over the sight of the enormous cupola, although nothing could block out the sounds of a hundred hammers. "There's so much wrong with this world, Darby, so much that's larger than all of us and makes our own worries seem small and petty. I feel completely *powerless*, and I can't begin to tell you how frustrating that is to me."

"I think I have some idea how you feel. My shame is that there are good men wandering the streets out there, men I led into battle, men who willingly followed me into harm's way, ready to die for king and country. Prinney is a fool, and probably shouldn't be expected to behave as anything more than a fool. But damn it, where is my excuse for turning a blind eye to those men who gave so much? And no," he said, smiling weakly, "that was not intended as a pun. I'm serious, Sadie. And not to be trite about it, you've made me see more with one eye than I ever did with two. I'm humbled, as well as ashamed."

"I don't know what to say to that," Sadie told him honestly. "I never meant to make you feel that way."

"It was time someone did. Tossing a coin to a beggar on the street is not sufficient. Returning soldiers, be they able to work or not, are never evicted from my estates, and their widows are not booted out of their homes. Taking care of mine own, that's one of the duties of a land-owner, a viscount. I've allowed myself to be soothed into thinking it was enough."

"It is more than many have done," Sadie told him, laying a hand on his arm.

"Is it? I have a seat in the House of Lords, you know. A seat I rarely occupy, a seat I've never risen from except to add an occasional halfhearted, *'Here, here!'* to what someone else has said. I've decided it's time for me to make my maiden speech, and probably lose a few friends in the process. It's time the Crown paid more than Prinney's outrageous debts."

"Are you certain you want to do that? I wouldn't care to think I…I goaded you into anything."

Now Darby did smile. "Madam, I pride myself in never being goaded into anything. All right, save for the night Gabe threatened to tell everyone I was a coward if I didn't steal the headmaster's top hat and stick it on the head of the dry grocer's horse. I had to cut a pair of holes in it, you understand, to fit over the nag's ears. Both of us were sent down for the remainder of the term, by the way. Rather than return to the cottage and face Camy, I traveled home with Gabe. Vivien and Basil were there, so the only lecture we received was one from Basil on how not to get caught when doing something one shouldn't do where one shouldn't be doing it. I'll spare you the examples he cited. Suffice it to say, much of my early education in certain subjects came by way of Basil and Vivien."

By this time Sadie had collapsed in giggles on one of the comfortably overstuffed couches. Definitely there were parts of Darby she would never wish to see change. "You're never serious for long, are you? I don't think you can help yourself."

"Probably not. I've never really thought about it." There was a knock at the door. "Ah, and that should be heralding the arrival of hot water for our baths. You have an hour, Sadie, and then we go in search of Sam Dobson. Here's a thought. We could save time by sharing a tub."

"I'm ignoring that," she said as a half dozen servants carrying pails of hot water entered the large room, half of them heading for the bedchamber to the right, the others to the bedchamber on the left.

Behind them came a manservant and a maid in a crisp white apron and cap, the maid curtsying before saying, "My name is Bettyann. If you'll be so kind as to follow me, my lady?"

"Yes, thank you." A bath and clean clothing sounded splendid after their long, dusty drive. Although it did give her stomach a small turn as she watched Darby heading off behind the manservant, already stripping off his neck cloth and actually giving it a quick wave above his head. She highly doubted he was employing it as a white flag of surrender.

Honestly. That man.

In only a few minutes, he would be naked in his tub and she would be similarly devoid of clothing in her own, with only thirty feet or less and two closed doors between them.

It was enough to give an unmarried woman pause—or, unwisely, another bout of the giggles. As Lady Nailbourne, however, she could only lift her chin and follow after the maid while at the same time attempting to follow Darby's lead—by trying not to be serious *all the time*.

The door had barely closed behind the servants and their now-empty pails before Sadie began stripping out of her gown as Bettyann set out soap and towels, as well as a lovely white robe that would cover a person head to toe. Well, most people, as Sadie felt certain the hem would only fall somewhere above her ankles.

A random thought entered her head: with both of them so tall, would their children all be tall, as well? This was followed by a panicked thought: could she already be carrying Darby's child? And if not yet, perhaps by the end of the day?

Now is not the time for such thoughts, she told herself, *even if you do understand the reproductive process. You're still too new at the first part of it, even as you seek to broaden your education.*

"I can manage my bath on my own, Bettyann," she said nervously, still quickly working at her buttons. "If you'd just see if the yellow gown and its blue redingote are reasonably free of wrinkles—I imagine they'll do with just a good shaking out—you may return to your other duties."

The maid made short work out of locating the items in Sadie's small portmanteau. "I'll take these right off downstairs and give them a good pressing. But, my lady—I'm to assist you in your bath, as well."

Sadie could hear Clarice's warnings about *place* ringing in her ears. "And I'm certain you would do so admirably. However, His Lordship has indicated that he will most probably be joining me shortly."

The maid cocked her head and looked at Sadie owlishly.

Sadie grasped at the only straw she could think of: "We...we're very recently married."

"But I—oh. Yes, my lady," Bettyann said, her brown eyes growing wide. "I'll be taking myself off right this minute, and then return these to the sitting room so as not to...to disturb my lord, that is."

She curtsied her way out of the room, and then probably ran all the way back to the kitchens to report on the randy couple occupying one of the suites and bound to be splashing tub water all over the carpets for her to sop up later.

Oh, that man! He could embarrass her even when he wasn't present.

Sadie stepped into the tub, gritting her teeth as she settled into the hot water. She reached for the soap and a cloth, and made quick work out of soaping and rinsing herself. She'd had long practice at bathing in two minutes or less, thanks to both the small, uncomfortable tub at the infirmary and the fact that she was forced to bathe in the kitchens, in front of the only fireplace they'd ever kept fully stoked in the wintertime.

For all her haste, she was only just pulling tight the sash of the toweling robe when she heard the *snick* of the latch being depressed, and turned about to see Darby standing there, clad in a similar robe and, clearly, nothing else save for the fairly wicked smile on his face.

Well, at least this time there would be fewer "practical matters that must be addressed." *It's also possible I've been spending too much time around Vivien and Clarice...*

"And here I'd hoped to arrive in time to help wash your back. What did you do with Bettyann? Toss her out the nearest window?"

Sadie clasped the lapels of the robe close against her breasts. "She's very young. I didn't feel I needed to add to her education."

"She could probably add to yours," he countered amicably, advancing on Sadie even as she retreated, never taking her eyes off him. "You look lovely, Sadie. Fresh, and dare I say *dewy*, rosy warm from your bath, a few enticing damp golden tendrils caressing that long, slim throat."

He put out his hand and touched the side of that throat, employing his fingertips to trace small circles against the sensitive skin just behind her ear. "You like that. I've noticed."

She closed her eyes as she allowed her head to tip slightly, giving him more access, sighing as he bent to press a kiss against her skin, lightly suck at her earlobe before running the tip of his tongue down the side of her throat. New, yet amazingly already familiar feelings dared to all but snatch her breath away.

"Do...do we really have time for this?"

"For what, Sadie Grace? Why, whatever do you have in mind?"

"Me? It wasn't me—I—who suggested we bathe together."

"Oh, you took that as an invitation to seduction, did you?" he teased, his hands now on her shoulders as he employed his thumbs to lightly knead at the skin below her collarbones.

"You...you came in here without knocking, wearing nothing beneath that robe."

"Only to find you similarly clad, or should I say similarly *en déshabille*. Should we call that a happy coincidence?"

He was slowly driving her insane, and he knew it. She'd already told him that she was more than ready to let someone else take the lead after so many years of having to make every decision on her own. And she certainly couldn't have taken the lead the other day at the cottage, because she had no idea where she was going, now did she?

But that was then, and this was now.

She wasn't the same person now as she had been then. That wasn't precisely his *fault*, but she felt it only fair to warn him.

Without answering his outrageous question, Sadie reached up and grabbed the lapels of his robe and pulled them out and down, rather *capturing* his upper arms while leaving his chest bare.

His voice was light and teasing. "Why, Sadie Grace, what *are* you thinking?"

"No more thinking," she told him. "Isn't that what you said? There comes a time when no more thinking is necessary. Or talking." With that, she reached up on tiptoe and proceeded to kiss him with all the pent-up anticipation brought on by his teasing touch.

He moved hands onto her buttocks and slid his thigh between her legs, pulling her close, grinding against her as she felt her entire body melt like heated wax, made entirely conformable to every part of him, the heat and strength of him.

The next thing she knew he had caught at her weakened knees, scooping her up high against his chest, their mouths still melded together, and carried her to the bed.

"Get rid of those pillows and pull down the covers," he said against her mouth, bending so that she could reach out and do what he said. The next thing she knew she was lying on the sweet-smelling sheets and her sash was open and he was kissing her.

Kissing her, touching her, driving her mad as he'd done the first time, but this time he was more sure in his touch, apparently knowing just what moved her, caused her breath to catch in her throat, painted multicolored rainbows behind her eyelids.

It was her turn to learn him.

She reached down to grasp his wrist, and pushed one bent leg against the mattress as she levered him over onto his back, ending lying half across his chest.

Now it was her hands that moved, that stroked, that found and captured, her mouth that trailed kisses, her tongue that tasted and teased.

Give to me, as I gave to you. Give me all of you, not just the parts you want the world to see. Break down

the barriers, Darby, let yourself free, make us both free.
Trust me. Trust me. Let it go. Let it all go...

Did she only think the words? Or did she say them?
She didn't know, would never know.

She only knew she was on her back again and he was
over her, his arms braced as he slid inside her, deep inside her, and began to move.

Sadie clasped her hands around his forearms as he
looked down on her, as she lifted herself to him, watching as he seemed to struggle for control, his chest heaving, his every muscle straining. She raised her legs,
lifting them up and onto his back, holding tight so that
he could move inside her but couldn't leave her. Never
leave her, never leave her...because she was with him,
joined to him, and they would be one, because the time
was past for them to be two.

Now, Darby. If not now, what are we doing?

"Sadie. Oh, God... Sadie..."

CHAPTER NINETEEN

DARBY KNEW HE would have to think long and hard to remember another time in his life that he had been left speechless, or as nearly so as to feel he wouldn't be quite coherent if he did say something.

Darby Travers, speechless, with not a single quip or even a self-deprecating joke meant to put everyone at their ease—perhaps including himself? He'd record this extraordinary event in his diary, if he kept one.

And there it was again. Even inside his own mind, he refused to remain serious for long. *If he kept a diary, which he didn't.* Not any of his best work, but still, he was right there again, attempting to make light of the serious.

Because what had happened a few minutes ago between he and Sadie had been deadly serious. She'd all but ripped his heart out with her impassioned, almost sorrowful words as he'd taken her to the brink. Had she even realized what she'd said to him, how she'd pleaded with him...how she'd succeeded in forcing fully open a partially closed door deep inside him for the first time in years, decades, allowing all of his past out in a single moment, taking all the bits and snatches that haunted him and putting them on a plate in front of him, daring him to consume it—face it all—at one time?

He held her as she slept against his shoulder, her arm

laid across his chest, recovering from their long ride through the countryside, no doubt, but also from her lovemaking, his unexpected loss of control as he plunged into her, calling out her name as the two of them melded together, becoming one. Truly becoming one...

She stirred in his arms as a shaft of sunlight he'd been watching make its way across the bed finally reached their faces, causing him to blink.

"Is it morning?" she asked him as she snuggled closer, burying her face against his chest. "Make it go away."

"Normally, your wish would be my command, but I'm afraid turning off the sun is beyond even my extensive abilities. It's not morning, Sadie Grace, but late afternoon, and we need to seek out Sam Dobson, remember?"

"Oh, my God!" She pushed herself up, nearly knocking the breath out of him as she used her right hand and his stomach as her launching point. "How did you...why did you let me sleep?"

He was already out of the bed and reaching for his robe. "Because you were exhausted? Because we arrived in Brighton too late for a morning call and too early for an evening visit? Because I could have happily held you forever, your long, utterly wonderful body snuggled warmly against mine?" He pulled the sash on the robe around his body and tied it. "Yes, I think it's that last one."

"You're imposs—no, you already know that. We have to get dressed. My hair is probably in a wretched tangle—"

"Your hair looks beautiful in a tangle," he interrupted as he planted a kiss on her cheek on his way back to his own room. "We're still too early to bang on Dobson's door, so I'll ring for some small snack for us and meet you in the other room in ten minutes." When he opened the door, she was right on his heels, tying her own robe shut. "Why are you following me?"

"Because my gown is in this room," she said, gathering up the garment. "I don't fully know where the rest of me is, so yes, some tea would be welcome. I'm a long way from awake."

"Don't worry, Sadie, I'll soon take care of that."

She rolled her eyes. "Darby, we don't have time for—"

"My stars, woman, is that all you can think about? I've created a monster."

He winced in exaggeration as the door to her bedchamber shut with a slam, and then smiled. At least she was fully awake now, and remembering how maddening he could be.

He'd have to ease himself into telling her what she needed to know, somehow sensing she hadn't ever seen all of him. But how? Perhaps because she'd been harboring a quite large secret these past days, she could recognize the signs of others who weren't entirely forthcoming.

All he could conclude was that it all went back to their first, disastrous meeting, when he'd looked into those magnificent eyes of hers and had felt his world tilt beneath his feet. Had he known even then that she was the one? The one who held the key that would finally help him close and lock the heavy door to his past and take him to a new and better future?

He heard the servant's knock as he was just finishing tying his neck cloth in a faultless Waterfall—one of his lesser talents, but a useful one at the moment. He spared a moment to smile at the memory of his friend Coop fumbling with his third attempt at a simple knot as he told his friend he'd become the target of a black-mailer. Coop had triumphed, as he always did, but only with the blackmailer. It had been left to Darby to tie the man's neck cloth that day. Ah, those who can keep their heads in any situation...*probably had more experience with fooling others into thinking they're more in control than they really are...*

"I thought I heard a knock," Sadie said a few minutes later as she entered the sitting room, closing the bedchamber door behind her.

"That was more than ten minutes, Sadie Grace," Darby pointed out as he waved her to the couch placed behind a low round table that now held their refreshments. "Don't tell me you stopped to make up the bed in order to spare Bettyann's blushes."

"I admit it was difficult, but I restrained myself. Remember, I've spent my entire life picking up after myself because nobody else would if I didn't, so I have to slowly adjust to being slovenly. I suppose it just came to you naturally?" she jabbed back at him as she sat down beside him. "You've already poured the tea? Thank you."

"Ouch...and you're welcome. Sadie, do you mind if I tell you something?"

She looked at him curiously over the rim of her tea-cup. "I suppose not."

"It's something you do in bed." Still easing into it... giving himself a chance to change his mind.

She put down the cup. "Oh, Lord. I snore, don't I? I've always wondered."

He reached over and took her hand. "No, Sadie, you don't snore, and I wasn't referring to sleeping in bed, but to another activity that takes place there, at least for the most part. You talk."

She pulled her hand free. "I—I *talk*? So I didn't just imagine it? I actually *said* those— Darby, I'm so, *so* sorry."

"No," he said quickly. "Never sorry. God, no. But now it's my time to talk, and well overdue. Twenty years overdue, some would say."

She raised her hand and laid it on his, which was when he realized he'd been rubbing at his temple, the headache pounding on the door of his skull, demanding entrance.

"Let me help you," she said. Before he could say it wasn't necessary, she'd gotten up and walked around the table, to come kneel behind him, reaching for the ties to his patch. "It only gets in the way," she told him, allowing the patch to drop into his lap. "Face away from me. Sometimes talking is easier when you don't have to look at the person."

"I'm not the only impossible person in this room, Sadie Grace," he told her, but then gave in and did what she'd instructed. "Have you figured it out yet?"

"That the headaches aren't caused by your wound? Yes, I believe I have. You've had them for a long time, haven't you?"

It was now or never. "Since I was about ten or eleven, yes. When I began to remember. It took years until I could piece it all together. The nightmares, the headaches…"

She moved her hands down onto his shoulders and began kneading at them.

"You've never told Gabe or the others, have you? Nobody knows. Are you certain you're ready to tell me?"

"They've all made vague guesses of an…an unhappy childhood. But no, I've never told them, and they've never pushed. You don't push, either, Sadie Grace. You *shove*, and it's more than time somebody did."

"You listened to me. You healed me."

"So you've forgiven John?"

"No, not yet. But I've forgiven myself, and that may have been the most difficult thing to do. The rest will come in time."

"Forgive yourself, and the rest will follow. I hope you're right. Your hands are still magic, by the way. Which is not to say I want you to stop."

"Darby, I won't stop. But you have to start. That's the most difficult part, I know. What did you try so hard, not to forget, but to not remember?"

The headache was still there, still trying to get in, but its attempts were losing strength, becoming more feeble as he could imagine himself growing stronger, fighting it, not giving in.

"I was seven. Like Marley, or close enough for me to see her in me, the me I was when my world fell apart. I...I wish I could have kicked someone, and probably I did, but I don't remember."

"You told me you came to the cottage when you were seven. Did Camy and her husband know why you'd been brought there? It was obvious to me from that first day that they hold you in deep affection. Couldn't they have helped you?"

"They tried. But they only knew the reason they were given by my then-guardian, an uncle who never visited, and died just after I'd reached my majority. I should probably tell you something else. I'd stopped speaking, not so much as a single word, until I was ten or so, and was sent off to school a year later."

Sadie's fingers stilled against his temples. "You…you didn't speak? For three years? Not at all?"

"I've since made up for that lack—in spades, some would complain—but yes, I was silent as a clam, as it's said. I believe there was some talk about *putting* me somewhere, but Dr. Whiting, the local physician Camy had called in to care for me, said I was fine, and I would talk when I had something to say. He was a lot like John, now that I think about it."

"I'm sorry, Darby, I keep interrupting you. Please, go on, right after I say thank God for Camy. No wonder she's so protective of you."

"Nearly dragon-like, but you passed her test in one afternoon. I should have known then, shouldn't I?"

"Known what?"

"Nothing. As I told you, my memory of that day came back in pieces, over time, years. I'll spare you that, and just tell you, beginning to end…or perhaps not to the end, as the past apparently is not yet done with me."

"These headaches."

"They're an embarrassment, yes, and come on at the damnedest times, like a guilty conscience, perhaps. All right, let's get this over with," he said, sitting up, and not bothering to tie on his patch as he turned to face her. In truth, he'd forgotten he wasn't wearing it…and what did it matter, now that he was baring the rest of him to her?

"We were in residence at the home estate for the summer, which was a happy thing for me because it meant I was presented to my parents once a day for ten minutes, to bow, to recite something I'd learned that day and receive a kiss on my forehead from my mother before being hustled back to the nursery. She was so beautiful, my mother. She smelled of flowers, I suppose, and her laugh was like the tinkling of small bells. I wasn't taken to London with them for the Season, you understand, and I only saw them those few weeks in the summer, and again over Christmas unless they were invited elsewhere. Those days, when I was called to the main saloon to perform, to be kissed, are burned into my memory.

"They were exotic, rather like a pair of Basil's birds, I suppose, and I was so proud that they were my parents, even when my father insisted on those long hours in the chapel every Sunday. He believed a man could do as he pleased all the week through, as long as he said he was sorry on Sundays. I can't begin to tell you how I hated those damned gargoyles.

"The day it all ended, my tutor, Mr. Trembley, had ordered me to bed for a nap I didn't think I needed, so while the nursery maid slept in a chair beside my bed— yes, *she* snored—I sneaked out of the nursery and down the servants' steps and outside. I've always been good at locating seldom-used doors and servants' stairs."

Sadie smiled, and laid her cheek against his chest.

"I was chasing a butterfly through the gardens when I heard my mother's voice. She sounded strange, calling out, and I ran to investigate. And found her. I...I, um, watched for a few moments. I'd been wrong—she hadn't been calling out in fear, or whatever I'd thought. She seemed to be very happy where she was, but I wasn't. I screamed, *'Stop it, get off Mama or I'll kill you,'* and leaped onto Mr. Trembley's back, pounding my fists against his head."

"Oh, Darby. Oh, God."

He'd get through the rest as quickly as possible.

"My screams, Trembley's attempts to order me to silence, Mama's shrieks as she struggled to push down her skirts—it was mayhem, Sadie. Like something out of a very bad farce. Until my father showed up. He'd just come back from hunting grouse or some other bird and had taken the path through the gardens on his way from the stables. He had his hunting guns with him, opened, draped over his arm, but still loaded.

"He saw me and ordered me back to the nursery, but I refused to go. Mama held on to me, held me in front of her, as a shield I've since realized. I told him Mr. Trembley was hurting Mama and I was protecting her, but my father just laughed and told me again to leave, because he'd take care of Mama now. By then he'd pulled up the barrel of one of the guns and was aiming it at Trembley."

"You were a child. You can't feel blame for obeying your father."

"On the contrary, Sadie, I thought my father was going to shoot Trembley, shoot him dead for what he'd done to my mother. I had no problem with that, but I wanted to watch, so I only retreated far enough to be hidden when I crouched down behind one of the yews. Seven is a fairly bloodthirsty age.

"Even birdshot can be effective from the correct range, aimed at a vulnerable target. Trembley went down first, as my mother screamed and begged, but nothing was going to save her. The sound of that second blast of gunfire was the loudest sound I ever heard, until I heard cannon fire in the war. Several hours later, when the butler found me lying on the stone floor in the chapel, I was still trying to explain to the gargoyles that Papa was very sorry, so could everything be all right again, please."

"Oh, Darby…"

"The butler informed me that, as the new viscount, I was to get my sorry self up from the floor and come with him. I apparently fell ill in the cold chapel, and a week or more later, when I woke, I was told my parents had both perished from the same fever that had nearly claimed me. I didn't contradict anyone, although even to a child it was obvious that my father had killed himself rather than face what he'd done. Shortly after that, I was sent off to the cottage. I know now, or at least I think I do, that my younger self believed if he had only kept his mouth shut, his parents would still be alive. So that younger me stopped talking, and stopped remembering, as well."

"Until the headaches began."

"Until the headaches began, yes. The younger me was right, you know. If I'd only behaved, stayed in the nursery that day, hadn't attacked the tutor, on and on, my life could have been totally different. It was Gabe and the others who saved me, really. I was assigned sleeping quarters with Gabe at school, and he always included me in anything he and Coop and Rigby were up to, and they were always up to something. Add to that Vivien and Basil, with their lighthearted silliness. Life was to be enjoyed, and I set out to enjoy it. Why bring everyone else down with the truth, once I'd fully remembered it? In truth, Sadie Grace, you see before you a by and large happy man. A happy man, and a lucky man, as I am prone to say."

"Except when the headaches come on," she said quietly. "My heart breaks for the little boy you were, but I'm so proud of the man you've become. Your friends love you, the duke and duchess do, as well, and Camy and her husband clearly adore you. If you were forced to build Darby Travers up from the ashes, you did a very good job. And…and while I'm speaking of people who love you, I'd like to add my name to that list. I love you, Darby, and probably have even when I longed to box your ears, and I love you even more now."

He looked at her for long moments, saying nothing, before realizing his vision was blurry because he wasn't wearing his patch and covered his eye with his hand.

She reached up and once more took his hand from his wound. "I love that part of you, too. Well? Aren't you going to say anything?"

He would always be Darby Travers; he couldn't help himself. "Oh? Was there something in particular you wanted me to say?"

She threw back her head and laughed out loud. How brilliant she was, his Sadie Grace. She could make the sun come out and light up every last corner of his world.

CHAPTER TWENTY

"I LOVE YOU. How many times does that make?"

Sadie looked across the dim interior of the hackney cab while pretending to count on her fingertips. "Thirty-two, I believe," she said as Darby leaned in to kiss her cheek. Honestly, the man couldn't seem to keep his hands off her. Not that she was about to lodge a complaint.

"I'll try to make it an even three dozen by the time we've returned to the hotel. Have you been considering what you'll say to Sam Dobson?"

"Congratulations, Darby. You've successfully kept my mind free of worrying about just that for most of the day. What do you think I should tell him? There's a part of me that still worries he'll immediately declare himself Marley's legal guardian."

"Ah, but you've forgotten this tall, strong viscount beside you. I look forward to impressing you with my persuasive powers."

"Your powers in themselves, or your uncanny ability to persuade people to think the way you do? And before you ask for an example, allow me to remind you that dearest Basil believes himself rescued from his nonexistent curse, not to mention the fact that Vivien is already shopping for a few new pieces to add to her wardrobe, items that might *go well* with camels. She's entirely forgotten that Madame Royale wasn't a true fortune-teller. I actually stand amazed at that, I admit."

"People believe what they want or need to believe. Right now, *I* want to believe that Sam Dobson is a tired old man whose heart we are going to break, but not without also telling him that his Susan lives on in Marley. Are you prepared for what is not going to be a particularly pleasant conversation, especially when we tell him we believe his life may be in danger?"

"I'm still attempting to tell myself we're not on our way to a funeral. Even after all these years, telling Mr. Dobson Susan is dead will be new information for him, the poor man."

"Perhaps we should have brought Marley with us. To help soften the blow. In any case, it appears we're here."

Sadie looked out of the hackney to see a row of fine-looking houses, all attached to one another. "How beautiful. Which one is his?"

He told her the number. "The houses, taken in total, go by the name of Royal Crescent. My father's house here, or should I say *my* house here, is located in the North Parade. He and Prinney weren't the closest of chums, I've learned, but friendly enough that he felt it necessary to purchase lodgings for himself. I've never seen it, by the way, what with going off to war for five years and then one thing or another, and it has been rented out on and off for years. Would you like me to put an end to the lease next year, and we can bring Marley to the sea?"

Sadie shook her head in amazement. "If some other man said what you just said, I'd think him a pompous braggart. Darby, it's all right for you to be the viscount. The title, and all that came with it, are yours as your birthright. It's not your fault if your forebears were…

were bloody wealthy. It's what you make of what you have that matters."

"I'll take that as your consent to bringing Marley here next year, to be dunked in one of those cursed bathing machines. And thank you. I've an excellent man of business—three of them, in fact—and he's installed good stewards at each of my estates, but you're right. I've yet to stop avoiding who I am. I was happy as a student, fit well into the soldiering life, but for the last year and more I've been busily doing nothing. We'll begin with a trip to Nailbourne, as good a place as any to start, I suppose. I do love you, Sadie Grace. Three more to go before sundown. Now let's go knock on Mr. Dobson's door and get this over with as best we can."

He hopped down to the cobbles, informing the driver to wait for them, tossing him a coin and promising more to come.

She let him help her down from the cracked leather hackney seat and slipped her arm through his as they made their way up three marble steps to a large round-topped white door.

"Sadie, look."

She did, and noticed the inch-wide strip of black grosgrain ribbon wrapped around the brass knocker. "Oh, no. Do you think he's—"

"Only one way to find out." He banged on the knocker and they were rewarded less than a minute later with the appearance of a rosy-checked woman still wiping flour-dusted hands on her large white apron.

"The viscount Nailbourne and his lady wife, to see Mr. Dobson."

"Mr. Dobson ain't receivin'," she said, her accent taking Sadie back to Liverpool. "Him's in mournin'."

"A thousand apologies, my good woman," Darby said, already stepping past her and into the narrow foyer, Sadie close on his heels. "May I inquire as to the identity of the deceased?"

The maid, or cook, or whoever she was, squinted for a moment, as if attempting to decipher some foreign language. "Oh! Who died? Could have jist said that. Miss Susan, that's who, and it tain't yesterday that it happened. But he only jist found out, poor man, ya see. Hasn't quit his bed for a fortnight now. Think he's comin' on ta die, that's what I think. Broken heart, ya know? Everyone's bin sent away exceptin' me and one of the maids, so's to keep the house quiet. Now will you go away? M'lord, m'lady."

"Agatha? Did I hear the knocker? Who are you talking to?"

Both Sadie and Darby looked up the long, steep flight of stairs, to a curved landing and the man who stood there, his hands on the railing, peering down at them.

"Why, hullo there," Darby cheerily called up the stairs. "Dearie me, perhaps we're a few minutes early? Lord and Lady Nailbourne at your service, with an appointment to see Mr. Dobson. You can't be he. Fetch him, would you?"

"Uncle Samuel makes no *appointments*."

"*Au contraire*, my good man." Darby reached inside his jacket. "I've his invitation right here if you're so silly as to doubt my word. Viscount, you understand. Not used to having my word doubted—I'm probably spoiled that way, being a child of privilege and all that. Mr. Dobson was most anxious to meet with my lady wife and I after I wrote to him about his granddaughter."

Sadie sucked in her breath at his audacity, and his

easy ability to make a fool of a man he clearly already did not like. She hadn't expected him to admit to Marley's existence quite this quickly, and to a person who could be anybody, although she was fairly certain she was looking at Ellesmere Odling. A tall man, thin as the proverbial rail, his clothes badly tailored. She noticed the black mourning band on his upper right arm. He looked more like an undertaker than he did a man who managed a coal mining empire.

"What are you doing?" she whispered, trying not to move her lips.

"I don't like him," Darby responded just as quietly.

"Yes, I've deduced that much on my own. But what are you *doing*?"

"Other than getting a crick in my neck? I'm getting us upstairs. Follow me."

"Aren't I supposed to go first, so you can catch me if I fall?"

"True, Miss Prunes and Prisms, but since I doubt you're going to grab him by that atrocious excuse for a neck cloth and walk him backward into Dobson's drawing room, you'd be best following me."

"I suppose that's reasonable, for you," she murmured, picking up her skirts, smiling at a bemused Agatha and following after Darby.

True to his word, he reached the landing and immediately shot out a hand to fist it in the layers of Odling's neck cloth.

"Your sister also in residence, Ellesmere? It is Ellesmere, isn't it? Horrid name—have you ever forgiven your parents?"

"Unhand me!"

"I don't think so, no. Call her. I can see that the staircases are open all the way to the attics, so she'll hear you. Go on, call to her. 'Oh, Edythe, please join me in the drawing room, sister dear.' *Do it*."

"Are…are you going to kill us?"

"Why, I don't know." Darby turned to look at Sadie. "Are we going to kill them? It's up to you, you understand."

"I…I think we should simply adjourn to the drawing room after he summons Miss Odling." Oh, how *lame* that sounded, when Darby was doing so splendidly. "Then we'll decide if we'll kill them."

"That's my Sadie."

"Edythe!" Odling cleared his throat, as the name had come out as more of a squeak, and tried again. "Edythe! We've visitors! Come down at once. Um, please?"

Please?

"Please?" Sadie repeated as they all made their way into the small drawing room, Ellesmere being seated first, thanks to Darby having given him a good push into a chair. "Are you beginning to wonder just who is in charge?"

"Picked up on that, did you? I doubt Ellesmere here could safely be put in charge of minding blind mice at a crossroads. Sadie, the moment the sister arrives, take yourself off and locate Sam Dobson. The cook thinks he's dying, remember?"

"I do. Perhaps he is?"

"Perhaps. And perhaps he's being helped along on the path to the pearly gates. Ellesmere here is too nervous."

"A big bad pirate of a man wearing an eye patch and hints of a beard since you refused to take the time to shave again just burst into this house and nearly choked him. Of course he's nervous! Look at him—he hasn't dared to move, even while we stand over here, possibly plotting his demise."

"So we agree he's awaiting reinforcements. I'll block his view of you and keep him busy while we wait with him. Get yourself to the doorway and stand to one side of it. The moment she enters, take yourself up the stairs. Dobson's probably on the next floor. You can do this, Sadie."

"I know that," she said somewhat testily. How did he know her heart was racing, her palms had gone all sweaty and she had begun wishing she not only knew how to use a pistol, but that either Darby or herself had thought to bring one?

"Now," he said as a clicking of heels could be heard on the stairs, and Sadie quickly positioned herself aside the door, her back against the wall. She watched as a round-bodied woman whose height nearly matched her own rather *rolled* into the room. Her hair was the gray of ashes and tied in a topknot, her gown was black, but her mood was jubilant.

She was waving a thin sheaf of papers over her head.

"We did it, Ellesmere. He finally signed them." Then she noticed Darby. "Who are you, and what are you doing in my house?" she all but bellowed.

"*Your* house? I was under the impression that one Mr. Samuel Dobson owns this house," Darby answered, walking over to the fireplace to rather *drape* himself against the mantelpiece. "I'm here to see him, at his invitation."

"That's impossible. Ellesmere, don't just sit there. Get this man out of here."

"Ah-ah, Miss Odling, don't look to your brother," Darby said silkily. "Look at me. I'm about to explain everything to you."

Sadie was already out of the room and on her way up the stairs, followed close behind by Agatha.

"I'm not going to hurt him, Agatha," she said. "I only want to speak to him."

"'Bout his grandbaby. That's what himself said. Is it true?"

"It's true, Agatha. Where is he?"

"Top o' the stairs and to the left. I thought there 'twas somethin' fishy when they showed up and sent everyone else away save me and that layabout maid. Cain't eat without a proper cook, can ya? I've been doin' for Mr. Sam for forty-odd years, came here with him an' all. They but broke his heart, tellin' him 'bout his Susan."

Sadie was out of breath by the time they got to the head of the stairs. "When…when did they arrrive?"

"Two weeks or more, jist the way I said. Mr. Sam says he don't believe 'em, but I thinks he does. But he won't sign the papers."

Sadie stilled with her hand on the latch. Edythe had been waving papers, sounding triumphant. "Papers? What sort of papers?"

"Don't be askin' me, m'lady. I jist know Mr. Sam won't sign 'em. Told me. Said, 'Aggie, I tain't signin' no papers.' Then he said somethin' about vultures hangin' over a not-yet-dead body, think it was, but I didn't understand that none, neither."

"And now he's ill. How was Mr. Sam's health before he was told about his daughter's death?"

The cook smoothed down the apron covering her ample bosom. "Good enough to give me a fair chase until I let him catch me. I told ya, been with him forty years now. We came here after that besom of a wife of his cocked up her toes, and nobody needs know our business, that's what Mr. Sam says."

"Mr. Sam is correct. Perhaps you should go in ahead of me?"

Sadie followed the cook into a fairly large but stale-smelling room. Somewhere there was an overflowing chamber pot, and from the odor of sweat hanging over everything it was doubtful Mr. Dobson had been bathed in days. The drapes were all drawn and only a small fire burned in the fireplace, a single candle next to the bed the only other light.

"Oh, goodness, Agatha," Sadie exclaimed, waving a hand in front of her face. "Push back those drapes. Open all the windows. Mr. Dobson?" she asked, approaching the bed. "Mr. Samuel Dobson? I'm Sadie Hamilton. John Hamilton's sister. Mr. Dobson? Do you hear me?"

As she spoke, she made her way around to the side of the bed and the small table holding the candle, along with a tooth glass, a spoon and a small brown bottle. Even before she uncorked it and lifted it to her nose, she was certain of the bottle's contents. *Laudanum.* She was painfully familiar with the smell, and its effects.

Not again, she told herself. *Definitely not again!*

"Mr. Dobson?" Sadie put a hand on his shoulder and shook it, gently at first, and then with more vigor. He moaned softly, which was the only way she knew he was still alive. But for how long?

"Here, now, what ya doin' to the man? Can't ya see he's sleepin'? That's most all he does now."

"He's more than sleeping, Agatha. They've dosed him with laudanum. Keeping him quiet except when they need him, asking him to sign the papers he won't sign. But now he's signed them and I doubt they think they need him anymore. What horrible people! Pull a chair in front of the window and help me get him to his feet so we can walk him over there. And…and coffee. You do have coffee in the house, don't you? I know the duke drinks pots of it. Once we have him in front of the window, go tell the layabout maid to bring coffee up here immediately or I'll have her sacked, and then come straight back up here. Agatha! Don't just stand there—help me!"

Once Marley's grandfather was slouched in the chair and Agatha on her way to the kitchens, Sadie returned to the bed and grabbed up the spoon. But first she had to get him at least partially awake.

Well, she knew how to do that, too, if only she could find—ah, there it was, a pitcher of water sitting on a small dressing table in the corner. Moments later its lukewarm contents were pouring down over Sam Dobson's head and he was sputtering and giving a halfhearted attempt to avoid the deluge. But he couldn't avoid a determined Sadie, who then grabbed at a hank of the man's thick, snow-white hair and pushed the round end of the spoon into his mouth, all the way to the back of his throat, until he gagged and gave back whatever was in his stomach.

"Here I am, m'lady," Agatha called out breathlessly as she ran back into the room. "Oh, laws, what a mess! Mr. Sam? Mr. Sam, are you all right?"

"I think he'll be fine now, Agatha, but try to slowly get that coffee into him as soon as it arrives. And keep talking to him. Tell him about Marley. That's his granddaughter. Marley. She's seven years old and looks just like her mama. Can you remember that? I have to go downstairs now."

"Yes, m'lady," Agatha said, tears streaming down

her face. "I don't understand any of this, but thankee. Thankee."

Sadie had acted quickly and, she hoped, correctly, but she'd also left Darby downstairs with the undertaker and the harridan, so she picked up a brass candlestick as she headed for the stairs, just in case.

She shouldn't have bothered.

When she entered the drawing room it was to see Darby one by one feeding what had to be the papers Edythe Odling had been waving about so happily into the fireplace.

But there was nothing to be seen of the Odling siblings.

"Where are they?"

Darby turned from the fireplace, the last paper slowly curling at the edges as it caught fire. "Should I have kept them here? I didn't realize you had hopes of going on the attack. I can always call them back if you want to get in a whack or two."

"What?" She looked at her hand, and the candlestick. "You should be impressed," she told him as she put the candlestick down on the nearest table. "I was coming to protect you, throw myself into the fray, since you're too much the gentleman to strike a lady."

"But you could conk her over the head without hesitation. To *protect* me. I'm speechless with gratitude, truly."

"You're never speechless," Sadie grumbled, collapsing into a chair, suddenly feeling weak as a kitten. "Mr. Dobson is fine, or he will be. Where are the Odlings?"

"Packing. They'll be gone within the hour. I've offered them our hackney—I hope you don't mind," Darby told her, handing her a glass of wine. "Here. I don't yet know quite why, but you look as if you need this. Sip it."

"They gave up that easily? How? They'd just gotten what they wanted. Mr. Dobson signed the papers. I heard Edythe Odling say so."

"The papers, as you've seen—in point of fact, a bill of sale naming Ellesmere the buyer—have met with an unfortunate accident. As for the Odlings, once I'd explained the many and varied consequences of what they'd attempted if the court was to hear about it, they almost immediately saw the sense in retiring from the field. I was glad of that, as to strike an attacking Ellesmere would be rather like kicking a dog, and I wasn't quite sure I could manage to subdue an irate Edythe."

"And that's it? That's all it took, and they gave up?"

"As we've decided, I can be very persuasive. And perhaps magnificent."

"Well, that's true enough, I suppose. Oh, wait! They thought they'd just murdered their golden goose. They weren't afraid of *you*, they're afraid of the hangman. But I'm certain you were as magnificent as you said. I'm sorry I was otherwise occupied saving Mr. Dobson's life, and couldn't be here to see it."

The look on his face was amazing, and she'd yet to tell him about the laudanum, the dumped water and most especially the spoon. Sadie couldn't help herself. She began to smile, then laugh, before finally bursting into tears.

But as she told Darby later, once they'd spoken with a fairly alert Sam Dobson and were snuggled together in her bedchamber back at the hotel, it had been a long day...definitely outstripping both Roscoe Thatcher and his shoeing nail and Belinda Henderson's inspection of Marrakesh.

EPILOGUE

THE BIG DAY had finally arrived. The day of reckoning. The day of rejoicing. The day that, once passed, would mean Vivien would finally get to ride atop a camel. The day Darby and Sadie's engagement would finally be announced by none other than the duke himself.

Unless he *erped* first. There was always that, although nobody spoke of it. He'd made it this far, farther than any of his brothers, but there was still a long way to go.

Gabe and Thea had returned to town the previous evening, Thea still limping slightly due to her sprained ankle. Vivien had rushed to coddle her, as Gabe had predicted she would, but Thea was made of stronger stuff, and spent several hours holding court in a chair placed in the center of the ballroom, her foot resting on a padded stool as she gave directions to the servants carrying in flowers and festooning marble columns with billowy lengths of sheerest pink netting.

She would make a fine duchess someday, but as she'd told Sadie when she'd stopped her in the hallway to inquire about the duke's health, she and Gabe were in no hurry to assume the titles.

Dany and Coop had also come back to town as promised, but with her parents, her brother, her sister and her husband all coming with them, so that she sent around a note saying she was sorry but she couldn't join them until she somehow managed to get her sister down out of the treetops, nearly hysterical that their mother would go snooping everywhere when nobody was looking and their father would drink himself into a stupor before dinner. "But they *adore* Coop, that fabulous man. If only they'd stop asking him if he was *truly certain* he wished to marry me. I think they don't believe I quite measure up to a hero's standards."

But Minerva, Coop's mother, had arrived at the duke's residence bright and early, two maids following her with bandboxes and an actual trunk. She told everyone that she was torn as to what she should wear that evening and began demanding everyone's opinion on the three gowns she'd brought with her. She'd learned that a Mr. Jasper Hooper was anxious to meet her—the very wealthy Mr. Jasper Hooper—and it was imperative that she look her best. She was so nervous she only scolded Vivien twice for choosing pink bunting over purple before she realized that purple would only serve to make her positively fade into the background, as two of the three gowns were that color (the third was black, "just in case," but she remained hopeful).

As if Minerva Townsend could ever fade into *any* background. Her son had said that, subsiding into a chair when she finally took herself off upstairs, dragging Vivien with her. "Gentlemen, you have no idea what it's like to spend a week in the country with your betrothed's family. Add Minerva to the mix and know that twice Dany and I seriously considered making a run for Gretna Green. It was only our promise to be here today that kept us from it. Where's our man of the hour, by the way?"

When told Basil had been sent off to tour the Tower

with that same Jasper Hooper, along with Marley and her grandfather, he asked if it might be possible that the rest of them could make a similar escape.

"Just for a few hours, Sadie," Darby had told her, "since we're probably only in the way here," so that she reluctantly agreed, hiding her pleasure until they were gone, at which time she and Clarice fell against each other, laughing, because they'd been cudgeling their brains for a way to get them all out from underfoot without making them feel unwanted, the dears. Men were needed in many places, but not in a household preparing for a celebratory dinner for thirty followed by a ball for three hundred. Or three hundred plus five, if she were to count the cockatoo ice sculptures.

And then there had been the deliveries of food and ice and the arrival of specially hired servants who had to have their duties explained to them, not to mention having to listen to a solid hour of the pipers rehearsing with their bagpipes. There was quite the echo in an empty ballroom…

By the time she and Clarice were dressed, and Clarice had performed her magic with both Vivien's and Sadie's hair (Minerva had settled on the purple turban over the, well, the other purple turban), they had all agreed that this had to be both the longest and shortest day in their lives. So much to do, with too few hours to do it all, yet now with what seemed like hours and hours of doing nothing but waiting for the clock to strike midnight with the duke still vertical.

"My Jerry told me there are several wagers written in the betting book at one of his clubs as to whether or not he'll make it, you know. The duke isn't mentioned by name, but these silly men act as if nobody would know who the bettor means because he scribbles in *Duke C-dot-dot-dot-etc.* instead of *Duke of Cranbrook.* I'd be more worried if Madame Royale hadn't been so certain."

"Yes," Sadie had said as the gong rang and they rose to go down to the drawing room. "Quite the wonder, wasn't she?" *Oh, Lord...*

Darby was just climbing the curved staircase up from the entrance hall as Sadie and Clarice descended from the second floor.

He bowed to them both. "Ladies! How beautiful you look this evening. I'm fairly dazzled."

He looked fairly dazzling himself. "Darby," Sadie said, "there's a parrot on your shoulder."

"You noticed, did you? We're all wearing parrots this evening, in homage to Basil. This pretty thing is Harry-Harriet, by the way."

"What a strange name. I suppose you now want me to ask why."

"I was told nobody's quite certain, as Harry-Harriet is, and I quote, 'right friendly with everyone.'"

Sadie refused to laugh, but she did smile. "You still haven't told me the whole of that story, you know, but now isn't the time." As Clarice wandered off in search of Rigby, who could always be counted on to be somewhere close by, Sadie took Darby's arm and led him down the hallway to the music room. "I hadn't realized how involved it can be to play the role of hostess."

"And you thought you'd have nothing to do all day as a viscountess but twiddle those magic thumbs of yours."

"I know. It might have helped if Vivien wasn't a firm believer that fairies come in and do everything, but Thea and Clarice and I have managed, which is remarkable in the fact that none of us has any real experience in the area. Oh, and the ice cockatoos have already begun to melt, but I refuse to worry about them. I just want the clock to strike midnight without any *real* disasters."

"And what would you consider a *real* disaster?"

"Don't make me say it."

"Erp?"

Sadie made a face. "Yes, that would be it. I haven't told anyone else, but Marley apparently regaled the gentlemen today with her fine impression of Madame Royale's Henry. It's only because Vivien threatened to leave him that the duke is even going to make an appearance tonight."

"Oh, the poor man! Ah, I keep forgetting that Marley is rather like having another parrot in residence. Is she upset?"

"I don't think she realizes what she's done. She and Grandfather Hobson are having tea and cakes with her doll Lucy and Max in the nursery. He's spending as much time with her as he can, since he and Jasper Hooper are leaving tomorrow to travel home to see how much of a shambles the Odlings made of everything. They're both such dear men, and apparently quite excited about taking up the reins on their businesses again. Mr. Dobson has promised to come to Nailbourne for Christmas, and he knows he can visit Marley anytime, that there will always be a place for him at our table."

"If you manage me half as well as you seem to manage everything else, it will be me twiddling my thumbs all day."

"I wouldn't think to manage you. Especially since you're now going to be taking a more active part in overseeing your estates. Oh, but that does remind me. Mi-

nerva said to tell you that Coop is studying the proper
growth of turnip crops, so that you might want to apply
to him for information."

"Really," Darby said flatly.

"Yes, but since Vivien then immediately went off into
peals of laughter, perhaps she was only making a joke."

"I'd go with the latter, yes. I'd also like to point out
that we've been here in the music room for a full five
minutes, and I haven't kissed you yet. Not through any
disinclination, but for the fact that you've yet to stop
talking long enough for me to do what I followed you
here to do."

"Oh, is that so? Well, then," Sadie said, eyeing the
parrot on his shoulder, "if Harry-Harriet doesn't mind—
kiss me, you impossible man."

"What a marvelous invitation. But first, come sit
down over here," he said, leading her to a gilt chair. It
wasn't until he got down on one knee that she realized
what was about to happen.

"Oh, Darby…"

"Shh, I've rehearsed this, but I'm afraid my memory isn't as singular as Marley's. Miss Hamilton. Sadie
Grace. My affections for you know no bounds. It would
be my honor and privilege if you were to take my hand
in marriage, and I promise to love and cherish and put
up with you for all the days of our lives."

Sadie gave an exaggerated sigh. "And you were doing
so well for most of it. Yes, my lord, I would be honored
to be your wife." And then she smiled. "Somebody has
to laugh at your silliness."

He kissed her fingertips, and then reached into his
pocket to extract a small velvet-covered box. "This is
the Nailbourne betrothal ring worn by all the Nailbourne

wives, including my mother. I thought…I thought we might want to give it a fresh start. If that's all right with you."

"Oh, Darby, I do love you. Now kiss me."

…you impossible man! Squawk!

"A TOAST, EVERYONE," Gabe said, standing up from the dinner table, a glass in his hand. "To my uncle Basil, loved by all and tolerated by most everyone else—may he live long and prosper!"

"Here! Here!"

"Wasn't that lovely," Vivien said, wiping carefully at her eyes. "Sunny, you always say the nicest things."

"I think the duchess has been drinking her way to midnight," Darby whispered to Sadie. "Basil's making a game try at it, but he looks as if he's expecting the sky to fall on him at any minute."

"I know. I think he's putting a brave face on everything for Marley's sake. It was so sweet of him to include her tonight, even seating her at his right. Look at her, she's all but dancing in her chair, but she assured me she will be on her best behavior because Grandfather Dobson told her he has a present in his pocket, but she only gets it if she's a proper little lady at table. He showed it to me. It's a locket of Susan's he's carried with him ever since she ran away with John."

The mantel clock in the dining room struck the hour of eight and Vivien raised her glass. "To eight o'clock!" she announced in a loud voice.

"Here! Here!" That was Minerva, who also lifted her glass. Most everyone else followed.

"If they keep this up, by midnight those two ladies will be under the table, drunkenly searching for their wits," Darby whispered as Sadie pretended to sip at her glass of ratafia.

"They've been toasting the passing of every hour since ten this morning, and if this didn't taste so vile, I'd be tempted to join them," she told him as servants began placing yet another course in front of them, this one a meat course.

"Everything's marvelous, Sadie," Dany said, leaning across Darby to give her compliments. "And that ring is beyond beautiful, what with all the stones and gold and such. Is it heavy?"

Sadie looked down at the ring. "No, not really. But I imagine it could be, on someone else's hand."

Dany nodded. "That's just what I was thinking. My sister's seems to drag on her hand like an anchor, but yours appears to have been made for you."

"Sadie was *made* for me," Darby said, lifting Sadie's hand and kissing her fingertips. "The ring was merely a happy coincidence."

"You sweet man," Dany said, laying a hand on his arm, "you've positively *mellowed*, haven't you? Isn't it wonderful? Gabe has his Thea, I have my Coop, Clarice most definitely has her Rigby and now the two of you. I doubt even Miss Austen could conjure up such a happy—*oh, Lord!*"

Everyone had turned to look to the head of the table, where Basil was clutching at his throat with both hands.

Minerva was the first to speak, and quite loudly at that. "Good God—he's *erping!*"

Sadie tossed her serviette onto her plate and pushed back her chair, not knowing what she could do to help, but there had to be *something*.

And there was.

Marley, who had spent many a day in the infirmary with Sadie and her father, climbed down from her chair before pulling it closer to the duke. She hopped onto the cushioned seat, balled her small hand into a fist and began taking whacks at his back.

"Begone!" *Thwack!* "Begone!" *Thwack!* "Begone!" *Thwack!*

A fairly good-sized piece of half-chewed beef flew out of Basil's mouth and onto the table.

Sadie subsided into her chair, realizing the crisis was over.

"I don't think Miss Austen would have written that," Darby said just before he stood up, glass in hand. "A toast, good ladies and gentlemen! To Marley Hamilton, heroine, to the duke himself and to all of us! Not to happy endings, but to happy beginnings!"

"And to camels!" the slightly inebriated duchess added.

"Why in blazes not? To camels," Darby said, and then bent down and gave his future wife a kiss.

* * * * *

If you loved Darby and Sadie Grace's story,
don't miss the complete LITTLE SEASON *series:*

AN IMPROPER ARRANGEMENT
A SCANDALOUS PROPOSAL
A RECKLESS PROMISE

Available now from
New York Times *bestselling author Kasey Michaels*
and HQN Books!

Can't get enough romance?
Keep reading for WINTER'S CAMP,
a special bonus story from
New York Times *bestselling author Jodi Thomas!*

WINTER'S CAMP

Jodi Thomas

CHAPTER ONE

Ransom Canyon, Texas
1872

JAMES RANDALL KIRKLAND took one last look at the sun's blinding light before heading into the canyon's narrow entrance. Shadows danced along the jagged walls as if holding secrets and danger below. The beauty of the rocks ribboned in the colors of the earth almost calmed his fears. Almost.

The only way to get to Ransom Canyon from the south was along one path barely five feet wide and far too steep for a wagon. Midday seemed to pass into early evening in a flash as the walls grew higher above him and the temperature dropped. Winter already whispered through the fall air, warning him of how little time he had left to prepare.

The trades he'd make today would restore his staples even if the trip down into the canyon might be dangerous. James had lived with risk all his life and bore the scars to prove it.

Anyone in Ransom Canyon who didn't want him showing up today would have a clear shot from above. But even among outlaws and Comancheros, there was a code. For a few weeks every year when nature turned from green to brown, any man could ride this trail and trade for what he wanted or needed. With the nearest trading post more than two hundred miles away, supplies were hard to come by in this part of Texas. Winter was coming on early; James knew he'd need blankets, food supplies and at least two more horses.

He had crossed the plains of this northernmost part of Texas before. Once in 1866, when the need to roam open country to clear the blood of war from his mind had grown too strong. It hadn't worked. Dreams of drowning in blood still haunted him. He had ridden over the Llano Estacado again in 1869 as a scout for the army. Settlers were moving into Texas fast and the army knew the fort line would have to be extended to where Comanche and buffalo roamed.

James might not live to see his thirtieth birthday. A wanderer's life was the only one he had known since running away from a mission in San Antonio at the age of twelve. All was adventure and freedom then. Now he longed for what he'd never had: roots. Deep roots so generations of Kirklands would live out their lives on the same land.

A priest had once told James he came from noble English blood. But all James knew was that his family blood must have been thin, for his father had been gunned down a few months after they'd arrived in Texas and his mother and little sister had been dead before their first winter in Texas had passed.

Now, as he and his companion, a buffalo-hunter-turned-guide, rode into Ransom Canyon, James kept his rifle over one arm and his Colt ready to slide from its holster at the slightest sound. He didn't trust the men they were about to meet or the buckskin-clad man who rode beside him. It had taken a war and several gunfights to make James realize he couldn't afford trust.

"I know you don't like this, Kirkland." Two Fingers broke the silence that had lasted all morning. "But you need horses and supplies to last the winter on the plains." The old ex-slave, who'd lost his middle two fingers on a bet down in Fort Worth, scratched his neck with his thumb. "I can speak enough of any language we come up against in this place, but like I told you before, you'd be better off to ride south with me and not stay on this land. We could winter near a fort and both still have our scalps come spring."

"I want to be alone out here for a while. I plan to scout this land and find the best spot for a ranch. Then, come spring, I'll stake my claim." James did not add that he had saved enough to buy a hundred head of cattle. The money, along with a small inheritance from his father that he had never touched, was waiting for him in a bank.

"If these traders know you're squattin' near here, they'll come calling and think nothing of killing you and taking back their goods. You might have been the great Captain Kirkland in the war, but out here alone you'll be nothing but dead if they find you."

James nodded. It had been seven years since the war and he still couldn't shake his past. Even Two Fingers, who hadn't known him long, had picked up on how some of the men had treated him in Fort Worth. Halfway into the War Between the States, he'd gone mad and ignored danger. He had been lucky to have survived but in the years since, his legend had seemed to grow, not fade, as he wished it would.

When he'd hired Two Fingers, James's plan had simply been to scout the land, but once he'd seen the beauty he'd known he would have to stay awhile if this was the place he planned to live out the rest of his life. With his hunting skills and more supplies, he could survive the winter alone.

Now that Two Fingers had started talking, he couldn't seem to stop. "A man without a horse in this country might as well whittle his own headstone."

When James didn't answer, Two Fingers continued. "Most of the men we'll run across today are just traders. A few might even be rangers looking for captives taken in raids." He shook his head. "Lots were kidnapped during the war years without menfolk around. The children and the women go wild or crazy after a while. Lawmen do them no good by taking them back."

James had heard the stories. "I'm not interested in captives or the slave trade. I'm only here for horses." The war against slavery might be over, but no one had told the outlaws and Comanche. Ransom for captives could pay well.

As they moved into the crossover shadows, James made out a dozen men camped at the bottom of the canyon along the riverbank. Goods were laid out on blankets and stacked in wagon beds. Movement in the cedars told him more traders with mule teams were in the shade. He noticed Comanche traders and what looked like outlaws from both sides of the Rio Grande. They were hard, weathered men who wore their supply of bullets crossed over their chests.

He spotted a makeshift corral with thirty or more horses. Most looked like half-wild mustangs, but they'd do. He needed horses or mules to pack supplies in and hides out come spring. If the hunting was good over the cold months, he would make enough to stock the new place for a year, maybe more.

As they walked their horses closer only a few people in the clearing seemed to notice them. A small group of Apache camped by the water, the women mostly doing the work while the men traded. The chief stood tall in the center of the camp even though he had to be over fifty. They were a ragged group, the leftovers of a tribe whose young braves had been killed in battle. The few ponies they had looked too young to break to saddle. One sported an army brand.

James was about to turn away when he caught sight of a woman standing at the edge of the Apache camp. She was wrapped in a dirty blanket as mud-covered as her face and hands. She simply stood staring at the ground; not moving, not interested in his passing.

One of the older women in the tribe walked near and struck her with a stick. The muddy woman, with hair so matted it might never comb out, finally looked up.

For a moment James could only stare. Her huge eyes, framed in dark circles, looked wild and mindless, but they were the crystal blue of a mountain lake.

"Best move along, Kirkland," Two Fingers ordered.

They moved on toward the main camp. "Did you see the color of her eyes?" James whispered. "She has to be a captive."

Two Fingers shook his head. "When I was a boy, I ran away thinking I'd be free, not a slave like my ma, but Apache found me. I was lucky. I was taken in by the tribe, treated as good as if I were a real son. I learned the language and had a grand time living the life, but now and then I'd see a woman who'd been traded from tribe to tribe as though she was nothing but a horse. No—a woman like that is lower than a horse. If they were lucky, if you want to call it that, they were taken in as a third or fourth wife. They'd do all the work the other wives didn't want to do and only eat when there was plenty. The number-one wife usually had the right to beat the last wife and did regularly."

Two Fingers swore in Spanish. "If they weren't so lucky, they fought for scraps with the dogs. Once they started looking and acting like that woman we passed, there was no hope. If they didn't kill themselves or get beaten to death, they were left to die. Her mind's gone, Kirkland. Don't look at her. Some say if you do, she'll steal your soul and take it down to hell with her."

James thought he was beyond caring about anyone but himself; that his heart and soul had hardened to rock. He'd lost every friend he'd had in the war. He had lived so long without a family he'd decided he never wanted one. Never wanted anyone to die on him. Never wanted someone grieving when he died. It didn't matter that he felt sorry for the woman covered in mud. He could not save her or heal her.

"She's mad," Two Fingers said again as they climbed off the horses. "Forget her. I knew an Irish trapper once who bought a woman crazy like her. She stabbed him in his heart the first time he fell asleep. In some tribes when a woman covers up in mud like that the tribe calls her 'no one.' She's nothing to anyone. She's no more than part of the dirt."

"Why don't they just kill her?" The leather creaked when James leaned his long frame forward in the saddle.

Two Fingers shrugged. "You don't kill *nothing*, Kirkland."

They moved into the group of traders. James forced

himself not to look back for a while. But when he did, the woman was just standing as before, wrapped in her ragged blanket, her eyes glazed over. The rest of the tribe moved around her as if she wasn't there.

James traded for the supplies he'd need and paid five times what he would have at a fort, but he didn't have the time to make the long trip back to a settlement or town.

As he packed the supplies on the two mustangs he'd bought, Two Fingers moved up to his side. "We'd better be getting out of the canyon. If we have to camp here tonight, one of us might wake up dead." He pointed a thumb at James.

"What makes you think it would be me?"

"Same reason rattlers don't usually strike each other." He glared at James. "I'm one of *them*. I may have been born a slave, but I consider myself Apache. The reason you're still alive, Captain Kirkland, is that I figure I might need you one day. Times are changing in this part of the country. Maybe not this year or the next, but they're changing. I can feel it in my bones. When they do, men like me won't be tolerated. Men like you will run this country. I do this for you, Kirkland, and you'll return the favor one day."

"What makes you so sure?" James asked.

"'Cause you're an honorable man. The only one in this canyon, I'm guessing. So whatever else you need, I'll help with the bargaining. When we leave, we part ways, but you remember me and one day I'll ask for that favor."

"All right, Two Fingers, but I have a small request before we go. I want you to bargain for one more thing."

"What's that, Kirkland?"

"The woman." James glanced toward the mud woman. All day, she had barely moved. Twice he'd seen the old woman hit her with a stick to move her farther from the campfire. Both times the blow had almost knocked her down. Now, she was so far away from the fire, she could not have felt the heat, assuming she could feel anything at all.

Two Fingers shook his head. "You don't want her. She's mostly dead already."

"You don't understand. I don't want her. I want to help her."

Two Fingers waved his hands in the air with the two remaining fingers on his left hand pointing to the sky as he swore. Finally he turned to James, still cussing. "I knew I shouldn't have gotten mixed up with an honorable man. If I even suggest trading for her, the old chief will think we're both crazy."

"Make whatever deal you can," James ordered in a tone he hadn't used in years. Pulling an old pocket watch from his pack, he added, "See if they'll take this. I've nothing left to offer."

Two Fingers looked at the watch. "Does it work?"

"No."

Two Fingers grinned. "Then we might have a chance. Trading something worthless for something worthless might just work. They'll see it as a joke. The Apache love a good joke."

James watched as the old buffalo hunter walked over to talk to the Apache chief. He pointed at the woman, then pointed at James, and the whole tribe laughed.

Finally, Two Fingers pulled out the watch James had carried with him since the day his father had been killed.

He remembered the ranger who had stepped in after the gunfight that had caught James's father unprepared. The lawman had collected his father's belongings and made sure he and his mother were on the next stage to Houston. As the ranger had said farewell, he'd told James's mother to put her money in a bank the minute she reached Houston and then he'd handed James the watch.

Two Fingers walked toward him carrying the stick the old woman had used to hit the mud woman. "Well, if I weren't the best trader in the south, this wouldn't have happened. They took the watch for her and threw in this stick. Apparently the only way to get her to move is to hit her."

James took the branch and stared at the woman still looking with dead eyes at the dirt.

"We'd better ride," Two Fingers said. "Trust me, you don't want to be here much longer."

Handing Two Fingers the reins to one of the pack-horses, James approached the woman with his horse and the other mustang he'd bought.

She didn't look up, not even when he stood two feet in front of her.

For the first time he noticed how small she was, barely over five feet. With the mud and the blanket she'd looked rounded, but up close he saw her hands and arms were so thin they were almost birdlike.

He lifted the stick.

She raised her head and waited for the blow.

He took the branch in both hands and broke it across his knee. For an instant he thought he saw a hint of surprise flash in her eyes.

"If you'll come with me, I swear I'll never raise a weapon or my hand against you. It seems you've been lost for a long time. I'll do my best to get you back to your people. I'm not looking for a slave or a wife. I want to help you."

She showed no sign of understanding a word he'd said.

He reached down and took her hand. For a moment all he did was brush off the dried mud. Even with the dusting of dirt over her skin he could see the bruises. "It's time to go," he said as he turned, tugging her hand gently.

To his surprise, she followed.

When he lifted her up onto the mustang, she pulled her hand from his and dug her fingers into the horse's mane. He knew without asking that she wouldn't fall off during the ride.

"You're going to be all right, Little Dove," he said, knowing she probably wouldn't understand.

The gash on her wrist he had noticed earlier was still bleeding. He pulled off his bandanna and wrapped it around the wound, wondering how many others were on her body.

When Two Fingers joined them, James whispered, "We ride out with her between us."

"Why? You think she'll bolt?"

"No," James answered. "Because she's the most precious cargo we carry."

CHAPTER TWO

MILLIE WATCHED THE man carefully. He was tall and lean with a strength about him. His words sounded familiar, as if she had once understood them a lifetime ago.

Of late she paid little attention to what was going on around her but she knew all the people came to the canyon to trade, and she seemed to be one of the things traded. It did not matter. She had been traded before. Only, no one had ever put her on a horse.

She had been twelve when the Comanche had taken her from her home. She'd been too much of a woman to be adopted into the tribe and too much of a child for any brave to claim her. Three summers later they'd traded her to an Apache tribe and given her to the chief's blind mother. The old woman had kept her tied to her camp by a long rope. When she'd needed her, she tugged on the rope. The old woman had been neither cruel nor kind. Millie had quickly learned that she was nothing.

When the old woman had died the next winter, she'd been traded again. These past two winters with the woman and the stick had been the worst. Millie knew she wouldn't have lasted much longer. Stick Woman had grown tired of having her around and begun to hit harder every day.

Now, at eighteen, Millie faced another change. In her life change meant things usually got worse, never better. This man of the canyon looked strong enough to kill her with one blow.

Not that it mattered. Nothing mattered anymore. Days passed, seasons passed. That whole first year she'd thought her father would come for her, but he hadn't. She remembered seeing her mother dead, facedown in the mud the day the Comanche rode onto their farm. Mother was dead and Father never found her. How could he? She moved from tribe to tribe like something worthless shuffled off. After a few years, she'd given up hope and tried to forget about her life before. It was too painful to remember.

The dark-skinned man with only two fingers on one of his hands frowned at her as they rode out of the clearing. The other man, with hair the color of the yellow walls of the canyon, talked as if trying to tell her something. She did not care where they were going. Away could be no worse.

Her new owner smiled at her now and then when he said something, but she didn't know how to answer. For as long as she could remember, any sound she'd made had caused someone in the tribe to hit her.

Slowly, the canyon man's words settled her. He never yelled. He was not young. The sun had wrinkled the corners of his eyes. But he was not old, either, because he had all his teeth and rode with the skill of one who had been born to ride.

They were long onto the plain flatland when they stopped to camp. The tall man lifted her down from the horse carefully as if he thought he might hurt her. He looked worried, as though he feared she might try to bolt. He could not know that running had been beaten out of her years ago.

She stood still and silent in the dark as he built a fire. When he moved her close to the fire, he tried to pull off her blanket, but she held tight. To her surprise, he laughed and gently pushed her to the ground closer to the fire.

The men talked a language she had not heard in years. Words drifted around her, reminding her of another life. The canyon man gave her food. She watched him eat his and followed suit.

"Spoon," he said, holding up the tool he ate with. "Cup."

The dark-skinned man in buckskins shook his head at the canyon man, but he watched her as though considering roasting her on the fire. She did not like the way the man breathed through his mouth as he glared at her.

"Cup," Canyon Man said again as he caught her attention. She didn't answer, but she stored the knowledge away.

"James," he said as he patted his chest. "I'm James."

She looked away. Inside her mind she'd remembered her other name before the Apache and Comanche called her names. Sometimes all that kept her sane was whispering *Millie* in her mind.

Millie, she thought as she patted her chest. *I'm Millie.* But she didn't trust this man enough to say her secret word aloud.

The dark-skinned man never spoke to her. He curled up in the shadows to sleep, but James stayed by the fire, his hand resting on his weapon.

Millie watched him until he fell asleep, then she moved closer so that her blanket almost touched his. She didn't sleep for a long while, waiting to be beaten and made to move away from the fire.

Finally he rolled over and looked at her, saying words she didn't understand. His hand reached across the dried grass and patted her mud-covered fingers.

Millie closed her eyes. She would not be hurt tonight. Maybe tomorrow, but not tonight.

CHAPTER THREE

JAMES WASN'T SURPRISED to find Two Fingers gone at dawn. He *was* surprised to find the woman still curled by the fire.

When she looked at him, he patted his chest and said, "James." Maybe she'd get the hint and give him her name.

No answer. Just those huge blue eyes staring up at him. Fear sparked in her gaze this morning. James wasn't sure it was an improvement over the dull, dead eyes he'd seen yesterday.

As he began to make coffee, she stood and moved silently toward the stream. Since the horses were in the other direction, he doubted she planned to run. If she did, he'd have no trouble catching up to her. In this part of Texas, he could see for miles in every direction.

He watched her by the water. She wasn't washing. She was applying a new layer of mud. She disappeared from sight for a while, but he decided he'd give her some room. Even a mud woman needed her privacy.

It was full dawn when she came back. If possible she looked dirtier than when she'd left. Her muddy hands were cupped, carrying something.

She offered him a half dozen eggs.

He'd seen the prairie chickens last night, but had no idea where their nests might be.

"Breakfast." He smiled and took the eggs. "Thank you."

She moved away without looking at him. James almost asked how she'd like them cooked, but he knew she wouldn't answer. He scrambled the eggs while the coffee boiled, then handed half to her on his one plate while he tackled his half from the skillet.

He talked while they ate, wondering if anything he said was getting through to her. As he loaded up the horses, he realized she was watching him, not simply glaring at nothing. Once he was ready, he walked over to her and took her hand. "We'd best be heading out. I've got a campsite picked out about twenty miles from here." He brushed the dirt off her hand as he talked, then he tugged her to the horse and set her up bareback.

When he turned loose of her hand, he patted his chest one more time and said, "James."

Shyly, in a whisper he barely heard, she said, "Millie."

"Millie." He laughed. "Nice to meet you, Millie." She had gone back into her shell and was not even looking his direction.

They rode hard all day, stopping at noon to let her rest and drink from a canteen he'd insisted she keep and a few times to water the horses. He found a good place to camp before sunset. Taking his time, James studied the land, thinking about where he'd someday build his home. He liked the idea of using the canyon cutting across the land for miles and miles as a natural border. He'd also need a creek or stream for water. Land was almost free, but without a good water supply it would be worthless.

When he lifted her down from the mustang, she didn't look at him, but she helped build the campfire this second night they shared.

As before, when he handed her dinner, she watched him before she ate. James tried to talk, but it wasn't easy carrying all the conversation. He finally took her hand and led her down to the water. He washed the dishes and his hands and face, hoping she'd understand what he was trying to teach her.

She watched, looking as though she feared for her life.

He didn't want to frighten her more, so he simply walked back to the fire. She stayed by the water for a long while. When she returned, she curled on the grass close to where he sat and closed her eyes.

James didn't move. He studied the muddy woman beside him. "Millie," he finally whispered, thinking that he was making no progress. Trading for her had seemed a good idea. He'd wanted to help her. Only now, out here a hundred miles from civilization, how could he help her? At least she wouldn't be beaten, he reasoned. He'd take care of her. Maybe this calm land would allow her to heal. Come spring, he'd get her to people who could help her.

The rise in the ground where they'd camped made a natural wall that hung over them almost like a rocky roof. By building the fire beneath the overhang, the smoke drifted over the roof through tiny openings and disappeared into the night. No one would see their fire or the smoke from it. The rock behind them also offered a break from the wind that constantly blew.

James made his bed on the other side of the fire, facing out into the shadows. He loved the sounds of the night. That's why he'd come back to this land. Here, he would start fresh.

He drifted to sleep listening to the bubbling sound of the stream, the swish of the tall grass and the rustling

of the dead leaves still clinging to the cottonwoods near
the water. He relaxed, thinking that someday every man
for miles around would know this was Kirkland land.
His land.

At dawn he woke to a cold fire and blue eyes watching him. Sometime in the night, she'd moved beside
him. It crossed his mind that if she'd walked the distance without waking him that she could have easily
killed him in his sleep. His hunting knife lay beside the
fire where he'd left it.

"Morning, Millie," he said.

Blue eyes stared at him with less fear than yesterday.
They were making progress.

He showed her how to make the coffee, frowning
when the coffee beans went into her dirty palm. They
ate from the supplies he'd bought at the trading day. He'd
bought enough for one. Now, with her to feed, they'd not
last the winter. He'd have to take time to hunt more. He'd
also have to find more firewood and close off at least
one more side of his camp. He didn't mind waking up
to frost covering him, but he didn't like the thought that
Millie'd wake up frozen. She didn't have enough meat
on her bones to keep her from freezing.

Plus, he was getting real tired of the filthy old blanket around her shoulders. Maybe if he could keep the
half-cave warm, she'd take the blanket off at least long
enough to wash it.

He spent the morning building a corral for his horses,
then decided to go exploring. If he went a different direction every day, he'd know the land before long.

It was almost dark when he returned.

She'd started a fire and had made a soup out of a potato and jerky the way he'd showed her the night before.

James took care of his horse and sat across the fire from her. She didn't look at him when he praised her but he noticed her hands were clean. Maybe the coffee wouldn't taste like mud tonight. A dozen eggs sat next to the supplies. She'd done her share of the hunting for food, it seemed.

She wasn't mad as Two Fingers thought her to be. She wanted to stay alive, but she didn't want to communicate with him.

He talked to her as they ate, telling her all about what he'd seen that day. She fell asleep without giving any hint that she was listening to him. James leaned back on his saddle and relaxed. Just before he dozed off, he watched her move near him and curl deep into her old blanket. Maybe she wanted to be near him, he thought, or more likely she was simply afraid of the dark.

Smiling, he decided Millie might not like him, but she felt safer close to him.

The next morning when he washed his hands and face, she did the same. The sight of her face, clean of mud, angered him. Deep bruises ran along one jaw and under her left eye. Along her throat were signs of rope burns.

For the first time he was thankful for the blanket because James knew it covered more bruises and scars. If he could have, he would have gone back to Ransom Canyon and made every one of the Apache pay. Only, deep down he knew wrongs were done on both sides, just as they had been committed during the War Between the States. Maybe Millie was more like him than James had thought. She might just want to get away from people for a while.

He reached to touch her, but she jerked away.

Give her time, he thought. Let her have control over herself. He had a feeling it had been a long time, if ever, since she'd felt she had any say in her own life.

Keeping his voice low, he began to show her how to fish. While he waited for her to accept him, he'd teach her to survive.

The day was warm by the time they'd caught enough for supper. While she watched, he pulled off his shirt and boots, then waded into the water to wash his shirt and body.

He knew she'd have to remove the blanket to wash even though that one filthy, ragged blanket was her armor. As long as she held it around her, she had a buffer against the world.

That night, in the light of the campfire, he shaved with his hunting knife, then combed his hair. He offered her the comb.

She tried, but her hair was too matted.

"I guess you'll just have to cut it off." He laughed, thinking that her hair looked like a tumbleweed packed with mud.

She gave up after several tries and handed back the comb.

That night, when she moved to his side, he reached across the foot of grass separating them and took her thin hand in his. "Good night, Millie," he whispered.

"Good night, James," she answered in a voice that sounded as though she hadn't used it in years.

"Your mind's not gone." He smiled. "Whatever you had to go through didn't drive you insane. When you come out of this dark place you're in, I'll be waiting to help. Just remember, they didn't break you. You're not mad."

THE NEXT AFTERNOON when James returned to camp, he changed his mind.

Millie sat by the fire, his hunting knife in her hand, her scalp bleeding from a dozen tiny nicks. Almost all of her muddy hair was piled in front of her.

Looking up with those huge eyes, he saw her sorrow. She'd done what he'd suggested. She'd cut off her hair. He wasn't sure if she thought his words had been an order. If she did, this mess was all his fault.

Kneeling beside her, he took the knife from her fist, then walked to the creek and wet his two clean bandannas.

Still sitting by the fire, she didn't look up when he came near her. She'd gone back to that place inside herself where she must have gone every time she'd been hurt. That safe place where nothing registered, nothing mattered.

"Millie," he started, "I'm not going to hurt you. I'm going to clean the cuts so they don't get infected."

She didn't move as he carefully cleaned the blood and dirt away from her head. Then, as if he were shaving, he scraped the last few tufts of hair from her scalp.

When he walked to the creek for water to fill the coffeepot, he thought he heard her crying, but he couldn't be sure. The whole night seemed to whisper sorrow from the lone coyote's call to the wind whining through the trees.

Without making any effort to talk, he untied the rabbits he'd killed for supper. As he skinned them and roasted them, he was surprised to see her begin to work with the furs, stretching them out on stick frames.

He ate alone, watching her, wondering where she'd gone in her mind as her hands worked.

An hour later she moved toward the roasted rabbit he'd left on their one plate and began to eat like an animal who feared someone would snatch the food away at any moment. The thought occurred to him that maybe, in the tribe, she'd never been allowed to eat until the work was done.

Before he turned in for the night, he built the fire a bit higher, worried that she'd be cold. But, as she had every night, she waited until she thought he was asleep and curled up beside him. She might only be six inches away, he thought, but it might as well be an ocean between them.

He thought of reaching out to touch her hand, but guessed she'd pull away. Silently, he promised he'd keep her safe. Maybe she had family? Maybe one of the missions would take her in.

Silently, James swore he'd not leave her until the fear in her huge eyes was gone.

CHAPTER FOUR

EVERY NIGHT MILLIE watched the canyon man who called himself James. He never yelled at her or hit her. And he never stopped talking no matter how hard she tried to show him that she wasn't listening. Days passed, the last of the cottonwood leaves fell, the wind howled of winter at night and still he talked.

She couldn't stop observing his every move. He took the time to show her things. He taught her each detail as if one day he'd leave her alone and she'd have to know how to survive on her own. Fishing, cooking, washing. All the while, he talked and each day she understood more of what he said.

Three nights after she'd cut her hair, he presented her with a hat made of rabbit skins. A week later he tried to make her moccasins out of more hides. As soon as he left camp the next day, she finished the job with much more skill. For the first time since she'd outgrown her boots, she had new shoes. Fur-lined. Warm. A perfect fit. Over the years she'd made many, but they'd always been taken away.

Canyon Man was a good provider. Millie hadn't gone hungry since he'd traded for her, but hunting wasn't the reason he was going out each morning. James was looking for something.

As the days passed she took on more of the cooking,

finding that she liked being alone all day and didn't mind his company at night. She wasn't sure what she was to him. If a Comanche had traded for her, she might have been a slave for his wife or mother, but James had no wife or mother, and he never treated her like a slave. She thought that maybe she was his wife, but he never touched her. Besides, a man like him could find a better wife than her.

The moon made its second cycle over the big, empty sky and Millie felt her mind calm. Her favorite time was at night when he'd lie on his back and point out the stars. He'd sometimes say that his father had known many of their names and that someday he'd know them all.

Each week she watched James wash in the creek but she never joined him. The habit seemed strange, but she remembered years ago being clean. She'd washed in a house with a fire, warming the air even in winter. Slowly the memory of her mother, her father, her little brother, drifted into her mind and for the first time in years, she let them settle there for a while. Another time. Another world. Her world once.

One warm morning, after James had left, she took his soap and went to the water. Slowly she removed her blanket and stepped out of the bloodstained shift she'd worn for years. She remembered she'd had a dress once, until it had fallen off, piece by piece. Then she'd had a petticoat and shift. Now she only had a shift.

As she walked into the cold water, she almost ran back to the shore, but a bath was long overdue. There was no reason for the mud anymore. No one would try to touch her now.

Slowly, one limb at a time, she washed. Her body was so thin. A girl's body, she thought, not a woman's.

She'd started her bleeding three maybe four years ago. The mark of a woman. Two months later the flow did not come back. That winter had been hard. Food was short and she was always the last one in the tribe to eat. The bleeding that made her a woman had never returned.

As she scrubbed off the dirt, she realized she was no longer the last to eat. James always ate with her, and he cut each portion in two as if they were equal.

Cleaning her inch-long hair with the terrible-smelling soap, she decided she could not put on the shift again, so she walked back to the campsite nude and cut a hole in a blanket James had tried to cover her with several times. Poking her head through the hole, she tied her waist with a rope and pulled on her moccasins.

When he returned, she would have a stew of meat and a potato cooking.

Whirling, Millie felt grand. She was clean and dressed in clothes no one else had tossed away. She couldn't wait for James to see her. Her name was no longer Mud Woman.

An hour later she watched James climb off his horse downstream from her. He studied her, shaded his eyes as if to make sure what he saw, then yelled, "Millie, is that you?"

She looked down. "I washed."

As he walked toward her he continued to talk. "You look great, Millie. I almost thought someone else was in our camp when I rode up. Without the mud and that old blanket, you seem half as wide." His hand lightly brushed over her clean hair. "Your hair is chestnut brown, not mud color. I'm telling you, Millie, in that clean blanket you are quite stunning."

She moved away from his touch, but didn't jerk in

fear as she had before. Over the weeks together, she'd learned not to be afraid of him. If he had planned to hit her, he would have done so when she'd spilled coffee on him one morning or when she'd forgotten to start the fire one afternoon, or when she wouldn't answer him no matter how many times he said her name. But he never hit her. James just kept talking as he smiled and shrugged off his frustration. Her canyon man was a good man.

While he staked his horse, she finished cooking supper.

They ate in silence, then both watched the fire. The air was still for a change, whispering around them. Now and then the wind moved in the dead leaves, sounding almost like someone walking.

Finally, when it was long past the time he usually turned in, he looked at her and said, "Talk to me, Millie. It's so lonely out here with me doing all the talking. I know you understand most of what I say. Just talk to me. I know you can, you spoke today when I rode in."

"James," she whispered.

He laughed. "That and 'good night' are all I've ever heard you say."

Millie thought about what she should try to say to him. Finally one thing came to mind. "Sleep beside me."

Standing, he grabbed the extra blanket and spread it out full on the ground beside the fire, then reached for his bedroll blanket and floated it on top. Pulling his boots off, he lay between the two blankets and lifted the top one. "I'd say come to bed, Millie, but I haven't seen a real bed in so long I've forgotten what they feel like."

She curled in beside him, pressing her back against his chest. The nights were getting colder and his warmth along her back felt so good.

To her surprise, he wrapped his arm over her and tugged her closer. "I'm going to have to fatten you up if we're going to cuddle through winter."

She fell asleep on his arm feeling something akin to happiness.

BY THE TIME the moon turned from full to a slice she'd grown used to him sleeping beside her at night. She liked the way his low snoring tickled her ear and how he often covered her shoulders with the blanket in the night. Now frost would be on the top of their blanket at dawn, but she always felt warm.

On clear nights he'd point out falling stars, laughing as he counted them as if each one was putting on a show just for him.

One cloudy night he asked her to talk to him again, though she thought she was managing several words a day. Her body had filled out a bit and her hair was now almost as long as her little finger. It seemed to curl around her face and she didn't mind when he brushed his fingers through it.

"Talk to me," he said against her ear.

Millie shook her head. She didn't know the words to say.

"Tell me what would make you happy, Millie." He rested his hand on her waist. "I don't have much out here but if I could make you smile, I'd count myself a lucky man."

She had no words. How could she tell him about all the things she was grateful he never did? He didn't yell at her. He didn't beat her. He never made her go to sleep hungry. He hadn't been angry when she'd cut up one of his blankets or forgotten how to do the things he'd showed her.

James sounded frustrated. "What can I do, Millie? Except when I feel you next to me at night, I'd swear I'm invisible to you most of the time. There must be something that you want."

She'd had enough talk. "Sleep with me," she whispered.

"I am. I keep you warm, don't I?"

She covered her hand over his resting at her waist and moved his fingers up to her breast. "Sleep with me," she repeated.

He rose to his elbow and looked down at her. "Are you asking what I think you're asking? Do you want me to…to mate with you?"

She nodded, thinking maybe "mating" was the word she had been looking for. She'd seen the old chief mate with each one of his three wives in the shadows of the tepee. They did not seem to mind at all. Once he tried to climb on her, but his first wife had pushed him off. She'd screamed at him that night and the next morning she had beat Millie so badly she could barely walk for days.

After that she'd put more layers of mud over her and slept outside unless the ground froze.

Maybe she was not James's wife, maybe she would never be anyone's wife. But, she wanted this. It had been so many years since she had been close to anyone, or cared if anyone around her lived or died. She wanted to feel a kind touch. It might wash away a few of the shoves and hits and slaps.

Deep inside she knew her need was more. Millie couldn't explain why, but she *wanted* James's touch. He mattered to her and for some reason she seemed to matter to him. She might not understand much of what happened between a man and a woman, but Millie knew she wanted to press her heart against his and know she was alive.

Without a word she rose and pulled off the blanket she had made into clothing. Then she huddled back under the cover and waited. Whatever this mating was, she wanted it to happen with someone she cared for. James had made her want to live again.

It took him a while to make up his mind, but slowly he began to touch her and, as he had done with a hundred other things this season, he taught her how to mate.

At first she was not sure she liked it. It hurt a little and he'd whispered that he was sorry and promised it wouldn't hurt next time. She had lain awake wondering why the first wife had wanted it or why the other wives never cried out as the old chief had moved from one to the other's blankets. The coupling felt strange, awkward. She liked when he touched her lips with his and she felt warm when he moved over her, but it brought her little pleasure.

He held her when they were finished and fell asleep. She stared into the night sky and tried to make sense of what had happened.

Deep into the night, she shook him awake, asking him to do it again.

This time he did not hesitate so long. He seemed better the second time, more comfortable in touching her. Millie decided all he needed was practice and all she needed was to learn how to do what he liked. Next time she would touch him.

At dawn she awoke to the sound of him whistling as he worked on a shelter for the horses. When she sat up and smiled at him he came to her and knelt down beside her. His hand moved beneath the blanket and brushed along her body as he kissed her lips.

When he backed away, he looked worried. "Are you all right, Millie?"

She nodded once, thinking again how kind this strong canyon man was. His heart rested over hers in the night. She knew its rhythm.

"Again, James," she whispered.

He laughed. "Tonight. The weather promises a storm. I'd like to get the road from the east marked off. When or if I return to this land I want to have everything planned and staked out." He cupped her face in his hands. "I'll be back soon."

While they ate he talked of how he'd mapped the land making sure there was water every mile and where he'd put barns someday.

They didn't talk about what had happened in the night. Not that morning or the next or the next. Millie silently understood. What happened in the night was not mentioned in daylight.

Someday was not a word either of them knew how to use.

So, as winter raged, she woke him at least twice a night so they could practice until one morning, just before dawn, she decided they got it just right. Finally, she understood why James did not talk about their mating. There were no words.

Leaning back, she let her breath slow as his hands slid along her damp body. She liked this part as much as the mating. He always took his time touching her after they mated, as if she were something very special, and she drifted into sleep knowing she was safe.

CHAPTER FIVE

JAMES RODE THE boundary of what would be his land come spring. His thoughts should be on cattle and building his herd, but his mind kept drifting to Millie. He felt as if he knew her body, but he didn't know her. They'd never talked of love, or even caring for one another. Most nights he felt as though they were simply two strangers surviving the winter together. Soon she'd be stepping into a world she hadn't known in years and he'd be back on this land building. Strange, he thought, he'd miss her even though they didn't talk. He'd miss her more than he'd ever missed anyone.

It had to be February. Another month and they'd be packing up and heading to Fort Worth. He'd file papers and buy his land. He'd pick out stock and hire a few hands to help him haul all he needed to build a house and proper corrals.

He might even buy furniture and hire real carpenters to help him. The money his father had left him had been sitting in the bank for years. Half his salary since the war had added to his account. He wanted everything ready and right once he found the land. Everything seemed to be falling into place, except for one thing.

Where did Millie fit into all this? She still never said a word to him except when she had to. Most days he wasn't sure she even liked his company. When she got tired of listening, she seemed to slip someplace in her mind that he'd never be able to reach.

Plus, just because he had paid her ransom with a broken watch didn't give him a right to sleep with her. There was something childlike about her and he was taking advantage of that, no matter that she had asked him to mate with her. She couldn't be more than eighteen or nineteen. That would make him almost ten years older. Old enough to know better. He hadn't said a word about love. Hell, he didn't even believe in love. And he didn't know if she understood what marriage meant so there was no point talking to her about it.

Only, he loved the way she made love. There was something wild and untamed about it. As if she'd never been told to hold back, to be a lady or not to act as though she enjoyed it just as much as he did.

He smiled. When they slept together she never made him feel as though he was taking a thing from her. If anything, she took from him. She might go along with everything he said all day, but in the darkness of their cave of a home, she demanded his attention. James grinned. If he didn't take the time to satisfy her, he knew she'd be poking him in a few hours. He'd roll over and ask what she wanted and she'd whisper "you" in that low, sexy voice that he could never refuse.

Not that he was complaining. He'd give her what she wanted no matter how many times a night she asked.

What would he do about Millie once they stepped back into civilization? What they shared here was like a dream. Come spring, they'd have to live in reality.

When they got to a town, he'd have to notify the rangers. What if she had a family searching for her? She'd never answered a single question he'd asked about when she was captured. Every time he'd asked, her eyes would glaze over and she'd go to that place out of his reach.

James had never found a woman he wanted to do more than spend a little time with. As soon as his troops moved on, or the cattle drive started, he was usually more than ready to leave any woman's bed. In his day-dreams of the future, he'd considered the possibility of marriage a few times over the years. If he got the ranch started, and things calmed down in this part of Texas, he might ride into some settlement and pick out a wife. Someone who'd be a good cook and look after the children. He wouldn't even care if she was pretty as long as she gave him sons.

James shook his head. He'd heard men talk about their wives and not much of it sounded good. Seemed as though they always complained about being nagged and none ever mentioned being awakened at night to mate.

Maybe he should just keep Millie. He might get used to her silence, and he could find someone to teach her to cook. The mating thing, she had down pat. If folks came by the ranch he'd just say they were married. As little as she talked, no one would ever hear otherwise from her.

Only, keeping her didn't seem right. What if one day his son or daughter asked them about their courtship? James would have nothing to say except, "Oh, I traded a broken watch for her and she asked me to mate with her so I kept her."

His offspring would probably haul him down to Austin to the insane asylum, and Millie would just wave goodbye from the porch without saying a word.

James swore. He'd never been a man to worry. Maybe if he didn't think about it things might just keep going on as they were.

He'd stay here, studying his land, mapping out the spot he'd build his headquarters and roads. Then, as soon as he trusted the weather, he'd ride to town and make the dream he'd had all his life come true.

Three weeks later when most of the supplies had begun to run out and the weather turned milder, James packed up. It was time to travel to Fort Worth. This part of his life would have to become a memory. By next winter he'd have a cattle ranch that spread for miles.

He could tell Millie didn't want to leave the campsite. The next morning she unpacked about as fast as he packed. When he growled at her, she walked away.

A few hours later, when she returned, she refused to look at him.

He sat in the camp cutting down a pair of trousers to fit her. When she walked past, he said without any greeting, "Put these on."

She did as he'd told her, but never spoke.

"I want you wearing them in the morning," he said as he turned away to hand her the last meal they'd cook at the winter camp.

She didn't talk to him that night. He was surprised she cuddled next to him after dark. Without a word, he made love to her, wishing he could read her mind. He knew every curve of her body, but he knew nothing of her hopes and dreams.

The next morning she wore the trousers and her blanket, but she refused to look at him or to speak. As he broke down the camp, he snapped, "We have to go, Millie, and that is all there is to it. So stop acting like I'm not taking you with me and climb up on the horse."

She looked at him, her blue eyes swimming in tears. "I go, too?"

He saw it then. The fear, the hurt she must have felt when she'd thought he was leaving her. He dropped his last bag and walked to her. "Of course you're coming with me."

She hugged him so tightly he knew he could never let her go. A part of her would always be cuddled into his heart.

When he finally pulled her arms from his neck, he tried to get control of feelings he'd thought were long-ago dead. "Now get on the horse, Millie. We need to make twenty miles before nightfall."

She did as he asked.

They rode southeast, eating up the distance faster than he'd thought they would. She was healthy now and rode as well as he did. The trip seemed easier with two people working to make camp every night. He'd often hunt while she built a fire and took care of the extra horses now loaded down with pelts.

At night he'd hold her as they watched the sky. He thought of her as his falling star. There was no telling where she'd land.

SPRING WARMED THE days as they rode closer to Fort Worth. He knew he could have gone into several settlements along the way, but James wanted time with her. This winter had been the most peaceful of his life.

Logically, he told himself that his bank was in Fort Worth so it made sense to go there. Cattle would be easier to buy at the stockyards. Men trained for what he needed would be there.

But he knew the real reason was that he couldn't let go of Millie. Whatever happened once they reached civilization, things would change. As they rode closer and closer to Fort Worth, her blue eyes grew wider. She'd point, wanting to know about everything she saw. Farms, barns, trains.

As they crossed through the streets of the town, she stopped again and again, looking into windows or staring at people. She'd grab his hand and hang on as if she feared all the population might sweep her away. His grip was solid but he could feel her slipping away.

A block from the ranger station he stopped in a café and they drank coffee and talked. He tried to prepare her for what was going to happen, but he wasn't sure he knew. She spoke slowly, answering questions he'd never asked. She must have felt change coming, also. Two hours later he knew her story. Looking at her now, her warm brown hair curling around her face and her big blue eyes holding his attention, he marveled that such a delicate creature could have survived.

Finally, armed with her name and the few facts she remembered, James walked into the ranger station in Fort Worth.

"I'VE FOUND A captive woman," he said simply to the first ranger he saw, a broad-shouldered fellow of not more than twenty. The circle star on his shirt marked him as a ranger, but James guessed he was yet to see any battles.

The young ranger at the desk nodded as if he'd heard the story before. "Is she alive or did you find a body? Does she know her name or where she was kidnapped from? Where'd you find her?"

James felt as if he'd fired off a few rounds in the small office. It had been so long since anyone had talked to him using so many words, he had to fight to keep from backing up.

He stepped outside and lifted Millie down from her horse. She didn't want to go, but he held on tight to her hand as he walked back into the station.

The young man with a badge stood as she entered the ranger office.

"Go slow, mister, or you'll frighten her," James ordered. "She's been through enough. We're not going to make this any harder on her than we have to."

The ranger nodded and offered her a chair. "My name's Drew, miss. Ranger Drew Price. I'm here to do the best I can to help you. If you've got family, we'll see you get home safe."

James stood at her side, guessing she wouldn't say a word to this stranger. "Her name is Millie O'Grady. She was kidnapped from a farm near Jefferson, Texas. She thinks she's eighteen or nineteen. She was twelve when kidnapped. She says her mother is dead but her father may be alive. She said she did not see his body. A little brother—she called him Andy—was also kidnapped. They were separated after the first night. She doesn't know if he's alive or dead but she remembered his hair was red like her father's."

The ranger glared at James. "Can the lady talk for herself?"

James grinned when Millie shook her head.

The young lawman knelt in front of her. "Are you injured, miss? Do I need to call a doctor?"

She looked up at James and he knew she'd lost a few of Ranger Price's words.

He smiled down at her. "She had many cuts and bruises when I found her. But she's fine now. I don't think there is need for a doctor."

While Ranger Price wrote up the report, James studied Millie. She was afraid but not terrified. He'd promised her no one would hurt her in Fort Worth.

When the ranger left to send a few telegraph messages to places that kept up with missing people, James pulled a chair near Millie's and talked to her in a low, calm voice. Slowly, she relaxed.

Another ranger came in; older and battle-scarred from the war, James guessed. The minute he met the ranger's eyes, James knew the man recognized him. The ranger straightened as if coming to attention. "Wilson, sir," he said. "How can I be of service, Captain Kirkland?"

James repeated all the facts he'd just given the young ranger. Neither he nor Wilson mentioned the war. They may have fought together once, but those days were long buried.

Wilson offered them coffee and was very polite when he spoke to Millie. He seemed to understand what she'd been through.

"We get several parents dropping in every year, hoping for news of their children. The odds aren't good, but now and then we get lucky and find one."

When Millie looked away as if not listening, the ranger continued to speak quietly to James. "Women have it the worst, I figure, Captain Kirkland. The tribes seem to like children, even adopt them as their own. The men are usually killed, not kept as captives, but the women, they go through hell. This one must have been too old to be adopted into the tribe and too young to be taken as a wife."

James didn't want to talk about what she'd been through. He'd already guessed that covering herself in mud may have saved her life.

A few hours passed and James insisted on walking

Millie down the street to a café for dinner. He invited
the ranger to join them, but Wilson said he was on duty.

"You will be coming back, Captain?" Wilson asked
when they reached the office door.

"We will. If there is news, you can find us at the first
café." James relaxed his shoulders. "And, it's just James
Kirkland now. I'm no longer a captain."

"Yes, sir." Wilson nodded once. "Mr. Kirkland. If
no news comes tonight, we've got a sweet widow a
few blocks over who'll take Miss O'Grady in for a few
nights. Her man was a ranger."

James wanted to insist that he'd take care of Millie,
but she wasn't his. She never had been. He'd meant to
save her, to get her to safety, to turn her over to her family. *She wasn't his.*

They took their time eating at the café. She did what
she always did; she watched how he acted and mimicked
his every move. But this time Millie merely picked at
her food, obviously troubled.

He could think of nothing to say. He had no idea how
to comfort her. Part of him wanted to simply hold her
as he had all winter, but he couldn't do that now. People
were all around.

So, he just looked at her. The bruises were gone and
her cheeks were no longer hollow. Her chestnut-colored
hair curled softly around her face. Even in her blanket of
a dress and his old trousers, she was beautiful. All the
months together, he'd never really noticed.

He'd caught people staring all morning and thought
it was because of the clothes or her unfashionably short
hair. Suddenly, he realized, they were admiring her.
Somehow this beautiful creature had survived, wrapped
in a filthy blanket with mud covering her body.

After they'd finished their meal, he ordered dessert. First one, then two, then every one on the menu board. Millie loved them all. She took tiny bites of each, closed her eyes and drank in the sweetness like fine wine.

Smiling, he thought of all the good things she was about to experience and realized he wanted to be the one to show her, to teach her.

About dusk, the young ranger they'd first met rushed into the café, his fist full of papers. "I have news, finally," Ranger Price said, taking the chair opposite James. "It took me longer than I thought it would. I had to telegraph Austin twice and Dallas several times to make sure my facts were right."

James leaned forward. Millie moved her chair closer to him.

The ranger smiled up at Millie, but she looked away. He addressed his news to her, anyway. "We've found a record of your father's death, miss. You have my condolences. Your father passed away three years ago in Jefferson. After you were taken, he stayed on the farm, hoping somehow you'd find your way back."

Both men watched her, but no emotion showed. If she understood, she didn't seem to care.

James cupped her face and turned her head toward him. "Millie, your father is no longer alive. Do you understand?"

She didn't try to speak, but one tear bubbled over and trickled down her cheek.

He brushed it away with his thumb. "I'm sorry, Little Dove."

Price shuffled his papers. "That's not all. I have some good news and some bad, I'm afraid. A boy, who might be her brother, was located. He's the right age—

about thirteen. He has red hair. He was caught stealing
horses a few months ago down near Austin. The sheriff tried to hold the boy, but he escaped. He was recap-
tured two weeks ago and, according to the sergeant who
telegraphed me back, he's been raising hell down near
Fort Richardson ever since. Claims he's Apache. Won't
speak a word of English."

James raised an eyebrow. "Is that the good news or
the bad?"

"The bad news is he shot a guard. Almost killed him.
They're hanging the kid as an adult at dawn four days
from today."

A tiny cry came from Millie. She leaned closer to
James and pressed her face into the hollow between his
shoulder and throat. "No," she whispered. "No."

James looked at the ranger. "Can I get there in time?
If I don't bring him back, we'll never know if it was her
brother or not."

"It would be a hard ride, but you could make it."

"Telegraph the fort and tell them to hold off the hanging until I get there. Tell them family is riding in to see
the boy."

Price looked at James. "You family, Captain?"

James wasn't surprised Wilson had passed on a few
war stories about him to the younger ranger.

"Joe told me who you were," the young ranger admitted. "Said you were the bravest man who ever fought for
the South. They say most bluecoats thought you were
the devil come to fight."

"I'm just a rancher now, Drew. The war has been over
for a long time." James thought about how it seemed
more like a lifetime than seven years. "I think this boy
might be the only one who can heal Miss O'Grady. The

kid's all the family she's got left. It's worth a try to bring him here."

"You want me or Wilson to go along?"

"I doubt I'll need help with a kid, but I'd appreciate it if one of you would check in on this lady. Talk to her, tell her what's happening. She might not talk back, but she'll understand. I'll wire when I can."

Price looked at James. "I'll do what I can to delay the hanging, Captain. If there's a ranger at the fort, I'll send orders to burn the gallows if he has to." He turned to Millie. "I'd be happy to visit her every day. Widow Harris feeds every ranger that drops by."

James stood and shook hands with Drew as he added, "Show me the widow's house." He swung Millie up into his arms. "This little lady has had about all she can take tonight. I'll see her safe and then I'll ride."

The ranger followed James out. "Before you leave, stop by the office. Wilson said you should be sworn in before you go after the kid. We'll give you a list of places that will trade out horses with rangers. If it doesn't rain, you'll make it."

CHAPTER SIX

MILLIE TRIED TO understand what was going on. James had left his other horses at the ranger station, and they rode away from the main street through dark roads hemmed in by cold, windowless buildings. The brick walls formed a canyon without beauty. James held her tightly in front of him as the ranger trailed behind. He talked but she did not listen. All that he'd told her in the café whirled around in her mind. Her father was dead. Her little brother might be alive, but it meant James was leaving her. Sorrow, joy and fear were at war in her mind.

"I swear I'll be back," James whispered against her ear. "I'll leave you somewhere safe, I promise. If this boy at Fort Richardson is your brother, I'll bring him back."

Pressing her cheek against his chest, she fought tears. He had never lied to her.

His hand brushed over her shoulder. "You'll have family again, Millie. You'll have Andy back."

She nodded slightly. That world she had been ripped from long ago seemed more a dream than real. Her life was with James now, even if he did not see it or speak of any future.

All too soon they reached the edge of town where a cottage sat in a forest of fruit trees. A round little woman with sunshine in her smile greeted them. Millie liked her right away. The kind woman spoke slowly and waited for Millie to answer or nod before she moved on.

Millie understood she had to stay at this place, but when James stood to leave, she could not seem to turn loose of his hand. "Take me, James. Take me with you."

Mrs. Harris was a kind old woman, but Millie wanted to go with him. She had to stay with him. Nowhere else in the world was safe.

He knelt beside her chair in a house filled with so many things she could not look at them all. "Millie, listen to me. I'm coming back."

She shook her head. In her experience people never came back.

"I want you to rest here. Do what Mrs. Harris tells you. The rangers will check on you. If I can, I'll let them know what I find at the fort." Slowly, he pulled his hand from hers. "I'll let you know when I'm on my way back with Andrew."

Turning his back to Millie, James handed Mrs. Harris a pouch. "Take what you need from this for her keep. Buy her clothes and anything else she needs."

Millie closed her eyes. James was not trading her away. He was paying someone to take care of her. He'd told her many times at the camp that all he wanted was to start a ranch. His dreams were in the money pouch, he'd said. Now he was giving part of what he had saved away to pay for her care.

"Millie, listen to me." He surprised her when she opened her eyes and found him close. "I'll be back in a few days and when I do I expect you to have learned to make an apple pie as good as the one we just ate. Mrs. Harris will teach you."

She tried not to listen, but he was too close to ignore.

James smiled at her. "If you could make a pie like that, you'd be just about perfect, Millie."

She remembered all the nights he had wished for a dessert. She had not remembered desserts, but James would rhyme off all the things he loved. Apple pie was always the first on his list.

Moving closer, Mrs. Harris smiled at Millie but spoke to James. "I'll be happy to teach her, Mr. Kirkland. She can sleep and eat all she wants, but if she wants me to teach her to cook, I'd be tickled."

Millie followed him to the door as he said goodbye to the others. On the porch, he pulled her against him and kissed her. "I'm coming back for you, Millie. I swear. No matter how long it takes, a few days or a month, I'm coming back."

Nodding, she straightened. This man had never lied to her. She would believe him now.

He smiled down at her and said, "Stay here. Learn what you can." For once the words seem to come hard for him. "You hold my heart, Millie O'Grady."

Then, as if he had said too much, he was gone.

MILLIE STOOD STARING into the night, wishing she could see one more glimpse of him, but the brick-and-wood canyon of the town gobbled him up. She fought to keep from trembling. He had said she would be safe. He had to go find Andrew. She had no choice but to stay and wait.

The porch door creaked and Mrs. Harris stepped outside. "This is a place of peace, child. You'll like it here."

Millie turned to the little, round woman. "Thank you." For the first time since the day she'd seen her mother die, she trusted someone quickly. James would be back. Until then, she had Mrs. Harris.

"I want to learn everything." Millie straightened her back.

"Then we'll have long days," Mrs. Harris said. "And some fun talking."

Millie kept to her promise. She learned all she could each day, but during the nights, she cried for her canyon man.

CHAPTER SEVEN

DAWN FEATHERED ALONG the eastern sky as James rode into Fort Richardson. The sight of so many men in blue uniforms bothered him. Memories and nightmares danced in his thoughts, but he pushed them aside as soon as the gallows came into view. Three nooses hung empty, waiting above the ten-foot-high stage. James couldn't change the past, but if he was lucky, he might be able to change one boy's future.

Walking up to the guard on duty, James announced, "I'm here to see Sergeant Gunther." James straightened, trying to not look as tired as he felt. "I'm..." He hesitated, almost saying Captain Kirkland for the first time in years. "I'm James Kirkland from Fort Worth."

"Yes, sir." The private stared at the badge James wore. The circle star marked James as a ranger. "This way, Ranger Kirkland. We've been expecting you."

James thought they'd take him right to the stockade, but the private marched him into post headquarters.

"The sergeant is at breakfast but will be in as soon as he's finished with muster. Our captain and the lieutenant are in Austin, so Gunther is in charge." The private nodded toward two chairs in front of a massive desk. "Please, Ranger Kirkland, make yourself comfortable."

The room was still cast in morning shadows, but a

freshly lit fire warmed the frosty air. James was asleep
in one of the chairs almost before the door closed.

He dreamed of cold nights at his winter camp. Millie was curled in at his side, sleeping so soundly she did
not wake when he ran his fingers into her soft curls and
kissed her forehead.

James woke when footsteps sounded just outside the
door. He had no idea if it had been five minutes or five
hours. A moment before the door popped open, James
noticed full daylight filled the window.

A sergeant whom he assumed was Gunther—wide
as the door—stormed into his office, followed by two
men dragging five feet of chained trouble between them.
The prisoner was dressed in traditional Apache clothing. From the looks of his leather and beaded vest he, or
his adopted father, was of high rank in the tribe. Braids
hung over his thin shoulders. Red braids, the same shade
of the Red River mud.

James stood and stared. Every inch of skin showing
on the kid seemed to be covered with bruises or cuts or
dried blood. One of his eyes was swollen closed and the
other glared straight at James with pure hatred.

Blue eyes, James noticed. The same color as Millie's.

The sergeant took command. "I'm assuming you are
the Kirkland the rangers have been telling me is coming."

"I am."

"Well, here's the boy you wanted to see. Claims he's
Apache. Won't speak a word of English, assuming he
knows any. I don't like the idea of hanging him like a
man. Anyone can see he ain't full grown, but no one will
claim him. In coloring and age he matches an O'Grady
child who disappeared several years ago. I've no place

to send him, and if I let him go, he'll keep stealing and trying to kill anyone who gets in his way."

The kid jerked and jabbed his elbow into the ribs of one of the guards holding him. When the soldier folded over in pain, he slammed his bound hands against the man's face, drawing blood where the chains connected with his jaw. The other guard responded, almost knocking the prisoner down with one swing.

The boy slumped, too hurt to fight back.

James studied what might be Millie's brother; her only living relative as far as he knew. "Your men put all these bruises on him?" James stared directly at the man in charge.

"For every one he's got, I've got a guard who's got two." Gunther swore. "I've seen tornadoes cause less damage to the fort."

"He's just a boy," James said, guessing the kid wouldn't stop fighting until someone hit him too hard and he died. He must be scared and angry and alone…and deadly.

Sergeant Gunther stood almost nose-to-nose with James. "Ranger Wilson said to grant you with full authority of the rangers behind you. If you want him, Kirkland, he's all yours, but if you find out he's not the boy you are looking for, you're not to bring him back here. Do I make myself clear?"

James knew if he *was* wrong, he'd be in real trouble. He walked over to the kid, who raised his head until one blue eye glared up at him.

"You're coming with me, Andy. Your sister Millie is waiting for you."

The flash sparked in the boy's eye so fast James would have missed it if he hadn't been staring. But it was there. His name, or maybe his sister's, had brought back a memory.

Turning to the sergeant, James said, "I'll need a wagon and all the rope you can spare. I'm taking him back to his family."

"You want chains?" Gunther grinned, happy to see one of his problems leaving.

"No. I'll tie him up so he doesn't run. I don't consider him a prisoner." James raised his voice. "If he cooperates, there will be no need for chains."

The sergeant looked at one of the men. "Loan him a wagon and all the rope you can find. Pull down the third noose and toss that in, too." The big man glared at James. "You're taking quite a risk, Kirkland. What's the kid to you anyway?"

James shrugged. "I think he's about to be my brother-in-law."

The sergeant's laughter shook the building. When he finally calmed down, he ordered everyone to help tie the kid in the wagon. As they walked outside he added, "I married a woman once without meeting her mother. When she came to live with us, I swore she was the devil's sister, but, Kirkland, she was nothing compared to this kid. If I were you I'd give up sleep permanently."

Six men saddled up to escort James far enough away to be out of the fort's territory. After that, they would be on their own. For a moment James feared he might not be up to the task. They had many miles to cover, and he couldn't stay awake all the way back even with a bloodthirsty wild kid waiting for his chance to kill him.

While two men stood guard the first night, James tried to catch up on sleep, but the boy worried him. First, he feared Andy might kill one of the guards trying to get away, or if he tried and failed, the guards might gang up on him and murder Andy while James slept. All six seemed like good men. They also all had bruises, and none treated Andy as though he was anything more than an animal.

Traveling by wagon was slow. They would be lucky to make half the distance he'd made on horseback. With the wagon, they had to follow roads and couldn't cut across country.

By the third day James was tired of listening to the prisoner kick and struggle with the ropes, so he started talking.

He wasn't sure if his talking bothered Andy, but it sure bothered the guards. They said their quick farewell as soon as James woke the fourth morning on the trail. All at once he was alone with a tied-up kid.

Unlike Millie, Andrew O'Grady, if that was his name, didn't silently ignore him. James might not know the language, but he had no doubt that he and all his ancestors were being cussed out. Every time James said something, Andy shot back with what had to be an insult.

Judging from the fire in his eyes, Andrew would happily murder James if he got the chance.

After two sleepless nights James was happy to see a town. He talked the sheriff into locking the boy up, his hands and feet still tied. While Andy gulped down a meal, James went to sleep a few cells away.

The kid must have been just as tired because the sheriff said they both slept the clock around.

The next day as they started off, James didn't secure Andrew with as many ropes as usual. Dark clouds promised rain and the boy looked as though he planned to sleep the day away. Some of the fight must have gone out of him, or maybe Andy had realized James meant him no harm. Though James still talked about the ranch he would build someday, Andy stopped yelling back. He might not be listening, but at least he was quiet. James saw that as progress.

That night, both were soaking wet by the time they made camp inside a rough lean-to built for travelers. James let the kid sit by the fire and eat his supper. He wasn't friendly. For the most part he simply ignored James—until Andy took a few swings at him. James tied him to the wagon wheel but left enough lead so that Andy could curl up under the wagon to sleep.

The next morning when James woke, the boy was gone. After he cussed himself for a few minutes he realized two things. Andy hadn't taken any of the horses and he hadn't tried to kill him in his sleep.

Both facts pointed to one thing: the boy was in a big hurry. Must've been almost first light when he'd worked himself free.

Using skills he'd learned in the war, James began to track the kid. The rain had stopped, but the mud made tracking easy. Five hours later he found him asleep in a pile of leaves at the base of a tree. He must have run as far as he could and then collapsed in exhaustion. The boy was dirty, cold, bone-thin and still rough as they come. If he lived to be a man, he just might be worth the knowing.

Funny, the tough kid didn't look near as mean curled up in sleep. He looked more like a frightened child.

James stood above him, really seeing him for the first time. Despite all his fire and anger, he was still just a boy.

Slipping a rope gently over Andy's wrists, James circled a loop around the tree behind Andy and secured it. He tugged hard and sat on the boy's chest.

Andy woke with a start, but couldn't move. His hands were pulled above him and James's weight held him down.

"Now, I'm only going to say this once, Andy." James hoped the kid understood. He pointed south. "I'm taking you to Millie. If you keep fighting and running, we're never going to get there... She told me your mother called you Andrew Jackson O'Grady when she was angry. So, Andrew, listen up. We're going back to your sister one way or the other. You're all the family she has and Millie remembers you whether or not you remember her. Now, will you go along without a fight or should I just sit awhile right here?"

The boy simply stared for a long moment. Then, to his surprise, Andy nodded once.

James had gotten through to the kid. He could see it in the boy's eyes. Andy might still hate him, but he remembered his sister's name and if he had to, he'd put up with James to get to her.

Slowly, holding the rope tight, James stood. If they didn't reach some kind of a peace he doubted either of them would make it back to Fort Worth.

Andy waited for him to remove the rope from the tree, then the kid followed James, his hands still bound.

"Millie," James said as he waited for the boy to climb into the wagon.

To his surprise, Andy nodded once and rolled into the wagon bed.

It might not be peace, but at least it wasn't all-out war. James could live with that, he decided as he looped the ropes over Andy's hands and feet. "I'll get you back to Millie. I promise."

James secured the kid to the wagon during the day, but Andy no longer fought or yelled. He seemed to be waiting to see what would happen next. As the days passed, James gave up trying to talk to the kid but he never let his guard down.

He thought about Millie and what he'd say to her when he finally made it back. There was so much he'd never said. At night he dreamed of holding her. Each day he pushed the horses as hard as he could, but the trip seemed endless.

Deep inside he knew Millie was waiting, missing him just as dearly.

WHEN THEY REACHED Fort Worth, James stopped by the ranger office for Drew Price. If the ranger thought it strange that James had a boy tied in the back of the wagon, he made no comment.

"I dropped by Mrs. Harris's house every morning, Captain," Drew said as if reporting in. "Your Millie is doing well. I've always heard that the widow could do wonders, but I'd never seen it before. Two days after you left she had Millie wearing proper clothes. Yesterday, the two of them were talking so much, laughing about their cooking lessons, that I could hardly get a word in."

"Millie was talking?" James had seen her smile a few times, but never laugh.

"Sure. She talks. Goes slow sometimes, like she's tasting a word before she spits it out, but she's talking." Drew hesitated. "Is she your woman, Captain, or are you just helping her out?"

James didn't want to answer the question. The hundred times he'd sworn he'd never marry sat in his mind. He ached to hold her, but if he were being honest he'd have to admit she didn't belong to him. "She's not mine."

When he glanced over at Drew, James frowned. The young ranger was smiling.

Telling himself he needed to check on her, James wouldn't admit that he couldn't wait to see her. He slapped the reins. A few minutes later they were climbing out of the wagon and hauling Andy into Mrs. Harris's house with them.

The fight was back in the boy. He struggled to get loose, but it wasn't full-out war. Maybe he was finally afraid of something…facing a world he'd once known.

When James stumbled into the parlor the two women turned from their sewing. Mrs. Harris looked surprised, but Millie jumped up and ran to him. She was dressed in calico and lace; a proper young lady now with combs in her hair and an apron around her waist.

She was almost in his arms when she spotted Drew Price in the doorway, holding the boy.

She went pale, and for a moment James thought she might faint. She moved slowly to the door and stared at the boy. They were almost the same height. Even through the layers of dirt and bruises on Andrew there was no doubt that the two were related.

Reaching out, she gently touched the bruises that marked his arms, then glanced back at James.

"He was in worse shape when I picked him up," he said. "Fought everyone who came near. Not one bruise is my doing, Millie. You have my word."

She nodded and turned back to the boy. "Andy," she whispered. "My brother."

The boy watched her, not as accepting or trusting as

she was. Finally he spoke to her in Apache. Only a few words, but Millie seemed to understand.

She nodded, then translated his words for James. "He asked if I am from his tribe long ago."

James let out a breath that he felt he'd been holding for almost two weeks. He'd found her brother.

He watched as Millie untied Andy's hands and pulled him to the table. Drew, James and Mrs. Harris watched quietly as brother and sister talked, mixing Apache with English.

An hour later Mrs. Harris served them pie, which Andy ate with his hands. As soon as he finished his slice, he pulled the pan over and began to finish off the entire pie.

Without comment, Millie moved to the seating area off the kitchen so she could talk to the others and still watch Andy. "He says he will not run unless I go with him." She smiled at James. "I told him I wish to stay with you. I'd like to go back to the winter camp and help build your ranch. You've done so much for me, it is the least I can do."

James smiled. "How did Andrew like that idea?"

"He says if you raise a hand to me, he wants to be close enough to kill you." She hesitated a minute, then added, "He said if I raise my hand to you, he'll hold you for me."

"The open spaces might be a better place to settle the O'Grady clan. I can't see your Andy walking the streets of Fort Worth dressed as he is."

"Then we travel northwest with you, James." She put her hand on his shoulder and leaned her hip against his side.

"It's time I said good-night," Drew announced, disappointment in his gaze as he stared at Millie's hand resting on James's shirt. "Thanks for the pie, Mrs. Harris, but I hate to see a family fight, especially this one. I have a feeling there are going to be a few before they even get the horses loaded up."

James laughed. "I was thinking I'd better tie the kid up tonight or, better yet, use one of your jail cells."

Millie shook her head and James knew that would no longer be an option.

An hour later when he finally pulled Millie into his arms in the hallway, he whispered, "I missed you, Little Dove. Let's go to bed." He kissed her soundly, loving the smell of her clean skin and starched clothes.

She pulled away. "No."

"No?"

"Mrs. Harris said not to lie with a man until marriage."

"What?" Up to now he'd liked Mrs. Harris. "But, I know you missed me as much as I missed you." His hand moved over her body, but so many layers of material seemed to block the feel of her.

"If you force me, I will tell my brother." She stood her ground. "Before there were no rules, but you brought me here and I learned, just as you told me."

James frowned. He had never forced her into anything and he never would, yet all at once she had this guardian devil watching over her. The kid still looked like he'd gladly run a blade through his chest. Which meant no sleeping together.

The chances of him getting a good night's sleep were looking slim.

He reluctantly put some space between them. James frowned. He needed to think. All he'd worked for since the war was about to come to fruition. He'd have his ranch and a starter herd. To make a go of it, he'd need

every bit of his energy for a year, maybe more. He didn't
have time to take on a wife and her wild little brother.
And he wouldn't be hurried into marriage by what Mrs.
Harris said.

A man had a right to make up his own mind about
what was right for him and when was the right time.
Only, he couldn't head back without Millie. Any terms
she set were fine as long as she came with him.

He stared into her beautiful blue eyes and promised,
"I'll never hurt you, Millie. I broke the beating stick, remember? I'll never force you into anything and no one,
including Mrs. Harris, will force me into marriage. It's
something a man has to step into willingly, not be forced
into, if he's going to settle down and be content."

The urge to sweep Millie up and ride back to their
winter camp was powerful. He wanted the peace of the
days on what would be his land and the wild, wonderful nights with this woman in his arms. He wanted what
they'd had, but layers far heavier than cotton were keeping them apart.

Big tears welled up in Millie's blue eyes as she nodded
and turned away. Silently she walked down the hallway
and disappeared. To James, it was as though she took a
piece of his heart with her. She had no idea how much
she was asking. He'd been alone, totally alone, almost
all his life. He'd survived the war for five long years by
never getting close to anyone, not the men he fought
with, not the women he'd met along the way.

Marriage was something far in the future, if at all.

Yet somehow this quiet woman and her wild brother
had become his family whether he wanted it to happen or not.

He went back into the kitchen where he found Andy

bedded down on the floor by the low fire and Millie asleep on the sofa a room away.

Walking toward the little room off the back porch where Mrs. Harris had told him to sleep, James decided he hated himself because no matter what happened he'd regret this decision in a year. If he married Millie, she'd be unhappy. Millie was beautiful, even Ranger Price had noticed. She wouldn't want to be stuck on a ranch with him. And if he didn't marry her, he knew he'd miss her and worry about her every day left of his life.

He lay in his bed wishing he could see the stars instead of the ceiling. Sleep didn't seem to be an option, so he just waited for dawn. In his brain he began list after list of all he'd need to buy and collect to make the trip. He'd have his ranch before fall. Only, he'd be alone.

An hour, maybe more, passed.

Then, as gentle as a breeze, Millie climbed into his bed.

James thought of fighting, or arguing, or demanding they talk, but instead he did something Captain James Kirkland had never done in his life.

He surrendered.

CHAPTER EIGHT

SPRING WARMED THE air in Fort Worth as Millie waited for James to return from his business dealings as she did every night. Now that her brother was always with her, her canyon man didn't talk to her as much.

He was busy making all the dreams he had told her about when they were at the winter camp come true. He had land to buy and cattle to choose for breeding his herd. Even when James was near her, there always seemed to be something between them. She missed his rambling about one subject or another. Their nights under the endless sky when they watched for shooting stars were over. She longed to feel him next to her, holding her safe and warm as he slept.

Millie missed the James she'd known. Now everyone called him Captain or Mr. Kirkland. Mrs. Harris whispered once that there was no doubt he would be a very important man one day. The men he hired to work for him were all cut from the same cloth as James. Most weren't far into their thirties, but they'd been hardened by war and seasoned from cattle drives. All wore chaps and spurs and guns strapped to their legs.

Millie felt as if he'd stepped up as a leader in a world she couldn't enter. Every night men circled the table poring over maps and numbers. Every morning James was gone before dawn.

Mrs. Harris continued to teach her to cook and sew, and Millie worked with Andrew every day. Her brother wasn't as hungry to learn as she had been. He gave in to bathing, but he still insisted on wearing his Apache clothes. He spent his mornings beside her, but disappeared into the wooded area every chance he got. In the afternoons he wandered the garden, picking tree branches to fashion into bows.

Late one afternoon, as she watched Andy in the yard, James appeared at her side. "What's the kid doing?" he asked.

Millie folded her arms, frustrated at her brother. "He's building an arsenal."

"I figured that." James put his arm lightly around her waist. "He sees himself as a warrior. He's preparing for battle."

"Who is he going to fight, James?" She fought tears, afraid of the truth.

"Me, I'm thinking."

For a moment she leaned into James. For years she hadn't cared about anyone and now the two men she loved seemed destined to be on different sides. James didn't trust Andy and her brother had told her once in Apache that James had cold eyes, the eyes of a killer. She knew he'd been in the war. She'd heard Ranger Price talk of it. Millie didn't know that side of James Kirkland. She only knew the one who was gentle, the one who touched her heart.

When James pulled her closer, his voice stayed calm in case Mrs. Harris was within hearing distance. "What do you and Andy talk about, Millie? Does he ever mention his home or your parents?"

"He wants to talk to me only in Apache, telling me

of the great adventures he's had. After a few days, I realized my years as a captive were a lower kind of hell, but for Andrew, those years were heaven. He never went hungry. He learned to hunt and fight, but was never beaten. He said he was adopted as the son of the chief and has three brothers. Over and over he tells me he would go back if he could, only he will not leave me. I'm his blood. He said when we were first separated, he cried every night for me until the chief told him it was time for him to be a man."

"He's thirteen, Millie. Even if he'd argue the point, he's still more boy than man. Give him time. He'll come around."

She nodded, but didn't believe. Sometimes she wondered if the little boy in Andy remembered her and her mother as one. When she looked in the mirror now, at her hair pulled back with combs, she thought she looked exactly like her mother.

"You'll always be kind to him, James."

"I will."

She pulled away. "And if we leave your ranch one day, you will let us go."

He closed his eyes and nodded before whispering, "I will." Slowly he smiled and added, "The woman I traded for a broken watch is gone. You've a mind of your own, Millie, and I'll respect that no matter how much I want you near."

"I'm here now," she admitted, "but I have to belong to me before I can belong to anyone else ever again."

For a long while he just held her, both feeling the world changing.

Finally he shifted and switched into a casual stance.

"Did I mention that your brother slipped into my room a few nights ago? He stole my hunting knife."

"I know. I saw him with it. He's also taken a few of Mrs. Harris's kitchen knives. I tried to make him give them back, but he refused."

"Let him keep my knife." James shrugged. "After all, if he planned to murder me in my sleep, he's already had the opportunity. Once we're on the road, he might need them to hunt."

"Is there a chance of trouble on the road?"

James nodded. "Apache might attack. Or outlaws robbing travelers. I think I could count on Andy's help with outlaws, but if it's Apache, he's liable to fight for the other side."

She laughed. "Maybe you should work on building a friendship?"

"Not much chance of that. He still won't speak to me."

James took her hand and they walked in to dinner. As they climbed the steps, his fingers moved over her back; a tender caress no one saw but that warmed her insides.

Andy retuned to the house after dark and ate alone, then curled into his blanket by the fire. In her world, his behavior had become the norm. Tonight, as she sat helping Mrs. Harris quilt, Millie didn't worry about her brother. Her thoughts were on James as he talked with his men a room away. She could still feel his touch.

The next evening Millie waited for James on the porch, hoping for another moment alone with him.

Only, the sun set and he did not come. The thought crossed her mind that maybe he'd left without her. Rain rumbled in but she couldn't seem to budge from her chair on the porch. She needed to see him.

Finally, slicing through the rain, he stepped onto the

porch. For a moment she saw the worry and exhaustion in his face before he spotted her and smiled.

"Millie," he whispered, and she was in his arms. "Millie," he said again as he held her so tight she couldn't breathe.

Then, like a man starved, he kissed her. His hands moved over her with need. When he broke the kiss, he laughed low against her ear. "You're filling out, my little dove. I've missed holding you something fierce. I know we agreed to sleep apart, but that doesn't stop the need I have for you."

She smiled, loving knowing he still felt about her as she did about him even if he wouldn't say the words she longed to hear. She told herself it was enough that he thought of her and she could be near him, if just for a few minutes every evening.

Mrs. Harris opened the door and they moved apart. She was a kind woman but she didn't approve of a man who didn't offer marriage touching a girl. If she'd known that Millie had slept with him that first night he'd returned with Andy, Mrs. Harris would have been outraged.

Millie didn't really think of it as right or wrong. It just was. Part of her felt as though she belonged to James. Part of her wanted always to be with him. She didn't want to be treated like a third or fourth wife. Even though no other women stood between them, Millie still felt as if she was down the line in importance. She'd rather be alone in her bed than matter little to a man.

"I hired a few more men today." James broke into her thoughts as he held the door for her to step into the house.

She wished he would say he missed her, but talk of

the ranch always came first. As they ate, she listened while Mrs. Harris asked questions. James was in his world of planning.

He was still talking of supplies when they moved into the parlor with their coffee. A box of Andy's clothes sat between them. Or what was left of them. He'd used James's knife to cut every pair of trousers and all the shirts into long strips.

James picked up what had once been a jacket. He hadn't said a word to Millie about the clothes or the cost. "Your brother will kill me one day. I see the hate in his eyes."

"He will not." She said the words strongly as if she could make them true but she knew her gaze mirrored the worry in James's eyes.

"He's not ready to live among people. If we take him to the ranch with us he's just as likely to go wild as to settle down."

Looking up at him, she picked her words carefully. "Are you sure you want me to go with you? Maybe everyone would be happier if I stayed here. I'll not leave Andy."

"I'd like you to come along, Millie, and your brother would be safer on the ranch."

She nodded, knowing he was right.

James hurried on as if worried that she'd ask questions he wasn't ready to answer. "Once we get to the ranch, I won't have time to watch him. I'm having lumber delivered for the house. The men will stay to help me get the house framed out. If Andy runs, I can't chase after him, Millie. I lost enough days this spring going to fetch him. We have to work hard to get ready for winter. I'll have cattle to brand and fences to build, not to mention the barn and a house." He stopped and looked at her. "For as long as you stay, the house will be yours. I'll not step foot in it unless I'm invited. If you'll come back with me, you come on your own terms. The way you want it to be. As far as I'm concerned your brother does the same."

She wanted him to want her with him, not just to invite her because of her brother. "We will be trouble for you. Are you sure you want us to come?"

"Yes." He leaned forward, almost close enough to touch her. "We got along in the winter camp, didn't we? It'll be much better with a house and supplies. If you like, I'll get you one of those new sewing machines. Both you and Andy will have a place to call home for as long as you like."

Millie spoke her mind before she lost her courage. "I'll not sleep with you again, James. Not until the time is right." How could she tell him it was more than just marriage she wanted? She wanted to be important to him. No. More than that. She wanted to be vital in his life.

"I dreamed you were in my bed the other night." He smiled.

Millie shook her head. "The dream will not follow us to your ranch. Mrs. Harris said you do not own me even if you traded for me."

James watched her so closely she was afraid to move. "Mrs. Harris is right. I do not own you. You can leave me if you want to, Millie."

She knew he was setting the rules. Giving her the choice to go with him. Only, he didn't want to tie her to him in marriage. If she went without being his wife she would be nothing again. But if she did not go, her heart would break.

"I will go, James," she said simply. "You are right about Andy. He is not ready to stay among people yet. But I may not stay with you for long." He had to know. He had to understand that she was free.

For a blink she saw anger and hurt in his gaze, then it was gone. For the first time she wondered if this man who had always been kind might not let her go so easily.

A tiny idea had settled into the corners of her mind. She'd seen the money James collected for hides and furs. If she and Andy were on their own, they could hunt and survive. Ranger Drew had told her that her father's small farm was east of Dallas, still waiting for her. Maybe she and Andy could live there? Once they got settled she'd buy chickens and a milk cow and raise pigs. Mrs. Harris had taught her how to make butter and bake. She remembered plums and cherries growing wild on their farm. They wouldn't need much.

Andy wouldn't fit in now, but he would one day. He was still a boy. He needed to learn a few things first about ranching and how to use a rifle. James could teach him that. Once her brother knew more, they would make their choice to go or stay. Until then, she would go and help James set up his dream. She'd learn and grow, but she would not be his *nothing woman* no matter how much she longed to be near him.

TWO WEEKS LATER they moved out of Fort Worth like a small wagon train with a hundred head of cattle, thirty horses, two wagons of supplies, pigs, chickens, four wagons of building materials and another wagon carrying all they'd need to set up a windmill on the land. Millie drove one of the small covered wagons with all the household items. Two hired men had brought their own wagons covered in wood as if they were houses on wheels. Their wives, dressed with colorful scarves around their heads and waists, drove the wagons. James had told her the men were farriers with blacksmithing skills. As Gypsies, the men had a hard time getting work in Fort Worth, but with their knowledge of horses they'd be invaluable on the ranch. James had let Andy pick out his own horse. She thought maybe James wouldn't care if the boy ran away, but she knew Andy wouldn't run without her by his side. She felt his commitment to her. If only James could feel the same.

WHEN THEY STOPPED for the night, Millie would work with Andy on the words he'd lost over the six years he'd been with the Apache. She soon noticed the Gypsy women moved closer to them and listened in. Slowly, she included them and felt as though she was teaching a class in a language she was still learning herself.

She slept in the household supply wagon each night with all her things around her: a trunk of clothes and dishes Mrs. Harris had insisted she take. A new sewing machine. Quilts and blankets. Four chairs for a table not yet built. If all this were truly hers she would be a rich woman indeed, but only the clothes and one quilt were hers. Everything else belonged to James.

Andrew slept beneath her wagon, his horse staked out a few feet away. He seemed happier now they were in the open air. The cowhands James had hired mostly avoided him, but one boy not more than two years older than Andy showed him how to use a rope. By watching him, her brother learned how to work the cattle.

Along the trail they sometimes passed small settlements. James or one of the men always went in for supplies. James had hired an older man and his wife to cook on the trail, so Millie didn't have to cook when they camped each night, which was fine with her. The jerking and bucking of the wagon left her exhausted and sick at her stomach most nights.

The older couple talked to her now and then, but, as with everyone, they didn't quite know what Millie was there for. She wasn't James's wife, or even his woman. James seemed to pay no more attention to her than he did to anyone else. So she held her thoughts and her sickness to herself.

Andy was the only one who noticed. One evening he disappeared for a while and brought back a root that he told her to chew on. She did and her stomach calmed.

"You are sick?" he whispered in English.

He might never speak to anyone but her, but he listened to everyone. She answered him in English. "I'm not sick. I just don't like riding in the wagon."

"You ready to leave?" he asked in Apache. "We could travel faster alone and not scar the earth like these men do."

She shook her head. "No. We've much to learn. If we decide to go back to our father's land, we must be ready. There may be no one to help us then."

"I know enough, but I will not leave until you are ready," he said in English. "When you leave, I will go with you. You do not need to be afraid."

Looking at him, she noticed he was now a half inch taller than she was. He wouldn't be a boy much longer. How could she explain that it would break her heart to leave James, but that she couldn't stay with him if she didn't matter to him?

THE MORNING DAWNED cold and rainy. Millie felt no better, but she climbed onto the wagon bench and watched the land go slowly by. They'd been on the road three weeks now. James always spoke to her at supper, and now and then he'd ride alongside her to see how she was. When the traveling was easy, she drove the wagon, but on rainy days or on uneven ground, one of his men would tie his horse to the back of the wagon and drive the team.

Millie always lied when James asked how she was doing. All those years of traveling with the tribes, she had learned that sick people might be left behind. Especially if they were no one to the others in the tribe.

This morning he rode close and smiled. "We're almost there, Millie. Another week at the most if this rain doesn't slow us down."

She nodded and tried her best to look excited.

"How're you doing?" he asked and leaned closer.

She didn't answer. She was cold and sick at her stomach and lonely and afraid. If she started telling him, she might never stop.

Tying his reins around the saddle horn, he lifted his arms to her. "Come on, Little Dove, ride with me awhile."

She slipped from the bench into his arms. He opened his coat and wrapped it around her and she felt warm for the first time in days. As he walked his horse at the pace of the wagons, she cried softly against his chest. Her warm tears mixed with the rain.

She wanted to share his joy. James seemed happy, excited. For the first time in his life, he'd have a home, a real home. But all she could feel was change turning her world upside down again.

"Don't cry, Millie," he whispered. "Everything is

going to be all right. We'll have the house built by winter."

When she didn't answer, he asked, "You want me to sing you a song?"

She sniffed. "You can't sing."

"The cows don't seem to mind." He kissed her forehead. "You've been listening to me sing the cattle to sleep for a month and now you tell me I can't sing."

Directing his horse away from the others, he whispered, "I love the feel of you next to me. I've missed you." All the wagons and cattle disappeared in the fog, but she could still hear the harnesses clanging and the rumbling sound of a hundred cattle slowly thumping the ground.

She liked the way the rain closed in around them, almost making her believe they were alone once again.

This was the first time he'd made an effort to hold her on the journey. There was no privacy on the trail. He must have missed her, too, for he whispered, "I've thought of coming to your canvas door at night, but that brother of yours is always right outside. I swear, one night he smiled as I came near, as if he was itching to slice off one of my ears if I came too close."

Giggling, Millie didn't argue.

"I thought about it, anyway. After all, I got another ear and I was missing holding you something terrible."

She shook her head. "If you only had one ear, your hat would fall off."

"You got a point." They rode for a while before he spoke again. "When we get to the land, we'll settle in and get this worked out between us. I've never thought of myself as a marrying man, but I don't like the idea of living here without you. All I've ever wanted and worked for was to own my own spread. I feel like if I think about anything else right now it might just slip through my hands. I can't let that happen. Will you wait for me awhile, Millie?"

James was asking her to wait while he followed his dream. Well, he might be able to push back his life, but she knew she could not push back hers. Disappointment clouded her heart. She leaned against him, knowing that from this point on she needed to store up memories to take with her.

She was leaving her canyon man. Not today, or next week, or maybe even next month, but she was leaving. She might never be the most important thing to anyone, but she couldn't stay with James and be less than that to him.

That night, when she was alone with her brother, she told him to be ready.

Andy nodded. Silently he reached and placed his hand on her stomach. The boy saw what the man hadn't noticed.

CHAPTER NINE

JAMES THOUGHT HE might explode with pure pride as he crossed the canyon and rode onto his land. This was the place he had looked for half his life. There might be trouble with the Indian Wars to the north and cattle sickness to the south, but here on his land there would be peace.

The wagons were a day behind him, but he couldn't wait. He had to see what was his. As the cattle and wagons circled miles north so they did not have to cross the deep part of the canyon, he set up camp on the spot where he would build his house.

James Randall Kirkland could see it all in his mind. His headquarters, spread out like a small town. The main house. The barns. A bunkhouse. A smoke shack. Millie would probably want a hen cage, too, and a big garden just like Mrs. Harris had back in Fort Worth. Packed away with her few belongings were bags of seeds that would do well in the fall. Potatoes, pumpkins and beans.

The dream that got him through the dark nights during the war and the lonely years of drifting was finally happening. He'd never touched his small inheritance or any of the money he'd deposited after cattle drives, anticipating the day he found the perfect land so he would have money for a real start. Here he'd watch the sun rise and set every day for the rest of his life.

The memory of an arrow landing inches from his

boot one night on the trail flashed through his thoughts. James decided he might want to build a little place for Andy, maybe over in the cottonwoods. The idea of sleeping in the same house with the wild boy bothered him. They had been traveling together for a month, and the boy had not said a word to him but he carried his bow and full quiver strapped to his saddle.

Andy usually glared at him with that wish-I-could-kill-you look in his eyes. The arrow that night had simply been a reminder that one day he'd finish the job.

James pushed dark thoughts from his mind. He focused instead on the wide porch he would build on the house, and someday he might buy Millie and him rocking chairs to use in their old age. If she would have him… He had asked her to wait. Surely she knew that as soon as he had the ranch up and running he planned to ask her to marry him. The idea had settled in slowly, and he would not say more before he had a real home to offer her.

At twilight a lone figure rode up from the canyon and waved.

James laughed. "I figured you'd hear us coming, Two Fingers."

The hardened ex-slave slid off his horse and walked toward the campfire. "I knew you'd be back, Kirkland. I was camped down in the canyon near where we traded for that mud woman when I got word. Took me two days to ride here. Passed that wagon train of supplies you got coming in." He looked around. "See you got rid of the crazy woman."

"Yeah, she's gone." James grinned to himself.

Two Fingers smiled. "Run off, did she? You're lucky

she didn't kill you first. I tried to tell you, once they go mad they never come back."

James didn't want to talk about Millie. "How'd you know I was near?"

"Trappers stopped by and said you were heading toward where the canyon snakes north." Two Fingers rocked on his boots for a few seconds as if debating with himself. "Word is, raiders are planning to hit you as soon as you settle."

"Apache or white?" James figured he would have to fight off one attack, maybe more, before he convinced outlaws he wasn't worth bothering. Every cowhand he'd hired knew how to fight.

Two Fingers shrugged. "They're a new gang that's been roaming this area for a few months. Got a little of everything in their mix. Mexicans who've been cattle rustling over in the Badlands, Apache too bloodthirsty to live with any tribe, a few rebels still mad about the war and a couple of outlaws willing to kill for a dime. They're like a pack of wild dogs, so mean they'll eventually turn on each other."

James watched the horizon. "How long before they hit?"

Two Fingers's grin was missing even more teeth than last time James had seen him. "A month, maybe two," he said. "They might let you settle in, then come after the cattle. If they're smart, they'll leave you alone and just take the stock. Then, they could come back in a year or six months and hit your place again."

"Are they smart?"

Two Fingers shook his head. "My guess is they'll take everything they can sell and kill the rest. This land is settling all around. Their kind will die off soon. If

Mackenzie ever stops Quanah in the Palo Duro Canyon north of here, this part of Texas might calm down. When that happens, I'm moving on."

James had worked most of the day marking off where each wagon coming in would unload. Now all he wanted to do was to sleep, but the ex-slave's words would keep him awake. Quanah was said to be a great Comanche Chief and Colonel Mackenzie never backed down. The Palo Duro would run red with blood before the battle was over.

"You're welcome to share my meal. I got beans and biscuits."

"I'll do that." Two Fingers pulled off his saddle. "I'll share your fire, too, if you've no objection. The canyon's not a safe place to be after dark."

"I'll be glad for the company," James lied. In truth the old scout smelled so bad he would need to be a mile away before the air cleared.

They drank the coffeepot dry and talked about the past before Two Fingers drifted off to sleep midsentence.

At dawn the next morning James stood waiting for his life to begin. All the years of having nothing slipped from his shoulders. He was a rancher now. He would carve his place right here. He'd build something to be proud to pass down. Something that would last for generations.

Finally the wagons appeared on the horizon.

Two Fingers crawled from under the buffalo hide he'd slept in all night and stood beside James. "Holy hell, Kirkland. You've hauled the whole damn town up here."

James laughed. "Tell the raiders, when you see them, that we'll be waiting. If they ride onto my land, they won't be riding off."

Two Fingers watched as wagon after wagon came into view. "This is too many people. I think I'll be moving on."

"You're welcome at my table anytime," James said as the old trapper loaded up.

"A man so settled he's got a table is too settled for me, but I might ride by and check on you now and again, Kirkland. See if you still got that pretty lady driving one of the wagons in." He shaded his eyes for a better look. "I'll bet it cost you plenty to talk her into coming out here."

"A small fortune," James admitted. "One broken pocket watch."

Two Fingers shook his head. "No. Impossible. That's the Mud Woman?"

"Afraid so. I told you she was of great value." James glanced to the east. "Too beautiful for the likes of me."

"True," Two Fingers said. "Maybe I should go over and introduce myself. I was told a few years back that I'd be quite a catch."

"You can try, but the lady drives a hard bargain. It's marriage or nothing, I'm afraid."

Laughing, the old tracker saddled up. "Too high a price. But if she's heading this way, she's already won, my friend. You're just too mule-headed to know it."

James slapped the tracker's horse and waved as he galloped off.

THE WORK BEGAN. Most days James was up and dressed an hour before dawn and worked until long after dark. He saw Andy sometimes riding with the other cowhands but he rarely saw Millie.

One night he felt a longing just to say her name. He

knew the ranch needed far more work before he talked
to her, but he wanted to know she was all right. As he
stood around the campfire eating a hearty chili with
hunks of sweet corn bread crumbled in it, James asked
one of the carpenters named Patty if he'd seen Millie.

"You mean, Miss Millie? She's right fine, she is."
Patty blushed to the top of his bald head as if he had
said too much.

"Go on," James encouraged. "How is she getting on
out here all alone?"

"Oh, she ain't alone, Captain. The two women in
those wagons work with her most days. She's teaching
them to quilt and they've been helping her with the garden. Mrs. Sands drops over to her place, too. I think they
have tea together. Funny, out here in this wild country
women work hard, but they still do their visiting."

"She's working?" James asked. He'd never told her to
do anything but fix the house up the way she wanted it.

Patty nodded. "She helped us frame up the house
the first week. Swung a hammer as well as most men
I've seen."

When James stood silent, waiting, the carpenter
continued. "When Old Man Sands had to quit cooking
'cause his wife got down in her back for a few days, Miss
Millie did a far better job than the old couple together
ever did. You ask me, Sands should go back to preach-
ing. His wife helps when she can but Miss Millie told
Sands to help build the barn and she'd cook. You'll not
find a carpenter or a cowhand complaining."

"I've never noticed her by the chuck wagon." James
always rode in dead-tired, but surely he would have seen
Millie if she moved among the campfires.

"Oh, you won't. After she gets the meal ready, Sands

takes over serving and cleans up. He claims she's too fine a lady to hear the rough talk around the campfires."

James nodded. "Good point." When he glanced toward the house where Millie stayed, the carpenter vanished into the shadows. James didn't care. He had learned what he'd needed to know. Millie was all right.

Slowly, one change a day, the headquarters took shape. By the time the carpenters left a month later with their wagons empty, James felt as though his dream was materializing.

He slept around the campfire most nights, knowing that if he stepped inside the house, he'd want Millie. He needed her so badly in the stillness of night he couldn't sleep. When he finally saw her a few evenings later, she looked tired and sad. The work was wearing on her, he thought. He'd told her to slow down, but he could see she wasn't listening.

For some reason she was turning away, going to that place where he couldn't reach her. Even the old woman said that the pretty lady rarely spoke. Maybe this life wasn't right for Millie. Maybe it was too hard for her out here. She used to laugh when she'd lived with Mrs. Harris; he had not heard her laughter since they'd left Fort Worth. The last time he'd held her, she'd cried in his arms.

At night James walked toward the house and watched her moving in the kitchen. What would he do if she wanted to leave? Was he strong enough to hold her? Could he be strong enough to let her go?

Finally, when the first hint of fall whispered in the air, the memory of the day he'd traded for her at Ransom Canyon wouldn't leave his thoughts. That evening he walked to the house wanting to thank her for all she'd done to help. His men were well fed thanks to her cooking, and the garden she had put in when they'd arrived looked as though it would feed them well all winter.

"Millie," he called as he neared the porch he had finished off while she'd cooked one morning. "Millie?"

She stepped out onto the porch but didn't say a word. Her hair was down, brushing her shoulders, and her big blue eyes warmed his heart. "Missing her" was not powerful enough to express how he felt.

"I think it's about time we had a talk." He made it two more steps before one of his men rode between him and the house.

"Captain Kirkland, we got trouble in the north pasture. Looks like someone shot one of our cows." The cowhand added, "Rustler's moon tonight."

James turned away from Millie and started yelling orders to his men. He'd seen a few signs of someone camped just beyond the border of his land. He knew Two Fingers was right: a raid would come one day.

As he swung onto his horse, James glanced back at the house. Millie wasn't there. She must have gone inside. Like a shot firing through his heart, he realized how afraid she must be. She had been in a raid. She'd seen her mother die. She knew the terror of being captured.

He wanted to comfort her. To pull her into his arms and tell her everything was going to be fine; that he wouldn't let anything hurt her. He had prepared for this. But there was no time to hold her. He had to ride. He had to protect the ranch. He had to protect her.

His men knew their jobs. Some would go with him; a few would take lookout posts in the loft of the barn and around the perimeter where they wouldn't be easily spotted. They would protect the headquarters while he and his best hands would make sure outlaws never came near.

As he circled the men riding, he spotted Andy among them. He carried a long bow and arrows filled the quiver strapped to his back. The kid had grown a few inches since James had reunited him with Millie. He was more of a man now, but not enough to join this fight. James would not insult Andy tonight. Not in front of the men he fought so hard to ride equal with.

James shouted as he rode near, doubting the kid would listen to any order. "Stay at the headquarters, Andy!" James yelled over the thunder of hooves. "I trust you to protect your sister. Do whatever you have to, but keep her safe."

The kid didn't look happy, but he nodded and dropped back.

If James had a minute, he would have told Andy that Millie would never speak to him again if he got her brother hurt...

Andy hated him, but now wasn't the time to worry about it.

James and his men rode hard toward the north pasture. Cattle were on that section, not enough to risk a life to steal, but maybe enough to draw men to a fight. As he cut across his land, he planned. No matter how many years had passed, part of him would always be a soldier.

By the time they reached the north pasture, the last light of the sun allowed him to see across his land. One calf lay dead. Two wolves were twisted and bleeding beside it.

One man, walking his horse, moved toward James. The horse had no saddle.

James raised his rifle. "I'd stop right there, stranger, if you want to live."

The man raised his hands. "No trouble, mister."

The trespasser's voice was laced with a thick German accent. James nudged his horse closer but didn't lower his rifle. "Want to tell me why you're on my land?"

The stranger didn't look armed and even in the shadows James could see that he wasn't dressed like a cowboy. His was big, though. Well over six feet with a broad chest and big, beefy hands.

"I come for work. Heard a big outfit come to this place. Do I talk now to Mr. Kirkland?"

"You are," James said as he stopped his mount five feet away. "Who are you? And what do you know about that dead calf?"

"Name is Wagner." He pronounced it *Vahgner*. "I carpenter by trade. The wolves kill calf. I kill them with ax, then think I have to come tell you even if it means no job."

"You alone?" James didn't trust a man who waited until dark to show up.

"*Nein*. I have wife and children with me. We travel from Fredericksburg to Fort Worth. Ranger named Drew Price told us to find you. He said if I say his name you give me job."

James lowered his rifle and dismounted. "Why didn't you ride into headquarters?"

"I plan to tomorrow. *Die* wife, she want to wash clothes first. Tonight I walk to the peak and try to see your camp."

James waved the other men in. Any man who could kill two wolves with an ax would be good to have around.

He offered his hand to Wagner. "Welcome to the

ranch, Wagner. We'll talk about your job in the morning, but if Drew Price sent you I'm guessing I'll be lucky
to have you."

James called out to the cowhands as they neared,
"Help Mr. Wagner and his family get back to headquarters. Make sure they have supper and get bedded down
in the barn."

The big man smiled. "I try to shoot wolves before
they kill cow, but I not a good shot so I run to them
with my ax."

"Can you make rocking chairs?" James thought of
the man's first project.

Wagner's chest swelled even bigger. "Best in state."

"How many children you got?" James liked the idea
of children running around.

"Seven," Wagner whispered. "All girls, maybe boy
for next time."

A few of the men laughed and then stepped forward
to shake hands.

James climbed back on his horse and nodded once at
Wagner before he turned back to find Millie.

He wanted to be the first to tell her that everything
was all right. Tonight he would try to put into words how
much she meant to him.

She filled his thoughts as he rode home, but when he
got to the house, not a single lamp burned. He searched
the campsite thinking she might have thought she'd be
safer somewhere else like the barn where men stood
guard, or the smokehouse buried halfway in the ground.

When he didn't find her there, James checked the barn.

The boy was gone, too. When he asked about her, no
one, not even the men who'd been on guard, had seen
Millie or her brother.

Storming through the house, he searched every room. All was neat, every towel folded, every dish clean. It was as if no one lived there. As if the house had been readied but not lived in.

Slowly he circled one last time. Fear set in as the thought that someone might have taken her settled over his panic.

Finally he remembered what wasn't in the house that should have been. Her trunk that she'd used to pack her few dresses and the seeds for her garden. The roll-top box with a sewing machine inside. The quilt she and Mrs. Harris had made those last few days they were in Fort Worth.

Anger and heartache ripped through his chest. She'd left him.

He had said he would let her go, but he couldn't. He couldn't live without her. She was his. He had paid her ransom. She was his. And he loved her.

James stood on the porch where he imagined they would grow old together and realized one fact. She wasn't his.

He was hers.

CHAPTER TEN

JAMES CIRCLED THE headquarters looking for any sign of Millie or her brother. Nothing made sense. How could they have disappeared?

As the men settled in around the campfire, James grabbed a lantern and continued to search. The Wagner family were all tucked in the hayloft. As he walked through the barn, he heard Wagner's wife singing the baby to sleep and two of the girls giggling.

James forced himself to concentrate. He passed the two Gypsy wagons. There, he heard the soft sounds of couples whispering and the memory of how he'd held Millie at the winter camp drifted in his mind. They had cuddled beneath their blanket and watched for shooting stars.

He glanced up thinking that if she had truly left him, he'd never study the night sky again. How could she have become such a big part of his life and him not know it? When he thought a raid was coming, all that mattered was Millie. Not the ranch or the cows, just Millie.

He walked around to the back of the corral where extra mounts shifted in the shadows.

The lantern swung at his knee. For the hundredth time he glared down at the dirt, but this time he saw something that made no sense. Horse tracks scarred the ground leading away from the fence. It looked as if three

of the extra mounts had simply walked through the fence
where no gate had been cut.

Setting the lantern down, he knelt. It took him a minute, but he solved the puzzle. The three fence boards had
been shaved where they went into the posts. No nails
held the fence railing up at this spot, just notches cut into
the cedar pillars. Someone had taken the time to make
it where they could slide the slats, let the horses out and
then replace them without a sound. He, or she, wouldn't
leave a trail unless one of the men walked around the
back of the corral, and no cowhand was likely to do that.
This far point almost bordered a jagged cliff where an
arm of the canyon dropped down.

James circled back to the barn and saddled the nearest horse as he pieced it all together. Andy had made the
invisible gate just in case he ever needed it. He had taken
Millie. The third mount must be carrying the trunk,
the sewing machine and probably enough supplies to
last them a few weeks. They both knew the way to Fort
Worth, though he doubted that was their destination.

Part of him wanted to believe that Andy had taken
Millie against her will, but he knew that wasn't true.

Maybe they'd thought he wouldn't let them go. That
would explain why they'd picked a time to slip away
when no one would be watching.

James fought the urge to yell for all his men. They
could spread out and find a kid and a woman within an
hour, but this was something he had to do by himself.
The men might hurt the kid when he protected his sister
or Andy might hurt one of them.

He rode to the edge of the canyon. The land was flat
until the sudden drop. It looked as if a man could see the
curve of the earth in all directions, but the canyon ran

for more than a hundred miles, wide as a mile in places, almost small enough to jump across in others. The canyon branched out like fingers of a huge root, barely scarring the ground in places and dropping a thousand feet in others.

He looked down at the shadows below where rocky ground left no tracks. They had picked their way before dark. Now, if he started into the canyon at night, he'd be risking his life. Dark rocks and holes looked the same and shadows hid any path.

Without hesitation he started into the canyon.

He might never find them. Not tonight or after a month of searching. They could turn left or right a dozen times and if he missed one turn they would be miles away before he could backtrack.

James felt his world shattering. He would give up everything he owned, all he had saved and planned for all his life, to have Millie back at the winter camp where they had one blanket to share.

Only, he had lost her. In all the talking he had done since they met he'd forgotten to tell her how much she mattered to him.

A shooting star flashed across the sky as if reminding him of a wasted future without Millie.

James swore. He should have told her how he felt. He should have married her when she'd wanted him to. He should have stormed the house and slept with her so she wouldn't have looked so lonely.

Another star arced across the sky, adding a flash of light for him to see the path. The light dimmed as it peaked and fell, winking out before it hit the ground.

James looked up at the night. Shooting stars don't arc.

Another tiny light shot up out of the canyon.

James turned toward the light. It took two more flashes before James realized what he was seeing. Arrows. Flaming in the almost moonless night sky. Flaming arrows showing him the way.

Ten minutes and a dozen arrows later, he saw Millie and Andy on the canyon floor. Andy stood still holding his bow in front of a tiny fire. The strips of a shirt James had bought him lay scattered by the fire. Millie was wrapped in her beautiful quilt.

James dropped the reins of his horse and ran toward them. When he was ten feet away, he saw that Millie wasn't moving. Her eyes were closed, as though she were sleeping.

"What happened?" he demanded as he knelt beside Millie and brushed her beautiful hair away from her face.

"She fell. I should have moved slower." Andy stared at the fire, not meeting his eyes. "I knew you would come. I only had to show you the way."

James glanced at Andy, who looked terrified. "It wasn't your fault, Andy. It was an accident. Your arrows may save her."

As gently as he could, James moved his hands over her, trying to find where she was hurt. He felt blood in her hair and found a knot and a small cut near her forehead.

"Why'd you bring her out here?" James didn't bother to look at Andy as he worked. He found no cuts or broken bones on her arms or shoulders. She was warm, still breathing, but he wouldn't move her until he knew where she was injured.

"She said we had to go." Andy's words were cold, full of hate.

"Why?" James asked as his hands moved down her sides.

Andy pulled the last arrow from his quiver. "Because a man who does not want a woman will not want the child she carries."

The boy's words struck James just as his hand spread over her rounded middle.

If Andy had pulled his bow and shot an arrow through James's chest it could not have hurt more. She was carrying his child and she feared him. Afraid he didn't want her.

"We have to get her back," James said, his hands shaking as he tied his bandanna around her head wound. Looking up, he saw Andy standing there, arrow at the ready.

There was no time to tell the boy how wrong he and Millie had been. All that mattered was trying to save her and the child. "I'm taking her home, Andy." James gently lifted her. "She's my life, whether you believe it or not. If she dies, let that arrow fly and bury me beside her."

Andy glared at him. "I will do that," he said calmly, as if it were a promise.

They didn't say another word. James held her close as he rode and Andy led them out of the canyon.

The kid pulled open the corral, then followed James to the shadows of the barn where he raised his arms to lift Millie down.

James lowered Millie off the horse, then climbed down and took her gently from Andy. "If you'll close the corral, I'll get her to the house."

Nodding, Andy stepped back. "I will go back for the other horses when I know she is safe."

"Good." James knew the kid would not leave her now.

The night guard spotted them as he walked out of the barn carrying Millie. By the time James reached the porch, people were coming from every direction.

Mrs. Sands ran toward him as fast as her legs would carry her. In her white nightgown and nightcap she looked more ghost than woman.

"My wife is hurt," he said. "I'll need your help. She's had a bad fall."

The chubby woman starting giving orders like she was second in command. "I'll need water and bandages and one of the Gypsy wives to help."

He didn't know the names of the farrier's or blacksmith's wives, but he saw both of them hurrying toward the house.

When he laid Millie on the bed, Mrs. Sands told him and Andy to get out.

"I'm not leaving her." James stood his ground.

"I will not go," Andy echoed.

James had a feeling that if Millie died, he'd feel the arrow through his chest before one tear could fall

"Then stay out of my way, the both of you," Mrs. Sands announced.

Wagner, a little girl on each arm, poked his head in to say his wife wanted to help. "No English, but she know about babies."

Mrs. Sands nodded once. "Tell her to come in, then you stand outside the door and yell back in English anything she says. It's not time for the baby to come, but the fall may have hurt her."

The newly hired carpenter disappeared and his wife waddled into the room, obviously near time to deliver that boy Wagner had been waiting for.

Mrs. Sands held the quilt while the German lady

examined Millie. James turned his head, fearing Mrs. Wagner's hand would appear covered in blood.

The exam took several minutes before she said something in German. Her husband yelled back the translation. "*Das* baby to be all right. No blood. Three more months to carry."

A cheer went up from the other side of the bedroom door and James let out a breath he'd been holding. He looked at Andy. The kid finally set aside the bow he'd had in his hand.

"Does everyone on the ranch know Millie is with child?"

"Yep," Mrs. Sands said as she cleaned the blood out of Millie's hair. "We just didn't know you two were married. Neither one of you said anything about it, but a blind person could tell you loved each other. She listened for you each night and you watched the house."

"We've never said the words but—"

Mrs. Sands shook her head. "Ain't no buts. You either are or you're not. If you haven't said the words, you're not."

"I'd say the vows right now if we had a preacher." James didn't want there to be any doubt that he loved Millie.

"Wait till she comes to, Captain. A woman usually likes to be conscious at her own wedding."

He sat by the bed until Millie finally opened her eyes, then they talked softly late into the night. He never touched more than her hand, but the knowledge of how near he came to losing her rocked him to his core.

The next morning James put on his only clean shirt and waited on the porch for Millie to appear. She'd agreed to marry him, but Mrs. Sands suggested Millie sleep on it first. Her exact words were, "A man too dumb to admit his love is probably too dumb to come in out of the rain."

James had glared at her, but the old lady had just smiled, letting James know she planned to pester him until one of them died.

Andy swung over the railing and stood at the door as if still on guard. He frowned at James with death-threat eyes as usual.

"I see you found a shirt and trousers. You giving up being an Apache?" James didn't add that he'd done the worst job of cutting his hair that James had ever seen except for when Millie had cut hers.

"No. I must stay. I be uncle soon. I should look like the rest of the cowboys if I stay." Andy glared at him.

"You giving up hating me, kid?"

"No. Your blood will mix with mine when the child is born. I will not kill the husband of my sister unless he deserves it."

"Fair enough. Nice to have you in the family, Andy." Darn if the kid wasn't growing on him. "If you stay and work this land, I'll cut you off a piece of it when you're eighteen."

Andy shook his head. "You pay me for work and I buy my land." He pointed across the canyon.

Grinning, James realized Andy's land would be out of arrow range.

Millie, her bandaged head wrapped in a beautiful scarf, came out of the house on the arm of Mr. Sands.

The old guy might not be much of a cook and no better as a carpenter, but by the time the wedding was over James had no doubt that he was fully married and the old man could preach.

THAT NIGHT WHEN they held each other tightly in bed, James told Millie just how much he loved her. When he was out of words, he looked over and noticed she'd fallen asleep while he'd talked.

He lay awake thinking he was the happiest man alive. He had a wife, a baby on the way, land to pass down to the next generation and a brother-in-law who'd gladly kill him if he didn't get it right.

An hour later Millie poked him.

"What do you want, wife?" he asked as if he'd been asleep.

"You," she answered.

James Kirkland did what he knew he'd always do.

He surrendered.

EPILOGUE

THE INDIAN WARS on the plains of West Texas ended a year later in 1874.

COLONEL MACKENZIE WON the war with the last great Comanche Chief Quanah in a battle in the Palo Duro Canyon. Mackenzie died a few years later of wounds suffered in battle. Quanah Parker took the last name of his mother, a captive, and lived out his days as a rancher, a judge and a lobbyist in Congress.

ANDY O'GRADY BOUGHT a farm twenty miles away and married one of Wagner's daughters. He was buried in moccasins and reportedly carried a bow and arrows to every family dinner at the Kirkland Ranch.

JAMES AND MILLIE KIRKLAND lived long enough to use the rocking chairs as they watched their grandchildren play. They never talked of how James had bought her from an Apache tribe in Ransom Canyon, but Millie gave him a watch every anniversary.

HE OWNED FIFTY-THREE when he died.

Don't miss SUNRISE CROSSING, the new
RANSOM CANYON *romance from Jodi Thomas,*
coming soon!

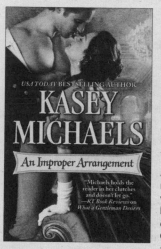

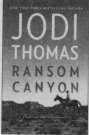
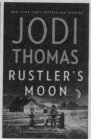

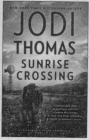

REQUEST YOUR FREE BOOKS!

HARLEQUIN®

HISTORICAL

Where love is timeless

2 FREE NOVELS PLUS 2 FREE GIFTS!

YES! Please send me 2 FREE Harlequin® Historical novels and my 2 FREE gifts (gifts are worth about $10). After receiving them, if I don't wish to receive any more books, I can return the shipping statement marked "cancel." If I don't cancel, I will receive 6 brand-new novels every month and be billed just $5.69 per book in the U.S. or $5.99 per book in Canada. That's a savings of at least 12% off the cover price! It's quite a bargain! Shipping and handling is just 50¢ per book in the U.S. and 75¢ per book in Canada.* I understand that accepting the 2 free books and gifts places me under no obligation to buy anything. I can always return a shipment and cancel at any time. Even if I never buy another book, the two free books and gifts are mine to keep forever.

246/349 HDN GH2Z

Name _____ (PLEASE PRINT)

Address _____ Apt. #

City _____ State/Prov. _____ Zip/Postal Code

Signature (if under 18, a parent or guardian must sign)

Mail to the Reader Service:
IN U.S.A.: P.O. Box 1867, Buffalo, NY 14240-1867
IN CANADA: P.O. Box 609, Fort Erie, Ontario L2A 5X3

Want to try two free books from another line?
Call 1-800-873-8635 or visit www.ReaderService.com.

* Terms and prices subject to change without notice. Prices do not include applicable taxes. Sales tax applicable in N.Y. Canadian residents will be charged applicable taxes. Offer not valid in Quebec. This offer is limited to one order per household. Not valid for current subscribers to Harlequin Historical books. All orders subject to credit approval. Credit or debit balances in a customer's account(s) may be offset by any other outstanding balance owed by or to the customer. Please allow 4 to 6 weeks for delivery. Offer available while quantities last.

Your Privacy—The Reader Service is committed to protecting your privacy. Our Privacy Policy is available online at www.ReaderService.com or upon request from the Reader Service.

We make a portion of our mailing list available to reputable third parties that offer products we believe may interest you. If you prefer that we not exchange your name with third parties, or if you wish to clarify or modify your communication preferences, please visit us at www.ReaderService.com/consumerschoice or write to us at Reader Service Preference Service, P.O. Box 9062, Buffalo, NY 14240-9062. Include your complete name and address.

HH15

Turn your love of reading into rewards you'll love with

Harlequin My Rewards

**Join for FREE today at
www.HarlequinMyRewards.com**

Earn **FREE BOOKS** of your choice.

Experience **EXCLUSIVE OFFERS** and contests.

Enjoy **BOOK RECOMMENDATIONS**
selected just for you.

PLUS! Sign up now
and get **500** points
right away!

Earn
FREE
REWARDS
HarlequinMyRewards.com
Join
Today!

MYR16R